Praise for the National Bestselling Bookmobile Cat Mysteries

"Charming.... Librarian Minnie Hamilton is kind-hearted, loyal, and resourceful. And her furry sidekick, Eddie, is equal parts charm and cat-titude. Fans of cozy mysteries—and cats—will want to add this series to their must-read lists."
—*New York Times* bestselling author Sofie Kelly

"With humor and panache, Cass delivers an intriguing mystery and interesting characters."
—*Bristol Herald Courier* (VA)

"A pleasurable, funny read. Minnie is a delight as a heroine, and Eddie could make even a staunch dog lover more of a cat fan."   —*RT Book Reviews*

"Charms with a likable heroine, [a] feisty and opinionated cat, and multidimensional small-town characters."
—Kings River Life Magazine

"Almost impossible to put down . . . the story is filled with humor and warmth."   —MyShelf.com

"[With] Eddie's adorableness, penchant to try to get more snacks, and Minnie's determination to solve the crime, this duo will win over even those that don't like cats."
—Cozy Mystery Book Reviews

Titles by Laurie Cass

Cat with a Clue

A BOOKMOBILE CAT MYSTERY

Laurie Cass

AN OBSIDIAN MYSTERY

OBSIDIAN

Published by Berkley

An imprint of Penguin Random House LLC

375 Hudson Street, New York, New York 10014

Copyright © 2016 by Janet Koch

Excerpt from *Wrong Side of the Paw* by Laurie Cass copyright © 2017 by Janet Koch

Penguin Random House supports copyright. Copyright fuels creativity, encourages diverse voices, promotes free speech, and creates a vibrant culture. Thank you for buying an authorized edition of this book and for complying with copyright laws by not reproducing, scanning, or distributing any part of it in any form without permission. You are supporting writers and allowing Penguin Random House to continue to publish books for every reader.

Obsidian and the Obsidian colophon are trademarks of Penguin Random House LLC.

ISBN: 9780451476555

First Edition: August 2016

Printed in the United States of America

5   7   9   11   12   10   8   6   4

Dedicated to the memory of Eddie, a cat for the ages,
April 1999–March 18, 2016.
We miss you, little buddy. We always will.

Chapter 1

After almost thirty-four years of living, my most important discovery was that there are remarkably few things I absolutely had to do.

Yes, I had to feed and clothe and house myself, but besides those basics, there wasn't much that couldn't be put off for the sake of sitting for a few minutes in the morning sunshine, especially when said sunshine was smiling down on your very own houseboat, which was resting comfortably on the sparkling waters of a lovely blue lake that sat alongside Chilson, a picturesque town in northwest lower Michigan, which happened to be my favorite place in the whole world.

I lay flopped in my lounge chair, eyes closed and soaking up the sun, content with pretty much everything and everyone. Life was good, and there wasn't much that could make it better, other than making this particular moment last longer. Peace and quiet reigned throughout my little land. Nothing I had to do that day was so important that a minor delay would matter much and—

"Mrr!"

Of course, my idea of what defined important didn't always match my cat's.

I opened my eyes and looked at Eddie, my black-and-white tabby, who was approximately three years old and who had placed his nose two inches from my face.

"You know," I told him, "if you'd gone running with us, you wouldn't have so much energy."

For the past few weeks, I'd actually been exercising. Sweating, even. I'd been meaning to start something like this for a long time, but it had taken a number of gentle suggestions from Ash Wolverson, my new boyfriend, to get me to invest in some decent running shoes. A few more suggestions, and I'd started hauling myself out of bed early three times a week to run with him. Luckily, he swung by the marina four miles into his own run, so he'd already had a good workout by the time we got together.

"Think about it," I said to Eddie. "You'll sleep even better during the day."

He blinked.

"Right." I patted him on the head. "You never have trouble sleeping during the day. It's the nights that are a problem. What do you think about going for a run in late afternoon?"

"Mrr." Eddie pawed at yesterday's newspaper, which was sitting on my lap. I'd stayed at the library late the night before and had been too tired to do anything except reread a chapter of *84, Charing Cross Road* when I got home. Since my boss, Stephen Rangel, had left his job as director of the Chilson District Library, I was interim director until the library board hired someone. This was stretching me a little thin, because in addition to my normal duties as assistant director, I also drove the library's bookmobile and was out of the building almost as much as I was in it.

"Which section do you want to hear first?" I asked, picking up the two-section paper.

"Sports, please," said a male voice.

I looked over toward my right-hand marina neighbor. Eric Apney, a fortyish male with perpetually mussed brown hair and undeniable good looks, was sitting on the deck of his boat, eating a bowl of cereal while a mug of coffee steamed next to him.

My left-hand neighbors, Louisa and Ted Axford, had spent summers in the slip next to mine for years and would usually be in residence by now, but a new grandchild had captured their hearts, and Louisa had e-mailed me that they wouldn't be up until mid-July.

Eric, who lived downstate but spent as much time in Chilson as he could, was new to Uncle Chip's Marina. I'd met him a few weeks before and had turned down his invitation to dinner when I'd learned he was a doctor, and, worse, a surgeon. I'd recently dated an emergency-room doctor and had learned that with doctors, dates were things that were made to be broken. Maybe I was being prejudiced, but my reaction had been instant and instinctive.

Luckily, Eric hadn't taken the rejection to heart. He'd laughed and said I was smart to stay away, and we were becoming good friends.

"Mrr," Eddie said.

"What was that?" Eric's spoon paused halfway up.

I looked at Eddie. "He's tired of hearing about the lack of depth in the Tigers bullpen and would rather hear the law-enforcement report."

In a lot of ways, marina life was like being in a campground. Your neighbors were mere feet away, and if the wind was calm, you practically heard them breathing. Politeness dictated that you didn't mention how their snoring kept you awake, but it was hard to maintain the fiction that you didn't know what the person on the boat next to you was saying while on his—or her—cell phone. From unintentional eavesdropping, I knew Eric was a huge baseball fan, just as he knew that I ordered take-out dinners more often than I cooked.

"Really?" Eric asked. Soon after we'd met, he'd heard me talking to my cat as if Eddie could really understand what I was saying. He'd laughed with only the slightest condescension, but when Eddie had responded with a conversational "Mrr," he'd stopped laughing and hadn't laughed since.

"No idea," I said, flipping newspaper pages. "But I know I'm tired of hearing about pitching problems. Okay, here we go. Ready for the good stuff?"

It hadn't been until I'd started dating Ash, a deputy with the Tonedagana County Sheriff's Office, that I'd become interested in the law-enforcement tidbits that Sheriff Kit Richardson released to the newspaper. Ash said what made print wasn't the half of it, but the farcical half was certainly there.

"Mrr," Eddie said.

Eric shoveled in a spoonful of cereal. "Fire away."

I scanned the short paragraphs. "Here's a happy one: 'Lost six-year-old boy in the woods. Six-year-old boy was located and returned home safely.'"

Eric swallowed and toasted the newspaper with his coffee mug. "Score one for the good guys. What's next?"

"'Daughter called from out of state to have her elderly father checked on. Officer spoke with father, who said he turned off his phone because his daughter calls too late at night and wakes him up.'"

Eric choked on his coffee. "Seriously?" he asked, coughing.

"I don't make this stuff up, you know. Next is about a guy who called 911 to tell the sheriff's office that he'd been driving with his window down. A bee flew in, and when he was trying to get the bee out, he drove into a parked car."

"Good story," Eric said. "Wonder if it's true."

Smiling, I went back to the paper. "Here's a call that someone had broken into a garage the night before a garage sale. Nothing was reported missing."

"Mrr." Eddie thumped his head against my leg.

"Yeah, I know," I said. "Not that good a story, but they can't all be winners. How about this one? 'Caller wanted to see an officer because her cat was being mean to her.'"

"Mrr!"

"Okay," I said. "It was one sister being mean to another sister, and Mom took care of things before the officer arrived." I gave Eddie a pat. "Just wanted to see if you were paying attention."

"Some kid really called 911 because she was fighting with her sister?" Eric held up his cereal bowl and drained the last of the milk into his mouth.

I averted my eyes, swung my short legs off the lounge, and stood. "Last week some kid called 911 because his mom wouldn't let him play all night with his new video game."

"Well," Eric said, "now, that I can see."

"Mrr."

I turned around. Eddie was settling onto the newspaper, tucking himself into a meat-loaf shape. "Oh no, you don't." I rolled him gently onto his side and slid the paper out from underneath him, like a sleight-of-hand artist pulling a tablecloth out from under a table full of china. Unlike the china, however, Eddie yawned and stretched out with his front feet, catching the paper with one of his claws and yanking it out of my hand so it fluttered to the deck.

"Nice job." I crouched down to pick up the now-scattered newsprint. "You have a gift for making a . . ."

"A what?" Eric asked.

"Mess," I said vaguely, now standing with the newspaper in hand, looking at the page Eddie had opened. The obituaries. *Talia DeKeyser,* I read to myself, *died peacefully in her sleep on Memorial Day. Born on May 24, 1933 to Robert and Mary Wiley, Talia married Calvin DeKeyser in 1955—*

"Minnie, are you okay?"

I folded the newspaper and put it under my arm. "Fine, thanks." I picked up a purring Eddie and tucked him under my other arm. "See you later, Eric. I have to get to work."

My shower was fast and, since my annoyingly curly shoulder-length black hair didn't take well to blow-drying without turning into a mess of frizz, I toweled it dry and hoped for the best. And even though I knew from my mother's years of scolding that breakfast was the most important meal of the day, I didn't feel like stopping even for a quick bowl of cereal. There were granola bars in the vending machine at the library; one of those could count for breakfast.

I blew a kiss to Eddie, who somehow knew it wasn't a bookmobile day and was already curled up in the middle of my bed, and headed out into the brightness.

Normally there wasn't much I liked better than my morning walk through the streets of downtown Chilson, but in spite of the cheeriness of the day, I couldn't help thinking of that famous line from the John Donne poem, "Any man's death diminishes me."

And any woman's, too, because though I'd barely known Talia DeKeyser, she'd seemed to be one of those people who could light up a room with a smile. Aged, widowed, and suffering from Alzheimer's, Talia had nonetheless brightened the day of everyone at Chilson's Lake View Medical Care Facility with her unfailing cheerfulness and horrible riddles. Her family had moved her to Lake View soon after Christmas, and I'd met her when I'd stopped by with a pile of large-print books from the bookmobile.

I remembered her grinning up at me from her wheelchair, all ready to share a knock-knock joke, and had the sudden and certain conviction that she'd gone on to a better place. "Sweet dreams, Talia," I said softly, and felt my sadness curl up into a tiny spot in my heart. And though I wasn't quite thirty-four, I knew my sadness would eventually fade and be overgrown by memories of bad jokes and happy laughter.

"Morning, Minnie," Cookie Tom said. Tom Abinaw, the tall and amazingly skinny owner of the best bakery in the area, had always been a nice guy, but he'd elevated himself to saint status in my eyes when he'd volunteered to let me purchase cookies for the bookmobile at a special rate and, even better, from the back door, so I didn't have to stand in the long lines that snaked out his front door all summer.

"Hey." I stopped. "Beautiful out, isn't it?"

"Sure is." Tom looked up from his sweeping of the clean sidewalk. "Yet another day I'm glad I don't work in a big city."

I laughed. "Better to work seventy hours a week in a small town?"

"Far better." He smiled and returned to his unnecessary sweeping.

I went back to walking through the few blocks that constituted Chilson's downtown. The mishmash of old and new, single-storied and multistoried, brick and clapboard, brightly colored and faded melded together into a cohesive whole that worked so well that it couldn't possibly have been planned. Organic growth, urban planners said. Whatever it was, I liked every inch of it, from the far reaches of the slightly shabby east end, where my houseboat was moored, to the moneyed west end, where my best friend, Kristen, had her restaurant.

Of course, the east end soon wouldn't be as shabby as it had been for years, thanks to the efforts of my friend Rafe Niswander. By day, Rafe was the best middle-school principal Chilson had had in years. By night, he was the renovator of what had been a run-down wreck of a house within shouting distance of the marina, and he was taking his own sweet time about it.

Whenever I told him that he could have finished two years ago if he hadn't spent so much of his summer in the marina's office, hanging out with the manager and the manager's marina buddies, he would loftily say that perfection couldn't be achieved in a day, and walk away, whistling.

"Morning, Minnie!" Pam Fazio fingered a wave at me. She was sitting in a small slice of sunshine that was hitting the front steps of her store, Older Than Dirt, and cupping her hands around what was most certainly not her first cup of coffee that morning.

I gestured at her drink. "Number three or number four?"

Pam had moved north from Ohio a year earlier, fleeing the clutches of corporate life, and had vowed that she'd spend every morning the rest of her life sitting on her front porch and drinking coffee. She'd done so through last winter's abnormal cold spell without missing a single day and, though I suspected that the contractor I'd noticed parked at her house would soon be glassing in her front porch, her vow was still intact.

She held the coffee close to her face and breathed deep. "Two. I'm trying to cut down. And I'm waiting for a delivery."

"Is it container day?"

Pam went abroad two or three times a year, searching the nooks and crannies of Europe, Africa, Asia, and Antarctica, for all I knew, for items old and new to sell in her store. She had an uncanny knack for choosing things that would sell like hotcakes, and the arrival of the shipping container piqued interest across town.

She nodded and drank deep. When she surfaced, she said, "Should be here any minute."

I needed to get to the library, but I couldn't leave, not just yet. "Um, are there books?"

"Now, Minnie, you know I don't tell."

"You used to," I muttered.

"Sure, but that was before I figured out what a draw container day could be. Off with you. Come back when everything's unpacked, just like everyone else."

"But—"

"Go!" She pointed toward the library with an imperious index finger, but she was smiling.

"Greedy, manipulative retailer," I said as seriously as I could.

"Naive and sentimental public servant," she shot back.

Laughing, I told her to have a good day and moved on.

Moving faster now, I walked past the shoe store, past the local diner known as the Round Table, and past the women's clothing stores whose super-duper sidewalk-sale offerings were still beyond my budget. I admired the new fifteen-foot-high freestanding clock, a gift to the city from the chamber of commerce, and moved swiftly past the side streets, where I caught glimpses of the local museum and the Lakeview Art Gallery. Past the toy store, past the post office and the deli and the T-shirt shop and the multitude of gift stores, and then up the hill to the library.

I supposed there might be a day when I wouldn't smile with pure pleasure when I approached my place of work, but since it hadn't happened in the four years I'd been assistant library director, I wasn't sure it ever would.

Once upon a time, the two-story L-shaped building had been Chilson's only school. When the growing population had packed the classrooms to panting capacity, new buildings had been constructed to house the older students. Decades passed, computers came into their own, and the town eventually realized that a modern elementary school was needed. The old school, built to last and filled with Craftsman-style details, locked its doors.

And there it sat. For years. Then, just before it crumbled away into dust, the library board looked around and noticed that the existing library was packed to the rafters, with no room to expand. *Hmm,* they collectively thought. *You know, if we could pass a millage to renovate that old school . . .*

Smiling, I hopped up the steps to the library's side entrance. Even though I'd started working at the library only a few weeks before the library moved into its new home, and in spite of the fact that I hadn't been involved in a single renovation decision, I felt as proprietary toward the building as if I'd refinished every piece of trim myself.

It was beautiful. Gorgeous, even. One of the most comfortable public spaces I'd ever stepped into, and I was grateful beyond words that Stephen, my boss, and the library board had chosen me out of the dozens of applicants.

I inserted my key into the lock of the wooden door and amended my thoughts. Stephen, my former boss. Because even though, just the previous winter, he'd said he was grooming me to take over when he retired in a few years, Stephen had jumped ship when he'd been offered the directorship of a large library that just happened to be in a climate where snow was seen maybe once every two years.

We'd been directorless for going on two months, but the library board would soon be interviewing candidates. I was sure the board would choose wisely, but I was also wondering what the future would hold for the impetuous five-foot-tall, cat hair–covered Minnie Hamilton.

"Quit worrying," I said out loud, and pushed open the door. The library didn't officially open until ten, but there were things to do, so here I was, walking into the building two hours early, happy that my best friend, Kristen Jurek, couldn't see me.

"You're salaried," she'd say flatly. "You make the same money if you work forty hours a week or sixty, so why are you working seventy?"

A huge exaggeration. I'd never once worked seventy hours in a week. Sixty-eight was my absolute tops, and that was only because one of the part-time clerks had called in sick. And if Kristen ever said that to me again in person, I'd point out that, as the owner of a top-notch restaurant, she routinely worked more than I did.

Then, if the past was any guide to the present, she would retort that at least she made lots of money, slide a bowl of crème brûlée over to me, and I'd agree with whatever she said.

The library's door shut quietly behind me and I breathed deep, drawing my favorite smell into my lungs: books. Flowers were all well and good, but what could compare to the scent of stories, of knowledge, of learning, of history?

My soft-soled shoes made little sound as I crossed the lobby on the way to my office. I flicked on the light, dropped my backpack on the floor, and, just as I started to sit down, saw the stack of reference books I'd meant to put away last night.

To shelve or not to shelve, that was the question. Whether 'tis nobler in the mind to—

"Oh, just do it," I told myself. Though I could put the pile onto a cart for a clerk to file, I enjoyed putting books in their proper homes. I snatched up the books and made my way back through the lobby.

I didn't bother to turn on the pendant lights as I entered the main hall; enough sunshine was streaming through the high windows of what had once been a gymnasium that the extra illumination wasn't necessary. I also didn't bother to look at the call numbers on the ends of the bookshelves; I knew the library so well that I could practically have put books away blindfolded.

Which was why, instead of looking where I was going, I was paging through the top book in the stack, a foreign-language dictionary, seeing if I could stuff a few words of Spanish into my brain before I shelved it, and which was why I didn't understand what had happened when my foot hit . . . something.

This made no sense at all, because I was walking through nonfiction, call numbers 407 through 629. There shouldn't have been anything on the floor here except, well, nothing.

Frowning, I stopped reading and looked down.

My sharp gasp was loud in the quiet space. The books fell with soft thumps to the carpeted floor, and I dropped to my knees, reaching forward, hoping that the woman lying on the floor was simply sleeping in a very strange place and in a very strange position.

But her skin was cold.

I swallowed, pushing myself to my feet.

And noticed the knife sticking out of the woman's back.

Chapter 2

I called 911 straightaway, and the first police officer on the scene was from the Chilson Police Department. He took one look and called the police chief. When the police chief arrived, he took a slightly longer look, then called for the next level up, the Tonedagana County Sheriff's Department.

"We don't have the staff or the training for a full-out murder investigation," the city's police chief said as we were waiting outside. "To tell you the truth, I'm happy to hand something like this over. Make one mistake and you can get a case tossed out of court. And the paperwork?" He shook his gray-haired head. "Inwood's free to take this one, with my blessing."

"Thanks so much." Detective Inwood said.

How long he'd been standing behind us, I didn't know. A gift for invisible lurking was probably an asset in his profession, but it creeped me out.

"Ms. Hamilton," Inwood said, nodding. "You called this in, I hear?"

The detective and I had met a number of times, and while our working relationship had occasionally been strained, we were reaching a point where we could converse without me wanting to yell at him for being narrow-minded. Likewise, he hadn't called me interfering in weeks. This was all very nice, because Ash, my new boy-friend, was standing next to and slightly behind Detective Inwood at what appeared to be the regulation distance for a deputy who was training to be a detective.

"That's right," I said.

Inwood looked at the police chief. "Have you identified the body?"

"Andrea Vennard," he said. "Found her purse. Driver's license says she lives downstate. Brighton." He shifted from one foot to the other. "You want me to notify the relatives, Hal?"

"I'll take care of it." Inwood tipped his head in the direction of the library. "Ms. Hamilton, we're going to have to—"

"I know," I said hurriedly, not wanting to hear any details. "The whole library is a crime scene, and we won't be able to open to the public until it's been . . . cleared out."

He nodded. "We'll let you know when you can open." He shook hands with the chief, opened the library's front door, and stepped inside.

The police chief glanced my way. "Let me know if I can help, Ms. Hamilton," he said, and returned to his vehicle.

For a moment, all was quiet. Birds chirped, leaves stirred in a slight breeze, and the sun shone down. It was June in northern lower Michigan, and it was a beautiful day.

"You okay?" Ash stepped close, his handsome square-jawed face frowning with concern.

Of course I wasn't. I'd just seen a murdered woman

on the floor of my library. And, once I'd called 911, it hadn't felt right to leave her alone, so I'd had time to think about things far more than I'd wanted to, which included wondering how she'd gotten into the locked library. Then I'd wondered how the killer had managed to enter the locked library. This had been followed by the stark realization that the killer might possibly still be in the building, and I'd done the remainder of my waiting outside. On the sidewalk. Next to the street.

"I'm fine," I said, summoning a smile. "Only, can I use my office? Now, I mean."

He glanced at the door. "Let me check. I'll be right back."

My hand itched for my cell phone, but I'd left it in my office that morning, years ago, before I'd found Andrea. I'd called 911 from the reference desk.

For the moment, there was absolutely nothing I could do, so I sat on a nearby bench and did exactly that. Of course, now that I was sitting, all I could think about was that knife sticking out of that poor woman's back and the puddle of red that—

"Minnie?" Ash was standing in front of me. "You sure you're okay?"

"Fine," I said as I jerked open my eyes. Far better to see the good-looking male specimen in front of me than recall the morning's earlier sight. "Did you ask about getting into my office? I need to make phone calls."

"You're good to go." He held out his hand and helped me to my feet. "But you'll have to stay in there until we're done."

I held on to his hand for a moment, welcoming the warmth of his skin. He reached out and gave me a half hug with his other arm. My cheek mushed uncomfortably against his badge, but I didn't mind. "Thanks," I said, smiling a little as he released me. "I needed that."

He gave the top of my head a quick kiss. "I did, too," he said. "Just don't tell the boss."

"Detective Inwood or Sheriff Richardson?"

Though he'd half smiled when I said the detective's name, he blanched when I mentioned the sheriff. "Not her," he said. "Anyone but her."

I almost laughed. Kit Richardson was fiftyish and formidable, and everyone except me seemed to be scared of her. Which wasn't a bad attribute for a sheriff to have, I supposed, but somehow the fear hadn't made its way to me. "She's not as scary as you think she is," I said.

Ash made a fast move and opened the front door for me. "Don't see how that's possible," he said. When we were inside, he turned the dead bolt. "The techs will be here soon. I'll let you know when we're done."

I started to ask how long that might be, but stopped myself. They'd get done when they were finished, and that was all I truly needed to know. "Thanks." I kept my gaze away from what I knew still lay in the library, and walked purposefully to my office.

Stephen was gone. There was no library director. It was up to me to do what needed to be done.

So I went to do it.

Three hours later, I'd talked to the library's board of directors and the entire library staff, touched base with a couple of the major donors, and told the newspaper and both the local television news programs that we were "deeply saddened, and have complete confidence that the sheriff's office will bring the murderer to justice soon."

I leaned back in my chair, thinking. Just as I was coming to the internal conclusion that there was no one else I needed to talk to, the phone rang.

For a moment, I debated letting it go into voice mail. For another moment, I wished the library's budget stretched to caller identification. Then, since I could almost see my mother frowning at me, arms crossed and foot tapping, I reached for the receiver and picked it up. "Chilson District Library. This is Minnie speaking."

"And you were going to call me when?" a severe female voice asked.

I flopped back into my chair, pulled out a low desk drawer, and put my feet up. "Why didn't you call my cell if you were so eager to talk?"

"Did," Kristen said. "A zillion times."

"It's so refreshing to talk to someone who never exaggerates."

"And it's so nice to know that I'm last on the list of people you'll call in an emergency."

"Not last," I corrected. "That would be my mom." Because as much as I loved my mother, she wasn't much help in a crisis. She was great at hugs and sympathetic tears and cooking up comfort food, but for straight-out practical help, not so much.

"True enough."

I heard a muted thumping noise and knew Kristen was in her restaurant's kitchen, chopping up who knew what for lunch. Kristen had a PhD in biochemistry and had once worked for a major pharmaceutical company, but she'd chucked it all to come home to Chilson and run a restaurant that specialized in serving locally grown foods.

During the restaurant's conception stages, she'd been pulling out her long—and straight—blond hair over the lack of local fresh foods available in winter. I'd suggested that since she hated snow anyway, to just close the place in winter. This had given the place its name, Three Seasons, and given Kristen an opportunity to spend the cold, snowy months in Key West, where she did some bartending on the weekends and as little as possible during the week.

"So," she said now, "are you okay? I heard you fainted dead away when you found the body."

Frowning, I sat up a little. "Who told you that?"

More thumping noises. "Can't say. Promised Rafe I wouldn't tell."

I slid back down. "Rafe's making it up."

"Well, duh. So. Are you okay?"

"Haven't had time to think about it, really, but—" The library's other phone line started beeping. "Hang on. There's another call coming in." I put Kristen on hold. "Good morning. Chilson District Library."

"Is it true?" a familiar male voice asked.

"Hang on," I said, and punched out a sequence of buttons. "Conference call," I told them. "And Rafe Niswander, I have never fainted in my life."

"You told her," he said to Kristen.

"Of course I did. You knew I would."

"Well, yeah, but you promised."

I didn't have to see the six-foot-tall Kristen to know she was rolling her eyes.

"Promises from a girl to a boy don't have any power over confidences between girls," she said. "You should know that by now."

"In theory, yes. It's reality I have a hard time with."

Rafe wasn't the only one having a hard time with reality. I blinked away the memory of what I'd seen that morning and tried to focus on the present. "Sorry—did someone ask a question?"

"For the billionth time, I asked if you're okay," Kristen said. "I mean, now that you've had time to think about it and all."

Yes, the last minute of my life had been very meditative. I half smiled, which I knew had been her intention. "I'll feel better when the police figure out who did this."

But how had it been done? Detective Inwood had already been in my office, asking about the maintenance schedule (five p.m. to one a.m., five nights a week) and the library's security system (doors that were securely locked every night). I'd passed on the phone number of Gareth Dibona, our custodian and maintenance guy, and Inwood told me that Gareth had said he hadn't seen anyone in the building after closing time and that he'd locked up as usual. To Detective Inwood, I'd confirmed that I'd had to unlock when I'd arrived that morning.

The detective's eyebrows had gone up when I'd told him about the locked doors as security, and I'd felt compelled to explain that a full-fledged security system had been part of the renovation plan, but increased construction costs had made cuts necessary.

If the library ever received the large bequest we'd been promised in the will of the late Stan Larabee, a security system would be installed lickety-split, but the will was being contested by numerous family members and it was a toss-up if we'd ever receive anything.

"No fainting, then?" Rafe asked.

"You sound disappointed," I said. "Did you bet anyone on it?" Rafe and I had a longstanding practice of making five-dollar bets on everything from which snowflake would make it to the ground first to what year Thomas Jefferson was born.

"Well, it would make a better story," he said. "You fainting, your knight in shining armor rushing to the rescue, dampening your brow with love-struck kisses, you blinking to life and—"

Kristen made a rude noise. "Have you been watching the Hallmark channel again?"

"Hey, no making fun of Jane Seymour. She's hot."

This was undeniably true. And now that I was being reassured that I had good friends who cared about me—even if they were moving on to a discussion of how all actors on the CW network looked alike—I was indeed feeling okay. Or at least a lot better than I had been.

"Thanks for calling, you two," I said into the middle of a mild argument regarding a plot point of *Arrow*. "But I need to get going."

"You sure you're okay?" Kristen asked.

"She's fine," Rafe said, and somehow his saying so made me feel stronger. Of course, that could have been because I wanted to prove him so very wrong about the fainting thing. He could be such a putz.

"Do you think . . ." Kristen paused.

"Let the woman go," Rafe said. "You heard her: She has things to do. Places to go. People to see. All sorts of—"

"Do I think what?" I interrupted. Rafe would go on like that for hours otherwise.

"That having the library be the place where someone was murdered will be a problem?"

"Not really. Ash figures they'll be done soon."

"That's not what I meant," Kristen said. "What if the murder hurts the library's reputation? What if people don't want to come to a place where someone was killed? I mean, this is safe little Chilson, where nothing bad ever happens, but now . . ." Her voice trailed off.

"It'll be fine," Rafe said, but this time his assurance didn't instill me with confidence. Because Kristen was right, and I was suddenly frightened for my library.

There was a quiet cough. Detective Inwood was standing just outside my office doorway. "Ms. Hamilton? I have questions about library procedures."

I nodded. "It'll be fine," I told my friends, then hung up, hoping it was true.

It didn't take long to answer the detective's questions, and soon after that, he told me I was free to open the building.

"There's limited value," he said, "to a deep crime-scene investigation in such a public space."

I nodded. Evidence that Suspect A had been in the library wouldn't prove anything unless Suspect A tried to claim that he (or she) had never been in the place, and what was the point of saying you'd never been in a public building?

"You have a bit of a mess over there." Inwood gestured toward the nonfiction section. "If your maintenance staff is like most, they won't have any idea how to clean it up."

"Clean what up?"

"Fingerprint powder. It's extremely fine-grained," he said. "I'd vacuum as much as you can, but that won't get all of it. Try putting a little liquid dishwashing soap into a spray bottle with warm water for what the vacuum doesn't pick up."

"Thanks so much," I said, but I wasn't sure my sarcasm showed enough, because Inwood said, "You're welcome," and then, "Deputy Wolverson will notify you when the victim's family has been contacted. At that point you can give out Ms. Vennard's name. I'll call if I have any questions."

He strode off. Ash, who'd been standing nearby, sent me a smile that made me go a little mushy inside, then followed him.

When they were gone, I was the only one left in the library. This wasn't unusual either early in the morning or late at night, but I couldn't think of a circumstance in which I'd ever been the only person in the library at one in the afternoon.

It was just too weird for words.

I wandered out to the reference desk, picked up the phone to call our maintenance guy, then put the receiver down. Gareth didn't start work for a few hours. If I asked him to come in now, he would, but it would result in overtime pay, and that particular part of the budget was tight after the recent repairs and cleanup expenses from a big storm.

Happily married and older than me by well over a decade, Gareth was a solidly good guy. We'd become friends soon after I'd moved to Chilson when, during a summer festival, we'd looked up from the opposite ends of a picnic table to see the other eating an identical, horribly delicious junk-food dinner of corn dogs, elephant ears, and cotton candy.

We'd made a pact not to tell a soul—especially Gareth's nutritionally minded wife and my budding restaurateur of a best friend—and ever since, we'd traded recommendations for restaurants with the best fried food.

So, budget in mind, instead of Gareth, I called Holly Terpening, one of the library's clerks and my good friend. As I waited for her to pick up, I couldn't help myself; I glanced over to where I'd found poor Andrea.

"Oh no," I breathed.

"Minnie?" Holly asked. "Is that you? Are you okay?"

"Fine. Sorry. It's just . . . I've been given the all clear to open the building, so come on in. And, Holly?" I tried not to wince at the vast amounts of fine black powder that covered the bookshelves. "If you have a couple of spare spray bottles, please bring them."

I made three similar phone calls, then, before anyone else arrived, I jogged upstairs to Stephen's former office for the mat he'd used for his winter boots. Its black rubber didn't exactly match the medium gray tweediness of the downstairs carpeting, but it would cover that stomach-lurching dark red stain until I could get some carpet guys in.

Half an hour later, Holly, Donna, Kelsey, and I had managed to clean up the worst of the powdery mess. Josh, our IT guy, another good friend of mine, had volunteered to work the front desk while the women did the dirty work.

"I'm not very good at cleaning," he said, sidling away.

"Just like a man," Kelsey called after him.

"Just trying to get to the coffeemaker before you do," he said, and he slid out of sight.

"He has a point," Holly said, and Donna and I agreed. Kelsey had a tendency to make coffee strong enough to rule the world and, though I always made the first pot of the morning, every one after that was a race of sorts.

"Someday," the thirtyish Kelsey said airily, "you young things will grow to appreciate the virtues of real coffee."

Donna, a seventy-year-old marathoner and snow-shoer, said, "Real coffee? The only good coffee is coffee that's laden with cream and sugar." Kelsey gave what didn't appear to be a mock shudder, and we all laughed.

The chatter went on as the cleaning continued, and I knew we were trying not to think about what had happened in that spot a few hours earlier. Maybe we were being shallow and callous, and almost certainly we were being inappropriate, but I was starting to understand why law-enforcement officers joked at crime scenes. There was only so much sorrow you could let yourself feel before it consumed you; humor was a method of keeping the pain at bay.

"I think we've got it, ladies," I said, stepping back and looking over our work. Though, if I looked hard, I could see minute traces of fine black powder in some crevices, we'd cleaned every surface that anyone would touch and we'd made sure the books were spick-and-span. We wouldn't pass the white-glove test, but, then, a library rarely did. "Thanks so much for helping."

Donna and Kelsey murmured that it was no problem, and Holly rolled her eyes. "Don't be such a twinkle toes. Of course we'd help."

I squinted at her as the other women went to put away the cleaning supplies. "Twinkle toes?"

She grinned. "It's Wilson's new phrase."

Wilson was her eight-year-old son. Her daughter, Anna, was six, and though Holly's husband, Brian, was currently working out West, all seemed well with the Terpening household. "Where did that come from?"

"Twinkle toes?" Holly shrugged as we walked toward the main desk. "Your guess is as good as mine." She lightly elbowed me. "Would you look at that?" She nodded toward the stocky thirtyish Josh. "Who knew he was such an excellent desk clerk?"

Josh slid her a look that could kill. The two had recently been at odds over what he saw as interference on her part regarding the decorating of his first house purchase. Josh had ostentatiously ignored each and every one of her suggestions; then, at his housewarming, she'd discovered that the small home was decorated precisely as she'd recommended.

He'd found the whole episode tremendously funny. Though Holly had been thrilled at how well her ideas had turned out, she'd also been annoyed at Josh's game playing. That had been a few weeks ago, and their respective feathers were only now smoothing down. Now, instead of listening to them go at it like brother and sister, I sent up a very shiny distraction.

"They're talking about setting up the interviews," I said.

Both their heads whipped around.

"They?" Josh asked. "You mean the library board?"

"For Stephen's job?" Holly inched toward me and looked around. No one was close by, but she lowered her voice to ask, "When's your interview?"

"Yeah," Josh said, nodding. "You need to tell us so we can help you prepare. I'll be the board chair." He dropped his voice an octave. "Ms. Hamilton, please tell us what you think qualifies you for this position."

Holly crouched down about five inches to mimic my height. She twirled her straight brown hair and said in a voice startlingly like mine, "Mr. Chairman, I worked under Stephen Rangel for four years, and I'm quite sure that anyone smarter than a box fan would be more qualified than he was."

"Yes, I see what you mean," Josh said in his chairman's voice. "Still, we would like to hear specifics about your credentials."

Holly, still crouching, said, "As you can see from my resume—"

"No, they can't."

My friends stopped their playacting. "What do you mean?" Holly asked, standing up and narrowing her eyes.

"Well," I said, inching away, "I haven't actually applied for the job."

"What?"

"Shhh," I told them, making shushing gestures with my hands. "This is a library. No loud exclamations of surprise allowed."

"Don't care," Josh said. "Why haven't you applied? What have you been doing the past month?"

"Minnie, you have to apply," Holly almost wailed. "Who knows what we'll get if you don't. Didn't Stephen practically promise you the job?"

What Stephen had told me was that he was grooming me to be his eventual successor. But that had been before his departure had been accelerated by multiple years. "The library board," I said, "hires the director, not Stephen. Besides, I'm not sure I want the job."

Holly pointed her index finger straight at me. "You're the obvious choice. Don't mess this up, Minnie."

"Yeah," Josh said. "Get to work on your application, or we'll fill it out for you."

Holly's face brightened. "That's a great idea! I bet we could write up a better one for Minnie than Minnie would."

"And we'd do a lot better job on her resume, too." Josh started laughing. "She'd be all accurate about every single freaking thing. No one does that."

"When you're done," I said, "let me know. I'll have it bound and shelved in the fiction section." I gave them a bright smile and headed to my office.

Instead of going home to the marina after work, I walked to the boardinghouse of my aunt Frances. She was sitting on the front porch's swing and spied me as I turned the last corner.

"Minnie!" She jumped off the white-slatted swing, letting it bounce up and down in its chains. Down the creaky wooden steps she hurtled, then ran the last yards toward me with arms flung open wide.

I braced myself for a jarring thud, but she gently enfolded me in her embrace and, once again, I knew how lucky I was that my father had such a wonderful older sister. Not only had she invited a young Minnie to spend her summers in Chilson, where I'd met Kristen and Rafe and many others, but she still welcomed me back to her home every fall when it got too cold on the houseboat. Come spring, of course, she kicked me out, but I was happy enough to move.

Not that I disliked the people who replaced me; I always liked them very much. No, it was more that I would have been a fifth wheel to the summer boarders and might have messed up my aunt's careful calculations. This was because, though my aunt's summer guests didn't know it, they'd been selected based on compatibility with another guest.

Yes, Aunt Frances was a secret matchmaker, and in all the years she'd been setting people up, she'd never had a flat-out failure. Sometimes the people intended for each other rearranged themselves, but everyone had always ended up happy.

This year, however, was turning out a little different. For the first time since my uncle Everett had died, decades ago, Aunt Frances had a love interest of her own. She and her new across-the-street neighbor, Otto Bingham, had been smiling into each others' eyes for months now, and I was wondering how that would affect the summer matchmaking.

She gave one last squeeze and released me. "I'm so glad you called this morning. Right after we talked, the phone calls started rolling in, asking if I'd heard the horrible news, if you'd been hurt badly, if I'd heard that you captured a killer."

Which was why I'd called her. The speed of light had nothing on the speed of gossip, and I'd wanted to give my aunt a heads-up before it hit her full force.

"I'm fine," I said. "It's awful that someone was killed, but I'm sure the sheriff's office will make an arrest soon."

"I hope so," she said, turning and linking her arm with mine. Though this was a little awkward for both of us, since I was half a foot shorter than my angular aunt, it wasn't far to the front porch and the side-by-side companionship was welcome.

We climbed the wide front steps and went inside, the screen door banging gently behind us, and plonked ourselves down in the large living room, a space that oozed relaxation.

The massive fieldstone fireplace hinted that comfy fires and marshmallow toasting were in the near future. Regional maps tacked onto the pine-paneled walls whispered tales of upcoming adventures. A bookshelf stacked with decks of cards and board games ensured that boredom was never possible, and the couches and chairs were populated with cushy pillows and cozy blankets, all promising the ease of a long nap.

Through an open doorway, the dining room was laid with dishes for the upcoming dinner, and beyond that, a screened porch looked out into a backyard so filled with trees, you could imagine that you were in a treehouse.

Something tapped me lightly on the shin. I jerked

out of my reverie and looked around. Aunt Frances was sitting diagonal to me, her foot still extended from the kick.

"Sorry," I said. "Did you ask me something?"

"How you were doing," she said, her eyebrows raised. "Preoccupied, clearly."

"Oh, it wasn't . . ." I stopped. Yes, I'd been thinking about how much I loved this house, but that had undoubtedly been avoidance behavior. I didn't want to think about the murder. Didn't want to talk about it, didn't want to speculate about it, and certainly didn't want to relive the morning. "I'll be okay," I said eventually. "It'll take a while, but I'll be fine."

My aunt scrutinized me, then nodded. "You'll tell me if you're having problems."

"Promise," I said. "And I'll tell my mom about it, too. Just as soon as the police put the killer in jail."

Aunt Frances grinned. She'd known my mom longer than I had and knew how over-the-top her reaction would be. "Sounds like a plan."

"So." I slid down on the couch and put my feet up on the coffee table. "How are the summer romances going?" I looked around. "And where is everybody?" I settled down for a long chat, but there was no response from the only blood relative I had within three hundred miles. I asked the question a second time.

"Hmm?" was the response.

"Boarders," I said a little louder. "Where are they?"

"Oh." My aunt blinked out of her trance. I'd noted the direction of her gaze, which was fastened upon a book sitting on the corner of the coffee table. Titled *Ice Caves of Leelanau County*, it was filled with fascinating photos of Lake Michigan ice formations. It had been a Christmas gift to her from Otto. "The boarders are fine," she said. "Victoria and Welles are on a day trip to Mackinac Island."

The first time Victoria—widowed, almost seventy, a grandmother of five, and a retired registered nurse—had met Welles, divorced and recently retired from dentistry, romantic sparks had flown high into the sky. Their match was almost guaranteed. I moved on.

"Eva and Forrest?" I asked. They were the young ones, at forty-five and forty-two, respectively. Both were long divorced, both were teachers, neither had children, and both were huge fans of mountain biking. They'd vowed to bike every single mile of trail in the region before they left in August. In the three days they'd been north, they'd already biked a hundred of those miles, so I had full belief that they'd reach their goal.

"Eva?" My aunt's gaze wandered back to the book. "Forrest. They went down to Bellaire, if I remember correctly. Glacial Hills—is that right?"

It was. "How about Liz and Morris?" I prompted.

They were my favorite intended couple. At fifty-seven years old, Liz was taking a "summer sabbatical" from her life. An extremely successful sales representative for a clothing manufacturer, she'd woken up one morning and been too exhausted to drag herself out of bed. She needed a rest, her doctor had told her, so here she was, not resting all that much, but having a wonderful time.

Her intended match, Morris, was a little different. At fifty-three, Morris was a middle-aged man who'd for years slid from one job to another without a specific career goal in mind. He made a lot of friends but not much money, at least until one of his buddies introduced him to a guy who know a guy who produced voice-over advertising. Morris's voice was now ubiquitous on radio and television, and he'd made enough money in five years to take a nice, long break.

The two of them had been the summer's first arrivals at the boardinghouse and, from the second day, had been inseparable. They were spending a lot of time on the multitude of beaches on the many area lakes and had started a blog about their observations.

"Liz and Morris." My aunt sounded puzzled. "Liz and . . . oh yes." She smiled. "They've gone to a beach."

I did an internal eye roll. "The matches are going well this summer?"

"Mmm." She thought a moment. "Well enough, I suppose."

I peered at her. If I didn't know better, I would have said she didn't care about the matchmaking results. Which was odd, because making sure her pairs paired up properly had been the focus of her summers for umpteen years. "Are you feeling okay?" I asked.

"What?" She blinked again. "I'm fine. What makes you think there's something wrong?"

I held up my index finger. "For one thing—"

She laughed and got to her feet. "Out, favorite niece." Since I was her only niece, this meant nothing, but hearing her say so still made me feel warm and fuzzy. "Or stay for dinner," she said, "but you'll have to eat all your vegetables."

"Got to go," I said, jumping up. "Eddie is waiting, and you know how he can get. I'll see you later."

I was halfway to the door when Aunt Frances said, "Minnie, I'm sorry about the woman who was killed, but . . ." Her voice caught on itself. "But I'm really glad it wasn't you."

Turning back, I gave her a quick, hard hug. "Me, too," I whispered.

* * *

"What do you think?" I held out a forkful of shrimp pad Thai:

Eddie, sitting across from me, with his chin almost resting on the houseboat's compact dining table, sniffed at the food, then blew out a quick breath and disappeared. A second later, I heard his feet *thump-thump* to the floor.

"Yeah," I agreed. "A little too spicy." But since this was the only food I had available, other than cold cereal, I forked it in, anyway, alternating bites of pad Thai with swallows of milk. "The take-out place has a new cook," I said. "I'll have to be careful next time I order."

My cat was supremely uninterested in my culinary concerns. He was far more interested in planning his jump to the boat's dashboard, where he would have an excellent view of the seagulls wheeling about over the lake's waving waters.

Janay Lake, twenty miles long, was connected to the mass of Lake Michigan by a narrow channel that was just out of sight. Chilson had come into being because back in the mid-to-late 1800s, it had been a transportation hub for logging, favored both for its natural harbor and for the railroad that skimmed around the north shore.

"Did you know that Alfred Chilson was the first postmaster?" I asked Eddie. "That's where the town got its name."

Eddie didn't seem to care about this, either. His body made a long arc in the air and he hit the deck.

"Need something to do?" I asked, getting up from the dining booth. After leaving Aunt Frances, I'd gone back to the library and worked a little longer. By the time I was done, it was far too late to cook anything—how unexpected!—so I'd picked up dinner at the local Chinese-Thai place and patted myself on the back for supporting the local economy.

I ran the water warm and started washing my minimalist dishes. "It was a little creepy," I said, "being in the library when everyone was gone." I'd jumped every time the ventilation system had kicked in. "I ended up locking my office door. I felt silly, but you won't tell anyone, will you?"

"Mrr," Eddie said.

"And if I'm jumpy about being in the library, I bet other people will be, too." And that couldn't be allowed to happen. Libraries were safe places. Havens. Harbors. Refuges. Places to learn. Repositories of knowledge. Locations of possible wisdom. Knowing that the Chilson library—*my* library—had been violated was an affront to everything I believed in.

Right then and there, I vowed to do whatever I could to help the police find Andrea's killer and to repair any and all damage to my library's reputation.

"Mrr."

That time his voice sounded a little too close. I turned.

"Hey!" I flicked soap suds at him. "Get off the counter! You know that's not allowed, at least not when I'm home. What are you thinking?"

"Mrr." He chin-rubbed the corner of the knife block—which had been a joke gift from Kristen, because she'd put bookmarks into the slots instead of the utensils for which it had been designed—one more time and jumped off the countertop.

"Cats," I muttered, or tried to, because a yawn interrupted the single syllable, turning it into something that sounded more like, "Caaa."

"Mrr," Eddie said from the top of the short flight of stairs that led to the bedroom.

"Hold your little kitty horses," I said. "Humans brush their teeth before going to bed." I'd heard of people brushing the teeth of their pets, but unless Eddie developed a health problem that threatened to shorten his life, I wasn't ready to try.

In short order, I was sliding between the sheets. "What do you think?" I asked. Eddie was walking around me, clearly trying to decide which of my body parts he wanted to cut off the circulation to the most. "Jane Austen, Tess Gerritsen, or L. A. Meyer?"

He flopped down on the bed, rested his chin on my right hip, and started purring.

"You know," I said through another yawn, "you could be right. It would probably fall on my face, smashing some pages in the process, and that's never—"

Eddie reached out and put his front paw across my lips.

"Eww." I turned my head. "I know where that paw has been."

"Mrr," he said firmly.

"Fine." I turned off the light and rolled onto my side. Eddie restarted his purr and, despite the morning's event, I fell into a dreamless sleep.

Chapter 3

The next morning was a bookmobile day—or, more accurately, thanks to my current schedule, a bookmobile three-quarters of a day—and I shut myself up in my office to steam through as much work as I could before hightailing it for Tonedagana County's lake-strewn, rolling countryside. I even filled my favorite Association of Bookmobile and Outreach Services coffee mug with Kelsey Coffee rather than waiting for a fresh pot to brew.

"Brave woman," Josh said, as I headed back to my computer. "Are you brave enough to send your director application to the board?"

"Working on it," I said over my shoulder. *Sort of.*

Back at my desk, I had just set my hands to the keyboard when my phone rang. I was tempted to ignore it. There were few phone calls I got these days that lasted less than fifteen minutes, and time was a-wasting, but my politeness reflex kicked in (thanks so much, Mom) and I picked up the receiver.

"Ms. Hamilton?" asked a warm male voice.

I leaned back, smiling. "Deputy Wolverson. How may I help you this morning?"

"I'm feeling stressed and overworked," he said. "No, hang on. It's you that's feeling stressed and overworked, isn't it? Either way, I think it would benefit both of us to take the day off and do as little as possible."

Since I could hear office noises in his background, I knew he was at work and wasn't about to run off into the sunset with me, but the idea was interesting. "Sounds good," I said. "How about I pick you up in the bookmobile in two hours? No one will know that I'm not making my appointed rounds."

"Isn't that the post office?"

"We have a lot in common."

He laughed. "I bet you go out in weather the mail carriers wouldn't touch. But believe it or not, I didn't call to entice you into an unplanned play day."

"Well, rats. I'd already shut down my computer," I said, expecting him to laugh again, and was surprised when he didn't.

"Sorry." His voice was sliding into formal cop mode. This was not a deeper voice, but was slower, measured, with sentences that were simple and direct. I'd been told that he'd had a severe stuttering issue as a kid, but I'd never detected a trace of it. "The city police chief," he said, "has contacted Andrea Vennard's family. Her name is being released to the press."

My emotions sagged. "Thanks for letting me know."

"No problem."

"Does this mean I'm free to talk about this?"

"Sure," he said.

I perked up a little; I'd detected a definite move out of cop speak. "Do you have any idea what happened?"

"Minnie . . ."

"I know, I know. You can't talk about an active investigation." I thought a moment. "How about this: Is it safe to be alone in the library late at night?" It hadn't been until last night, when I was working late, that I'd thought about the bad guy coming back. Something else I wasn't going to tell my mother.

"Safe?" he repeated. "Is anywhere truly safe?"

"Ash . . ."

"I know," he said. "Most people are good folks, and I shouldn't assume that bad guys lurk behind every corner."

It was a conversation that, in the short time we'd been together, we'd already had multiple times.

"Exactly," I said.

"That doesn't mean the bad guys aren't out there," he pointed out.

"But it also means the vast majority of the corners don't have bad guys anywhere close by."

Ash was silent for moment, then said, "But there was a bad guy, Minnie. And he was in your library."

Yes, he had been. And how icky did that make me feel? Very. "I know."

After a few beats, he said, "Take care, Minnie. You set for tomorrow morning?"

"Bright and early. And, Ash? Thanks for caring."

"No problem, ma'am," he said. "You have a good day, now."

Smiling, I hung up the phone and picked up my empty coffee mug. How I'd managed to down a full mug of Kelsey's brew in such a short time, I wasn't sure.

Holly was in the break room, opening up a plastic tub. "Leftovers from the last day of school," she said. "Have at it."

I peered in and pulled out the smallest brownie. Holly's treats were the stuff of legend, and it wouldn't do to offend the creator. "Ash called," I said, after swallowing the chocolatey goodness. "They're releasing the name of the woman who was killed."

Holly sat heavily. "I don't like to think that someone was murdered in our library."

Neither did I, but we had to move on. "The police are working hard to find the killer. I'm sure it will all be over soon."

"Will it?" Holly's face turned to mine. "Will it, really?"

No, and we both knew it. I couldn't conceive of a time when I wouldn't look at that aisle of bookshelves and not be reminded of what I'd seen. We would always remember what had happened, and it would always be a part of the library's history.

I gave her a vague half nod, half head shake, and said, "Her name was Andrea Vennard. She was from downstate. Brighton, I think."

"No, she wasn't."

Holly and I looked up to see Donna walking into the room.

"Andrea was from here," she went on. "She may have lived downstate, but she was born in Chilson, grew up here, and graduated from Chilson High School."

"Never heard of her," Holly said. "Or the name Vennard."

Donna went to the coffeepot and held it poised over her mug. "Who made this?"

"Josh," I told her.

She nodded and filled her mug. "Vennard was her married name, though she got divorced a number of years ago. She was a Wiley."

"No kidding." Holly sat back. "Why didn't I know her?"

"Older than you by ten years, I'd say." Donna shrugged. "And she was Bob's daughter."

"Bob, not Rob?"

The two of them dropped deep into a discussion of Chilson genealogy and, within seconds, since I hadn't grown up in Chilson or been provided with visual aids, I was totally lost. Which was okay, because it was relaxing, in a way, to lean against the counter and let the conversation wash over me. Normal. Everyday. Typical. For a couple more minutes, I could stand here and think about nothing while—

"Wiley," I said, cutting into something Donna was saying.

Donna glanced at Holly, then at me. "What about them?"

"If Andrea was a Wiley, was she related to the DeKeysers?" I asked, remembering Talia DeKeyser's obituary.

"Hmm, let me think." Donna frowned and stared at the ceiling. "Yes," she finally said. "She must have been a great-niece of Talia's."

She went off into an explanation, but this time I wasn't even trying to pay attention, because my brain was too busy thinking, connecting A to B.

Andrea Vennard lived downstate.

She was a great-niece of Talia DeKeyser.

Talia DeKeyser had recently passed away.

Andrea had, most probably, returned to Chilson for her aunt's funeral.

So . . . what? Nothing, really, was the conclusion I reached as I reached for another brownie. Because none of those facts answered the question of why Andrea had been in my library.

I waved at Donna and Holly, but they barely noticed

my leave-taking. As I walked back to my office, my brain was already on the things I had to finish before the book-mobile could back out of its garage, so when a large voice called my name, I jumped high enough to slop coffee over the side of my mug and onto the tile floor.

"Oh, geez, Minnie, sorry about that. Here, hang on." Mitchell Koyne, when standing, was well over a foot taller than my five feet. On his knees, using a grimy handkerchief to mop my spill, he was all arms and legs and awkwardness.

Mitchell was my age, but as far as I knew, he'd never held the same job for longer than six months. He bounced from summer construction labor to ski-lift operator to hauling firewood to plowing snow. Last year he'd started his own investigation business, but he'd never had a client and was still living in the attic apartment of his sister's house. He was clueless about almost everything, so totally clueless that it was easy to dismiss him as an Up North hick who'd never set foot in a real city.

But the thing was, Mitchell was smart. Extremely smart. In his untucked flannel shirt, ratty baseball cap, worn sneakers, and unshaven face, Mitchell would spend hours in the library, reading books and maga-zines, and I'd once watched him read an encyclopedia. Why he didn't translate some of that knowledge into useful skills, I did not know.

"What are you doing here?" I asked.

"Checking out books?"

"Not a chance," I said. "Your overdue fine is still the highest in the library's history, and just because Ste-phen's gone doesn't mean I'm going to let you start checking out books until your account is down to zero."

"Doesn't hurt a guy to ask," he said, grinning.

"But it's not even close to noon." I tipped my head in the direction of the wall clock. "You're never here before noon. Ever."

"Yeah." He took off his baseball hat, scratched his head, and put the hat back on. His hair, I noted, had been cut recently, which was unusual. Mitchell would go for months without a haircut; then he'd go to the barber and get it buzzed close to his skull. Neither the long hair nor the buzz was a good look for him, and it was interesting that his habits were changing.

Very interesting.

"So, Minnie," he said, "I got a question for you."

I made a come-along gesture and started walking again. Mitchell's long legs took two strides to every three of mine. "What's your question?" I asked. "But, just so you know ahead of time, I can't say anything about yesterday morning." More like "didn't want to" than "couldn't," but Mitchell didn't need to know that.

"Huh?" He peered down at me. "Oh, right. That Andrea Wiley got killed, didn't she? No, it's not about that."

I breathed a small sigh of relief. In the past, Mitchell had tried his best to insert himself into police investigations; that he wasn't inclined to do so now could only be a good thing.

"It's about Bianca," Mitchell said.

Then again, maybe it wouldn't be so horrible if Mitchell could be distracted by a murder investigation. Because if his girlfriend had dumped him, even if it was weeks past the latest guess from the library pool that Josh had started, Mitchell would need serious amounts of distraction.

"How is she?" I asked. Bianca Sims was one of the most successful real estate agents in the area. Blond, attractive, energetic, and outgoing, it boggled the mind that she and Mitchell had gone out on more than one date, let alone been seeing each other for two months. While I understood that Mitchell had his own variety of charm, I'd long held the opinion it was an appeal that was more attractive at arm's length. Still, there was no accounting for what attracted people to one another, a fact for which I should be grateful.

"She's great," Mitchell said gloomily.

I quirked up my eyebrows at his tone. "She's great, but there's a problem?"

"It's not her. It's me."

Now, that I could believe, but it didn't make sense that Mitchell was coming to me for advice on how to change his life. First off, Mitchell was one of those people who never seemed to recognize that improvements needed to be made. Second, while we'd been friends of a sort for years, we'd never shared soul-baring confidences.

"What's the matter?" We'd reached my office door, and I stopped to look up at him. Talking to Mitchell in the hallway was one thing, but I flat-out did not have time for him to come in and sit for a long, cozy chat.

"You're like her," he said. "I mean, you're short and she's nice and tall, and you have all that curly black hair and she has that nice smooth blond hair. Plus you read all the time and she's more fun and—"

"So how are we alike?" I asked, cutting into the brutal blow-by-blow comparison.

He shoved his hands into his pockets and looked at the floor. "You're both smart. Way smarter than me.

And you're both, you know, going places. I'll never be anything different from what I am right now."

I blinked at the naked truth of his words. Who knew that Mitchell was so self-aware? Served me right for thinking that I had him all figured out. Once again I realized that we could never truly know what went on inside someone else, and my heart ached for him. "If Bianca likes you," I said, touching his arm, "she likes you just the way you are."

"But will she ever, ahh, you know"—he shrugged and kicked at the floor—"love me. Like the way I'm getting to love her."

Whoa. I was not qualified to give romantic advice. My previous relationship had fallen to bits in less than a year, and before that I'd fallen out of love with the guy I'd become engaged to in graduate school, so slowly it had taken a total lack of interest in bridal magazines to make me realize what had happened.

"Mitchell," I said, "there are only two people who can help you."

"Yeah?" He perked up. "Do you have their numbers? Because I'll take any advice I can get, even if I don't like it."

But I was shaking my head. "The only two people who can help are you and Bianca. Talk to her, Mitchell. Tell her how you feel."

He sighed. "Not going to happen. I use the L word now, and she'll run for the hills. I need her to love me before I say anything, see?"

"How do you know she doesn't?"

"Why would she?"

The conversation was starting to circle around. "Do you two have a good time together?"

"Well, yeah."

"And she calls you to make dates?" He nodded, and I said, "Then she obviously likes you, Mitchell. If you love her, give her time to fall in love with you."

"But what if—"

"But nothing," I said firmly. "Give her some time, Mitchell."

"What should I do while I'm waiting?" he asked.

That I could answer. "Stay busy," I told him. "Best way to not think about something is to stay as busy as possible."

He nodded slowly, then more vigorously. "Okay, yeah. That makes sense. That makes a lot of sense." A wide grin lit up his face, almost making me forget about the four days' worth of beard he hadn't bothered to shave off before going into public. "Thanks, Minnie. I knew I could count on you."

I watched him saunter off, the swagger already back in his walk, and wondered what I'd done this time.

Two hours later, I hurried through the back door of Cookie Tom's. On bookmobile days, I had a standing order for two dozen of whatever he had plenty of, and even though I was running late, I didn't want to show up at the first stop empty-handed.

"Hey, Tom," I said, standing at the end of the glass display cases. Though it was late morning, there was still a line of people in the bakery's main room. Which could only mean that, no matter what the calendar said, it was officially summer. Pam Fazio, a tall travel mug of coffee in hand, was in the middle, listening to a sixtyish woman not much taller than me, who was saying how much she'd like it if Pam would purchase her collection of china cups and saucers. Pam caught my eye and toasted me. "Morning," she said.

Tom nodded my way. "Hang on, Minnie, I'll be

right with you." His summer helper, a high school girl, was ringing up orders while he was stuffing white bags and boxes with doughnuts, cookies, croissants, and muffins. I averted my eyes from the custard-filled chocolate long johns and dug the appropriate amount of cash out of my wallet.

A twentysomething man who was standing in line looked vaguely familiar, and I gave him a genial nod, trying to remember where I knew him from. The diner? Maybe. Or did he look like someone I'd gone to high school with? Then again, it could indeed be someone I'd attended high school with, even though I'd lived my early years in the greater Detroit area. Or it could be an actor from a hit movie I'd never seen. In a tourist town like Chilson, you never knew who you might run into.

"Mostly chocolate chip." Tom plopped a bag in front of me. "Some raisin, some oatmeal. Tossed in some broken peanut butters, too."

"You are a gentleman and a scholar," I said, handing over my money. "A prince among—"

"Hey," the sort-of familiar guy brayed. "Why does she get to cut in line?"

I flicked a glance at Tom. In all the months I'd been getting early dibs on cookies, we'd never once had anyone comment. "Sorry," I said, "if this—"

"No apologies necessary," Tom said, smiling at me, then turned to face the complainer. "This is my store, and I get to choose how I do business. Ms. Minnie here drives the bookmobile and she buys cookies for the patrons out of her own pocket. Getting her on her way quickly is my contribution to the bookmobile."

"Yeah," the guy said, "but—"

His objection was drowned out by the happy chatter and smiles of everyone else standing in line.

"There's a bookmobile in Chilson? That's wonderful!"

"Every time my grandson sees the bookmobile, he wants me to read him a story."

"Someone told me the bookmobile has a cat. Is that true?"

"Is there any way to make a donation?"

I smiled, handed out some business cards, and said I'd be happy to talk to anyone if they called me during library hours. Angry Guy folded his arms and didn't say a word. "Sorry," I murmured to Tom as I picked up the big white bag.

"Don't worry about it," he said. "Go forth and deliver books."

So I did.

Not much later, I was behind the wheel of a thirty-one-foot-long moving library, complete with more than three thousand books, CDs, DVDs, jigsaw puzzles, and games. Also along for the ride were the sixtyish Julia Beaton, and the thirteen-pound, three-year-old Eddie, who was in the strapped-down cat carrier at Julia's feet.

"Oh, my dear," Julia, my part-time bookmobile clerk said, when I finished telling her about Andrea Vennard. "What a wretched thing to have in your memory."

Her empathic reaction made my eyes sting. Then again, if anyone knew empathy, it was Julia. She'd grown up in Chilson, but had hightailed it for the bright lights of New York City to make it as a model or bust as soon as her parents had given the nod.

Bust as a model she did, but her second-choice career, that of acting, served her to the tune of multiple Tony

Awards. However, since she'd stuck to Broadway and never set foot in Hollywood, and with Chilson being Chilson, she'd never achieved much local fame. Julia being Julia, she found this extremely funny and welcome. "Why would I want complete strangers staring at me when I'm not onstage?" she'd asked, and I gave her the point.

I'd looked up reviews of plays in which she'd once starred and read that one of her strengths as an actor was in understanding people, so it shouldn't have been a surprise that she had so quickly sensed what kept returning to my thoughts and too-vivid imagination.

"How did you sleep last night?" she asked.

"Surprisingly well," I said. "Then again, I had some help from our little pal down there."

Neither Eddie nor the patrons would have been pleased to have a bookmobile absent of its bookmobile cat, so, after leaving the library that morning, I'd carefully driven the extremely expensive vehicle from the library down the narrow road that led to the marina, sat it temporarily in the parking lot, and run in to fetch Mr. Ed.

Julia leaned forward and reached her long fingers in through the wire door to scratch Eddie under the chin. "You did a fine job, my furry friend. Keep up the good work."

"Mrr," he said.

Julia sat up, pushed back her long strawberry blond hair, and laughed. "There are times when I really do think he understands what we say to him."

"I sincerely hope not," I said fervently, earning another laugh.

"Just think of it," Julia mused. "Eddie sees all, understands all, knows all."

"If so," I said, "why doesn't he make himself more useful?"

"That's not what cats do."

"What do they do, besides shed and eat and make a mess of the paper towels, no matter where I put them?" Eddie had a penchant for paper products and not in a loving way. He liked to shred them to bits, strewing pieces in every room possible.

"They purr," Julia said.

I grinned. "They do indeed." Which more than made up for every cat hair that ever had been or ever would be shed upon my person. "And they're excellent at convincing people to take naps."

Julia nodded. "Plus they help keep the mice population down."

And it was a cat, Eddie in particular, who had brightened the day of a little girl with leukemia the day he'd stowed away on the bookmobile. Brightened it so much, in fact, that he'd become a permanent bookmobile feature. At the time, I'd been intent on keeping Eddie's presence on the bookmobile a secret from Stephen, who'd been rule-bound to the extreme. But it had all worked out in the end, and Brynn Wilbanks, who was now six years old and attending kindergarten, was in remission and melted my heart with her wide smile every time I saw her.

"You realize, of course," Julia said, "that the primary reason for the existence of humans is to take care of cats."

"Eddie has mentioned that." I glanced down at the carrier. "But I thought he was exaggerating."

"Mrr!"

Julia laughed. I shook my head and flicked on the turn signal in preparation for our first stop of the day, in the parking lot of a township hall.

In less time than it takes to tell, I'd swiveled the driver's seat around to face the front desk and readied the computer, Julia had reached up to pop open the ceiling vents—at five foot eight, she could do it without the help of a step stool—and gone to the back of the bus to fire up the rear computer. I unlatched Eddie's carrier and, after a pause of almost half a second, he leaped out and jumped up on top of his latest favorite perch, the passenger's-seat headrest.

"Are we all set?" I asked.

"Ready," Julia called.

"Mrr."

I patted my cat on the head, watched a few black and white hairs fly in multiple directions, and opened the door.

"Good morning, Bookmobile Ladies!" A woman with short graying hair bounced up the steps. "And how is the Bookmobile Cat today?"

Eddie blinked at the woman, whose name was Faye, and said, "Mrr."

She laughed delightedly. "You are a treasure. Minnie, if you ever get tired of him, I'll take him home with me."

I smiled. "Sorry, but Eddie and I are bonded for life."

"Mrr."

Faye snorted out another laugh and patted him on the head. "Oh, Eddie, if only all cats were like you."

Someone else came stumping up the stairs. "Minnie! Are you all right?" Mrs. Dugan, a matronly woman in her mid-sixties, frowned at me, her firm white curls bouncing a little with the effort. "After what happened yesterday, I can't believe you're able to work, let alone drive the bookmobile!"

She flung her arms wide, and I had little choice but to stand up and get the stuffing hugged out of me.

"Poor Minnie," she murmured. "You're lucky you're so strong. I would have been a wreck, just a wreck. I take things to heart, and finding that poor woman would have sent me to bed for a week."

I murmured a thanks for her sympathy and extracted myself. To fend off further exuberances, I picked up Eddie, unashamedly using him as a shield. I made a mental vow to give him extra treats and asked Mrs. Dugan if she'd known Andrea Vennard.

"She was a Wiley, wasn't she?" Mrs. Dugan turned to look at Faye.

"Hmm?" Faye was perusing the new books and was just opening the cover of Sophie Kinsella's latest release.

"Andrea Vennard," Mrs. Dugan said. "Wasn't she Bob Wiley's daughter?"

"Is Bob married to Missy?" Faye asked. She looked up from the book and saw Mrs. Dugan nod. "Then yes, Andrea was a Wiley before she was a Vennard."

This confirmed what Holly and Donna had said. "How long ago did Andrea leave Chilson?" I asked.

Mrs. Dugan laughed. "That one? She left town right after high school."

Faye nodded. "Said Chilson wasn't big enough for her, that she had places to go, people to meet, things to accomplish."

I looked from one to the other. "And did she?"

"I live next to a high school friend of Andrea's,"

Faye said, "and she says Andrea was too busy to have kids or to get back home. I guess she owned a business downstate. Grosse Pointe? Bingham Farms? One of those fancy suburbs of Detroit, anyway."

Mrs. Dugan sniffed. "She came back fast enough when Talia DeKeyser died. That was her great-aunt, you know. Probably hoped she was named in the will."

"What kind of business did Andrea own?" I asked, but Faye didn't know. I shifted Eddie around a little, trying to ease him into a position that made him weightless. Thirteen pounds isn't much until you start shooting for the world's record in the Longest Eddie Hold. "Did Andrea have money problems?"

"Who doesn't?" Faye gave a crooked smile. "But I wonder what Andrea was doing in the library in the first place. From what my neighbor says, Andrea wasn't what you'd call the literary type."

"More a partying type?" I asked. If so, that could open up all sorts of possibilities for murder. I'd tell Ash tonight, and he would find a fast lead to the killer, and soon everyone would forget that the library had—

But Faye was shaking her head. "She was ambitious, mainly. There's a story about her high school boyfriend, Steve something. He was really serious about her, gave her an engagement ring on prom night. She laughed in his face, and I guess he went nuts. Got so angry that some other guys had to hold him back from hitting her. She got a personal protection order against him and left town the next week."

I shivered. "He doesn't sound like a good choice for a long-term relationship."

Mrs. Dugan snapped her fingers. "Guilder. Steve Guilder, that was his name. Didn't he move to Texas?"

Eddie, who up until that point had been purring quietly, started struggling to get down. Knowing that the cat always wins, I let him escape to the floor. "What did her folks say about her leaving home so young?"

"Normal stuff. That she was just a kid, that she had a lot to learn, that she didn't know everything, even if she thought she did."

So just adolescence, and no long-buried clue to the reason behind her murder. Maybe Andrea, in leaving town at eighteen, had taken her rebellion a step further than most kids, but even that wasn't too far from of the ordinary. Julia had done the same thing.

"I remember being that young." Mrs. Dugan sighed. "Life was simpler then, wasn't it?"

It had also been very limited, both in scope and in size, and fraught with self-doubt and self-esteem issues. "Personally," I said, "you couldn't pay me enough to—"

Crash!

I whirled around. "Eddie! What are you doing up there?" My cat had managed to dump a shelf full of books onto the floor. I reached for him, but he slid away from me and jumped in Julia's direction. "Fine," I muttered, crouching to pick up the books. "Be that way."

"Maybe he wants you to read to him," Faye suggested.

I eyed his selection. He'd dislodged the books in the Dewey decimal five and six hundreds: natural and applied sciences. "You could be right." I slid the gardening and philosophy books aside and held up *Cats: The Ultimate Beginners' Guide to Raising Healthy Cats for Life!* and *Think Like a Cat*.

Julia's laugh was loud and long.

"We can take one home," I told Eddie, who was

sitting in the middle of the aisle with his tail curled around his paws. "But only one. I know how short your attention span can be."

Eddie got to his feet and stalked past me without a glance.

Smiling, I watched him go. There really was nothing like a cat.

Chapter 4

"So," Lindsey Wolverson said that evening at the Round Table. "Your aunt tells me you have a knack for leadership."

I sent a panicked glance to my left at Ash, but he was busy sprinkling malt vinegar onto his fries and wasn't paying attention to either me or his mother, whom I was meeting for the first time.

Aunt Frances had known Lindsey for years, but I'd never met her. My aunt had told me of backyard picnics and dinner parties and watching Ash and his sister grow from roly-poly toddlers into adulthood, but she hadn't mentioned that his mother was so flat-out gorgeous that every person in the room—men and women alike—stared at her with dropped jaw. Not only that, but her chic yet casual attire was more elegant than anything I'd ever owned in my life.

It was a little intimidating, and I wish I'd known ahead of time. Then again, given Ash's innate good looks, I should probably have guessed something like this was possible. But mathematics wasn't my strong suit and I didn't always put two and two together.

So I smiled, added more salt to my fries than I really wanted, and struggled for something to say that didn't sound completely stupid. "I . . . I . . . uh . . ." I gave up. Stupid it would have to be.

Ash gave his fries one last dollop of malt vinegar, then screwed the top back onto the bottle. "You should see her with Sheriff Richardson. You'd think they'd been buds since day one."

Lindsey's perfectly plucked eyebrows went up. "Kit Richardson? That woman has awed me for years. She frightens men who have United States senators on their speed dial. Good for you. How did you do it?"

Basically, I had no idea, but it probably helped that I wasn't from Chilson. I hadn't known I was supposed to be nervous around the sheriff and had assumed she was like the other people I'd met from her office: helpful, courteous, and competent. Then again, it could have been because I'd knocked on the sheriff's front door early one morning, and it was hard to think of someone in terms of fearsome starch once you'd seen her in a ratty bathrobe.

I was about to explain parts of that when I accidentally caught the look on the face of a male passing our booth. He was staring at Lindsey, jaw dropped, eyes goggled, and there might even have been a small trail of drool leaking out one corner of his mouth, although that could have been my imagination. "I . . ." But whatever I'd been about to say had gone clean out of my head. "I . . . I . . ."

Lindsey's smile went from friendly to fixed.

I stared at the food on my plate. A burger and fries, all of which was rapidly growing cold and unappealing, but since I was losing my appetite even more rapidly, that didn't matter.

She hated me. My new boyfriend's mom hated me, and I hadn't uttered more than half a dozen words. A new record!

"How's business?" Ash asked. "Busy?"

Lindsey paused, her forkful of grilled chicken salad halfway to her mouth. "Do you realize that I've had this firm for nearly twenty years? And they said it wouldn't last."

Ash laughed. "Well, maybe that's what Dad said right after the divorce. I always knew you'd be a success."

She smiled at him fondly. "I just hired another employee. Who knew financial consulting would be so lucrative?"

My misery deepened. Not only was she beautiful, but she was smart and successful and could do math. There was no way she was ever going to approve of a mousy little librarian dating her son. Especially one who couldn't put two and two together and get a reality into which I would never, ever belong.

I picked up a French fry and thought about eating it, but its coating of salt crystals glinted in the light. While it was my opinion that fries had to have a certain amount of salt to make them edible, there was also a point at which too much salt made them inedible, and these fries had reached that point halfway through my use of the saltshaker. Poor fries, doomed to end their life in a garbage bag, never to be—

"Minnie?" Ash nudged me with his elbow. "Did you hear my mom's question?"

"Oh." I blinked at him, then at the stunning woman sitting across from me. "Sorry. I . . . I . . ."

Thankfully, she cut into my repetitious soliloquy. "I hear you had a traumatic experience the other morning at the library."

Not nearly as traumatic as it had been for Andrea Vennard, but the thought was a kind one. I nodded. And since I didn't want to relive the experience any more times than my stupid brain was already forcing me to do, I returned to contemplating my dinner.

There was a pause. A long one.

"Well," Lindsey said, and though I'd known her for less than an hour, even I could hear the brittleness in her voice. "Have the two of you seen any movies lately?"

I glanced at Ash, who was in the middle of taking a large bite from his hamburger. He wasn't going to be any help. I looked at Lindsey and shook my head. "I—"

Ash's cell phone burst into life. He shifted his burger to one hand and pulled out his cell with the other. With a huge effort that happily didn't end with the necessity for someone to jump up and perform the Heimlich maneuver, he swallowed, then said, "Sorry— I have to take this," and thumbed the phone to life. "Wolverson." As he listened, he flicked glances at his mother, at me, at his food. "Okay. I'll be right there."

In one smooth movement, he slid the phone back into his pocket and stood. "Sorry, Mom. Sorry, Minnie. That was Detective Inwood. He needs me to—"

But his mom was already waving him away. "Duty calls. I understand," she said as he leaned down to give her a kiss on the cheek.

He looked my way, gave me a large wink that his mother couldn't see, and left me alone with her.

This time the pause was even longer.

"Are you a reader?" I asked.

"Of what?"

"Books. Magazines. Newspapers." Anything, really,

because if we could find some common ground, surely I would figure out something to say to this woman.

"Most of my reading is business oriented," she said. "Books on economics and financial forecasting. Trade magazines—that kind of thing."

"No fiction?"

Lindsey looked at me with an expression I couldn't interpret. "My father always said that fiction was the refuge of the unhappy. That readers of fiction were looking for an escape."

"But . . . but . . ." Then I stopped, because I did not want to get into an argument with my boyfriend's mother the first time I met her.

I turned my attention back to my hamburger, mainly because if I was eating, I couldn't be expected to talk. The resulting silence was awkward. With a capital *A*.

"Ran out on you, did he?" Sabrina, my favorite waitress at the Round Table, stopped by to top off our water glasses. "You ladies need anything else?"

"Just the check, please," Lindsey said. "And I'll take that right now."

"Gotcha."

Sabrina pulled the correct slip from her apron pocket without looking. As soon as she slid it onto the table, Lindsey picked it up and slid out of the booth. "Thank you. I'll pay up front. Minnie, it was a pleasure meeting you." She smiled politely and was gone.

"Wow," Sabrina said, watching her go. "That was Ash's mom, right? She's gorgeous."

I pushed my plate away. Ash's mother was everything I was not and never would be. Tall. Straight-haired. Articulate. Financially successful. Stunningly beautiful. Not to mention articulate.

Sighing, I started to slide out of the booth. I almost asked Sabrina how her husband, Bill, was doing. They'd met here at the Round Table and had been married less than a year. Then I decided to ask the next time I was in. Right now, all I wanted was to go home and snuggle up to my cat.

"How could I have been such an idiot?" I asked.

"Mrr," Eddie replied.

"Well, yeah," I said, pulling the lap blanket up over my legs. We were sitting outside on the houseboat's front deck. The sun was slipping down into the horizon and the temperature was dropping. "Everyone's an idiot some of the time. Except you, of course."

"Mrr."

"You're welcome." I patted his head. "But I'm relatively self-confident. I haven't had major self-esteem issues since I talked Mom into letting me get contact lenses."

"Mrr."

"Right. So, why tonight? Why couldn't I get out more than three words in a row?" I thought back to the nonconversation, then corrected myself. "More than one word in a row."

Eddie stood, stretched, and then walked up my body and flopped onto my chest. "Mrr." A front paw reached out to rest on my chin.

"When you do that, it makes it hard to talk," I told him.

"Mrr."

I laughed softly. "That's the point, is what you're saying? That I should just enjoy the sunset and your company and not worry so much about one dinner?"

"Mrr!"

So I stopped talking and concentrated on enjoying a cat's affection and the gloriousness of a summer sunset. And, long before the sky went completely dark, I'd put the Doomsday Dinner to the back of my mind.

Well, almost.

The next morning, life at the library was more or less back to normal. Work was piling up on my desk, Josh and Holly were trying to pin me down on when I'd turn in my application for library director, and the carpet guys I'd contacted had come and gone, leaving behind nothing but a faint new-carpet smell and a swath of carpet that held no bad memories.

Yes, there was still a killer on the loose and, yes, I was still disturbed by the fact that I had no idea how he—or she—had infiltrated my library, but I was determined not to lose my focus on the multitude of tasks that needed to be done. Because in spite of last night's miserable dinner, and no matter what Lindsey Wolverson must think of my character, I was a capable human being and people relied on me to do my job.

And in a just world, which would be where hardworking and almost-always-kind people were given dignity and grace, when one of those hardworking and kind person's cell phone rang, her brain would have used enough of itself to think about how she was going to answer rather than just pick up the phone absently and say, "Busy. What's up?"

There was a short pause. A male throat cleared itself. "Ms. Hamilton?"

I sat up, blinking away from the invoices on my desk whose numbers didn't match what the accounting program on my computer was telling me. "Detective Inwood.

Good morning." I darted a quick glance at the computer screen. *Yes, still morning. Excellent.* While I may not have been paying full attention to what my phone had been trying to tell me, at least I had the time of day correct by three full minutes. "What can I do for you?"

"The Sheriff, Deputy Wolverson, and I have decided to make you aware of the results of Ms. Vennard's autopsy."

"Oh." Did I really want to know this? No, I did not. I'd read far too many thrillers and seen far too many television shows that featured autopsies to want to hear any grisly details regarding a real human being. "Thanks," I said, "but I'm pretty sure I don't—"

"Ms. Vennard," he went on, paying zero attention to my wishes and desires, "was not killed by the knife."

"She wasn't?" Once again, I pictured the silver handle. "Then why was it there?"

"We do not know. The cause of death was strangulation."

That made no sense.

"The knife found in the body," he said, "was an X-Acto knife. The blade was thin and about an inch long."

"A what kind of knife?"

He repeated the word. "It's a brand name. Used by artists, woodworkers, and any number of hobbyists."

"So not unusual."

"Not at all. But it's puzzling," the detective said. "Ms. Vennard's fingerprints were sharp and clear on the handle. The lab's opinion is that no great force was exerted on the handle other than by Ms. Vennard. In addition, the X-Acto injury was postmortem."

I suppressed a shudder. "Why would she be in the library with an X-Acto knife?"

"That's why I called," Inwood said. "I'd hoped that as the acting library director, you'd have some insight."

"Sorry. It doesn't make any sense to me, either."

"Well," he said heavily, "we will do our best to keep all avenues of investigation open."

It was a phrase I'd heard before. "Do you have any new ideas about how Andrea got in the building?" I asked.

The working theory was that she'd walked into the library when it was open and simply hid. Gareth left at one in the morning, and searching for stowaways certainly wasn't anything he'd ever needed to do.

"Not yet," he said. "No signs of forced entry on any doors or windows; no record of any missing keys."

The possibility of a missing key would have been high in the old building, which hadn't had new locks since it had been built decades earlier, but Stephen had instituted a strict key-tracking system when we'd moved to the new building, and for once I was grateful for his persnicketiness.

But this scenario also meant that Andrea might have opened the door to her killer, which made—

A sturdy woman barged into my office, tossing back her short brown hair. "Minnie, I need to talk to you."

I held up my index finger and pointed to the phone. "Is there anything else?" I asked Detective Inwood. "Someone's just come in that I need to talk to." Didn't want to, but would obviously need to, since she was settling into my guest chair, no invitation required.

"If anything further develops," Inwood said, "I'll let you know."

I thumbed off the phone and looked up. "What's up, Denise?"

Denise Slade was fiftyish and the current president of the Friends of the Library. Just before last Thanksgiving, her husband had died tragically. I was trying to remember that, was trying to allow her time to work through her grief and come to grips with the loss of her life partner, but doing so was easier some days than others.

She pointed her index finger straight at me. "I have a problem, and I want to know what you're going to do about it."

I folded my hands on my desk. Denise had a lot of problems, but it wasn't likely that she was coming to me for advice on how to win friends and influence people. Then again, if she was interested in doing that, there were some books I could recommend.

"Can I get you some coffee?" I asked.

"If Kelsey made it, then yes. Otherwise, no. She's the only one who makes a decent brew around here. The rest of you are a bunch of coffee wimps."

"Holly made the last pot."

Denise shuddered. "I'd rather go without."

Then that's what she'd do. I smiled, trying my best to stay friendly and composed. "What's the problem?"

Her frown turned into a glower. "The book-sale room."

"What about it?" For eons, the Friends of the Library had been running a book sale. In the old library they'd been shoehorned into a basement room little bigger than a closet, but now they were in a spacious area on the second floor with room to grow. Donated books and books we took out of circulation were sold, and all the profits went to benefit the library.

The Friends purchased books for us, hosted author events for us, held children's events for us, and lent a helping hand whenever one was needed. I didn't want to think what running the library would be like without the Friends, and I was deeply grateful for everything they did.

"It's a mess," Denise said. "A huge mess, and no one is admitting to having done it."

This wasn't a huge surprise. A mess by Denise's standards would have been a comfortable clutter to anyone else. I'd once heard her berate a volunteer for walking past a shelf of sale books without straightening them to be flush with the front edge.

"How much of a mess are you talking about?" I asked.

"Come see," she said, and shoved herself out of the chair and to her feet.

Not for the first time, I realized that I hadn't given Stephen enough credit. When he'd been here, he'd been in charge of soothing Denise's ruffled feathers, and I was now realizing it must have taken more time and patience than I'd ever dreamed. I made a silent apology to my former boss and remained seated.

"Sorry, Denise," I said. "I don't have time right now." I nodded at the piles of papers on my desk. "Give me half an hour."

She huffed out a massive sigh. "And here I thought you were going to be a better director than Stephen. You're just as bad as he was at meeting the needs of the Friends."

Though it was disheartening to be compared to a man whom I'd never thought had an ounce of management skills, I was learning. Slowly, but I was learning. "I'll be up in half an hour." I smiled politely and went back to my papers.

Half an hour later, on the dot, I walked into the

book-sale room. "Wow," I said, looking around. "You weren't kidding."

Denise rolled her eyes. "I told you, didn't I? A mess."

For once, she was making a huge understatement. Books were on the windowsills. Books were on the tables. Books were scattered across the floor. It looked as if a huge wind had rushed through the room, sucking every book off a shelf and spitting them out every which way. It was a horrendous mess.

"You'd better stop," I told Denise.

"What?" She was crouching on the floor, picking up books, and sliding them onto the nearest shelf. "Don't be ridiculous. We have to get this room back in shape before tomorrow. That's sale day, you know."

Once upon a time I'd known when the Friends opened the room to the public for sales, but Denise had switched it around so much the past few months that I never told anyone the sales days without running upstairs and checking the dates taped to the door.

"The police need to look at this," I said.

"Police? That's nuts. This was vandalism, pure and simple. Some kids snuck up here and, without Stephen in his office down the hall, they had time to do all this."

I frowned. "Haven't you heard what happened?"

"Heard what?" she said crossly. "I've been downstate visiting friends. Drove up this morning and came straight to the library."

Oh, dear. If I'd had to make a list of the people who'd heard about the murder ten minutes after I'd called the police, Denise's name would have been at the top. She was related to half the people in Chilson and had gone to school with the other half. That she hadn't heard about Andrea Vennard might well be a sign that the world was about to end. I hoped not, though, because I had things to do. Like grow older.

I walked across the room and gently took the books out of her hands. "You'd better sit down. There's something I need to tell you."

Since murder had struck her own family less than a year ago, I thought she might take the news hard, and she did. She dissolved into sobbing tears after I'd told her a woman had been killed in the library, but after she'd recovered, I called the city police and they sent up the nice Officer Joel Stowkowski. He looked around, took notes, snapped photos, checked doors and windows, and offered a lot of sympathy, but he hadn't been able to promise much in the way of retribution for anyone who had the temerity to damage books in a library, even if they weren't technically library books.

It was all kinds of rotten, and I was glad to head home to the marina that evening and curl up with Eddie and a book. But that night the wind came up, slapping waves against the houseboat and rocking me into dreams that featured earthquakes and landslides. Then, as the dark edged into a gray, dreary, windswept morning, the heavens opened up and the rain came down.

Eddie and I sat at the dining table, me on the bench, Eddie on the back of the bench looking out at the wet world.

"It's a bookmobile day," I reminded him. "What do you think?"

There was no response from my feline friend.

"You don't have to go, you know," I said. "People will understand." Which wasn't exactly true. Once, last winter, Eddie hadn't been feeling well and I'd left him at the boardinghouse instead of dragging him out into the cold. I'd had to explain his bookmobile absence, and he'd received more Get Well cards than I'd received Christmas cards. Not that it was a contest, but still.

Eddie jumped onto the table and started to stick his head into my cereal bowl.

"Hey!" I pulled what was left of my breakfast away from him. "What do you think you're doing? This is mine. Yours is on the floor. You know, in the cat-food bowl? And get off the table. You don't belong up there."

He gave me a look, then started a slow ooze onto the floor.

"Faster," I said, giving his hind legs a slight shove.

"Mrr!" he said just before he landed.

"Yeah, well, back at you."

When I didn't hear anything else, I turned and saw that he was sitting on top of his cat carrier. "Ready to go?" I asked.

Cat fashion, he managed to rearrange his feet without moving, staring at me the whole time.

"I'll take that as a yes."

"Mrr!"

I laughed out loud. I was almost sorry I'd had Eddie fixed, because if I'd been able to find a girl cat who could tolerate him, their kittens would have been something extraordinary.

"Then again," I told him a few minutes later, as I fastened my car's passenger's-side seat belt around the cat carrier, "having an entire litter of you might be too much. Yes, I know that none of your offspring could possibly be an improvement on your own unique species, but just imagine four or five or six little Eddies, all trying to talk to me at the same time."

Months ago, I'd decided that Eddie had to be one of

a kind and named him *Felis eddicus*. Very like the more common *Felis domesticus*, but not quite.

"What kind of cat would be your mate of choice?" I asked. "Tortoiseshell? Another tabby? A Siamese? How about a Scottish fold? They're way cute."

"Mrr."

"Okay, no Scottish folds." I glanced over. My cat was flopped on his back, wedging himself into a corner of the carrier, waving his legs in the air. "Though a better question might be, what self-respecting lady cat would have anything to do with you?"

"Mrr!"

"Yeah, whatever." Grinning, I squinted through the rain. "You're out of practice, pal. As I recall, the last time you talked to a female feline, there was a lot of fur flying and you weren't the clear victor." Last winter, my aunt Frances's new love interest, Otto, had brought over his adorable little gray cat, hoping the two would become friends, but all had not gone well.

I flicked on the turn signal and made a right into the library's back parking lot, which was the only place Stephen had allowed me to site a garage for the bookmobile. It was a very small garage, not much bigger than the bookmobile itself. This made hefting books back and forth to the library more than a small chore, but at the time I'd accepted his conditions willingly, because it was either accept or not have a bookmobile at all.

"If that estate ever gets settled," I told Eddie, "what do you think the chances are that I'll get to use some of that money for a real garage?"

"Mrr."

"You think so?" Because he'd sounded optimistic. "That would be wonderful. And maybe the new Stephen will let me . . ." I trailed off. Holly and Josh and Donna and Kelsey and everyone else on the staff were still after me to turn in my application. "I could be the new Stephen. What do you think of that?"

"Mrr!"

I frowned. "It's not that unlikely. I'm doing an okay job so far. It's not that much of a stretch to—"

"MRR!" Eddie howled, banging his whole self against the carrier's wall, thumping so hard that I winced.

"Will you stop that? What's wrong with—"

It was then that I noticed the people door to the bookmobile garage wasn't closed up tight. In fact, it wasn't closed at all. I braked to a sudden stop.

There wasn't a single, solitary chance I'd left that door unlocked, let alone standing wide-open. There were things I routinely forgot, such as going to the dentist every six months and making sure I dusted the top of the kitchen cabinets, but I would never, ever forget to shut and lock the bookmobile's garage door.

So there were two possibilities. One, last night's wind had broken the door open. But since the door had remained firmly shut throughout the massive storm of a few weeks ago, when hundred-mile-an-hour, straight-line winds had rushed through town, that didn't seem likely. Unfortunately, the other possibility was far more troubling.

My heart beat fast as I put the car in park and opened the driver's door. I had to find out what had happened, I had to see what was—

"Mrr!"

I looked at my cat.

"Mrr!" he said again, glaring at me.

"You're right," I muttered, sitting down. "It would be stupid to go barging in there."

I reached down, pulled my phone out of my backpack's outer pocket, and dialed three numbers. Then I took a deep breath and unclenched my jaw so that I'd be able to respond when the dispatcher asked about my emergency.

"I'd like to report a break-in," I said.

Chapter 5

"**Y**ou seem to be making a habit of this," Officer Joel Stowkowski said, eyeing the mess that had once been a tidy bookmobile.

"Well," I said, still doing my best not to sit down on the carpeted step and bawl like a toddler, "you know what they say: Bad habits are six and a half times easier to create than good ones."

Joel quirked up a smile. He was probably fifty years old, and was known throughout town as a good guy. Ash, who had first worked at the Chilson Police Department before moving to the sheriff's office, said he had a nasty tendency to think puns were the highest form of humor, but so far that hadn't bothered me. "Six and a half times?" he asked. "You're making that up."

"Mrr," Eddie said.

Joel peered into the cat carrier, which I'd set onto the bookmobile's console. "Was he asking the same thing or coming to your defense?"

"He was wondering where his treats went." I nodded at the empty shelf near Joel's left shoulder. "They used to be up there. Now . . ." I looked at the thousands of books, CDs, DVDs, and magazines strewn all across the floor and, once again, felt tears prick at my eyes. *Buck up, Minnie,* I told myself. *You can't fall apart now; there's too much to do.* "He'll probably," I said, "turn up his nose at treats that have been handled by a burglar, and demand new ones."

"Yeah," Joel said. "Cats are like that." He reached out and patted the top of the carrier absently. "Well, Minnie, I'll do what I did yesterday upstairs—take pictures, take a close look at the doors and windows, and take fingerprints in the appropriate places."

I nodded. If I ever got tired of working at the library, maybe I'd start a forensic-cleaning business. After all, I now had more experience getting rid of fingerprint dust than most people would get in two lifetimes.

"This is probably a stupid question at this point," he went on, "but do you see anything missing?"

I just looked at him.

He grinned. "Told you it was a stupid question."

"The computers are still here." I gestured at the two laptops—one up front, the other at the back. "Of course, they're bolted in."

"I'll take prints on those, too. We already have yours for elimination. Is there anyone else who uses the computers regularly?" After I told him I'd have Julia stop by the police station to get fingerprinted, he said, "Okay, then. Let me get the camera from the car and I'll get going."

He turned to go, then stopped and swung back around. His face, normally creased with a smile, was serious. "I have no idea what's going on here, Minnie, but we will find out. Between us and the sheriff's department, we'll figure out who did this and prosecute to the fullest extent of the law."

I swallowed away another round of pending tears. "Thanks, Joel," I said quietly. "That means a lot."

"Maybe it was just kids messing around, maybe it was someone else. But no one is going to get away with breaking into our library and our bookmobile."

"Our library," he'd said. "Our bookmobile." Was any librarian ever so lucky as I was? In the guise of scratching my face, I rubbed away my tears. "I believe you."

He gave me a sharp nod and trod down the steps. I sat heavily onto the passenger's seat, giving myself three minutes to cry.

When that was done, I started thinking. First, I had to call Julia. Then there were the calls to make to the day's bookmobile stops, giving them the bad news that the bookmobile wasn't coming. I hated to do that, but there was little choice. If Joel's work yesterday at the Friends' sale room was any indication, he'd be here for a couple of hours. And then all the books needed to be shelved and checked against the computer to make sure nothing was missing.

I looked over at Eddie, who was staring at me. "What do you think?"

"Mrr," he said.

"Yeah," I agreed. "It's way past time to install security cameras, isn't it."

"Mrr."

By lunchtime, I was almost ready to cry again, but this time from the wonderfulness of human beings. I'd called Julia to give her the news, and, without a word of suggestion from me, she, in turn, had called Denise, who had immediately harnessed the tremendous power of the Friends of the Library.

When Joel declared himself done with the documentation of the scene, half a dozen strong-minded men and women wielding vacuum cleaners, spray bottles, and rags went to work. Behind them came another equally strong-minded group who sorted and shelved and called out book titles to the people behind the computers.

"It's amazing," I murmured as I peered out my office window. Denise and her crew had banished me to the library, and I'd reluctantly done as they'd asked.

"Mrr," Eddie said.

He'd squeezed himself onto my office's narrow windowsill and, though he didn't quite fit, he didn't seem to mind that half of him was spilling out into the room.

"You look like a dork," I told him.

He looked at me, and I could almost see the thought bubble rising out of his head. "Whatever," it said, and he went back to working out how he could morph through the window glass and get at the birds swooping around the back side of the library.

"But it is amazing." I'd just wandered out for a quick check of the progress at the garage and, with all the hands that had come in to help, they'd be done with the whole kit and caboodle by midafternoon. Which, technically, gave me time to make the last scheduled bookmobile stops of the day. "What do you think?"

Eddie, still at the window, didn't reply. He was miffed because I was keeping him contained in my office. Yes, libraries across the world had resident cats, but even though Stephen had been gone for weeks now, I couldn't break away from his policies in a finger snap. Though Stephen had tacitly allowed Eddie's presence on the bookmobile, the main library was another story altogether.

"Plus," I told my furry friend as I turned back to work, "I'm only the interim director. That means I'm not the real one. Making drastic changes isn't what I'm supposed to be doing. I'm just keeping the seat warm for the next person."

"Which should be you." Holly poked her head into the room. "The library board's about to start the first interview, you know. Did you turn in your application yet?"

"As soon as you finish cleaning out your garage." The messy state of Holly's garage had been a constant lament for months. The possibility of it actually being cleaned out, however, was as real as the possibility of Eddie not shedding for thirty straight seconds.

Holly stuck her tongue out at me. "Do you have plans for lunch? Want to go down to the deli?"

"Sounds good." I thought wistfully of my favorite sandwich from Shomin's: olive and Swiss cheese on sourdough with Thousand Island dressing. "But I should eat the lunch I brought to eat on the road. Thanks, though."

Holly looked at the windowsill. "What about you, Eddie? Anchovies? Sardines?"

"He's fine with the cat food I brought," I said quickly. Anything else tended to upset his little kitty tummy.

"See how she is?" A straight-faced Holly asked Eddie. "Strict. Uncompromising. Inflexible. She'll make a perfect successor for Stephen."

"Mrr."

"What did he say?" Holly asked.

"That if you don't stop insulting me, he's going to make you wish you'd never been born."

"Really?" She looked at Eddie with some trepidation.

I laughed. "He's a cat. He's probably trying to figure out the most comfortable place to take a nap."

"He might be smarter than you think."

"Or not. You do realize that he can't really understand human speech?"

"If that's true, why do you keep talking to him as if he knows what you're saying?"

"Because I like to pretend."

"Uh-huh." She looked at me askance. "I'm not sure I believe you. I've heard the way you talk to him. Just like he's another human."

"He's used to the sound of my voice—that's all," I said. "Have you seen the size of his head? I mean, it's big for a cat, but compared to a human, it's tiny, and there's no way he has the capacity for cognition, not like we have, and—hey, Eddie, don't—"

A black-and-white shape whooshed past me and past my desk, then eeled through the gap Holly had left between the door and the doorframe, and ran into the freedom of the hallway.

"Eddie!" I called pointlessly. Like he was going to come just because I wanted him to.

Holly laughed. "You sure he doesn't understand what you were saying?"

"He saw an open door." I got to my feet. "Cats are opportunists."

"Doesn't that take brains?" she asked.

"Instinct. Natural reaction. Doesn't take any more intelligence than a . . . a horse getting out of a pasture, and I don't hear you saying that horses understand human speech."

By this time we were both out in the hallway, scouting left and right for any trace of a runaway feline.

"Hmm," she said. "Remember that television show, *Mr. Ed*? Maybe there's something about the name."

Right. "I doubt he ran into the main library or the children's section. All those people would freak him out. Can you check back there?" I nodded toward the front desk and the office spaces behind. "I'll check the reading room."

Holly headed off, and I hurried toward the reading room. And though I was doing my best to project nonchalance, I was actually a little worried. If Eddie had been close to an outside door when someone opened it, he could have zoomed out and—

"Stop it," I said to myself. It was a big library, but there were only so many places a cat could hide. It wasn't like a house where there were nooks and crannies everywhere. The building was mostly public space without much furniture. There was no place for him to hide in the main stacks, unless . . . My steps quickened.

Unless he squirreled his way in behind a row of books. The shelves were deep enough for a cat to fit behind there, especially a cat wanting to hide from a human companion who had been seriously disrespecting his mental capacities.

Maybe he didn't know what I was saying, but he certainly understood the different tones in my voice, and he'd been tossed into a brand-new environment just a few hours earlier. Cats like routine, at least Eddie did, and I hadn't taken enough time to make sure he was happy. I was a horrible cat owner and didn't deserve Eddie's friendship and—

"Mrr."

I stopped dead, just outside the entrance to the reading room. "Eddie?" I called. "Where are you?" I waited, but didn't hear him again. Which was frustrating, because

I hadn't been able to pinpoint his location from that one little "Mrr." For the first time ever, I wished he'd start howling.

The reading room, my favorite space in the library, was almost empty. Even on this dark day, natural light filled the space, streaming through the windows that lined one wall. A multitude of seating options were offered through window seats, upholstered couches, chairs, and large ottomans, some of which were clustered around the large tiled fireplace at the far end of the room. The gas fire wasn't turned on today, but I almost wished it had been, because its heat would have been a sure Eddie magnet.

"Shhh," an elderly male voice whispered. "If you don't tell, I won't. What do you say?"

I should have known.

Smiling, I walked around the back of a large wing chair to see one of my favorite library patrons, Lloyd Goodwin, feeding Eddie small bits of . . . "Is that beef jerky?" I asked.

Mr. Goodwin closed his hand over the meat. "I'm sure I have no idea what you're talking about."

"You," I said, crossing my arms, "are a horrible liar." Eddie, curled up on Mr. Goodwin's lap, reached out with one white-tipped paw and patted the closed fist. "Besides, Eddie knows what you have in there, and he doesn't care if you get caught eating in a room where food is forbidden."

Mr. Goodwin had noticed Eddie the day I'd walked home from the cemetery with a stray cat on my heels, and the two had met numerous times since, because Mr. Goodwin's summer walking route went right past the marina.

"That was," Mr. Goodwin said, "the leftovers from

my morning snack that I ate out in the hallway. I would never eat in this room."

"But you'll let him?" I nodded at Eddie, who was snarfing down the last bits of jerky from the hand that Mr. Goodwin had opened. "That stuff probably isn't good for cats."

"Cats are smart," Mr. Goodwin said. "They don't eat what isn't good for them."

I wasn't so sure about that, not in Eddie's case, anyway. "I need to get him back to my office," I said. "He's an escapee."

"This one?" Mr. Goodwin's age-spotted hand rested on Eddie's back. Eddie started purring immediately. "What's the harm in letting him roam? Pity about the bookmobile this morning," he added. "Makes you wonder what's next. And that Andrea Wiley." He sighed. "I don't like it when young people die. Such a waste. She had too many years taken away from her. And I'm so very sorry that you had to be the one to find her, dear Minnie."

That was not something I wished to revisit. "Thanks. Did you know her?"

He began to pet Eddie, eliciting even louder purrs. "My wife was a good friend of her mother's, so I heard about her until my Mary went away."

Two years ago, Mrs. Goodwin had gone to the emergency room because she was having trouble breathing. They'd diagnosed a serious heart condition and admitted her immediately for emergency surgery, but she hadn't survived. It had taken Mr. Goodwin more than a year to come back to being anything close to his former self, and only recently had he been able to speak her name without his voice breaking. I could only guess the depth of his grief, and still hadn't decided if I wanted to love someone that much. Not that we got the choice. Or did we? Something to wonder about tonight.

"The last time I saw Andrea," Mr. Goodwin said, "must have been when the library was in the old building."

I blinked at him. "What?"

"Now, don't go trying to confuse an old man," he said, smiling. "I may not be able to remember what I had for breakfast this morning, but I can remember some things."

I laughed. "You have a better memory than ninety-nine percent of the population, and that includes me. Better eyesight, too. And probably better hearing. Don't you go running down one of my favorite library patrons."

Mr. Goodwin arched his eyebrows. "Should librarians have favorites? Shouldn't they be like parents and claim to love all their children equally?"

Probably, but there was no way I was going to like Mrs. Suggs, who checked out nothing except books on how to improve other people, as much as I liked Reva Shomin, who had small children whose favorite thing in the world was to curl up in the big chair in the children's section and have their mommy read aloud to them.

"Then you saw Andrea about four years ago?" I asked. "I'd heard that she'd never come back to Chilson after she lit out of town right after high school."

Mr. Goodwin scratched Eddie's chin. Whenever I tried to do that, he turned his head away, but here he was, allowing Mr. Goodwin to scratch away and, even worse, purring as if that's what he wanted all along.

"Metaphorically speaking," Mr. Goodwin said, "I

suppose that's true. After that trouble with her high school boyfriend, she didn't come north for years. But eventually she came back for Thanksgiving, Christmas, that kind of thing. Her parents' fiftieth wedding anniversary. And"—he ran his hand over the length of Eddie's long body—"her great-aunt Talia's funeral."

All of which kind of put paid to my half-formed notion that Andrea had been killed because it was the first time she'd returned to Chilson in more than twenty years. That was too bad, because I'd already come up with half a dozen scenarios that would have worked, ranging from an unrequited high school love that turned deadly to a long-dormant posttraumatic stress disorder triggered by Andrea's return. Why her return might have reawakened a trauma, I hadn't yet determined, but I figured all I needed to do was watch a little more television and something would occur to me.

"Were they close?" I asked.

"Talia and Andrea?" Mr. Goodwin picked up the end of Eddie's tail and waved it around. Eddie purred. "Not to my knowledge, but that's not to say they weren't. My Mary would have known." He held on to Eddie's tail a little too long, and Eddie turned around to look at him.

"Mrr," he said quietly.

Mr. Goodwin smiled. "Apologies, Mr. Edward. I wasn't taking proper care of you, was I?" He chuckled and patted the top of the furry head. "From what I recall, Andrea was a squarish peg in a round hole. Ambitious in a family of folks who were accustomed to taking what was given them. Full of curiosity when those around her didn't question a thing. It must have been difficult for her, and moving away was probably the best thing."

Except that coming back had ended in her death. "Do you have any idea," I asked, "why she might have been in the library after hours?"

Mr. Goodwin was silent for a moment. "No, I don't," he finally said. "I have nothing to offer, and I've considered that question thoroughly." He frowned. "Beyond the appalling tragedy of Andrea's death, the entire event is extremely puzzling. I'm sure your Deputy Wolverson agrees, yes?" Mr. Goodwin's white and bushy eyebrows quirked up at me.

I smiled. "He doesn't talk to me about active investigations, but he has to find it weird."

And that's what I kept coming back to. The whole thing was beyond weird. Why had Andrea been in the library? It probably wouldn't have been that difficult to hide from Gareth for a few hours, but why on earth would she? Had she unlocked a door to let her killer inside? If so, why? She wouldn't have unlocked the door for someone who was about to kill her, but who would she have unlocked it for? Or could it have been the other way around, that the killer had been hiding in the library and let Andrea inside? Since we didn't have security-camera video, I wasn't sure we'd ever know.

"Mrr," Eddie said.

I looked down to find both Eddie and Mr. Goodwin looking at me with concern. "Did you go somewhere?" Mr. Goodwin asked. "You had an odd look on your face."

"Just thinking," I said. "Makes my face twist up sometimes."

Mr. Goodwin laughed. "And I suppose you want to take your feline friend back to your office, yes?" He tried to arrange Eddie into a pickup position, but

Eddie knew what was coming and wasn't having any of it. He went flat, dangling his legs and drooping his head.

"Nice try, pal," I said, scooping him up from Mr. Goodwin's bony lap. "Better luck next time."

"Good-bye, Eddie," Mr. Goodwin said, waving. "Come back again."

I held up one of Eddie's front paws and waved back, then walked out of the room, muttering to my cat. "Come back again? Not in this lifetime. You may be a bookmobile cat, but you're not a library cat. I'd be a wreck worrying about you."

"Mrr."

"Yeah, well, just so you know, some people worry a lot more than I do. I'm a very low-grade worrier, in the general scheme of things."

"Mrr."

We were nearing the front desk, and since there was no way to sneak around it, I'd have to barrel through with Eddie in my arms and hope no one took much notice of what I was carrying. "Compare me to some others," I murmured, trying to keep Eddie's attention on my voice so he wouldn't be frightened by all the new things around him. "Do you really think Aunt Frances would let you climb onto the houseboat's roof? No, she would not. And do you think Julia would be okay with you wandering all over the marina most of the summer? I don't think so. And—"

"Mrrrrr."

I slowed my brisk walk. That hadn't been Eddie's normal sound. It sounded like a howl, but not really that, either. What it had sounded like was the noise he made just before—

"And the front desk," boomed a stentorian voice, "is another highlight of our library. We paid a high price for the design and installation, but we think it was worth every penny."

I stopped stock-still in the middle of the hallway. In front of me was Otis Rahn, president of the library board, along with two other board members, and a sleek woman I didn't recognize. The small group hadn't noticed me and, if I was very lucky, they wouldn't.

Silently, I walked backward and was about to turn and beat a fast retreat to the reading room when Eddie let out a hideous and mournful howl.

"Mrroooooorrrrooo!"

He squirreled out of my arms, started to run, reached the ankles of the group of four, then stopped and arched his back.

I ran forward, reaching out, and just as my fingers touched my cat's fur, he hurled up all the beef jerky he'd eaten and half his breakfast. Then he took three backward steps, bumped into the ankles of the woman I didn't know, turned her way, and hurled up the other half of his breakfast onto the toes of her very expensive-looking shoes.

Still crouching, I looked up.

"And this," Otis said grimly, "is Minnie Hamilton, our interim library director. Minnie, I'd like you to meet Jennifer Walker, our first interviewee for the library director position."

Kristen's laughter echoed off the walls of her tiny office and bounced back into my ears over and over.

"It was not funny," I said, slumping in my chair.

"Seriously?" she managed to ask. "Eddie puking on

the shoes of the person who might be your next boss?"
She went off into more gales of laughter. "How could
it get more funny?"

I eyed her coldly. "You could have a little more sympathy for my situation."

"And you need dessert." She picked up the phone
and dialed the kitchen. "Harvey? No, not the crème
brûlée, not tonight. What she needs is a piece of the new
thing. You know. Thanks." She replaced the receiver
and leaned back in her chair. "Just think: If this Jennifer
person turns into the new director, you have nowhere to
go but up."

She had a point, but it was even more likely that Ms.
Jennifer Walker would want a new assistant director to
replace the one named Minnie, whom she'd fired her
first day on the job.

"What did everyone else think about her?" Kristen
asked.

I slid down a little farther. "They're begging me to
give the board my application."

The board had toured Ms. Walker through the
building and then taken her upstairs to the boardroom
for the interview. The staff had immediately congre-
gated in the break room to discuss the potential boss,
and their knee-jerk reactions had been overwhelm-
ingly negative.

"Did you see her face?" Kelsey had asked. "All screwed
up tight?"

"Well," I'd said, "Eddie had just heaved his stomach
contents onto her Italian shoes." Which I'd only known
were Italian because she'd told me so when I'd tried to
help clean them. "That's not likely to bring out the best
in anyone."

"She could have asked how Eddie was," Donna had said. "All she cared about was her stupid shoes. Who wears shoes like that in Chilson, anyway?"

My point that anyone would have expected their shoes to be safe in a public library was ignored.

"It was like she'd never seen a cat before," Josh had added. "Lots of libraries have cats. She looked at Eddie like he should never have been born."

The thought had chilled me. If Eddie had never been born, my life would be the lesser for it. He brought me comfort and companionship, and if Ms. Walker became the new Stephen, would she want to ban Eddie from the bookmobile? I'd bit my lip and tried not to worry. She was only the first candidate, after all.

"Minnie," Holly had said sternly, "you have to apply for the job. Just think if that . . . that witch is our new boss. She's just like Stephen."

Heads around the room had nodded, mine included, because from the little I'd seen of her, she might be even more strict and have even less of a sense of humor than Stephen.

"Then it's settled," Holly said, dusting off her hands. "Minnie's going to apply. They'll have to interview them all, just to say they did, but they'll hire Minnie in the end." She'd sent me a brilliant smile.

"But—"

I'd wanted them to know that all I'd been nodding about was that Ms. Walker was Stephen-like, not that I'd apply for the job, but my explanation was lost in the shuffle as everyone left the room, satisfied that life would be good from here on out.

Kristen *thump*ed her long legs up onto her desk. "And are you going to? Apply, I mean?"

"Do you have a date for Trock yet?"

She gave me a look, knowing that I was trying to change the subject, and decided to let me. "Yes. Tuesday."

"The second Tuesday in July, you mean?"

Kristen's restaurant was scheduled to appear on an episode of *Trock's Troubles*, a nationally syndicated television show hosted by Trock Farrand, who owned a nearby summer home. Trock also had an adult son, Scruffy Gronkowski, who was currently dating Kristen.

Three Seasons had been short-listed for the show before she'd met Scruffy, but it had taken a lot of Trock's convincing her that the other restaurateurs in the area wouldn't hate her for being on the show of her boyfriend's father. "They will love you for it," he'd said. "After the show, people will come to this adorably quaint town for a weekend, and since they won't be able to eat at Three Seasons three times a day, they will eat elsewhere, yes? Yes."

My friend leaned back and yawned. "No, I mean next Tuesday."

"What?" I squeaked. "Like the Tuesday that's"—I made a quick count on my fingers—"five days from now?"

"Just like." She put her hands behind her head, trying to act all nonchalant, but failed completely, since a huge grin was lighting her face from ear to ear.

"When did the date get changed?" Last I'd known, the taping had been scheduled for mid-July, with an October air date. That was unfortunate for two reasons; one, July was the busiest month of the year in Chilson, and tripping over a television crew wasn't going to help get dinners served any faster, and two, an October air date was worse than useless, because Kristen closed the place down around Halloween.

"Just yesterday," Kristen said. "A restaurant that was set to be on the show burned to the ground the other night, so they bumped me up." Her smile faded. "Horrible thing, to have your place burn. I hope they get back on their feet soon."

Knowing Kristen, she'd start a social-media campaign to support them in their time of need and send a hefty check. "And when will you be on TV?"

Her grin reappeared. "That's getting moved up, too. Scruffy says he'll rush the production and get it on the air the second week of August."

"Hmm." I squinted at her. "I'm trying to think of better timing, but I can't think what it could be. What did you do to deserve all this good fortune, anyway?"

"Not a thing," she said promptly. "Except this." She nodded behind me, and Harvey bustled into the room, carrying a tray and a tray stand. Smoothly, he set up the stand, settled the tray down, tidied the small arrangement of flowers, straightened the silverware and napkins, and pulled off the silver domes that covered the plates.

"Your desserts, madams," he said in a suave, butler-like tone that wasn't anything like his usual voice, and retreated.

I gaped while Kristen pulled her chair around the desk to sit opposite the tray from me. Four adorable little crepes the size of my palm were stacked with alternate layers of sliced strawberries and whipped cream. A massive chocolate-dipped strawberry topped the creation, and an artistic chocolate drizzle decorated the entire plate. It was almost too pretty to eat, but Kristen would have my head if I didn't put a fork into it, so I did. If possible, it tasted better than it looked. "You're a genius," I said solemnly.

Kristen nodded. "I know."

I took another bite, then asked, "Say, who should I talk to about the DeKeysers?" Kristen and Rafe, being Chilson born and bred, were my sources for insider knowledge. If they didn't know the dirt on someone, there was a roughly 99.9 percent chance they'd know someone who did. And since I was convincing myself that Andrea's death was somehow linked to Talia De-Keyser's passing, getting background on the DeKeysers was a good starting place.

My friend stared at me. "Does this have to do with Andrea Vennard's murder? Don't you dare tell me you're getting mixed up in that. Remember what happened last time."

"Yeah, I ruined my cell." The water resistance of cell phones clearly needed to be improved. Sure, I'd accidentally immersed the thing for nearly twenty minutes, but still.

"And you were almost killed," Kristen said accusingly.

"Like the man said, the report of my death was an exaggeration."

"Is that Shakespeare?"

"Mark Twain," I said, sighing and shaking my head. "See what a PhD in biochemistry got you? An unrounded education." I finished the last bite of dessert and laid my fork across the plate. "Can I come and watch the filming?"

"Not a chance."

"Please? I promise I won't make faces at you."

She snorted. "Now, that's a promise that you can't possibly keep. See? You're making a face right now."

I flattened my expression, which felt really strange. Something else I needed to work on. Next week, maybe. "So, who should I talk to about the DeKeysers?"

"No one," she muttered.

"You might as well tell me. Otherwise I'll ask Rafe, and he'll tell me without any lectures."

Kristen forked in another bite. She swallowed, then said, "Well, if you insist on being stupid about this—"

"I do."

"—you should talk to Dana Coburn."

I'd never heard the name. "Is that a female Dana or a male Dana?"

Kristen grinned, her good humor suddenly restored. "That's for me to know and you to find out."

Since Kristen wasn't being helpful, on the way home I stopped at Rafe's house to get more information. He was in his dining room, up on a six-foot stepladder and installing crown molding.

"Looks nice," I said, hitching myself up onto a battered wooden stool.

"You think?" He eyed the length of trim he'd just attached. "I wasn't sure about the proportions. Maybe half an inch more height would be better."

"Nope. It's good just the way it is," I said, exactly as if I knew what I was talking about.

"All righty, then." Rafe came down the ladder, moved it over a few feet, and went back up with another piece of trim in his hand.

I watched his efficient movements. Out of school, he had a tendency to play up his chosen role as an Up North redneck wannabe, but with only me for an audience, he was mostly himself. With his longish black hair, slim build, white teeth, and cheerful disposition, I wasn't sure why he didn't have a girlfriend or a wife, but, then again, maybe all the women in town knew him as well as I did.

"What's so funny?" he asked.

"Do you know a Dana Coburn?"

He laughed. "Kristen give you the name?"

"Yes." Lying was pointless, since if I denied it he'd call and ask.

"Did she tell you anything about Dana?"

"No. Why?"

He laughed again. "Then I'm not going to tell you anything, either."

"Not even an address? A phone number? How about where she—or he—works?"

"Works?" He snorted.

"Stop that," I said. "You sound like a pig rooting around for truffles."

"Yeah? How many pigs have you seen up close and personal, city girl?"

"You'd be surprised what I see out on the bookmobile, Mr. Niswander," I said loftily. Which was true, although it hadn't yet included many pigs. But with the bookmobile you never knew.

"And what do pigs eat, Ms. Smarty Pants?"

"Anything they want," I said promptly.

There was a short silence. "Okay, you got me," he said. "Let me make a phone call, and we'll see if I can give you Dana's address. Hang on a second—my cell's in the kitchen."

He clambered down the ladder and scuffed into what I called a kitchenlike area, since it lacked cabinets, dishes, and any silverware other than the ones that came with takeout. What it had was a utility sink, a battered refrigerator, and a hot plate, and I hadn't yet figured out how Rafe had wangled an occupancy permit out of the building inspector.

I heard a few sentences of muffled conversation, and then the refrigerator door opened and closed. Rafe returned, cracking open a water bottle, another one under his arm.

He handed me the open bottle and I took it, asking, "So? Am I in or out?"

"In, with qualifications." He tipped his head backward and took a long drink, then went back up the ladder, noisily crimping the empty plastic bottle and tossing it halfway across the room to land in a pile of sawdust and scrap wood. "Hand me that hammer, will you?" he asked.

I slid off the stool and reached for the tool he'd dropped on top of a box as he'd gone into the kitchen-like area. "What are," I asked, handing up the hammer, "the qualifications of which you speak?"

He turned and blinked down at me. "Oh, right. Dana. You know that house on Fourth Street, the big white one with the columns that's set back a little ways from the other houses? That's where Dana lives."

"Okay." I'd walked past that house dozens of times on my way back and forth to my aunt's and had often wondered who lived there. All I had to do was ask someone, but I'd never remembered to actually do so. "You still haven't told me the qualifications."

He pulled a handful of small nails from a pouch on his tool belt and put most of them into his mouth. "Stop there anytime tomorrow morning," he said around the nails. "All you have to do is be interesting."

I frowned. "It's hard to hear you when there's a pound of nails in your mouth. Because I could have sworn you said I had to be interesting, and that doesn't make any sense."

"No?" Rafe chuckled. "That's because you haven't met Dana."

And, try as I might to get more details, he wouldn't say anything else about the mysterious Dana Coburn.

The next day was Friday. I'd scheduled myself the morning off for an eye doctor's appointment. I knew she'd want to dilate my pupils for retina-examination purposes, and since my vision was nearly worthless for three hours afterward, there was no way I'd be able to work. I'd planned to go grocery shopping—I was down to condiments and wilted lettuce in my refrigerator—but I eschewed that in favor of tracking down Dana Coburn.

Soon after the appointment, I knocked on the front door of the house on Fourth Street. It was what I'm sure my father, an engineer who should have been an architect, had taught me was a Greek Revival. Columns ran from the porch floor to the bottom of the pedimented gable. There was a heavy cornice over a wide and plain frieze, and, above all, it was perfectly symmetrical. Two windows left of the front door, two windows right. Six columns across the front, with the front door centered between numbers three and four. Even the entry mat was perfectly centered.

The perfection was the teensiest bit disconcerting, and I'd had to make a conscious decision between tiptoeing my way across the front porch so I didn't ruin the symmetry with a single speck of dirt, and kicking the entry mat to an odd angle. And there was a puddle out on the sidewalk that I'd walked around. What would the house do if I tracked mud onto the porch?

The door suddenly swung open. "Why are you smiling?" a high-pitched voice asked.

I looked ahead and up and then finally down. Standing in front of me, instead of the elderly and wizened person my imagination had assumed a Dana Coburn would be, was someone little more than a child. She—or he—was shorter than my five feet and thin, with lank hair swinging past the jawline, wearing jeans and a plain T-shirt. There were zero indications of gender.

"Hi," I said. "My name is Minnie Hamilton. Rafe Niswander called yesterday. I'd like to talk to Dana Coburn." The kid's gaze didn't falter. "Is, ah, Dana here?"

"You didn't answer my question," the kid said. "Why were you smiling?"

I blinked. Social niceties were clearly not going to be part of this conversation. Which meant I could tell the complete truth.

"It's the porch," I said, nodding at the pristine floor. "I was picturing so much mud all over it that the house would want to shake it off like a dog shaking off water."

The kid stared at me. "Interesting. Ridiculous, but interesting." She—he?—walked away, leaving the door open. After a short hesitation, I followed.

"You're Dana?" I asked, hurrying after. There was no reply as we trekked through a large entryway, skimmed around the edge of a massive living room, and marched across a formal dining room. I gained an impression of old money and good taste. At long last, we reached a kitchen that was so clean and white, it almost hurt my eyes.

The kid sat on a stool at the corner of a white granite-topped island and pointed. I sat primly on the stool indicated and waited.

Dana, because I could only assume that's who it was, peered into my eyes. "Why are your pupils dilated? Are you taking recreational pharmaceuticals?"

"Eye doctor," I said. "She likes to check for—"

"Retinal detachment." Dana waved away the rest of my explanation. Not interesting enough, no doubt. "Mr. Niswander told my mother you'd like information about the DeKeyser family."

I wondered where the mother figure might be, but decided to keep on topic. "Yes." I looked at her. Him. "Do you want to know why?"

"I have two theories," the kid said. "One would be merely a spurious interest."

It took me a second to make sure I knew what the word "spurious" meant. *Fake. Not valid.* I frowned. "Why on earth would I fake interest in the DeKeysers?"

Dana shrugged. "Not enough information. But the possibility exists."

This kid had read too many Sherlock Holmes stories. "Okay, but that's not why I'm here."

"Then you're looking to connect the murder of Andrea Vennard with Talia DeKeyser's death."

"How did—" I held up my hand, not wanting to hear the kid say "Elementary, my dear Minnie."

"Never mind," I said. "You're right. I want to learn more about the DeKeysers, and I was pointed in your direction."

Dana gave me a straight, unblinking look. "Don't you want to know if I've made the connection between the murder and Talia?"

"If you had, you would already have told me," I said confidently. Someone like Dana wouldn't be able to keep from saying how she—he—had found the answer faster than everyone else. My brother had been like that. Spouting out the answer was practically an involuntary reaction for young folks with that much brain power.

The kid nodded slowly. "You're right. I would have. How did—" Dana's head went back and forth. "Never mind. I'll think about it later and learn from the exercise."

Why had I never met this kid before? Surely someone like this should be in the library on a regular basis. "I would, however, like to know why you're the local expert on the DeKeysers."

"Yes, I can see why you would be curious," Dana said. "It was a research exercise. I am homeschooled, and my parents wanted me to get familiar with the methods involved in genealogical research. Death certificates, birth certificates, property records, newspaper articles, and similar items." The kid eyed me. "This was before you were hired as the library's assistant director. I've been told that the new building has much more to offer than the old."

Old building? This meant the research had occurred at least four years ago. I desperately wanted to ask how old Dana had been at the time of the research, but let it go. "Why did you choose the DeKeysers?"

"I wanted a challenge," came the prompt reply. "By head count, they're the largest family in town. Having so many family branches to investigate made the project more interesting."

Interesting. That word again.

"And you're interested in Talia DeKeyser," Dana said. "Would you also like information regarding her husband, Calvin?"

"Yes, please," I said, and settled myself down to listen.

Dana leaned back on the stool, lifting one knee and cupping it with his—her—hands. "Calvin DeKeyser. Born 1928, died 2013. Would you like the months and days?"

"Not necessary, but thank you."

The kid nodded. "Talia DeKeyser, born Talia Wiley in 1933. Both Calvin and Talia were born in Chilson, went through the Chilson schools, and graduated from Chilson High School. Talia attended the Michigan Normal School in Ypsilanti, which is now Eastern Michigan University, and subsequently taught school for three years before she married Calvin in 1958."

At that point in Dana's precise factual recitation, my tiny little brain adjusted to the concept of a child with the vocabulary and sentence construction of a doctoral candidate. I stopped being amazed at the person in front of me and simply tried to absorb what was being said.

"Benton's, the general store in the downtown core of Chilson, was one of the first commercial establishments in Tonedagana County. Newspaper accounts indicate that the county seat was settled in Chilson primarily because of Benton's."

I started to ask a question, but stopped, not wanting to interrupt the narrative flow.

"Benton was the maiden name of Calvin DeKeyser's mother," Dana said. "Elijah DeKeyser married Dorothy Benton in 1920 and they had six children: five daughters and one son. The daughters married into other original Chilson families, and, as there were no Benton males, Calvin eventually came into ownership of the store."

Yes, folks, primogeniture had been alive and well in

northern lower Michigan in the 1900s. I stirred but didn't say anything. After all, maybe none of the daughters had wanted to run the store.

"Calvin and Talia," Dana was saying, "also had a large family." Dark eyes peered at me through long bangs. "Are you interested in Talia's ancestry?"

"As a matter of general interest, yes," I said, "but I doubt it's pertinent in this case."

"I agree," Dana said, and I felt an embarrassingly happy rush that a thought out of my small brain matched a thought out of the big one. "Talia had seven children who lived: four daughters and three sons. Would you like their names?"

I quickly pulled out my cell and opened the notes app. "Yes, please." I typed away as Dana dictated the names and birth dates.

Leslie, born 1953. Kimberly, born 1956. Thomas, born 1958. Kelly, born 1961. David, born 1962. Melissa, born 1965, and Robert, born 1968.

After that, Dana rattled off the names of the spouses, names and birth dates of the next generation of DeKeysers, and the cities in which they were born.

"Do the sons still run Benton's? Or one of them?" I asked, typing in the last few letters.

"There was a change of ownership after I completed my project," Dana said. "I don't have that information."

Well, stone the crows, as Rafe might have said. There was something the kid didn't know.

"The DeKeyser family," Dana went on, "is well respected in the community. There wasn't a hint of scandal in any of the newspaper articles I read, and none of them has ever died of anything other than natural causes or the typical diseases of their times."

"Any theories about a connection between Andrea

Vennard and Talia?" I asked. "And I'm not talking
about the genetic relationship. I'm talking about something that would be a motivation for Andrea's death.
Even a guess might be helpful."

The kid frowned. "I don't guess."

"Dana!"

Both Dana and I turned to see a woman standing at
the back door to the kitchen. She was probably a little
older than I was, with hair the color of Dana's pulled
back into a ponytail. Her forehead was streaked with
dirt and there was a scratch across one cheek.

"Dana, I told you to call me when Ms. Hamilton
showed up." She looked at me apologetically. "Sorry
about that. I'm Jenny, Dana's mother. I was clearing out
the backyard. Now that we're only here in the summers,
the spring-cleanup chores don't get done until June."

Which explained why I hadn't met Dana during the
school year, but not why I hadn't come across this
amazing human intelligence during the summers.

"Would you like something to drink?" Jenny asked,
toeing off her garden clogs and walking stocking
footed into the kitchen. "Water, soda, iced tea?"

"Thanks," I said, "but I need to get going. Dana was
very helpful and I'm grateful for"—*his? Her?*—"the
time."

"Did you get everything you need?" Jenny took a
glass out of a cupboard and went to the sink. "The
DeKeysers were a pet project of Dana's a few years ago.
I'm sure you were inundated with information."

I glanced at the kid. "I think I have everything."
Dana nodded. "Thanks again for the help. I really appreciate it."

"Stop by if you need anything else," Jennifer said as
she walked me to the front door. "Dana could use more

human interaction." She smiled wryly. "Even if it's just spouting off facts."

After thanking her again, I walked down the pristine steps thoughtfully.

I now knew all sorts of things about Talia, her husband, and their children. I had numbers and dates, facts and figures, straight data that might or might not be useful. But I didn't know what kind of people they were. Didn't know what made any of them tick. Didn't know what any of them thought important, didn't know what might move any of them to an act of crime.

Thanks to Dana's rapid-fire delivery, I had plenty of time for lunch at Shomin's Deli. Somehow I'd managed to leave the house without a book in hand, but there was a quick cure for that.

A wide block from downtown, some hopeful soul had recently opened up a used-book store. I went inside, walked around a sixtyish woman haggling with the clerk over a bag of books she wanted to sell, spied a Colin Cotterill book I'd never read, handed over my dollar plus tax, and was out the door in less than three minutes, which had to be a new record for me.

My steps were nearly jaunty. Yes, my library was in turmoil, what with a murder and the unknown leadership issue, and, yes, I had no idea how I was going to keep juggling my interim-director duties and the bookmobile without sliding into permanent sleep deprivation. Yes, the bookmobile, its garage, and the Friends' book-sale room had all been vandalized, and, yes, my boyfriend's mother hated me, but I had an unread book in my backpack and almost a full hour in which to read. What was there, really, to complain about?

I hummed a happy little tune as I walked through

the first block of Chilson's downtown. Past the real estate office in an old house, past the shoe store, past the pharmacy with its wood front painted this spring with a fresh coat of a disturbingly bright blue, past the toy store with its display windows filled with rocking horses and pedal cars and—

And Mitchell.

My pace went from Happy Traveler to Grandpa Shuffle. Yes, that was indeed Mitchell Koyne standing in the toy store's window. If I'd been asked to state a reason why Mitchell would have been in a toy store, I would have laid down money that he'd have been buying something for himself. Beanbags for juggling, maybe, or one of those three-dimensional brainteaser puzzles that would take me hours to figure out, but that my brother could take apart in three minutes flat.

Mitchell, however, wasn't buying anything. He was wearing the toy store's signature polo shirt. He had a feather duster in hand, and he was using it to dust. Mitchell was working.

I waved, but his concentration was so focused that either he didn't see me or he was ignoring me.

Either way, he wasn't being Mitchell-like.

"Who are you?" I asked softly, "and what have you done with the real Mitchell?"

He didn't answer, of course, and I moved on, troubled and more than a little sad.

Chapter 6

Iworked late into the evening on Friday, but left with plenty of time to hang out at the summer's first Friday-night marina party. Ash was on duty both weekend nights, but we'd made plans to get together Monday after I got off work. During our last morning run, I'd tried to explain how the dinner with his mother had gone wrong, but, manlike, he'd said not to be silly, that everything was fine, and he'd run off to finish his ten-mile loop, calling over his shoulder to tell me to bring my swimsuit on Monday.

After a night during which even the soft purrs of my furry friend didn't help me fall asleep, when I got out of bed on Saturday morning, I felt the need for a family connection. "Do you mind?" I asked Eddie. "It's a bookmobile day, so you'll have to stay in the car for a little while."

He yawned, sending bad cat breath straight into my nostrils, and said, "Mrr."

I took this to be assent and whirled through my morning routine in record time. In short order I was tromping up the steps of the boardinghouse and banging through the front door.

"Hello?" I called. "It's me." I found my aunt Frances in the dining room, reading the newspaper.

"Good morning, sunshine!" she said, smiling and reaching up to give me a hug. "I didn't know you were stopping by this morning. Let me set you a place." She set down the coffee cup she'd been holding.

"Can't stay," I said. "Too much to do at the library before we head out."

Conversation and the *tink* of pots and pans filtered out to us from the kitchen. My aunt provided her boardinghouse guests with dinner every night and breakfast six days of the week. Saturday morning, however, was the day she put her guests to work. Co-cooking the occasional breakfast with another boarder was part of the deal, she told her applicants. What she didn't tell them was that the task was designed to get them to work as a team, which would help them get to know each other, which would nudge them into love.

Aunt Frances gave me a brief appraising look and reached for her mug. "How about some of this?"

I looked longingly at the beverage, but shook my head. "Too many miles to drive and too few bathroom stops."

My aunt tsked at me and drank deep.

"Cruel, you are," I said, pulling out a chair.

"But funny." She waggled her eyebrows, and I couldn't help but laugh out loud. "So, what brings you to my humble abode this fine morning?"

I shrugged. "Nothing, really. Just felt like stopping by." She peered at me and I hurried into a question. "Who's cooking? Is that bacon I smell?"

Aunt Frances had known me all of my life, and

knew that I was throwing out a distraction, but she also knew I'd talk about whatever was bothering me when I was ready.

"It's Eva and Forrest's turn this morning," she said.

My night of half sleep and bad dreams had made my brain sluggish, and it took a moment for me to recall the details on Eva and Forrest. Teachers, I finally remembered, although I couldn't think where or what they taught. In their mid-forties, divorced. Both did a lot of mountain biking. "What's on the menu?"

"Straight up traditional breakfast," Aunt Frances said. "But with the twist of freshly made English muffins and clotted cream." She smiled at me over the top of her coffee. "Perked up at that, I see. You sure you don't want a plate?"

I glanced at the wall clock. "No time. Maybe next Saturday."

"How are things at the library?" she asked. "You've had a hard week."

Via phone calls and texts, I'd kept my aunt apprised of the multitude of events. As always, her deepest concern had been for me, and, as always, I'd begged her not to tell my mother about any of it. But though I could have burst forth with a long litany of concerns and questions, I really didn't feel like talking. "We're muddling through," I said. "How about you?"

Her eyebrows went up. "You think I had a hard week?"

"Busy, anyway," I said. "With the boarders and all."

"True," she agreed, her gaze flicking toward the living room. I had a feeling, however, that she was looking through the walls, across the street and into the house where Otto lived.

"How is Otto these days?" I asked.

She gave the vaguest of shrugs. "He's busy; I'm busy. We haven't seen much of each other the past few weeks."

Which was unusual, because they'd been hand in hand since December. I could hardly think of a time in the past six months when I'd seen one of them without the other. "You miss him, don't you?" I asked.

"Silly old me," she said with a wry smile. "Live without a man for decades, and now I hate to have a day go by without seeing this particular one."

We sat there a moment in companionable silence, thinking about things and not thinking about things. Then I got to my feet. "Time for me to go," I said. "Eddie's in the car, waiting, and you know how he gets."

"Sleepy," Aunt Frances said. "And if there's any sunshine on him, he's probably snoring."

I laughed. Last winter, my aunt and Eddie had become fast friends. She knew his quirks almost as well as I did.

We reached the front door and went through to the porch. Outside, the sun was shining, the birds were singing, and the road was beckoning.

"Minnie?" my aunt asked. "Are you okay?" Her voice was low and full of concern.

"I'm fine." I put on a smile. "It's been a long week—that's all. I just wanted to stop by and . . . and make sure you're still here."

She made a rude noise in the back of her throat. "I'm not going anywhere. It's too hot in the South, too dry out west, and too humid most other places." She gave me one last look. "Are you sure there's nothing I can do?"

I thought, then said, "Well, there's one thing. Can I . . . can I . . . ?" My voice faltered.

"Can you what?" Aunt Frances asked gently.

I swallowed. "What I'd really like is a big hug."

"Silly girl." My aunt reached out and pulled me into her warm embrace. "You silly girl," she said again, kissing the top of my head.

I did feel a little silly, like a kid again, going to my aunt and expecting that a hug would make me feel better, that some aunt comfort would fix everything.

Silly, yes, but the funny thing was, after a bit, I did feel better.

"What do you think is going on?" Julia asked, reworking her long hair. We'd just parked at the third stop of the day, in a church parking lot out in the southeast part of the county, and most of the conversation heard on the bookmobile that morning had been shocked questions and theories about the murder and the break-ins.

I watched Julia with a twitch of envy. Her smooth hair smoothly obeyed her long and limber fingers, going easily from a simple ponytail to a tidy bun. If I'd tried to do that with my curly hair, all I'd get was a red face and an unruly mess.

"Mrr," Eddie said. He stalked down the aisle and set his furry self onto the carpeted step near the nonfiction section.

"Nicely done," I told him. "You do realize you're right underneath the books on how to train your dog."

"Mrr!"

"That's what I think, too." Eddie had been even more Eddie-like than usual that morning. He'd insisted on being cuddled by a nice elderly lady wearing a floppy gardening hat, and had literally rolled around on the work boots worn by the foreman of a landscaping crew. Luckily, the guy had found this amusing, but I'd hauled my protesting cat away.

"Chill, already, will you?" I'd whispered. "I know you like footwear and all, but this is the first time this guy has visited us. And that was only because his crew was on break at the house across the street. What are you trying to do, embarrass me?"

Eddie had twisted away and hadn't replied, which I took as corroboration. If raising children was remotely like having a cat, I wasn't sure I was ever going to be ready.

Julia patted the back of her head, found two stray hairs, and tucked them in expertly. "Do you have any theories? Because a murder in the library, vandalism of the Friends' sale room, and a break-in at the bookmobile garage seem far more than coincidence."

It did to me, too, but I didn't see how the three events tied together.

"I have an idea," Julia said.

She'd had lots of ideas already, all of them outlandish, melodramatic, and completely unrealistic. My favorite had been tightly localized earthquakes, though her theory of a malevolent library ghost had come a close second. "What is it this time? Does it involve time travel? Because I've always wanted to believe it was possible."

"It's one of the library director candidates."

I opened the back door, letting fresh air waft through the bookmobile. Though Eddie blinked at the change, he didn't seem inclined to move. "Don't you start, too," I said.

"About your application?" she asked. "That is your business and your decision."

I was about to thank her when she added, "You would make an excellent director and the library needs you, but don't let my opinion sway you."

"Of course not," I said sardonically. "But please tell me how one of the director candidates could be involved with murder and break-ins."

Julia put her hands behind her back and walked up and down the aisle. Playing the part of an attorney, no doubt, and I wondered in how many productions she'd acted as one.

"Motive is everything." Her voice was calm and measured, and I steeled myself to disbelieve every word she said. If she tried, Julia would be able to convince a classically trained musician to purchase weekend passes to a rap festival.

"Okay." I wasn't sure I agreed one hundred percent, but playing along wasn't going to hurt anything.

"Let's say that getting this job means everything to one of the candidates," she posited. "Let's say that she—or he—has made commitments and promises and is now in a situation that demands she—or he—become the library director."

"I don't see it," I said. "What could possibly make that true?"

"Use your imagination, young lady! There could be a hundred good reasons."

I couldn't think of even one, but Julia had already waved off my objection and was moving on.

"An excellent way to get hired," she said, "is to demonstrate your value to an organization. All this candidate has to do is ride to the rescue by finding a scapegoat for the murder and the break-ins. Do that, and he's in like Flynn."

"Wouldn't finding a scapegoat be hard?"

This, apparently, was another difficulty not worth considering. "All he needs to do," Julia said, "is find someone who's close to being a killer. That will demonstrate his commitment to the library nicely enough to get him the job."

"What do you think?" I asked Eddie.

He shifted back and forth on the step, leaning left and right, then back to center, but didn't move his feet.

Julia frowned. "Interpretation, please."

Most likely he'd had an itch that he'd managed to scratch without going to much effort. "He thinks your idea would be better if it involved a cat."

"Hmm." Julia rubbed her chin. "He could be right. Let me work on it." She grinned. "Unless you want a time-travel version."

"I'd like to go back to 1978, please," said a new voice.

Julia, Eddie, and I turned. Lawrence Zonne, a newcomer to the bookmobile, was at the top of the steps, smiling at us. Mr. Zonne's sharply white hair and the wrinkles on his face were the only indicators that he was an octogenarian. He moved as easily as a twenty-year-old, had vision sharper than mine, and had a memory that rivaled . . . well, everyone's.

Mr. Zonne had lived in Tonedagana County most of his life and moved to Florida when he and his wife took early retirement. But after his wife died the previous winter, he'd looked around and realized that home was elsewhere. Though I was sorry he'd lost the companionship of his wife, I was glad to have him back in Michigan. His sharp intelligence and wit made every conversation a treat, and, besides, Eddie liked him.

"What happened in 1978?" Julia asked.

"The blizzard, young ladies. Don't you remember?"

I shook my head. "I wasn't born yet."

Mr. Zonne looked at Julia.

"I was living in New York City," she said. "When it snowed, I stayed inside until it was gone."

Mr. Zonne eyed Eddie. "And you?"

"Mrr."

"Exactly," Mr. Zonne leaned down to pat my cat on his fuzzy head. "Mrrr-low. As in Merlot, my preferred varietal of wine. You are a cat of great discernment, Mr. Edward. My wife and I spent the entire week of that blizzard without a decent wine in the house. If I could go back in time to just before the storm hit, I'd make sure to stock up. Just think how much easier we could have endured the snow and wind and cold with a case of good Merlot. But why, may I ask," he said, straightening, "are we discussing time travel?"

"We're not," I said. "Julia might be, but only to make up another wacky explanation for all the . . . the things that have been going on at the library."

Mr. Zonne nodded. "An odd litany of incidents. I can see why one would turn to unusual interpretations."

"Do you have a theory?" I asked.

He smiled. "Of course. However, I regret to say that while I am a man of great memory, my imagination is entirely earthbound. Limited, you might say."

"Your memory," I said, "could do us more good than a guess about alien invaders."

"Hey," Julia protested. "I never said anything about aliens." But she looked thoughtful.

"Did you know the DeKeysers?" I asked. "Especially Talia? Because it was her funeral that the murder victim came north to attend."

"The beautiful Talia," he murmured. "Yes, I did indeed. She was kind and generous and, to be blunt, a trifle shallow. Not the deepest thinker in the family. But she had a good heart, and what could count more?"

It was my opinion that it would count a little more if you could have a good heart and be a devoted reader, but I just nodded. "Andrea Vennard was Talia's great-niece," I said.

"One of the many." Mr. Zonne nodded. "And if I had a free afternoon and a large sheet of paper, I could sketch out all of Talia's relatives."

"Er . . ."

"Don't worry, Miss Minnie," he said. "I won't subject you to all that. But I can share a story or two about the beautiful Talia and the handsome Cal. They were a few years older than me, but their storied romance cast a long and memorable shadow."

"How did he propose?" Julia asked. "Do you know?"

Mr. Zonne laughed. "He'd asked her father for permission first, as young men did in that day and age, then purchased a ring chosen by Talia's mother. He took her out in his canoe one fine summer evening, held out the jeweler's box, and got down on one knee."

Uh-oh. "Um . . ."

"Miss Minnie," he said, "I see you know where this is going. Cal, in his efforts to be the gallant swain, tried a little too hard. He tipped the canoe, sending his lady love and himself into the waters of Janay Lake."

Julia sputtered with laughter and I asked, "What about the ring?"

"Ah, now, there's the rest of the story," Mr. Zonne said. "Cal, still being gallant, escorted Talia to shore, settled her down with a blanket from his jalopy, as such things were called, and dove back into the water to find the ring."

"Good thing it was Janay Lake," Julia said, still laughing, "and not Mud Lake."

"That small fact has not gone unnoticed in the DeKeyser family," Mr. Zonne said. "Many a family gathering has discussed the fate of Talia and Cal if

Janay Lake hadn't had clear water and a rock bottom. As it was, young Cal fished out the ring after a dozen dives, then, dripping wet and panting, once again offered it, on bended knee, to his ladylove."

An uncharitable thought crossed my mind. If my former boyfriend, Tucker, had dropped an engagement ring in a lake, he would have called the insurance company before going to any great personal efforts.

"Now they're both gone." Mr. Zonne sighed gently. "So many are." He stood for a moment, lost in his thoughts. Then he shook himself and looked directly at Julia and me. "If I can share a small piece of advice with you ladies, make friends with people younger than yourself. Don't, and someday you might wake up to find that all your friends are gone."

Julia slung her arm around my shoulders. "One down. How many do I need?"

Mr. Zonne laughed. "You can never have too many, but you know that. You both do."

We did indeed. I gave Julia a quick hug, then stooped down to pull Eddie up into a snuggle. Eddie, who made friends easier than any human I'd ever met. "What about Talia and Cal's children?" I asked.

Mr. Zonne slid his hands into his pockets and squinted at the ceiling. "Leslie. Kim. Tom. Kelly. Dave. Melissa. Bob. I think that's the correct birth order, but don't hold me to it."

I assured him we wouldn't. "Do you know anything about them?" Even the youngest ones were probably older than Andrea Vennard, but in a small town, who knew what slings and arrows had wounded whom?

Mentally, I spun out a scenario in which Andrea had stolen away the younger DeKeyser daughter's boyfriend, a hurt from which she'd never recovered. She'd snapped when she'd seen Andrea at her mother's funeral and tracked her down at . . . at the library? I shook my head. Every theory fell apart when you put the library into the mix.

"Most of what I know about them is secondhand," Mr. Zonne said. "They grow so fast and leave even faster. Talia and Cal invested thousands into college educations for their offspring. They all married years ago and have grown or nearly grown children of their own. If I recall correctly, the girls stayed in Chilson."

"And the boys?"

"Gone off to find fame and fortune in the wide blue yonder."

"Did they find it?" Julia asked.

"Depends on what you call success," Mr. Zonne said. "None of them are millionaires, but they're all solid citizens, from what I hear. Salt-of-the-earth types who spend time volunteering, donate money to nonprofits, and subscribe to newspapers instead of getting information from blogs."

He pronounced the last word as a curse, and I had a hard time keeping my grin to myself; Mr. Zonne and I had a difference of opinion on the usefulness of the Internet, and the twain would never meet.

"Anything else?" I asked.

"Nothing that would be useful."

Julia opened her arms wide. "Give us your all, kind sir. Give us the details, tiny and large, obscure and not, because one never knows what is important until the right moment."

I looked at her. "Is that a quote?"

"No idea," she said. "There are bits of so many plays in my head that I haven't had an original thought since 1987."

"The year Dave DeKeyser left Chilson for good," Mr. Zonne said. "And the year van Gogh's *Sunflowers* sold for almost forty million dollars."

I smiled. "Not sure that's pertinent, but, like Julia said, you never know. Do you remember anything else?"

"The DeKeyser women love to garden," he said. "From stem to stern and top to bottom, the whole kit and caboodle could spend hours talking about roses, manure, trilliums, invasive species, Gertrude Jekyll, and how to force lilacs to bloom in January."

"You can do that?" I asked, surprised.

"None of them seem to have any problem," he said, "but I never had any luck. Forsythia, yes, but not a lilac, not once."

The three of us started a discussion of Mackinac Island's annual Lilac Festival, which had ended the previous weekend, and my questions about the DeKeysers faded away from the conversation.

But not from my thoughts.

Late that night I was sitting at the dining table in my pajamas with a copy of C. J. Sansom's *Lamentation* in front of me. Eddie was disgruntled because we weren't in bed, where we should have been, but there was a good reason, which I had to explain to him every few minutes.

"Stop that," I said, pushing him off the book for the ten-thousandth time. "This book is compelling and wonderfully written, but it's also"—I flipped to the back page and read the number at the bottom—"six hundred and forty-two pages long. That's more pages than you have bits of kibble in your bowl."

Eddie looked down at the book, then up at me.

"No," I said firmly. "You don't need six hundred and

forty-two pieces of kibble in your bowl. For one thing, the bowl isn't big enough. The four hundred and fifty pieces in there are its maximum capacity." I'd made up the number, but Eddie wouldn't know the difference.

"Mrr," he said.

"Exactly," I told him. "Any book longer than six hundred pages is too big to take to bed. I might fall asleep and drop it on your furry little head, and we can't have that, now, can we?"

My cat rubbed his face up against the book, leaving a trail of Eddie hair across the rough-cut pages. "Nice," I murmured, and pulled him onto my lap. One more chapter and then I'd get to bed.

Two chapters and three pages later, my cell phone rang.

I blinked at it, then reached out and flipped it over. *Pam Fazio? Why on earth would she be calling at—* I glanced at the phone's time and was startled to see that it was past midnight. Well past.

Huh.

I thumbed on the phone. "Pam? What's up?"

"Oh, Minnie," she said raggedly. "I'm so sorry to call you at this hour."

"No problem," I said. "Eddie and I were up reading." I patted the top of my furry companion's head, making it bob up and down. "What's the matter?" Because something clearly was. Pam, who was extremely capable and very intelligent, was also one of the most self-reliant people I'd ever met, but her voice was tight and worried.

"It's a lot to ask," she said, "but could you do me a favor? Now, I mean?"

I almost made a joke about being willing to do anything for her, as long as it didn't involve quadratic equations or juggling, and especially not both. But

Pam had moved to Chilson not all that long ago, and she was still forming friendships and connections. I knew how hard it could be to insert yourself into the life of a small town, so I said, "Absolutely not a problem. What do you need?"

"A ride."

I blinked. "To somewhere or from somewhere?"

"To home," she said. "From . . . from the hospital." And then the brave and capable Pam Fazio did something that shocked me.

She started crying.

Chapter 7

The next day, after the police had come and gone, I stood in the back doorway of Pam's antiques store.

It was a horrific mess.

Linens, shoes, clothes, and books lay scattered everywhere. Slowly, I walked through the store, bits of broken glass and porcelain crunching under my feet, bits that had, until yesterday, been whimsical teapots, adorable mugs, stunning vases, gorgeous candlesticks, and hand mirrors that had probably survived two world wars.

Standing in the middle of the room, I turned in a slow circle. Even the framed prints and photos on the walls had been tossed onto the floor, their glass shattered and frames broken. The noise filled me, and I wanted to plug my ears against a memory that was only in my imagination.

I crouched and picked up a metal lunch box, one from the female-themed collection Pam had been growing the past few months. Supergirl was still flying, but one of her arms was a little dinged.

Just like Pam.

My friend had returned to her store late the previous night to make sure she'd turned off the coffeepot. "I always double-check before I leave," Pam had said as I drove her home from the hospital. "But when I was getting ready for bed, I just couldn't remember. I had to go back."

I'd nodded. Though the library's coffeepot had a timer attached, on my way out I always made sure there was no heat. Not that I distrusted electronics; I just trusted my own senses more.

"So I walked back to the store," Pam had gone on. This made sense, since her small house was only a few blocks from downtown. "It was a beautiful night. I was looking at the stars, thinking how lucky I was to live in a place where you could actually see the Milky Way without driving for miles to get away from the city lights. I cut down the alley, like I always do, and went to the back door. "But . . ." She gave a pained noise. "But the door was partly open. There was no possible way I'd left it that way. Something was seriously wrong."

She'd looked over at me. "I know I should have left right then and called the police—I know they do hourly rounds downtown all summer—but I had to look inside. I mean, it's my store."

Her last words were emphatic and heartfelt, and I knew exactly how she'd felt. If I hadn't had Eddie with me the morning I'd found the bookmobile garage broken open, I might have done the same thing. Sometimes the right thing to do takes second place to what you have to do.

Pam had continued on with her tale. That she'd pushed the door all the way open. That she'd seen a large shape moving around inside the shadows. That she'd called out in anger. That the shape had moved toward her, shoving her aside with so much force that she'd fallen hard against a counter. The shape had run into the poorly lit alley and vanished.

Struggling to her feet, Pam had put her hands on the floor to push herself up and fallen back down from pain. She'd extracted her cell phone from her purse and called 911. The city police had arrived quickly, the ambulance right behind them. In the emergency room, Pam was told she had a broken arm and that it would take eight weeks to heal.

"Eight weeks," she'd said, as I helped her out of my car and into her house. "I have a store to run. A store to clean up! I can't . . . I don't . . ."

"Shh," I'd told her, helping her out of her clothes and into her nightgown. "Don't worry about that now. Get some rest." I pulled back the bedcovers and tucked her into bed. "Sleep now. That's what you need more than anything."

"Sleep?" she had asked sleepily. "I can't possibly go to sleep right now. I have too much to do . . . too much to figure out . . . too much . . ."

And she'd been out.

I'd soft-footed it across the room and shut the door behind me. I turned to leave, then went the other way and stopped in the kitchen. After reassuring myself that she had food in the refrigerator edible for someone one-handed, I'd driven home and settled into bed with a purring Eddie, thinking that if I'd been a truly good friend, I would have offered Pam the comfort of my cat.

"What do you think?" I'd asked him, yawning. "Would you mind being someone else's security blanket for a few days?"

"Mrr," he'd said, lightly sinking the claws of one front foot into my arm.

"Okay, maybe it was a bad idea."

"Mrr."

"Okay, it *was* a bad idea."

"Mrr." He'd retracted his claws and snuggled up against my shoulder.

In seconds, he was snoring as only an Eddie could. I'd lain awake for a few minutes, thinking, then closed my eyes and, still making plans for the next day, had fallen sound asleep.

Now I turned in a small circle, surveying the damage. The stunning shock of seeing the shambles of Pam's geniuslike retail displays had retreated, and I started to take a hard look at the damage.

After a few minutes, I had a plan, and pulled out my cell phone to start its implementation.

"Tom? It's Minnie Hamilton. Sorry to bother you on your one day off, but— What's that? No, I don't need any cookies. Something happened last night, and I was wondering if you'd be willing to help."

An hour later, a small band of downtown business owners had converged on Pam's store. I handed out work gloves I'd borrowed from the marina office, told everyone to watch for broken glass, and put them all to work.

We piled and we sorted and we swept and we cleaned and we talked a little too loud, trying to keep the fear at bay. Chilson was a haven for so many of us, a place of calm and peace and serenity. Sure, unhappy things came around every once in a while, but to have something like this happen, something malicious and evil, well, this was different.

At one point, I held out my hand for cash donations and ordered a stack of pizzas from Fat Boys. When I came back, arms laden, I held out my hand again.

"Take your money back," I said. "Those guys heard what we were doing and wouldn't take any money."

But no one, from Cookie Tom to the Shomins to Shannon Hirsch, an attorney at the other end of downtown, would take their cash. "We'll leave it for Pam," the owner of the jewelry store said. "It's not much, but she's going to need it."

Everyone nodded.

"Even if her insurance company pays out," said the hardware store's owner as he picked up a slice of pepperoni and sausage, "it'll take weeks, if not months, to get a check, and she'll need cash to replace stock."

Which was far easier said than done, because Pam's buying trips were done in the slower seasons, not in the busy summer. We all knew this, but since there wasn't anything we could do about it, we ate and drank the soda and water that the Fat Boys had also donated, and got back to work.

Late in the afternoon, as Reva Shomin and the owner of the bike shop were trying to wrestle a corner cupboard back into the exact position we'd all decided it had been yesterday, a loud voice cut through the chatter.

"What on earth are you doing?"

The cupboard *thump*ed to the floor, rocking a little, then going still. Everyone looked at each other, then as one, they all looked at me.

I swallowed and turned to face Pam, who was standing in the front doorway with her hands on her hips. Well, technically, one hand on one hip because the other hand was poking out of a sling, but whatever.

"Um," I said. Earlier, I'd thought about calling her and making sure she was okay with us going ahead and cleaning up. But I hadn't wanted to wake her if she was still sleeping, and since she'd left her purse behind in my car, a purse that had contained the keys to the store, I'd figured I'd get started, then call her a little later.

"I meant to call you," I said lamely. And I had; I'd just ended up so busy I'd forgotten all about it. I suddenly remembered my mother's admonitions to think first and act second. Maybe next time I'd remember her advice at a moment when I could implement it.

"Hey, Pam," Cookie Tom said, nodding. He probably would have waved, but his hands were busy because he was hauling books from one of the carefully sorted piles. "Maybe you should sit down. You look a little pale."

He was right. I guided her to a tall stool that the owner of a local bar had hauled in for us to use. "Just sit a minute," I said. "You can direct everything from there."

"But . . . but I don't even know all these people," she said, bewilderment clear on her face.

This was because our work crew had accidentally hauled in some passing tourists who had seen the activity inside and been more than willing to roll up their sleeves and pitch in.

"They're people who want to help," I said, opening a water bottle and handing it to her.

"But—"

"Drink," I told her. "I'm willing to bet you haven't had enough fluids today, and I know they told you at the hospital to make sure you stay hydrated."

Not really paying attention to what she was doing, Pam took a sip of water. "How did . . . Why are . . ." She shook her head and glanced around, her eyes wide. "Everything's almost done. I thought this would take days."

"Many hands make light work," I said, nodding as wisely as I could.

Pam blinked. "I can't believe . . ."

Before she could go all teary, I nudged her hand, encouraging her to drink. When she was doing so, I started listing our accomplishments. "We decided to sort things into groups. Things broken beyond repair, things that were damaged but still saleable, and the things that weren't damaged at all." Her expression turned pensive, and I hurried on. "The busted-up pile was the smallest by far, and we took lots of pictures for your insurance claim."

"Got them right here," said Kirk, owner of the local photography studio, tapping his laptop. "I'm finishing up the file names."

"Same with the slightly damaged stuff," I said. "Kirk will burn DVDs so you and your insurance company will have records."

"You . . . will?"

"Not a problem," Kirk said, smiling at her. "Glad to help."

"Really?" she asked.

I rolled my eyes. "And over there, at the other laptop, Trudy is finishing up an inventory." Trudy, an accountant, waved a manicured hand in our direction but didn't look away from the computer. She'd been happy to help out, and even happier to know that her specific help wouldn't involve the lifting of anything heavier than her computer's mouse.

"When it's done," I told Pam, "Trudy will e-mail you the spreadsheet. We didn't know how you track your stock, so Trudy put the data into lots of columns. You can sort it any way you need and compare it against your existing list." I didn't have any firsthand knowledge of Pam's inventorying practices, but I knew without a doubt that this capable woman kept accurate track of the items in her store.

"I . . . don't know what to say." Pam clutched the water bottle hard enough to make the thin plastic crackle. "I . . ."

"Don't say anything," Kristen held up two large handfuls of antique cookie cutters. "Unless you want to tell me where these buggers go."

Without a pause, Pam said, "In a wire basket. It was on the butcher-block kitchen island."

As Kristen bustled off to display them properly, the owner of the shoe store held up a pair of large dolls and asked, "Pam? How about these?"

She slid off the stool and, within seconds, was deep into the business of directing the placement of the hundreds of items in her store.

I watched for a moment, making sure she was steady on her feet, breathed a short sigh of relief, and then returned to my self-appointed task of sorting the books.

"What's missing?" I asked Pam.

We were eating the last of the pizza, and everyone else was long gone. For the past hour, Pam and I had been comparing her inventory list against Trudy's list and the pictures Kirk had taken.

Pam swallowed a bite of mushrooms and olives and said, "To tell you the truth, I'm not sure."

"Bzz! Wrong answer. We've worked too hard for that kind of response. Try again."

She laughed, and I sent up a small prayer of thanks to whomever might be listening for the quick return of her warm laughter. "That's not what I meant," she said. "What I meant was, I can't see that anything has been stolen. It looks like this was just vandalism."

I studied the two lists and murmured, "Another one."

"That's right," Pam said. "You had two up at the library, didn't you? The book-sale room and the poor bookmobile. Well, they say things come in threes."

"They also say drinking coffee as a kid will stunt your growth."

Pam looked at me. "You do drink a lot of coffee."

"Didn't drink a drop until I was in college."

"Then why are you so short?"

"Because you can't breed midgets and raise giants," I said, quoting my grandfather, who had also told me to pay attention not just some of the time but all of the time. This was my mother's father, and she'd learned many of her stock phrases from him, but somehow I'd always found it easier to listen to Grandpa.

And somehow that made me think of something. I went to the back of the store, trying to put myself back in time to when I'd walked in that morning. After a moment, I asked, "Can you pull up the first pictures Kirk took?" Kirk had been my second phone call and, after I'd explained what had happened, he'd been the first to arrive, camera and lighting equipment in hand. He'd set up quickly and snapped away, finishing just as the rest of the troops trooped in.

"Hang on a sec." One-handed, she clicked open the appropriate computer file. "Are you looking for anything in particular?"

"Three things." I pointed toward the rear wall, to a display in the middle of the room, and to some shelving near the front door. "What do those look like in the pictures?"

"A mess," Pam said. "Hard to believe it looked like that a few hours ago," she said in a wondering tone. "And hard to believe that all those people would drop their plans for the day and help me. I barely know most of them. And you," she said, her voice cracking. "You've done so much for me, I can't—"

"What you can do is look at those pictures," I cut in. If she started bawling, I would, too, and soppy tears on top of too much leftover pizza wouldn't sit well in my stomach. "Really study them. Tell me if you see what I see." Which sounded a little too much like that Christmas carol, something completely inappropriate in June.

"All I see is a mess," Pam muttered, but she kept looking. "A big, fat mess. I had no idea I had so much stuff in here. How could I have accumulated so much in such a short time? And what's—" She stopped abruptly. "Hang on. The hatboxes are on the floor, but they're close to where they should be. Same with the linens and the wooden puzzles and everything else. There's only one category of item that's scattered far from where it should be."

"Exactly," I said. "The books."

The next morning was Monday, a library day, but I stopped at the sheriff's office before going into work.

"Good morning, Ms. Hamilton." Detective Inwood's greeting was a salute with a powdered doughnut. "If you don't make any jokes about cops and doughnuts, you're welcome to a pastry."

I blinked at the man. As far as I could remember, he'd never before invited me to partake of anything inside the office. Had he had a personality transfer since we'd last talked?

"Take advantage while you can," Ash said, walking

into the interview room, handing me an apple fritter
with one hand and a cup of coffee with the other. We
brushed hands during the transfer and smiled at each
other. "Hal got another grandkid yesterday."

"Congratulations!" I transferred my smile from
Ash to the detective. "Girl or boy?"

"Girl," he said, beaming. "Emily Grace."

It was a nice name. I said so, and his smile went a
little wider. For a second I was worried that the unac-
customed expression might send his face into spasms
that could end up freezing there forever, but it went
back to normal as he began to eat.

I breathed a sigh of relief. There was only so much
dramatic change I could take in any given time span.

"Have a seat, Ms. Hamilton," the detective said.
"Unless this won't take long?"

"Sorry to dash your hopes," I said, sitting, "but I
have a new theory." I'd texted Ash yesterday about
Pam's store, but hadn't said anything about what Pam
and I had both noticed at the end of the day.

True public servant that he was, Detective Inwood
didn't even blink at my statement, even though I was
sure he would have been content to never hear another
idea from me the rest of his career. He and Ash sat
across from me. "One of these days," the detective
said, "you'll sit on this side."

I glanced up at the stained ceiling tiles near the
doorway. A few months back, when I'd mentioned that
I'd thought the stain looked like a dragon, he'd said it
wasn't a dragon at all, that I needed to see it from that
side of the room. One of these days, I'd break out of
my rut and remember to actually do so.

"So, what's your new theory?" Detective Inwood
asked.

"This first part isn't the theory," I said. "I just wanted to make sure you knew about Andrea Vennard's old high school boyfriend, Steve Guilder. You know she had a personal protection order against him?"

Inwood brushed powdered sugar off his jacket. "Yes, Ms. Hamilton, we're very aware of the documents issued out of this county."

I colored the slightest bit. "Well, it was a long time ago. I just thought I'd mention it."

"We're exploring all avenues of investigation," Detective Inwood said, and I almost mouthed the words along with him. "That includes looking into any possible suspects from her business downstate."

"I heard she owned a business. What was it, anyway?"

The detective popped in the last bit of his doughnut. "The theory?" he asked around it.

I decided not to be miffed that he wouldn't tell me. There were lots of other ways I could find out. "It's about books," I said.

Ash glanced at his supervisor. His supervisor, who was still in the act of taking a pen from his shirt pocket and flipping open a small notebook, didn't glance back. He also didn't write anything down.

"What's about books?" Detective Inwood asked.

I almost said "Everything," but knew that would earn me raised eyebrows from the detective and a shake of the head from Ash. "The murder. The break-in at the Friends' book-sale room. The break-in at the bookmobile garage. The break-in at Pam Fazio's store on Saturday night."

The detective sat back. "The break-ins are the jurisdiction of the city police. If you have information, you should speak to them directly."

Which he would prefer, I was sure. "It all ties in with the murder," I said quickly. Though the city police were well trained and experienced, they weren't the ones investigating Andrea's death.

"How, exactly?" Inwood asked.

"It's all about the books," I repeated. He made a rolling motion with his hand, so I kept going. "As far as anyone can tell, nothing was taken from the sale room. And we know that nothing was stolen from the bookmobile or from Pam's store. But it was the books in her store that were examined most closely."

"What," the detective said, hunching forward the tiniest bit, "makes you think it isn't simple vandalism?"

"Two things," I said. "One is that there's been no real damage. Nothing has been taken, nothing maliciously destroyed. Sure, there were things broken at Pam's store, but we did an inventory, and, considering the number of breakable items that could have been shattered into teensy-tiny bits, the number of things broken was surprisingly small."

Thirteen, to be exact, and most of the broken bits had been from one large mirror. I'd swept up the pieces, hoping, for the first time ever, that the tale about the seven years' bad luck for whomever had broken the mirror was true.

"And number two?" Detective Inwood asked.

"It was too much work," I said.

His bushy eyebrows went up. "How's that?"

The librarian was about to explain vandalism to the law-enforcement officers. It was a good day. "Straight vandalism," I told them, "wouldn't have been so thorough. Vandals go in, destroy everything in sight, and leave. Whoever broke into the bookmobile garage, Pam's place, and the Friends' room was very methodical. There are three thousand books on the bookmobile," I said. "And each and every one was taken from its shelf and tossed onto the floor. Every one," I repeated, tapping the scratched table with my forefinger. "Would any vandal be so thorough?"

Inwood and Ash looked at each other, and I knew I'd scored a point. "They were looking for something," Ash said.

I nodded. "Had to be."

Detective Inwood made a noise of dissent. "There are no 'have to's when you're talking about crime," he said. "You never know what people will do. But"—he put up a hand to stave off my knee-jerk protest—"you have a valid point."

It took me a moment to realize that the detective had given me a compliment. Or, if not a compliment, at least it wasn't a brush-off, and with Detective Inwood, that was pretty much the same thing.

"So, what I'm thinking," I said, "is the person who killed Andrea is looking for a book. Andrea must have been, too, because why else would she have been in the library when it was closed? And since none of this happened until after Talia DeKeyser died, maybe the two things are linked. Maybe it was a book Talia owned, maybe it was valuable, and maybe both Andrea and her killer were trying to steal it."

The detective frowned. "That's a lot of maybes, Ms. Hamilton. And what book," he asked, tapping the tip of his pen onto his notepad, which was still as pristine as snow on a winter's morning, "could possibly be worth killing for?"

"Not that long ago," I said, "one of Audubon's first editions went up for auction and sold for almost twelve million dollars."

The two men across the table from me blinked, but then Ash thinned his eyes to slits. "That book is, what, three feet tall? There's no way one of those could be in the library without everyone knowing about it."

I grinned. Having a well-educated boyfriend was kind of fun. "Just an example, gentlemen. There are other rare first editions that sell for a lot of money."

"How much?" Inwood asked.

"There was a first folio of Shakespeare's that sold for over six million," I said. "And a *Canterbury Tales* that went for seven and a half."

"Okay," Inwood said, putting his pen to paper, "other than old first editions, what book could be worth killing over?"

"A signed copy of a rare first edition would send it to another price range, if the signature was authenticated." I thought a little bit. "Or it could have been some sort of tell-all journal that was given away by accident." I didn't see how something like that could have gotten into circulation at the library, but the breaker-inner/killer wouldn't necessarily know how the library put books into the system. Besides, the donations box for the Friends of the Library book sale had a sign that the library had first dibs on donations.

Inwood, who had been writing furiously, glanced up at me. "But why would something that rare be in the library or Ms. Fazio's store?"

"Haven't you ever watched *Antiques Roadshow*? Rare things are found all the time in weird places."

He thought, then nodded. "Anything else?"

"No, it's just . . ." I put my hands in my lap, not wanting Ash or the detective to see how they'd turned into hard fists. Pam's phone call was still fresh in my mind. *Could you do me a favor?* that strong and capable woman had asked hesitantly, as if she wasn't sure I'd help her. As if she'd had been dealt a blow almost too hard to bear.

I looked at my hands, then directly at Inwood, staring him flat in the face. "Just find out who did this to Pam."

Chapter 8

That evening, I intentionally immersed myself in lake water so cold that it made me feel as if the top of my head was going to blow off.

"It'll get better," Ash said. He was leaning off the back of a powerboat, ready and willing to give coaching advice.

"When?" I asked, teeth chattering.

"Soon as you're up!" He grinned, and large parts of my insides went a little mushy at the idea that this incredibly good-looking man was dating me. Then again, I was in sixty-two-degree water with a wide board attached to my feet. Sure, I had a life jacket and was being watched over by a professional law-enforcement officer who also had EMT certification, but he wasn't the one in the water, now, was he?

"It's the getting-up part I'm worried about," I said, loud enough to be heard over the noise of the motor. The boat behind which I was about to water-ski belonged to, and was being driven by, a friend of Ash's, whom I was pretty sure he'd introduced as Tank. There was undoubtedly a story there, but to me, a thin guy with long sun-streaked hair and an easy smile could have had a more appropriate nickname.

"Hang tight to the towrope," Ash said, "and remember the drills we went through on land."

"Arms straight," I said to myself. "Knees to my chin. Let the boat do the work."

"Got it?" Ash called.

I nodded. Excitement and anxiety were knotting up together in my chest. I'd water-skied before, but never had I tried to slalom ski, to get up on one ski. Ash and I had gone out boating a couple of weeks ago with a different friend of his, and I'd looked on enviously as they had cut left and right behind the boat, sending up large rooster tails of spray.

"Next time we ski," Ash had said, "if you want, I'll show you how."

I'd said sure, and now here I was, about to fail miserably. On the plus side, I had a ready-made excuse: Since I didn't have quality goggles, I'd taken out my contacts, and the world was blurry around all its edges. On the minus side, my vision wasn't that bad, so it wasn't that great an excuse.

"No," I said out loud.

"What's that?" Ash called, cupping a hand to his ear. "Did you say roll?"

As if. I took a deep breath and nodded. If I fell the first time I tried, it wouldn't be a big deal. If I fell twenty times, it wouldn't be a failure. I would fail only if I gave up. "Roll."

Tank pushed the throttle slightly forward and there was an immediate tug on the rope. The boat puttered ahead with me trailing afterward like a baby duck behind a great big momma.

"Arms straight!" Ash called. "Knees to your chest!"

I nodded, although I was mostly trying to figure out where to put the towrope. To the left of the single ski that was sticking out of the water or the right? This wasn't a decision you had to make when you got up on two skis. I tried one side then the other and settled on the right. Then, before I really thought about it, I tightened my grip on the handle and shouted, "Hit it!"

The boat's engine roared. I was hauled forward at an incredible rate of speed. Water rushed over my face and over my head. Then, miracle of miracles, I felt myself rise, felt the ski start to level out. I was getting up! I was actually going to get up! I was . . .

Splash!

I fell forward with a resounding crash. After a second, I even managed to remember to let go of the towrope. Coughing away the water that had shoved itself into my nasal passages, I took stock of my body and of life in general.

"You okay?" Ash was hanging out the front of Tank's open cockpit boat.

"Fine," I said, coughing. "I hear fresh water is good for your sinuses."

Ash laughed. "You were almost up. Ready to try again?"

"Sure. What did I do wrong?"

"Leaned too far forward."

Since I'd fallen on my face, that made sense. I vowed not to let that happen again. And so, a couple of minutes later, I was in position a second time. "Hit it!"

Splash!

A few minutes later . . . "Hit it!"

Splash!

"Hit it!"

Splash!

The boat circled back around. "You getting tired?" Ash asked. "This is hard work."

My shoulders were aching and my thighs were screaming, but no way was I going to quit, not now that I'd fallen every way possible. I set my jaw. "Hit it!"

Splash!

"Hit it!"

And then everything came together. *Arms straight, knees to my chin, let the boat do the work, all you have to do is stand up . . .* and I was up. On top of the water and skimming away. I let out a shout that was pure, unadulterated joy. I was doing it, I was slalom skiing, I was cruising, I was king of Janay Lake, I was—

Splash!

This time when the boat came back around to me, I'd pulled off the ski and was floating in the water, faceup to the blue sky, panting from the exertion, and happy with the world.

"Not bad," Tank's gravelly voice said.

"You did great!" Ash leaned over the boat's transom and hauled in the ski.

"Next time," I said, kicking my way to the ladder, "I'm going outside the wake."

"That's my girl." Ash helped me into the boat and handed me a swim towel. "You'll get it in no time."

"All those years I've spent lifting boxes of books weren't in vain," I said. "Who needs to go to the gym to lift weights when you're a librarian?"

Tank and Ash laughed, although I hadn't been trying to be funny; it was just true. I rubbed the towel over my hair, making it go all frizzy, and pulled on a fleece sweatshirt.

"You going again?" Tank asked, looking at Ash, who shook his head.

"No, thanks. Have a long run scheduled for tomorrow morning. Don't want to be tired starting out."

"Got your bet down?"

"What bet?" I frowned. "And what's with that 'keep quiet' gesture, Deputy Wolverson?"

"Umm . . ." Ash made himself busy with coiling up the towrope.

"He doesn't want you to know because you might get uptight," Tank said. "But I can see you're not like that, so I have no problem telling you there are bets at the sheriff's office and city police on what place is going to be broken into next."

"Why would I get upset about that?"

Ash took the towel from me and folded it up neatly. "It's more that I don't want to be the first one to break our agreement."

Now, that made sense. The morning of our first run after Andrea's murder, we decided that we wouldn't talk about the murder, or any other crime in which I was involved, on an official date. We'd decided that the first one to break the agreement would suffer severe consequences that would be named by the non-agreement-breaker, and sealed the deal with a kiss. Though placing a bet wouldn't violate the contract, a broad discussion would almost guarantee that one of us, at some point, would cross the line.

Of course, we had yet to decide what constituted an official date, but it's hard to get everything right on the first try.

"That used-book store," I said.

"What used-book store?" Ash gestured for me to sit

in the boat's front seat, across from Tank, and dropped into a backseat.

"It just opened a couple of months ago." Used-book stores had a hard go of it financially. Their margins were thin, and most advertising was beyond their budgets. I had high hopes for this one—their selection of mysteries and thrillers was outstanding—but only time would tell.

"Huh," Ash looked thoughtful.

"Too late, pal," Tank said. "You already placed your bet. Minnie, you betting?"

I shook my head. Putting down money on someone's future misfortune wasn't anything I'd want my mother to know about. Not that I told Mom a tenth of the things I did, but anticipating her reactions was a good way to judge how I should act.

"Maybe there won't be any more break-ins," Ash said.

"Who gets the pot if there aren't?" I asked.

Tank started the boat's engine. "Ash, man, you really got to talk to your girlfriend more."

"What?" I looked from one to the other. "Why?"

"Because he"—Tank jerked his thumb over his shoulder—"said if no one wins, the pot goes to the library."

He slapped the throttle forward and we zoomed across the lake.

A few hours later, back on the houseboat, I asked my cat a simple question: "Is Ash the nicest guy in the world, or what?" I opened a kitchen cabinet and, standing on tiptoes, rooted around in the back. "Ha! Found it." The vase was dusty, so as I cleaned it out I talked to Eddie, who was supervising my efforts from the dining booth. The back of the booth, to be exact, upon which he'd arranged himself into a three-dimensional rectangle.

"Do all cats do that?" I asked. "Make themselves into a meat-loaf shape?" There was probably a proper mathematical term, but to me he looked like a furry meat loaf. "And how do you do that, exactly?"

He blinked at me.

"No, seriously," I said. "When you stand up, you look like a normal four-legged mammal. But when you're like that, your legs disappear, your tail disappears, and sometimes—yeah, like that—you sink your head down and you're almost completely rectangular."

"Mrr," said the geometric shape.

"I suppose that's some sort of an answer." I poured water into the vase and opened a drawer. Once upon a time, my mother had given me a pair of kitchen scissors. I still didn't know what normal people did with them. I'd asked Kristen once, but her explanation had involved the naming of parts of chickens and turkeys that I hadn't known existed.

"Scissors work great for this," I told Eddie, clipping off the ends of the flowers Ash had presented as he'd dropped me off. "He'd had these in a cooler in the back of his SUV the whole time we were out water-skiing. Aren't they pretty?" I popped the flowers into the vase and arranged them as artfully as I could.

"Mrr," said the meat loaf.

"What kind are these? Well, those are daisies," I said, pointing. "And those are ... are yellow flowers, and those are blue ones." Maybe it was time to start studying the wildflower book that was in the bookmobile. I'd learned a lot about birds over the past year while driving around the county, and there was no reason I couldn't learn more things.

"Not that these are wildflowers," I told my critical

cat. "I've heard you're not supposed to take wildflowers from where they grow." Why, I wasn't exactly sure, but it probably had something to do with native and protected species and public lands, and that removing the blooms could hurt the flower's reproduction possibilities.

I moved the vase to the middle of the dining booth's table and turned it this way and that, admiring the colors. "Sounds weird, though, doesn't it? Flowers reproducing, I mean. Kind of makes you think about them sneaking around after dark and making out."

The image amused me. "Maybe that's how we get new species—adolescent flowers doing what Mom and Dad warned them not to do, and suddenly there's a brand-new flower in the family." Smirking at myself, I turned back to the sink and washed off the scissors. "Then there's this new flower, and it's not accepted by any of the other flowers and—"

Crash!

I whipped around. "Eddie!" I lunged forward, grabbing at the tipped-over vase with one hand and reaching for the flowers with the other. Water streamed onto the floor and puddled around my flip-flopped feet.

Eddie, who was now sitting on the table, just watched.

"Why on earth did you do that?" I shoved the flowers back into the vase before they could drip anywhere else. After refilling the water, I put the vase on the kitchen counter.

"These," I said, glaring at my cat and pointing at the flowers, "are not a cat toy. They are mine. Not yours. Understand?"

Eddie stared straight at me, then yawned, showing long and white teeth.

"Yeah, yeah." I pulled off a length of paper towels and knelt on the floor, reaching under the table to get the far end of the puddle. "How did you get water way back here? You're a mess maker—that's what you are. Like a matchmaker, only different. We could make up new lyrics to the song. How about—"

Crash!

"Eddie!" I started to stand, bonked my head on the underside of the table, slid out of the danger zone, and spun myself around on the floor, holding my hand to my head. "What is with you, cat?"

My furry friend was paying no attention to me. He was on the kitchen counter, his entire being focused on pushing a daisy out of the fallen flower arrangement and onto the floor. *Plop.*

"Off," I ordered.

"Mrr!" he ordered back, but he did jump down.

"And quit playing with my flowers." I pulled the daisy away from his outstretched paw. "Not a cat toy, remember?" For the third time, I put the flowers in the vase. After adding some water, I looked around for a safe home and quickly decided there wasn't anywhere both out of reach and viewable by those houseboat residents—which would be me—who would enjoy looking at the flowers.

"You are horrible." I put the flowers into the fridge. "I'll have to take those to the library to get any pleasure out of them."

Eddie pawed at the refrigerator door. "Mrr!"

"Really? How many times do I have to tell you? Not a cat toy."

He gave me a look of fierce disgust and stalked off.

"You're not going away mad, are you?" I called.

"Mrr."

"I love you, you know!"

He paused at the top of the short stairway and looked back. "Mrr," he said, and hopped down the stairs, pushed open the door of my tiny closet, and flopped onto my shoes, where he stayed the rest of the night.

Chapter 9

The next morning I woke up sore in all sorts of odd places. I sat on the edge of the bed.

"Mrr?" Eddie asked.

"Hang on a second. I'm still trying to figure it out." I stood, not bothering to stifle a whimpering groan, and hobbled around in a small circle. "Worst is probably the backs of my shoulders," I said. The trapezius? I tried to remember the diagrams from a high school physiology class. No, that wasn't right. I reached around with my fingers and tenderly poked at the sore parts. "Latissimus dorsi." I eyed my cat, wondering if he had a corresponding muscle. If he did, would he be able to water-ski? There'd been that video of a water-skiing squirrel; maybe I could make Eddie famous.

"Mrr," he said, stretching out a long paw.

"Sorry." I nodded. "Back to the inventory. Shoulders hurt the most; thighs aren't far behind. And my neck is stiff, although I'm not sure why."

Eddie flopped over on his side with a soft *thump*.

"You're right," I agreed. "It probably is from that last time I crashed. I hit the water pretty hard." I rotated my head around, trying to loosen up the muscles. "And all that crawling around on the floor of Pam's store, sorting out books, probably didn't help, either." Or the sleep I'd lost. But, hey, I was young and relatively fit, and I'd be able to catch up on sleep soon enough. All I needed was a hot shower and breakfast.

Eddie yawned and drew himself into a ball that was half his size, a miracle achieved on a daily basis by cats around the world.

"I wouldn't get too comfortable," I told him as I headed toward the bathroom. "It's a bookmobile day, you know."

His eyes opened wide.

"Would I mess with you about a thing like that?" I asked. "Yes, I might give you a hard time about your snoring, your tendency to sleep draped across my neck, and your complete disregard of the only ultimate demand I've ever had of you—you know, that one about staying off the kitchen counter—but I would never joke with you about the bookmobile."

"Mrr!"

He jumped off the bed, galloped through the bedroom and up the stairs, and only screeched to a stop when he reached my backpack, upon which he sat upright until it was time to leave.

The bookmobile day was crowded with patrons who wanted information even more than they wanted books. We were making stops in this part of the county for the first time since Andrea's murder, and by this time, even the people who eschewed newspapers had heard the news.

But even though the concern about a murder was real, what seemed to be upsetting people the most was the attack on the bookmobile.

"It's all right, isn't it?" asked seven-year-old Ethan Engstrom. He looked up at me anxiously, his face full of concern.

I'd met Ethan on the first stop of the bookmobile's maiden voyage, the one upon which Eddie had been a stowaway. Not wanting word of a cat hair–laden beast to get back to my boss, I'd emptied a storage cabinet and encouraged Eddie to stay inside during the stops.

Young Ethan was curious and helpful, and he'd opened the Eddie cabinet in hopes of finding a place to store the things I'd taken out of Eddie's cabinet and had to put on the floor. Eddie came out of the closet, and life hadn't been the same since.

"The bookmobile is fine," I assured him.

"They didn't hurt Eddie, did they?" asked Cara, the middle of the three Engstrom girls.

"Eddie was sound asleep in bed," I told her, smiling. "He wasn't anywhere near the bookmobile when it happened."

This, apparently, puzzled Emma, the youngest Engstrom girl. Emma was twin to Ethan. Cara was twins with Patrick, and the oldest of the statistically impossible Engstrom twins were Trevor and Rose, now thirteen. Last year Rose had been going through a princess phase, but she seemed to have grown past that and was now into horses.

Their father, Chad, worked from home designing educational video games, and homeschooled the kids with the help of a retired neighbor who'd once taught high school biology. His wife worked for Tonedagana County as human resources director, and one of these days I hoped to actually meet the woman who'd given birth to such a great collection of intelligent young people.

"Eddie doesn't sleep here?" Emma asked, frowning.

"Not at night," I said, because denying that he slept in the bookmobile would be ridiculous. Right that very second, for instance, he was sprawled on the dashboard, overdosing on sunshine. "At night he comes home with me."

"Oh," she said, her face drooping.

I felt like a heel. I'd obviously just destroyed one of her illusions. Accidentally, but that didn't matter. No one should have to suffer the destruction of an illusion without some compensatory relief, so I moved closer to her and whispered, "Do you want to know a secret?"

Her lips curled up in a slow smile. She nodded.

"Eddie knocked over a vase of flowers last night," I said. "Twice."

She giggled and slapped her hands over her mouth. "He was a bad kitty?" she asked through her fingers.

"The worst," I said solemnly. "He didn't even help clean up the mess afterward."

"Bad Eddie!" She giggled again.

"Hey, now. No laughing," her father said, mock sternly. "Not unless you share why you're laughing."

I shook my head. "It's a secret," I told him.

Still giggling, Emma ran off, singing, "Bad, bad, Eddie. Bad, bad, bad."

Her father watched her go. "Do you know what's going on?" he asked. "A murder, two break-ins at the library, and now another burglary downtown?" His face was serious now, and it wasn't a look that sat well on him. "Not that I really think crime in Chilson is going to spread over here, but you have to wonder, especially with six kids in the house."

"The police are . . ." I sighed. "Are exploring all avenues of investigation."

Chad squinted at me. "You did not just say that."

"Sorry." I half smiled. "Would it help if I told you it was a direct quote from the detective working on the case?"

"A little." He studied me. "But it would help even more if I knew they were close to figuring out what's happening."

"You're not alone," I said, and went to help Julia help Trevor find a book that would answer his questions about capacitors and inductors.

As soon as we got back to Chilson, I hurried through the post-bookmobile routine as quickly as I could, even to the extent of leaving some tasks for the next day. Julia said she'd be willing to work late, but I shooed her off, saying it was too nice a night, and locked all the doors behind us, checking them twice. And then three times.

I dropped Eddie off at the houseboat, sent him an air kiss, then hauled my bicycle out of my storage locker and hurried across town.

The parking lot of the Three Seasons was packed with vehicles of all shapes and sizes. Vans, cars, trucks, and SUVs littered the lot with no regard for where the lines had been painted. Black cables thicker than my wrist snaked across the asphalt, a tripping hazard to the unwary, which explained why the lot's entrance had been blocked off by bright yellow sawhorses.

I leaned my bike against the restaurant's white clapboard siding and went inside a way I rarely did: through the front door.

People wandered hither and yon, hauling lights and clipboards and rolls of tape. Most of them were younger than I was and were wearing black pants and black

T-shirts, looking extremely serious. I spotted two people I knew and made my way toward them.

"Don't tell me we're actually going to finish on time," said Scruffy Gronkowski.

A wild-haired woman in capris, flip-flops, and a tie-dyed shirt nodded. "If we get this last part in the can in less than two takes, we'll even be early."

"Lynn," Scruffy said, "you are a marvel."

"Ha. It wasn't me. It was your girlfriend. You sure she's never done this before?"

"Far as I know, she didn't even do high school acting."

"She tried out for a nun in a production of *The Sound of Music*," I said, "but it turned out she can't sing for beans."

"Hey, Minnie," Scruffy said, turning toward me and smiling. "You met Lynn last summer, didn't you?"

"Over pork tenderloin, if I remember correctly."

Lynn grinned. "And I'm still grateful that you steered Trock away from changing the menu." A distant voice called her name, a note of panic clear in the single syllable. "What now?" she asked, rolling her eyes. "See you two later."

I looked up at Scruffy. "How did it go today?"

He picked a piece of invisible lint off his tailored polo shirt. His nickname hadn't come about because of reality. "Outstanding. And would you please go tell her so?"

"Pulling a Kristen, is she?"

"Perfection is a worthy goal and all, but it's also an unattainable one."

Uh-oh. "Are they done in there?" I tipped my head toward the kitchen.

"If you walk fast, you might catch the last take of the sous chef cutting parsley into perfect tiny squares."

I blinked. "Harvey's going to be on TV?"

"Kind of," Scruffy said. "He froze up if he talked or if the camera was on his face, but he was fine with a hands-only shot."

The world righted itself. Harvey was a great guy, but if I'd been asked to describe his social skills, I would have backed away from the conversation, pleading a dire emergency somewhere else. Harvey was quiet around men and tongue-tied with women, and the concept of his blossoming in front of a television camera was nearly impossible to comprehend.

I went to the kitchen, where bright lights shone everywhere, highlighting everything to the point that I understood Kristen's recent obsession with cleanliness.

"And that's it, Harve," someone called. "We're good. Thanks."

"Okay," Harvey said, continuing to cut parsley.

"Um, we're all set, Harvey. You can stop now."

He shook his head, his attention on what he was doing. "It's for tonight. Kristen wants all this cut up."

Grinning, I cut through the back corner of the kitchen. That was Harvey in a nutshell. Who cared if there was a national television show being filmed in the restaurant that day, who cared if his hands were going to be broadcast across the land? What mattered was taking care of what Kristen wanted.

I walked along the wide hallway that led to her office, a little surprised to see that none of the boxes and trays and chairs and general restaurant miscellanea that always littered one side of the passage hadn't been cleared away. Then again, it was just like Kristen not to change anything for the sake of a TV show. I could almost hear her saying, "They can take me or leave me.

I'll clean, but I'm not about to transform myself. If they don't like who I really am, they shouldn't have come here."

Then I actually did hear her say to someone, "You shouldn't have come here at all."

A deep voice rumbled back, "Dear lady, you must not judge yourself. Leave that to me."

I pushed her office door open wide. "And me. I've had lots of experience, you know."

Kristen and Trock Farrand turned to face me. Kristen's expression was one I'd seen many times before, one that combined anger at herself with deep despair. Trock, on the other hand, was nothing but smiles.

He lumbered to his feet. "Dearest Minerva! I had hoped to see you this fine day." He leaned forward in a half bow, reaching out for my hand and lifting it to his lips. Postkiss, he straightened his rotund body and released my hand.

"You missed an exceptional day of filming," he said grandly. "This will go down in history as the episode of *Trock's Troubles* that absolutely cannot be missed. From beginning to end it was perfection. Nothing went wrong. The food was exquisite, and the presentation was superb. Kristen here could take over my job without blinking her deep blue eyes. Which," he added, beaming, "will show up brilliantly. I ordered as many close-up shots as they could manage."

"Nothing went wrong?" Kristen asked. "What about the strawberries? There was mold. Mold!" she practically shouted.

I winced, knowing that Harvey, poor soul, would have borne the brunt of her anger.

"Piffle." Trock waved away the problem. "Easy to

drop that on the cutting floor, as it were. My dear, the magic of television has an infinite capacity to show what it wishes to show, and I wish to only show the best."

"Mold," she muttered. "I can't believe it. They were fine this morning." She sat up straight, her chin lifted. "If you want to cancel airing this show, I'd understand completely. I won't hold you to the contract."

"Good gad." Trock blinked. He turned to me. "Is she serious?"

"As a chocolate soufflé."

Both Kristen and Trock frowned in my direction. "What's so serious about a chocolate soufflé?" Kristen asked.

I shrugged. "Didn't want to say heart attack, and I've heard a chocolate soufflé is hard to make. Seriously hard, see?"

The twosome stared at me a moment, then went back to their discussion. "My darling restaurateur," Trock said, "love of my son's life and highlight of my own, please believe me when I tell you the finished product will be wonderful."

Kristen crossed her arms across her chest. "Why should I believe you? You exaggerate from morning to night. You probably talk hyperbole in your dreams."

Which was most likely true, but there was one difference. "Not this time," I said.

"How can you possibly say that?" she asked.

"Because he never exaggerates about his show." She started to object, but I held up my hand. "He may talk on and on about a restaurant he's featured, and he may wax lyrical about a particular entrée that he made, but he never deviates from the absolute truth about an episode of the show itself."

Kristen's mouth opened, then shut. She stared at the ceiling and tapped her fingers together. "You're right," she finally said.

"Which means . . ." I held my hands out, palms up.

Her smile became a wide grin. "We're going to be famous."

"And rich," I added. The two looked at me again, and I amended my statement. "Well, maybe not *rich* rich, but you're certainly going to the most popular fine-dining establishment in northern lower Michigan for months, if not years."

"Bubbly!" Trock called out at the top of his robust lungs. "We must have bubbly! Scruffy, where are you, son? Get the glasses. Get the champagne. We need to celebrate."

Kristen laughed as Trock continued to yodel out commands, and I felt myself grinning like a jack o'-lantern, because there was nothing like a friend's success to make you feel happy inside.

"It was horrible," Holly said the next morning. "Just awful."

I looked at Josh, who nodded.

"She's right," he said. "It was horrible."

"Scary bad." Holly shuddered.

"What was his name?" I asked.

"Theodore," she said dolefully.

"Well, he can't help the name he was born with," I said. "And Ted isn't so bad. I have a neighbor named Ted and he's—"

But Josh was shaking his head. "He doesn't go by Ted. It's Theodore."

He spoke the syllables in a round, full, sonorous tone,

and I got a mental image of what Theodore must look like. Which was ridiculous, because who ever looked like their name?

"Minnie!" Donna hurried into the break room. "Did they tell you?"

"About what?"

"About Thee-o-door," she said. "He was awful. You can't let the board choose him as the new director— you just can't."

Holly and Josh, when grouped together during the morning break time, had a tendency to exacerbate any given situation. I'd been taking their comments about yesterday's interviewee with a large grain of salt, and had been thinking about stringing them along with hints that the board had thought highly of Theodore. But if Donna was agreeing with the Dual Voices of Doom, I had to take the situation seriously. "Tell me what happened."

"Thee-o-dore," Donna said, "was too friendly."

"Way too," Josh said. "The guy was creepy. Pretending like he knew us, calling us by our names even though he'd never met us before."

Okay, that was weird. It meant the guy had done his homework—there were pictures of the staff on the library's Web site—but it was weird not to let yourself be introduced first.

"And he kept talking about what he'd like to do here," Holly burst out.

"What's so bad about that? Any library director will have goals."

"You're not getting it," Josh said. "He was talking about the changes he was going to make."

That was different.

"Want to know the first thing he's going to do?" Holly

asked. I didn't, not really, but short of running out of the room and locking my office door behind me, I wasn't sure how to avoid hearing. "He wants to get rid of the—"

I steeled myself to hear the word "bookmobile."

"—sculpture garden."

My mouth dropped open. The library's sculpture garden was a labor of love for the entire town. Local artists had submitted designs, school art classes had constructed the pieces, and the installations had been celebrated events attended by hundreds.

"He doesn't know what it means to Chilson," I finally said. "That's all. Once he finds out, he'll change his mind."

Josh made a rude noise. "He said it was a waste of maintenance dollars."

I blinked. Gareth, our maintenance guy and my fellow junk-food maven, loved the sculptures. He took care of them on his own time, saying that it was his civic contribution to Chilson. The sole cost to the library was the occasional bolt or small can of paint, and I wasn't sure Gareth charged even that to the library.

"And," Holly ruthlessly went on, "he said it would save money to move the sculptures to commercial venues. That we'd be better off with a bigger parking lot."

"After that," Donna said into my look of stunned disbelief, "the next thing he wants is to get rid of all the DVDs. Says they have no place in a library."

"Are you sure he wasn't just nervous?" I asked. "That could make anyone act unusually."

"When he walked out," Holly said, "he was whistling."

It was hard to imagine a whistle coming out of someone who was anxious. "What was he whistling?" I asked, still trying to find a way to make excuses for this guy.

"The theme music to that last Superman movie."

Oh, dear.

"Minnie, you have to apply," Josh said.

"You mean you haven't?" Donna practically shrieked. "We need you. Thee-o-dore was horrible. What's-her-name wasn't much better. I'm not holding out much hope that the other interviewees will be any improvement."

"If you love us even a little," Holly pleaded, "put in your application. You have it ready, don't you?"

"Apply," Donna said. "Please?"

It was the question mark at the end that got me. Donna wasn't big on asking for favors, even when she really needed the help. I needed to tell them what I'd decided, and I needed to stop putting it off.

"Sorry, but I'm not going to," I said. "If I'm director, I can't drive the bookmobile, and that's too important to me."

There was a long silence.

Holly heaved a huge sigh. "I understand. I don't like it, but I understand."

"I get it," Josh said, nodding slowly. "But I'm with Holly. I don't like it."

I looked at Donna, who grimaced. "Yeah, yeah," she said. "Same as those two."

I smiled, glad to have the bad news delivered and done with. "Don't look so gloomy. Things will work out."

"Or not," Donna muttered, but I chose not to hear her comment, and went back to my office.

At lunchtime, I pushed back from my computer. I'd been staring at the screen for two hours straight and needed a break. Outside, I looked around, smiling at the high white clouds, blue sky, and sidewalks that were beginning to crowd up with the summer folks. It wouldn't get avoid-downtown-at-all-costs busy until the Fourth of July, but there was enough foot traffic to make it impossible to walk in a straight line.

I stopped outside Pam's store and peered in. Her clerk was showing off a collection of antique aprons, and Pam herself was at the register, totting up purchases with one hand faster than I could have with two.

When she finished, I popped my head in the front door and waved at her. When she waved back, I asked. "How about lunch?"

She looked around her store. At least half a dozen customers were milling about, and I moved aside to let two more inside. "How about tomorrow?" she asked.

I shook my head. "Bookmobile day."

One of the women who'd just walked in whirled around. "You have a bookmobile here? How wonderful!" She elbowed her female companion. "Did you hear that, Susie? They have a bookmobile."

"That settles it," Susie said. "I'm moving up here next week."

I laughed. "Hope you like snow." I looked back to Pam. "Lunch on Friday? No? Saturday is probably too busy for you. How about . . ." I had plans for Sunday, didn't I? And it seemed as if I had something on Monday. Tuesday was another bookmobile day, which left—

"How about September?" she asked, laughing.

I smiled at her ruefully. "Sounds about right."

"We'll figure out a day soon," she said. "And I'm paying. I owe you big-time for Sunday—don't think I'm going to let you forget it. All that work, not to mention the hospital trip."

Susie and her friend, who were still standing close by, looked at the two of us curiously. "Hospital?" Susie asked. She gestured at Pam's sling. "That's recent?"

"Fresh as a daisy," Pam said. "And it's all thanks to Minnie here that the store is even open today."

I could see where this was going, and I didn't want any part of it. "Nice to meet you," I said to the two women, "but I hear the library calling." I smiled and hurried off before I was forced to listen to any of Pam's tall tales about my good deeds.

Outside, I walked past the insurance agency and the shoe store, pausing only to use a stranger's cell phone to take a picture of said stranger's family, all of whom were posing under the new clock. As I handed the phone back and listened to their thanks, I eyed the large store across the street. Speaking of deeds, good and bad, there was Benton's, the store the DeKeyser family owned. And, I'd recently learned through a text from Rafe, still owned through a granddaughter whose name I'd come up with in a minute.

As I crossed the street, I remembered her name. "Rianne," I said out loud, and earned a sideways glance from a man wearing shorts, a polo shirt, and deck shoes. "Howe," I added, nodding.

"How do you do?" he asked pleasantly enough, but he kept to the far side of the sidewalk and didn't slow down.

Since I'd clearly spent enough time that day making tourists uncomfortable, I opened the store's front door. Once inside, I stopped and did what I always did when walking into Benton's: just stood there and breathed deep with my eyes closed.

Instantly I was transported back in time, back to the days of stores with wood floors and tin ceilings, when penny candy was sold from glass jars and herbs could be purchased in bunches that hung from a rack.

I opened my eyes and there it all was, from tin ceiling to wood floor, to candy in a jar and hanging herbs. The penny candy cost more than a penny and the herbs were for decoration only, but still.

A few customers milled about in the housewares section, exclaiming over the glass butter dishes and wire fly swatters, just like grandma's. A young man about twenty years old was standing behind the wooden counter, bagging up a small collection of toys and candy for a girl half his age. "There you go, miss," he said, pushing the paper bag toward her outstretched hands. "Would you like help carrying that to your car?"

She giggled. "No, thank you. Bye, Brian. See you next week!" She ran past me, flew out the door, tossed her purchases into the front basket of her bicycle, and was pedaling off in seconds.

"Next week?" I asked, coming up to the counter. "She's a regular?"

"She's in here once a week through mid-August," he said, nodding. "Her family spends the summer up here, and this is allowance day."

"Which is now all gone?"

He glanced at the cash register. "She has thirty-two cents left."

"Maybe Cookie Tom will give her a cookie for that much," I suggested.

"When I did the same thing when I was her age, he'd give me two." We laughed, and he asked, "What can I do for you?"

"I'm looking for Rianne Howe. Does she have a minute?" I gave him my name.

"Hang on." He picked up the phone, asked my name, and punched a few sleek buttons. The anachronism of a twenty-first-century telephone in a late-1800s general store bothered me a little, so I averted my eyes and studied the massive brass cash register instead.

"She said come on back." Brian clunked down the phone and nodded to the rear of the store. "See that curtain? Through there. There's a door on the right—that's her office."

I thanked him and made my way past the shelves of office supplies, then past the T-shirts, work boots, and overalls. I glanced at the far side of the store toward the colorful selection of fabric and kitchen supplies and strong-mindedly marched past the books. I pushed my way through the navy blue burlap curtain panels Brian had indicated and knocked on Rianne's office door.

"Come on in," she called.

"Hi," I said, and stopped short. I'd assumed her office to be one of two things: full of the castoffs from a store that had been in existence for more than a hundred years, or city sleek and modernistic. "Wow. This is . . ."

Rianne grinned. She was probably in her early forties, and her smile crinkled the corners of her eyes attractively. "What do you think?" she asked, pushing her reddish brown hair back behind her ears. "I love hearing people's first impressions."

"It's amazing," I said, soaking it all in. "And I mean that in the best possible way."

There were wide windows and wood-paneled walls and a high ceiling made of wood. There were built-in cabinets that looked like they'd been designed by a master, and brass light fixtures that harked back to the days of kerosene lamps. There was a wood floor and scattered area rugs and framed diagrams of Janay Lake and Lake Michigan.

But, above all, there was a massive wood ship's wheel attached to the front of Rianne's desk. My hands itched to take hold of one of the spoke handles and give it a spin, but since I was working on being a fully functioning adult, I kept my hands at my sides.

"Did you do this?" I asked.

She shook her head. "The only addition of mine is a dent in the desk when I was five, from riding my tricycle too fast. It was the last Benton to own the store, my great-grandfather, who did all this."

"By himself?"

"Pretty much, or so the family story goes. He'd wanted to go to sea, but as the only male Benton, he was obligated to take over the store. Back then they ran tabs for people and would sometimes trade. One of their customers paid for a full year of groceries with maple planks cut from trees he'd felled on his land. Great-grandpa sold some, but used the bulk of it for this." She smiled. "Or so the story goes."

"You don't believe the story?"

"In my family, the stories get better with every generation, so it's hard to know the truth." She tapped the desk. "Take this, for instance. I grew up hearing it had been given to Great-grandpa by President Roosevelt for saving his life during some hunt."

"Not true?" I asked.

"When I took over the store, I crawled underneath the desk during a cleaning frenzy and found the manufacturer's label. Made in 1923."

"Didn't Roosevelt die just after World War I?"

"In 1919."

"Hmm." I studied the desk. "Who made it? Maybe there was some association with the name."

"The desk?" She looked at it, too. "Something to do with kitchens. Something Furniture. Pot, pan . . ." She snapped her fingers. "Kettle. Kettle Furniture."

A report I'd written in sixth grade bounced out of my brain. "Kettle Hill," I said. "The Spanish-American War. Kettle Hill and San Juan Hill were where the big battles took place."

She considered the possibility for half a second, then shook her head. "Don't see it. Thanks for trying, though. By the way, I'm Rianne Howe," she said, standing up and holding out her hand. "You're Minnie Hamilton, and I'm not sure why we haven't met before today." After we shook, she waved me to a chair. "I love libraries, and I think your bookmobile is the best thing that has happened to this town since Cookie Tom opened up."

I beamed. "We welcome volunteers on the bookmobile. Julia and Eddie and I love to have new folks along."

"Sounds like adding one more might make it a little crowded."

"Well, one of us is a cat. He doesn't take up too much room." I thought about what I'd said, then added, "Most of the time, anyway."

Rianne laughed. "So, what can I do for you? I'd love to make a donation to the library, but I'm still trying to figure out how to make sure this store actually turns a profit."

"You haven't been running the store very long?" I asked.

"Technically I took over when Grandpa Cal retired six years ago. I was downstate then, managing some big-box retail stores. No one else wanted to run this place, and I couldn't stand to see it go out of the family, so I said I'd do it." She looked around the office, smiling. "But we wanted our youngest to graduate from high school first, so I hired a manager. Then when Brian graduated last June, we started making plans to move up. My husband's an RN. He got a job with Lake View Medical Care Facility, and here we are."

It wasn't an unusual story, but there was one part of it I was curious about. "It seems odd that with seven children and who knows how many grandchildren, you were the only DeKeyser who wanted the store."

"That's because you don't know how much work it is. My grandparents were wonderful people, but one of their strongest beliefs was that a strong work ethic made for strong character."

"Sounds like my mother," I murmured.

"Each and every DeKeyser relative," Rianne said, "worked in this store when they were kids. After school, on weekends, through the summer. Probably half the kids in town worked here, too, but it was the DeKeyser kids who had to work harder and better." She gave a wry smile. "No nepotism in my family. Raises? Not a chance. Holidays off? Not for a DeKeyser. It was our store, and we have to live up to its reputation."

"I can see how that would sour you on working here."

"Yet this is where I want to be," she said. "I even got a degree in retail management. Go figure."

"It was your fate," I said, although I wasn't certain I believed in fate.

"Maybe." She looked around the room again. "Though it's more likely," she said, half smiling, "that I just want to be able to play with the ship's wheel every day."

"Every office should have one," I said, slipping my hands under my thighs so I didn't reach out to give it a whirl. "But I'm not here for a donation. If you have a couple of minutes, there are a couple of things I think you should know."

"Sounds serious."

I sighed. "Sorry, but yes. I assume you heard about the break-in at Pam Fazio's store the other night?"

"Horrible thing," Rianne said. "I would have been over to help, but I was downstate last weekend for a wedding. How is Pam doing?"

"Cranky that she's going to get weird tan lines with a cast on her arm," I said. "And it's the break-in at Pam's store that got me thinking. I've talked to the police, but I'm not sure they're taking it seriously."

"Haven't I heard that you're dating Ash Wolverson? Isn't he training to be a detective?"

Sometimes this town was way too small. "Yes, and he's not sure I'm right about this."

"About what?" Rianne asked.

"I think everything that has gone on the last couple of weeks is all about books. Or maybe even one book."

"Not sure I'm catching this," Rianne said, leaning back in her chair.

Yes, folks, it's true. Everyone in town thinks Minnie Hamilton is a nutcase. Nevertheless, I forged ahead with my theory. "Your grandmother's funeral—and I'm so sorry for your loss—was what brought Andrea Vennard to town. That's when—" I looked at her. "Um, I haven't figured out the relations, exactly. Was Andrea your cousin?"

"She was a great-niece to Grandma Talia, which made her my . . ." She frowned. "Second cousin? Anyway, I knew her more from school than through family, and even then not very well. She was a few years ahead of me."

I nodded. "Andrea came north for your grandmother's funeral and was killed in the library. The Friends of the Library book-sale room was vandalized soon after that. Then the bookmobile was broken into, and Pam's store was burglarized." I held up the fingers I'd been using to count. "Four incidents that involved books."

Rianne looked puzzled. "But there was a lot more damaged in Pam's place than books."

"Yes, but when you look at the pictures we took of her store before we started cleaning, you can see that it was the books that were tossed around the most. Nothing was stolen from Pam's. Not one thing."

"Huh." Rianne leaned back a little farther and let out a long, slow breath. "That's downright weird."

Hurray! Finally, there was someone who understood my concerns. "So, there are two things I wanted to talk to you about. One, if you could think of any possible link between Andrea and your grandmother, something beyond the normal family connection."

Rianne's eyes grew distant as she tried to come up with an idea. When I could see that she was coming up dry, I said, "What about books? Did your grandmother have any valuable books? Or maybe a journal?"

"The only valuable thing my family has ever owned is this store," Rianne said, glancing around fondly.

Another brilliant idea bites the dust. "If you think of anything, will you let me know?"

She nodded. "Sure. What's the second thing?"

"If this is all about books, you should be extra careful." I thumbed toward the front of the store. "You have books, too."

Rianne blinked, then laughed. "Minnie, I appreciate your concern, but I can't think that our small selection of paperbacks is going to tempt anyone, no matter what this is all about."

I'd expected that kind of reaction, but I stuck to my theme. "We don't know what's going on. Until this is over, please be extra careful."

"This one be careful?" A tall man entered Rianne's office. He wore the unofficial summer uniform for Up North male professionals: khaki pants, a polo shirt, and a blazer. "She hasn't been careful since the day she was born, and probably was a problem to her mother in utero."

Rianne rolled her eyes. "So nice to see you, Paul. Minnie, don't ever hire an attorney who used to babysit you. There's just no respect in the relationship."

"From either side," Paul said. "For example, when her attorney asks her to get together the items listed in her grandmother's will for distribution to the family, she puts the list who knows where and says she'll look when she has time." He spread his hands. "And that will be when? October? Back before Cal died, I went through the house myself to put together the list, so I know there's not much. Meanwhile, the estate remains unsettled and the papers continue to clutter my desk."

His tone was jocular, but there was an undertone of annoyance. I stood. "Well, I should get going. Thanks for letting me take so much of your time, Rianne."

"Not a problem," she said. "I'm glad you stopped."

Paul held out a business card. "In case you never need an attorney," he said. "Any friend of Rianne's is a future client of mine," he said, laughing.

I smiled. I already had an attorney, Shannon Hirsch, who'd set up my will and advised me on some estate issues. Shannon had been one of the people who'd answered my call to help set Pam's store to rights. "Thanks," I said, taking the card and sliding it deep into my backpack. "You never know, do you?"

He grinned. "Nope. That's why we have insurance and lawyers. You can't prepare for everything."

"Sounds like a tagline," Rianne said. "All you need is a tune, and you'll have the best lawyer jingle in the north." She hummed a nonsense tune.

Paul laughed. "Lawyers don't do jingles. It's beneath our dignity."

"Oh yeah?" Rianne challenged. "Didn't I see you wearing the ugliest holiday sweater in the history of ugly sweaters?"

"That was twenty years ago." He dropped into the seat I'd just vacated. "Way past the statute of limitations for embarrassment."

I nodded my good-byes and walked out. As I made a left turn, back into the store, I heard Rianne say in a low voice, "What's going on with Aunt Kim—do you know?"

Paul gusted out a sigh. "All I can say is, Bob Parmalee hasn't been in to see me in months."

"The rest of the family is saying they're going bankrupt," Rianne said in a shaky voice. "I keep wanting to call, but you know how they keep to themselves. They spend more time in Petoskey than they do in Chilson."

"Almost makes me glad your grandparents are gone," Paul said. "They would have been devastated about a bankruptcy in the family."

I eased away, not wanting to be caught eavesdropping—*Sorry, Mom. I won't eavesdrop ever again, but if I do, I promise I'll feel horrible about it afterward*—and walked out into the store.

"All set?"

I looked at Brian Howe, latest in the long line of DeKeyser relatives to spend a summer working in the store. "Yes, thanks," I said, and headed out into the day.

But as much as the sun and the fresh air tried to distract me from my dark thoughts, on the way back to the library, all I could think about was how money was one of the most common motives for murder.

Chapter 10

"Excuse me," said a polite voice.

I jumped. "Sorry," I said, moving away from the middle of the grocery store's aisle, which was where I'd parked myself and a small cart. "I was just . . . thinking."

The sixtyish woman sent a vague smile in my direction and moved on past.

"Good job," I muttered. "Next thing is you'll start talking to yourself in public." I glanced around fast, but I was alone with the spices and baking supplies.

Which, truly, was a strange place for me to be, considering my inclination to cook as little as possible. Then again, even noncooks had to feed themselves once in a while in order to avoid spending too much disposable income in restaurants.

Then I remembered that eating out could be considered doing my bit to help the local economy. Commendable, that's what it was, not indulgent.

Cheered, I faced the spices and tried to remember what it was I used for the steak dry rub I'd made last summer and liked so much. I shoved my hands into my pockets and tried to think, but my brain kept going back to my chat with Rianne and the conversation about her aunt Kim.

It was easy enough to imagine that a pending bankruptcy could drive almost anyone to do deeds she—or he—would never have considered otherwise. But in this situation, I still had no idea if there was anything involved that was worth a lot of money.

"Maybe whatever it is, it's worth something that isn't money," I murmured. Which led me back to the possibility I'd posed to Ash and Detective Inwood, that this thing someone was looking for might be a tell-all journal. Of course, that didn't tie back to Aunt Kim's need for money, so maybe—

"Can I help you?" asked a male voice.

Startled, I whirled around to face the twentysomething store employee who'd asked the question. He wore black pants, a black cap, and a polyester short-sleeved shirt in a color that did nothing for his skin tone. "Uh, no, thanks. I was just . . . looking." As I manufactured a fake smile, I realized that I'd seen him recently. My fake smile grew fixed. This was the guy who'd looked vaguely familiar at Cookie Tom's. This was the guy who'd yelled at me for cutting in line. Angry Guy.

The expression on his face shifted from polite to hostile. He was recognizing me, and there was no Cookie Tom around to save me.

I put my chin up. I was short, but I was strong and invincible in many ways, none of which I could remember just then, but if I had a few minutes, I was sure I would. I didn't need Tom. I had myself.

"You're that *librarian*," he said, making it sound like a swearword. Certainly it was italicized.

I glanced at his name tag. Shane Pratley. "Hi, Shane," I said politely, holding out my hand. "Yes, I'm the bookmobile librarian. Minnie Hamilton. We got off to a bad start the other day. I understand that you're upset about the arrangement I have with Tom, but I think I can explain."

My arm was getting tired from holding my hand out for so long, but I gamely kept it up there. "Tom's a longtime supporter of the bookmobile, you see. He's a big believer in getting books to people who can't come to the library. His margin is so slim that he can't afford a big donation, even though he'd like to, so giving me a discount on cookies and letting me jump the line is his way of—"

"I don't care what Tom thinks." Shane pushed my hand away. "You got no right to take cuts. That's just wrong."

What was wrong was his rudeness. This was a man who was desperately needed to borrow an etiquette book from the library. Why was it always the people who needed a library the most were the least likely to visit one?

Of course, this was a tricky situation, because in principle I agreed with Shane; cutting in line was wrong. Then again, if I wanted to provide cookies to the bookmobile folks, and I did, zipping to the front of the line was the only way it was going to happen.

It was a moral question and an ethical dilemma and, for once, the voice in my head that sounded so much like my mother's whenever one of these situations turned up was silent.

"I understand why you're angry," I said. "If it was me in your position, I might—"

"But you aren't, are you?" He glared. "You're the fancy librarian, driving around, making yourself queen of the town, looking down on us little people."

"I . . . What?"

"Oh yeah," he said, sneering. "I seen you around, your nose up in the air, acting like you're better than everyone else. You and your friends with the restaurant and the art gallery and the boats and the big houses. You're not from here. Why don't you go back where you came from, you and all your rich friends."

Clearly, young Shane had no idea how little money a librarian made. Or that at least half my friends had been born in Tonedagana County. Yet he knew so much enough about me that my skin itched.

"I live here," I said firmly. "This is my home. I'm sorry you resent that I've moved to Chilson, but—"

"If you were really sorry," he snarled, "you'd leave Chilson to the people who belong here."

He spun and marched off, leaving me to gape after him. I'd run into his attitude before, that only people born here truly belonged, but it wasn't even close to the majority opinion.

I took in a deep breath, another one, one more, and went back to my shopping. But when I realized I'd started to add a jar of bay leaves to my empty cart instead of basil, I gave up, returned the cart to the front of the store, and headed back out into the sunshine.

Halfway home, my brain began to unscramble and I started thinking again. I mentally walked back through the events of the past couple of weeks and came to an abrupt realization.

"Huh," I said. Angry Shane Guy had caught me cutting in line two days before the break-in at the bookmobile garage. He clearly knew who I was and where I worked and, just as clearly, he didn't like me. Was it possible that he was on a one-man mission to rid Chilson of people who hadn't been born Up North? It sounded bizarre, but the guy's anger at someone he didn't even know was also bizarre.

Was it possible he'd made a mess of the bookmobile just to make my life more difficult?

And if he could do that, could he have killed Andrea?

"So, what do you think?" I asked Eddie.

My cat, of course, didn't reply. We were on the houseboat's front deck, and he was busy staring at my plate, which was on my lap. The two of us had started out on separate lounge chairs, but once Eddie had realized I was eating the sub sandwich I'd picked up for dinner at Fat Boys, he'd moved over to my chair. At first he sat at the end, down by my feet. Then he'd inched closer and closer, ever so slowly, and now that I was on the last two bites, he was on my thighs and practically had his chin on the edge of the plate.

I'd tried to gently shove him away and even onto the floor, but when Eddie decided to become an immovable object, no brute force in the universe could possibly dislodge him.

I tossed in the penultimate bite of veggie sub—see, Mom? I am eating properly—and chewed and swallowed. "No comment?" I asked Eddie. "I would have thought for sure that you'd have something to say about my two suspects."

The last bite of sandwich was still in my hand, and Eddie's eyes were intent on following its every move.

"There's Kim, a DeKeyser daughter, who people are saying is about to declare bankruptcy. If we're going to assume that Andrea was trying to steal something valuable—say, a book—maybe Kim knew what it was and killed her to get it.

"But wait," I said, popping in the last bite of sandwich.

Eddie watched it disappear. When I'd finished chewing and swallowing, I said, "There's also Shane. For whatever reason, he's mad at the world and he's taking it out on the folks he feels have invaded his town. Is he mad enough to break into places he's never been before? Did Andrea make him mad, too?"

I thought about that for a minute, wondering how I could find out if Andrea and Shane had known each other.

"Ash needs to know about Shane," I said, petting Eddie and watching a generous collection of cat hair slide off his back and spin away into the air. "Not sure what good it will do, but you never know."

One white-tipped paw slowly stretched out long, and I let Eddie try to gather up a crumb from the sandwich bun. "Don't make this a habit, okay? One time only."

"Mrr," he said, and reached out a second time.

"Say, you know what else happened on the way home?" I glanced over to the boat next door. No Eric, which was just as well, because I was about to enter the gossip zone. "Remember that construction site downtown, where they're renovating that old department store into condos and offices? You'll never guess who I saw hauling bricks in a wheelbarrow."

Eddie was paying no attention to me, so I pushed the last little crumb of bun his way. It was a bad idea, though, to let him take food off my plate. With Eddie, all it took was once to establish a bad habit. How long it took for him to establish a good habit, I didn't know.

"It was Mitchell," I told my uncaring cat. "Mitchell Koyne. You know, tall and loud and typically unemployed?" It wasn't unknown for Mitchell to take on summer construction jobs, but if he was working at the toy store, why was he doing hard labor? It was very unlike Mitchell, and I was starting to worry that aliens had invaded his body.

"What do you think?" I asked.

But for once, Eddie had nothing to say.

After I took care of the dishes (meaning I threw away the foam container and napkins, and washed the plate and the fork that I'd used to eat what had spilled out of the sandwich) I debated on what to do with the rest of my evening.

It was a beautiful night, and even though I could easily continue to sit outside and read, I felt a pull to get up and do something. The absence of yard work on a houseboat was usually a bonus, but today I could have used a few weeds to pull.

I considered the social possibilities. Ash was working. Kristen was working, Aunt Frances and Otto were at a concert in Petoskey's Bay View, Pam was working, Rafe was sanding drywall and being cranky about it, Holly had houseguests for a couple of nights, and, since it was past seven o'clock, it was too late to start calling around and finding out what my other friends were doing.

"What about you?" I asked my furry friend. "Want to go for a bike ride?"

Eddie, who was sprawled across the boat's dashboard, opened one eye a fraction of an inch, gave me a look of utter disdain, and went back to sleep.

"I take it that's a no?"

His mouth opened and closed silently.

Smiling, I kissed the top of his fuzzy head and headed outside.

* * *

Five minutes later, I was rolling along on two wheels, the sun on my face and the wind in my hair. Which would turn it into a frizzy mess later on, but I wasn't out to impress anyone, so who cared?

I pedaled up from the marina, riding around the edge of downtown to avoid the ice-cream-cone and fudge-eating tourists, and thought about who, if she or he had been in town, I might actually want to impress.

There wasn't a sports figure in the universe that I cared about enough to do more than make sure my shirt was tucked in. Same thing for actors, singers, and politicians. If I could go back in history, I'd have loved to meet Amelia Earhart, but wanting to talk to someone and impressing them were two different things.

No, the only kind of people I'd ever consider trying to impress were authors. Barbara Kingsolver, for one. Louise Erdrich for another. Plus Laurie R. King, John McPhee, Ann Patchett, Malcolm Gladwell, Mary Roach, and lots more. But, again, all those folks were people I wanted to meet more than to impress.

Of course, there was one person I'd recently wanted to impress but upon whom I'd totally failed to make a positive impression. And I was uneasily certain the consequences were going to last a long time. Ash was still saying that his mom liked me just fine, but he was wrong about that; he just didn't realize it yet.

"Seriously wrong," I said out loud.

"Are you sure?"

I stopped my slow pedaling, squinted, and looked around. Had I really heard someone say something?

"Is 'seriously wrong' a proper term?"

It was a young voice, it sounded familiar, and it sounded like it was coming from the sky, which made no sense. I looked left and right and finally focused on where I was. Right in front of the oh-so-symmetrical house in which the prodigy Dana Coburn lived. Only where was he? She?

"Are there degrees of wrong?" Dana continued. "Or is modifying 'wrong' as nonsensical as modifying the word 'unique'?"

"There's no modifying 'unique.'" I slid off the seat, straddled the bike, and looked up into a large maple tree.

"Glad to hear that." Dana slid backward on a large branch until he—she—came up against the massive tree trunk. Sitting up, the child asked, "Is it always going to be painful to listen to people assault the English language? My mom says I'll get used to it."

"Maybe," I said. "Maybe not."

Dana scrambled down the tree. "That's not a satisfying answer."

"No, but it's an honest one."

Two small feet hit the ground with a light and very Eddie-like *thump*. Dana ignored the dirt and bits of tree bark clinging to shirt and pants and faced me. "Explain, please."

"Sure." I leaned forward, putting my elbows on my handlebars. "You'll grow accustomed to some things people say, maybe even most, but there will always be a few things that drive you batty."

Dana nodded. "I understand. It makes me sad to hear anyone say 'ain't,' but I attribute that to poor education. Hearing people say 'kind of unique,' however, makes me want to tear out their hair in large clumps."

"You're not alone," I said.

"You're not like my mom." Dana grinned. "You don't talk to me like I'm a little kid."

"Well, you're not mine. That makes it easier."

"Mom's always after me to comb my hair and wash my hands." Dana looked down at the former tree parts still clinging to shirt and pants. "She wants me to wear dresses to Sunday dinner."

"Moms will do that," I said, wondering why, now that I had a solid answer to the female or male question, I was so satisfied. It was very possible that I put too much importance on gender. Did it matter so much to attach a pronoun to someone?

"I wish she wouldn't do so much of it." Dana kicked at the bottom of the tree. "All she wants to do is change me."

It was a feeling I understood well, but I also knew that Dana's mom was doing her best. Which meant it was best that I divert the conversation immediately.

"So I talked to Rianne Howe the other day," I said. "Have you ever been in the back office of Benton's?"

Dana's face lit up. "You've been there? I've only read about it. Is the ship's wheel still there?"

For once, she sounded like a normal kid. "I bet Rianne would let you give it a spin, if you asked. Especially since you know so much about her family."

"No, that's okay." Dana's expression went suddenly still. "I don't like . . . I mean . . . I don't go . . ."

Her voice trailed off and her words rose into the treetop and wafted away. Clearly, I'd wandered into territory where I didn't belong. "Anyway," I said easily, "the wheel is still there. And there are model ships all over the place. Maps of the lakes, too."

Dana, who had been studying the tops of her shoes, looked up at me. "Charts. Navigation maps are charts. Are they recent or old ones?"

"No idea," I said. "Why?"

"The older the chart, the more valuable it is as a collectible."

I squinted, trying to remember, but gave up quickly as to not tax my limited mental faculties. "They looked very chartlike is all I can say."

Dana shoved her hands into her pockets. "It would be unlikely that they're old, given the circumstances."

"What circumstances are those?"

The kid tipped her head to one side. "Perhaps I didn't tell you. My mother came into the room before I could completely finish describing the last few years of Talia DeKeyser. Mom says this part is gossip, anyway."

Before she could go all ethical on me, I jumped in. "Talia's great-niece was killed. A store has been broken into, along with the library and the bookmobile. Any information might be helpful."

"Yes, I can see that." Dana glanced toward her house, then back at me. "As you know, Talia DeKeyser spent the last few months of her life at the nursing home."

I nodded.

"One of the reasons Talia DeKeyser's children had her moved to the home was"—Dana looked at the house again—"that she was giving everything away."

I didn't grasp why anyone would care what Talia did with her possessions. Then I clued in. "Everything? Heirlooms, you mean?"

Dana nodded. "They weren't valuable things, just family items. It was when she tried to give the mail carrier a vase that their great-grandmother DeKeyser had brought over from Europe that the daughters caught wind of what their mother was doing."

"Alzheimer's," I murmured, and Dana agreed.

"From my research, I gather that it can be hard to

detect when it is late onset, which Talia DeKeyser's obviously was. I can imagine that it's easy to attribute forgetfulness to age instead of to consider more dire implications."

Though I'd already grown accustomed to hearing an adult vocabulary and sentence structure come out of a child, it was a jolt to hear her understand the reluctance to diagnose an elderly parent with a difficult and devastating disease. Not only was the kid bizarrely intelligent, but she also had empathy.

I looked at Dana, wondering if she'd been born this way or if something had already happened in her short life that had instilled that difficult emotion. It was hard to be empathetic; sympathy and pity you could assuage with a check to an appropriate nonprofit foundation. Empathy, though. That could spur you to acts of—

"Minnie? Hi!" Jenny Coburn came out of the house and down the center of the front steps. "How nice to see you. Dana, did you want to invite Ms. Hamilton inside? It's getting dark; the mosquitoes will be out soon. If you'd like to keep talking, why don't you come in?"

Dana and I shared a look. I wouldn't have minded getting to know my young new friend a little better, and I had the feeling she felt the same about me, but doing so under the watchful eye of Mom would be difficult.

"That would be nice," I said, "but I have to get going. Things to do, socks to wash. All that."

"Okay. See you later." Dana walked off to the house, going up the steps the same way her mother had come down them: exactly in the center.

Jenny looked after her, frowning a little, then turned back to me and smiled brightly. "It's hard to remember what time it is, the sunset is so late up here this time of year. I'm sure she didn't mean to be rude; she's just tired."

I blinked. I hadn't thought anything about Dana's abrupt departure and didn't know what to say. Happily, Jenny kept talking, and I didn't have to say anything.

"It's so nice that you're making friends with Dana. That's the one thing about this neighborhood; no children."

I glanced around at the stately homes, most owned by the same families for generations. "Aren't there grandchildren running around all summer?"

"Yes, but they tend to stay in their family groups, doing the same things they've always done with the same people they've always done things with." She sighed. "It's hard for a well-adjusted adult to break into an established social pattern, let alone someone with . . . someone like Dana."

"I think she's a great kid," I said.

"You do?" Jennifer looked at me. "You really think so? She's . . . well, you see what she's like."

"Different." I nodded. Which wasn't what Jennifer had meant, but that was the root of it. "And being different is hardest when you're young."

"True." Jenny sighed. "My husband and I, we're not like her."

I flashed back to how both she and Dana had trod the front steps and guessed that mother and daughter weren't as far apart as Mom thought.

"We try to understand her, but we just don't." Jenny looked back at the house again, then at me. "Do you have children?"

I shook my head. "All I can handle right now is one cat."

"Well, I hope you have kids someday. You have a knack for drawing them out."

I was pretty sure she was wrong. Most days I had no idea how to treat kids other than as short adults. People said when I had my own children it would be different, but I was also pretty sure I wasn't nearly mature enough to have kids. Besides, they'd be embarrassed to death if people knew that their mom talked to cats.

"Stop by again," Jennifer said. "Anytime."

I told her I would, wished her a good night, and pedaled off into the darkening evening, thinking about chance encounters and inappropriate gifts and about Talia and about the great mystery of what the future holds for all of us at the end.

"Minnie? Is anything wrong?" Otto, in jeans and a polo shirt, peered at me the next morning.

I was standing on his front doorstep, my skin prickly in the chill air. "It's time for breakfast," I told him.

"Yes," he said. "Yes it is. It is definitely that time of day." He raised his eyebrows, still waiting for an answer to the question he'd asked.

"Have you been to breakfast this summer?" I asked, nodding at my aunt's place.

"Well, actually, no." He looked at the big house across the street. "I haven't been invited, and I didn't want to barge in without being asked."

My aunt was an idiot. "Come on." I grabbed his hand and tugged. "I'm inviting you."

"I can't possibly." Otto pulled out of my grip. "Frances will—"

"When's the last time you saw her?" I asked, crossing my arms. "How many times have you seen her since the guests arrived?"

"Well." He rubbed his chin. "We had dinner . . . No, that was the day before the first one arrived. I think we had lunch last week. We were supposed to go to a concert in Petoskey the other day, but there was a plumbing emergency at the boardinghouse and she had to cancel."

"Otto, it's only June," I said. "If you don't make yourself part of the group, you're not going to see anything of her until after Labor Day."

He continued with the chin rubbing. "That's not what she led me to believe."

I rolled my eyes. "That's because she doesn't quite get how much work running that place is. Trust me. I've been watching this for four summers in a row. If she ever has the time to go out and do something with you, she's going to be too tired to do it."

"That sounds remarkably unappealing," Otto said. "I'd hoped to spend a lot of time with her the next few months."

"Well, then."

"I'm not sure what you mean."

"Get over there."

"Minnie, I'm not sure I should—"

"You may not be, but I am. Come on." I tugged at his hand a second time, and this time didn't let go until his front door was closed and we were crossing the street.

The entire way, he was hemming and hawing and sounding more like he'd sounded last December. Back then he'd been hesitant about introducing himself to my aunt, then, after a little push, had blossomed into the confident man who'd been squiring her around town for the past six months.

I ignored every one of his worried comments and practically dragged him up the steps and through the boardinghouse's front door. "Good morning," I called out. "Any chance you have a little extra?"

When I'd opened the door, I'd heard a congenial babble of voices and the tinkling of silverware. As soon as I spoke, however, the noises ceased. "Minnie?" my aunt said. "Is that you?"

A chair scraped backward and I knew she'd be standing up. "Not just me," I said, towing Otto toward the dining room. "I brought an uninvited guest. He said he's never had a boardinghouse breakfast, and I think it's high time he gets one."

"Did you bring Ash?" Aunt Frances appeared in the doorway. Behind her, the sun was streaming through the leaves of the trees in the backyard, slanting into the screened porch and the dining room. Her tall, angular figure was rimmed with sunlight, giving her a dazzling aura and making her look as if she'd walked straight out of the sun.

Otto caught his breath at the sight.

"Not Ash," I said, shoving at Otto's shoulder. "Just your across-the-street neighbor. He didn't want to barge in uninvited, but I made him come over anyway." I was about to add that I hoped it was okay until I saw my aunt's radiant smile.

She reached out for Otto's hands. "Why didn't I think of this before? Of course you should come over for breakfast. You don't need an invitation, for heaven's sake." She leaned forward to kiss him on the cheek, then turned and escorted him to the dining room.

"Everyone," she said, "this is my good friend Otto Bingham. Otto, going clockwise, that's Eva and Forrest, Liz, Morris, Victoria, and Welles."

All six of them greeted Otto with smiles and cheerful 'nice to meet you's. In short order, they were sliding chairs around and setting another place. Liz, who was at the buffet, getting out silverware, looked at me. "Minnie, are you eating?"

I shook my head. "Thanks, but there's no time. It's a bookmobile day and Eddie's in the car, ready to go forth and conquer new bookish territory."

My aunt wrapped a blueberry muffin in a paper napkin and put it into my hand. "Thank you," she whispered, "for Otto."

But there was no need for her words. Seeing the happiness on her face was more than thanks enough.

Chapter 11

"It's a shame your new young man couldn't make it tonight." Barb McCade looked at me over the top of her wineglass.

"That's right." Barb's husband, Russell, looked around as if Ash might be sitting somewhere else and waiting for an engraved invitation. "Where is that boy, anyway? Are we going to have to teach him manners?"

The only people sitting anywhere close were a six-tyish couple who were arguing over the price of something in the six-figure range. It seemed to be real estate, but if they were summer people, it could be anything from new landscaping to a new car.

"The boy," I said, "is close to six feet tall, runs ten miles a day, has a bachelor's degree in criminal justice, and is studying to be a detective."

Barb elbowed her husband. "And he's a cop. Bet he could take you down, Cade."

"Of course he could," Cade said calmly. "I channel my physical powers a different way."

"You do?" His wife frowned. "What powers are those? I didn't know you had any."

"I'm pacing myself." He grinned.

"Possible," Barb said. "But probable?" She held out her hand and tipped it back and forth.

Smiling, I shook my head. They were at it again.

I'd met these two clowns last summer when Barb had run in front of the bookmobile, waving me down because her husband was having a stroke. We'd raced him to the hospital, and it wasn't until I was relaying information to the emergency room via my cell phone that I realized the sick man was none other than the painter Russell McCade, known as Cade to his thousands upon thousands of fans.

Though his critics dismissed his work as sentimental schlock, his fans—which included me—defended it as accessible art. I'd loved his work from the time I'd received a birthday card illustrated with one of his paintings, but had never dreamed I'd actually meet the artist, let along become a friend of the family via a hospital visit and the letter *D*.

For reasons lost in the mists of time, the McCades had a habit of randomly choosing a letter and then finding words starting with that letter to fit the ongoing conversation. When I'd joined in the game the first time, I'd gone to visit Cade in the hospital, and our acquaintanceship moved into firm friendship. Who cared if they were twenty years older than I was? Who cared if they spent six months out of the year in a place that was warm and sunny? As long as we had the letter *D*, we were good.

"Pathetic," Cade said, sighing.

Or the letter *P*, which was also an excellent word starter.

"Penny for your thoughts?" I asked. "What's pathetic?"

"A pound would be better. There are profound thoughts up here." Cade tapped his head.

I searched madly for an appropriate *P* word, but couldn't find one anywhere.

"He was talking about you, Minnie," Barb said. "And you're not pathetic. You're preoccupied; that's all, right?"

Cade started studying me, and I felt myself squirming. Every time he looked at me like that, I was afraid he was thinking about how I'd look on canvas. Though I'd made it perfectly clear that I had no interest in being the subject of a portrait, I wasn't certain he'd paid any attention to me.

"There's a lot going on right now. The bookmobile, the library director, not to mention . . . well . . ." I glanced around.

We were in Petoskey, eating at the City Park Grill. One of its claims to fame was that it had once been the hangout of Ernest Hemingway, which was nice enough, especially if you were a Hemingway fan, but what I cared most about were the buttery garlic biscuits served as an appetizer. Warm, buttery garlic biscuits, moved with tongs from serving platter to your own individual biscuit plate by a server who would bring more; all you had to do was ask.

The McCades and I were sitting in the back of the restaurant. Cade wasn't exactly a recluse, but he didn't make any efforts to be a noted celebrity, either—much to the dismay of his agent—and I was happy enough to sit in the back corner, where it was a little darker and far quieter. From the six-figure couple, we were hearing an occasional tone of frustration from the man and a sporadic "Bob!" from the woman, but other than that, all was peace and calm. She looked vaguely familiar, and I surreptitiously studied her for a few moments, trying to figure out where I'd seen her before.

"The break-ins," Barb said.

"And the murder of Andrea Vennard, a former resident of Chilson," Cade added. "There is indeed a lot going on."

"You two were out of town when most of that happened." In Chicago at a show of Cade's work, specifically. "How did you know?"

"The newspaper," Cade said. "It's a marvelous invention. You should try it someday."

Barb shook her head, making her ponytail of graying brown hair flick around the sides of her neck. "Don't believe a word he says. He heard it from the neighbors first, then dug through the papers afterward."

"Corroboration." Cade sipped at his beer, a draft from Short's Brewing Company that was so hoppy I could smell it from across the table. "One must have corroboration."

Suddenly I remembered where I'd seen the six-figure woman. She'd been the woman at the used-book store, haggling with the clerk over books she was trying to sell.

"Does that detective have any ideas?" Barb asked.

"All avenues . . ." I said, then stopped.

Cade set his beer on the table with a sharp *bang*. "All avenues of investigation will be explored, especially wide-open and freshly paved avenues that could easily lead to the wrong person."

"Sorry," I murmured. Cade had been the lead suspect in a murder investigation last summer. "I didn't mean to bring up bad memories."

"Not bad," he said, "so much as annoying."

I glanced at Barb and, judging from the tight expression on her face, I wasn't sure she agreed with him. "Anyway," I went on, "Detective Inwood and Ash aren't telling me much. It is an active investigation."

"Ah, but you have some ideas, don't you?" Cade eyed me. "You are full of the things. Ideas ooze out of you."

I made a face. "Ooze? You make me sound like a mud puddle."

"Flow? Gush? Emanate?" Cade asked. "Exude. Escape. Discharge."

"Oh, ew."

"Percolate," Barb said.

"Excellent!" Cade exclaimed. "And a *P* word to boot. You win this round, my darling." He toasted his wife. "And now," he said, turning to me, "your idea. No denials; I can see it in the set of your shoulders, and slumping like that will not change the facts."

I sighed and straightened. It wasn't fair that a man who'd grown famous painting landscapes could see into my head by looking at my posture.

"And now, young lady, it's time to share." Cade made a come-along gesture. "What's your idea?"

"It's about books."

The McCades frowned, exchanged a quick glance, then looked back at me.

"What's about books?" Barb asked. "The break-ins or the murder?"

"Both."

"How do you figure that?" Cade asked.

I looked at him closely, but saw no trace of the Patient Look, the expression that meant I was being humored and coddled and been found amusing in a condescending way. My previous boyfriend had used that expression too often, and I was still sensitive to its use.

"There were three break-ins," I said, holding up the requisite number of fingers. "The Friends' book-sale room, the bookmobile, and Pam's antiques store. During each incident, every book was tossed onto the floor, but according to the records of both Pam and the bookmobile, no book was stolen."

"And the book-sale room?" Barb asked.

I shrugged. "No way of knowing. They don't need to track books the way we do. But someone was clearly looking for something, and since the bookmobile and Pam's store were both broken into after the sale room was, I figure he didn't find whatever it was."

"Or she," Cade murmured.

"Or she," I agreed, a little chagrined that a male had had to correct my gender usage.

Barb frowned. "But what about Andrea Vennard? How does she fit in?"

"That's when it all started," I said in a low voice, leaning forward. "Andrea was killed. Then the library was broken into, then the bookmobile, then Pam's store. In a town this size, it's hard to believe that all those crimes aren't connected somehow. My guess is that someone is looking for a book worth a lot of money, and Andrea got in the way. Maybe," I said slowly, thinking of a new possibility, "a book that's been in a family for a long time and no one realizes its value."

"Isn't there a new used-book store?" Cade asked. "Have they had a burglary?"

Ash had told me that they'd been incident free, and I told the McCades so.

Cade sipped his beer. "You think Andrea's murder was committed by the same person who's responsible for the break-ins."

I nodded.

"Does anyone know," Barb asked, "why Andrea was in Chilson?"

"Oh, we know why."

"We do?"

"Well, sure," I said. "She came up for her great-aunt's funeral. Talia DeKeyser."

It was as if I'd tossed a restrictive force field over them just after they'd witnessed a shocking sight. Both stared at me, unblinking and unmoving. Just at the point where I was beginning to wonder if time had indeed stopped, Barb turned to her husband.

"You're going to have to tell her."

"Yes," he said, breaking the spell I'd unwittingly cast.

"Tell me what?"

Cade pulled in a long breath. Then, instead of doing the expected thing and letting it out in a long, gusting sigh, he picked up his beer. When the only thing left on the inside of the glass was a sticky foam, he returned it to the table. "Sorry," he said to his wife, "but I do believe I needed that."

"Wanted, not needed." She patted his arm and half smiled. "It's all right. I have the car keys."

There was a long pause. I tried to be patient, but was on the verge of using my foot to whack at someone under the table in the hopes of kick-starting the conversation, when Cade started telling the story.

"This was when Cal, Talia's husband, was still alive. About five years ago, I'd guess." He turned to Barb, who nodded confirmation. "Barb and I had bought our lake house the year before, and we were still getting to know the area and the town. Still meeting people and getting to know the neighbors."

It was a familiar story. Newcomers, if they didn't use some sort of method to establish a social network— volunteer work, church activities, whatever—took a long time to develop friendships.

"We were in Benton's," Barb said. "Mr. Smart Alec

here was at the candy counter, trying to guess how many jawbreakers he could fit into his mouth before his jaw actually broke, when this tall, old guy spoke up and said he could take in fifteen."

Cade laughed. "And then an elderly woman, who was standing next to him, said his mouth was much bigger than that, he'd be better off guessing twenty, and did he want to try an experiment?"

I smiled. "That was Talia and Cal?" All the stories I'd heard about them, I'd never once heard they were funny.

Barb nodded. "We were instant friends, despite the age difference." She smiled at me. "One of these days we're going to have to get some friends our own age."

"Age is nothing," Cade said, waving off the issue. "What matters is that you laugh at the same things."

"I laugh at you every day," his loving wife told him.

He ignored her and said, "We went out to dinner with Talia and Deke a few times—"

Barb saw my puzzled look and interrupted. "Deke was Cal's nickname. From DeKeyser, and from his playing pond hockey into his sixties."

Cade barely slowed down. "One day they invited us to dinner at their home. Barb insisted on bringing salad and bread, so when we arrived, she and Talia went back to the kitchen, while Deke and I mixed drinks in the dining room."

It was an easy picture to summon; women and men in separate rooms, all four chatting easily and comfortably. Of course, the picture I was bringing to mind was incomplete, since I had no idea where the DeKeysers had lived, so I asked.

"Just a few blocks from downtown," Barb said. "In

the historic district." She described a house I had seen many times, a Victorian home of gingerbread trim, lace curtains, and creaking wooden floors, the kind of house where grandmothers grew up, the kind of house that could almost make you smell lilacs and taste home-made ice cream.

"In the dining room," Cade said, bringing me out of my historical fog, "the bottles and glasses were on a sideboard. Also on the sideboard was a stack of books."

Books?

Cade gave me a crinkly smile. "You are suddenly a little more interested in this story, I see. Yes, there was a stack of books. Picture books was what I noticed. Books to read to the grandchildren on a rainy day. *Blueberries for Sal*, *Stellaluna*, *Make Way for Duck-lings*, *The Little Engine That Could*."

I nodded at the names, all as familiar to me as the back side of my teeth.

"At that moment," Cade continued, "I just glanced at the pile. But then Talia called for Deke's help to reach a dish on a high shelf, and I was left alone."

"You looked at the books."

"Exactly," he said, nodding. "I was in the home of an acquaintance and didn't feel free to finish mixing the drinks, and I didn't want to sit uninvited. Yes, I could have stood there and been bored, but why do that when there are picture books at hand? An artist can always learn something from other artists. Our research never ends."

Barb coughed into her fist, but it was a multisyllabic cough that sounded a lot like the word "Plagiarism."

Once again, her loving husband ignored her. "So, of course I looked at the books. And there, at the bottom of that small stack, underneath the mass-produced copies of children's books that are in half the houses in the country, was a first edition of . . ."

He stopped for a moment, shook his head, then said, "Right there on the sideboard, well within the reach of grubby-fingered five-year-olds, was a first-edition copy of Chastain's *Native Wildflowers of North America.*"

Eddie, who was doing his best to sprawl across the full length of the dining booth's seat back, and doing a very good job, didn't look impressed at my story.

Clearly, he hadn't been listening.

"You must not have been listening," I said. "Chastain's *Wildflowers* is, well, it doesn't have anything close to the value of Audubon's book, but a complete copy in good condition is worth upward of half a million dollars." And possibly much more. Cade, a fan of Chastain's work, had said no first-edition copy had gone up for public auction in years.

That night at the DeKeyser's, Cade had told Deke about the worth of the book that was casually lying underneath a copy of the *Cat in the Hat.* Cade had also advised Talia and Deke to move the book to a climate-controlled environment, but, he'd told me wryly, "It's hard to communicate the value of a book that's been sitting on the same piece of furniture for close to a hundred years."

Over dinner, Deke had told the McCades that the book had been given by Robert Chastain himself to the then-matriarch of the family for her kindness in showing him a variety of wildflower he'd never seen. The family story was that Robert Chastain had been a nice gentleman who was a little nuts about flowers. The DeKeysers smiled at Cade's story of the book's value, and Cade had said it was obvious they didn't believe him.

"Thus, the sideboard," I said.

Eddie, unblinking, looked at me and flicked the tip of his tail up and down, up and down.

"Cade," I told my uncaring cat, "had even confessed that he was a hugely successful artist himself, and that he knew what he was talking about when it came to a first edition of Chastain's, but Deke and Talia just smiled and said they were fine with things the way they were."

And, I realized, maybe they were right. What did a happy elderly couple need with the headache of a valuable volume like *Wildflowers*? Let the next generation worry about it.

Which was exactly what was happening.

I'd driven home from Petoskey, thinking about it, and to me there was no doubt that Chastain's *Wildflowers* was why the book-sale room, the bookmobile, and Pam's store had all been broken into and tossed around into a huge mess. Someone out there knew about *Wildflowers* and was looking for it in all the places that Talia might have been expected to gift a book.

That someone had also killed Andrea.

"You know what else?" I asked the question of Eddie, but I was looking at the last two flowers from Ash's bouquet that hadn't dropped all their petals or been turned into cat toys. "I bet I know why that X-Acto knife was at the murder scene."

Either Andrea or her killer had expected to find the book in the library, and one of them had planned to slice out individual pages of the stunningly gorgeous flower paintings and sell them one by one.

The thought of that beautiful book being ripped into bits stirred up outrage in every cell of my librarian's body. "No," I said out loud. "I won't let that happen."

Of course, I had no idea how to stop it from happening, but there had to be a way.

And if there wasn't, I'd make one.

The next morning, I woke up late. Eddie did, too, but, then, he almost always did.

"You know," I told him as I stood, yawning, "if you didn't try to turn my head into your pillow, I'd sleep a lot better."

He opened one eye a fraction of an inch, then closed it again.

I tried again. "Experts recommend that you don't allow pets into your bedroom at all. They say pets on your bed disrupt sleep patterns and bring dust and hair and dander and who knows what into a space where you don't want any of that stuff."

Eddie wriggled himself deeper into the bedcovers. Half a second later, I heard the dulcet tones of his snores. Smiling, I patted him on the head and headed to the shower. What did experts know, anyway?

Fifteen minutes later, I was clean and dressed, and we were both on the boat's front deck, me with a fortifying mug of coffee.

"It's Saturday," I said to Eddie. "And I'm not working at all today." For the summer, I'd scheduled the bookmobile three Saturdays a month, and this was the off day.

Though I was tempted to go to the library and get some work done, Holly and Donna and Kelsey had all vowed to make my life miserable if I didn't get some fun into me. When I'd protested, saying that working at the library was fun, they'd said that alone was proof that I needed to get out more. Since it was possible they were the teensiest bit right, I'd agreed to stay away for an entire day and a half.

"Only what should I do with myself?" I scooped out the last bit of cereal, swallowed, and put the bowl onto the deck. Eddie slid off his chair and trotted over to get the last drops of milk out from the bottom of the bowl.

I listened, shaking my head at the *lap-lap-lap*. You'd think a creature as graceful as a cat would drink more quietly.

"Hey, Minster. Did you hear?"

I turned. Standing on the dock that ran between my boat and Eric's was Chris Ballou, the marina's manager. If I'd been forced to guess his age, I'd have said Chris was in his early forties, but he had a whippet-thin body that could be making him look fortyish even if he were pushing sixty. Then again, his speech patterns were those of a twenty-year-old. Since I hadn't taken enough advanced math to figure out how all that might shake out, I'd long ago decided not to think about it.

What I did need to think about was how to make a new deal on keeping my boat slip's reduced rental rate. Up until now, I'd been given a cut rate because no one else would take the slip next to the cranky guy who used to rent Eric's slip. Now that Eric was here, however, Chris should have upped my rate to normal. He kept dodging the issue, saying that what his uncle Chip didn't know wouldn't hurt him, but I knew that was wrong, and one of these days I'd get Chris to be serious about the situation.

"Hear about what?" I asked.

"Huh," he said. "Looks like I get to break the news."

My skin tightened. A hundred possibilities occurred to me. Something had happened to my parents. To my brother. My brother's family. To my aunt Frances. To

Ash. To Rafe or Kristen, or Holly or Josh or any of the library staff. Then, when I ran out of people, I wondered if something had happened to the bookmobile. Or the library. Or downtown. Or my hometown of Dearborn. Then I started wondering if something had happened to something bigger, like the Mackinac Bridge or the state capitol or the US Capitol or—

Eric's head popped out of the entry to his boat's lower regions. "What news?" he asked.

"Hey," Chris said, nodding a good morning to Dr. Apney. "I just wondered if Min-Bin here knew what happened."

Chris was a great mechanic, a solid marina manager, and a decent enough guy, but he had two bad habits. One, he enjoyed making new nicknames for me a little too much. Two, he couldn't relate simple facts without turning them into a long-winded story.

Eric squinted into the morning sunshine. "That's an extremely open question. I mean, it's a guarantee that lots of things have happened, after all. Tightening the time frame would be helpful."

And my neighbor was not helping.

"Well," Chris said, drawling out the word, "you got a good point there. I could narrow it down a little, make it easier for her to figure out."

This could go on all morning. I stood and summoned my Librarian Voice. "Tell me," I ordered.

Chris straightened imperceptibly. "Early this morning," he said. "There was a fire in Petoskey. At their library. I heard the janitor was in the hospital— breathed in too much smoke, you know?—and he probably won't make it. There was a bunch of damage . . . hey, Min, what're you doing?"

Paying no attention to Chris, I unceremoniously

dumped Eddie inside the houseboat and grabbed my backpack. When I came outside three seconds later, Chris was still talking.

"Hey, my pal Ed was liking it out here in the sun," he said, sounding aggrieved. "What's the matter with leaving him out here longer? Hey, where you going?"

But I was down the dock and gone.

Chapter 12

Detective Inwood stared at me over the top of a coffee mug. He blew off the steam, sending it my way, and lifted the mug toward his mouth. I looked away, hoping somehow that if I didn't look, I wouldn't be able to hear the slurping noises as clearly as I had a moment before, but, once again, the technique was a complete failure.

The detective's swallowing sounds filled the small room. I sat as patiently as I could. After all, it was a Saturday morning, and I'd expected to tell my concerns to the on-duty deputy up front. Once I'd started talking, however, he'd called the detective, and here we were, back in the interview room. Ash was off this weekend, helping his mom with some outside chores, and I hadn't wanted to bother him.

"My apologies, Ms. Hamilton," the detective said, setting the mug onto the table. "My daughter and our new grandchild are staying with us for a few nights while her husband is out of town on business. It's wreaking havoc on my sleep patterns. What do you have for me this morning? More mayhem, with dire complications for the future?"

He quirked up a smile. "And please tell me your cat isn't involved this time. The sheriff's been talking about getting an office cat ever since that night she spent with your Eddie."

That had been months ago. If Sheriff Richardson was serious about an office cat, I was sure she would have brought one in by now, but I put on a thoughtful expression. "I know of a litter of kittens that's almost old enough to go out on their own. I'll have to remember to tell the sheriff."

Inwood gave me a pained look, and I almost laughed out loud.

"What I wanted to tell you," I said, "doesn't have anything to do with cats." My imagination almost saw Eddie picking up his head at the flagrant heresy and sending me a loud "Mrr!" but I plowed ahead.

"You've heard what happened at the Petoskey library?" I asked.

The detective frowned. "I have not." I started to tell him what little I knew, but he put up his hand to stop my flow of words, pulled his cell phone from his inside suit pocket, and pushed some buttons. "Morning, Scott," he said. "What's with your library?"

As he listened to Scott, whoever he was, Inwood's gaze came my way but focused on something behind my head. The wall, maybe, or—I mentally summoned a map of the area—maybe he was seeing far past me, all the way to the library in Petoskey. It was a fairly new building, and I ached for the library director and staff and the hundreds of people who used it regularly. A fire had to be about the worst thing that could happen to a library. Even if the books hadn't actually burned, there'd be smoke damage or water damage from the sprinklers or firefighters.

I cringed to think of what it would take to bring a library back from a large fire, and started thinking about what we could do to help. First, I'd find out what books they needed most; maybe we had extras, or could at least lend them some of ours. Then, if they needed hands to help clean, I'd make phone calls to the libraries all over northern lower Michigan. For something like this, people would turn out to help in a heartbeat. Then, if they needed—

"The fire," Detective Inwood said, putting his phone away, "was limited to a meeting room. An exterior window to the room was broken, and an incendiary device of some sort was thrown inside. The smoke detectors went off at two a.m., and a night custodian entered the room. He used a nearby extinguisher to put out the fire, but inhaled enough smoke that he was taken to the hospital by ambulance. He was treated and released."

Inwood picked up his coffee mug. "The meeting room suffered damage to the furniture, walls, carpet, and ceiling, but there was no damage to any other portion of the building. Or its contents."

I slid forward on my chair. While I was beyond pleased that the library was essentially fine, that wasn't why I was here. "It was a diversion," I said. "Someone who didn't want to be seen needed uninterrupted time to look at their books."

The detective's eyebrows went up, but he didn't reply until after he'd upended the mug and drank down the last of its contents. "How so?" he asked.

So I told him. I told him about the kindness of a long-ago DeKeyser to an artist wanting to paint flowers. I told him how the artist had sent a copy of the completed book to the DeKeysers. I told him where Cade had seen the book. And, finally, I told him the current value of Chastain's *Wildflowers*.

Then I sat back and waited.

Which wasn't much of a wait, because he immediately said, "The X-Acto knife. That's why it was in the library. *Wildflowers* may be worth a lot of money intact, but if you cut it apart and sell it page by page, you probably wouldn't have to prove your ownership, and it's possible you'd end up with a lot more money."

I nodded.

"But why would anyone go to the trouble of doing that?" he asked. "Why wouldn't she or the killer simply steal the book?"

I'd thought about that. "They probably assumed the security at the library is a lot tighter than it really is. Most downstate libraries have a chip embedded in the book that sounds an alarm if it's not deactivated at checkout. And she probably figured we have security cameras that get reviewed for theft. Seeing someone walk out with a book in the middle of the night would be a huge red flag. Just seeing someone walking?" I shrugged. "If the cameras existed and we noticed it, we'd probably wonder, but if there wasn't anything missing, I doubt we'd do anything."

"Well." Inwood started to lift his mug, realized it was empty, and stood. "Now, that's worth brewing a new pot of coffee for."

He smiled at me, but I couldn't manage to return it.

Because I couldn't stop thinking that, somewhere out there, a killer was on the loose. And if he'd killed once in search of this book, would he hesitate to kill again?

* * *

Ten minutes later, my knees were underneath the large dining table at my aunt's boardinghouse, and I was enjoying the ebb and flow of conversation while eating a breakfast frittata made by the cooking team of Liz and Morris. I'd deciphered enough healthy ingredients in the dish—asparagus, tomato, and broccoli—to count it as my recommended daily allowance of vegetables. Plus, there were fresh strawberries and cubes of melon that looked good enough to be served in Kristen's restaurant. Breakfast didn't get much more nutritious, and I felt virtuous about my adultlike meal.

On a Saturday morning like this, the talk inevitably centered around what everyone was going to do with such outstanding weather. The forecast was for sun, light winds, and a high of seventy-seven degrees, a Chamber of Commerce kind of day.

Eva and Forrest, the fortysomething mountain bikers, were planning to ride the Little Traverse Wheelway between Charlevoix and Petoskey. Liz and Morris, once the kitchen was cleaned up, were headed east, over to Lake Huron, to explore the beaches near Alpena. Victoria and Welles, the couple in their sixties, had announced their intention to tour the Music House Museum, just north of Traverse City.

Aunt Frances, who hadn't eaten much but had spent most of the meal looking out the windows to the screened porch and beyond to the trees of the backyard, blinked at the mention of the Music House. "If you're going there," she said, "you should stop at Guntzviller's."

"What's Guntzviller's?" Victoria asked.

I grinned. I'd stopped there once and had been entranced by the blend of retail, taxidermy, and museum featuring wildlife and Native American artifacts. "Don't be scared by the howling," I said, then wouldn't say any more.

Welles, the retired dentist, who with his fit frame and white blond hair, didn't look nearly old enough to be retired, glanced at my aunt. "What are your plans for the day, Frances?"

She started at the question. "Me? I'm afraid I have chores to do."

"How annoying," Eva said, grimacing. "I hope they're outside ones, at least."

Aunt Frances smiled, but it didn't last long. "I'd best get going." She rose, but when she started stacking her dishes, Liz put out a hand to stop her. "Forrest and I will take care of this. It's our day, right?"

Typically, everyone cleared their own place, but this time my aunt simply nodded at the violation of her own rules. The seven of us sat and listened to her footsteps cross the living room, climb the stairs, and enter her room. When there was a light *thud*, indicating that her bedroom door had shut, the six boarders all turned to face me.

"What's wrong with your aunt?" Victoria demanded. I blinked. "Umm . . ."

"We're getting concerned," Morris said. I'd almost grown accustomed to hearing a well-known voice at my aunt's dining table, but there were times when I had to force myself to stop looking around for the radio.

"Um . . ." I said again, not sure where this was going.

"The scrapbook," Welles said.

And then everything became as clear as the summer day outside.

The first year my aunt took in boarders, she'd purchased a scrapbook and invited everyone to fill it up. It was the perfect activity for a rainy day, and past guests had created pages of drawings, notes, postcards, ticket stubs, restaurant napkins, and cardboard coasters. Most of the pages had handwritten comments about the fun times, the weather, the lakes, the food, even the late-night card games and board games that often took place on the screened porch.

There were also, I remembered, many entries about my aunt. My aunt, who, in previous boardinghouse summers, was a participant in the games. Who, in the past, had often sat on the front porch swing with a guest or two. Who, for as many summers as I could remember, spent many an evening crouched in front of the living room's fieldstone fireplace, convincing her boarders that s'mores were best with a mini Reese's Peanut Butter Cup.

"She's not the same as in the scrapbooks," Eva said.

I shook my head, not so much disagreeing as not wanting to talk about this.

"In the books," Forrest persisted, a frown of concern on his face, "she was more active. Participating with guest activities almost every day."

"But she's not doing that," Liz said. "Not this year. So we're wondering . . ." She bit her lower lip.

"We hope she's not ill," Welles said, sighing, and I had the sudden and frightening thought that, as a dentist, he must have seen dozens or hundreds of patients who'd been seriously sick. Was it possible that Welles had detected something about my aunt's health that I didn't know? Had she been diagnosed with something so life threatening that she didn't want to share it with anyone?

My throat constricted so tight that I had to cough it loose. And, in doing so, I rattled my brain enough that some thoughts fell out.

"If she was sick," I said, "she would have told me." She also would have made me promise not to tell my parents, which included her brother, until she was good and ready. "We made a pact about that very thing when I moved to Chilson."

This was true. It had started as kind of a joke. Aunt Frances had been reading a novel about a man diagnosed with a fast-moving internal cancer, but he hadn't told anyone, even his wife, until the day he collapsed while walking up their basement stairs, carrying a wooden stool he'd just finished mending. He'd died two days later, and the bulk of the novel was about the wife trying to forgive him.

My aunt had looked at me over the top of the book and said, "I promise I'll tell you if you promise you'll tell me."

"Deal," I'd said, and we'd bumped knuckles to seal the pact.

It had been a lighthearted moment, but since then, we'd both made references to the promise. It was reassuring, in a way I wasn't sure I wanted to think about much, so I usually didn't.

Now I looked at the concerned faces. My heartstrings were well and truly tugged. These folks cared about my aunt. They wanted to know that she was all right, and they certainly looked ready to step in and roll up their sleeves if she needed any help.

But I knew what my aunt needed, and there wasn't any help they could provide.

Instead of taking a direct walk back to the marina, where I was going to meet Ash in a couple of hours, I wandered through downtown. It was still early; the only places open were Cookie Tom's and restaurants that served breakfast. This meant the sidewalks were empty enough of tourists that I could walk without paying too much attention to where I was going.

So it shouldn't have been a surprise that, when I was staring up at the few clouds in the sky, wondering if the wind was going to stay low or if it was going to whip up into something that would put a damper on the afternoon's activities, I didn't hear Denise Slade calling until she planted herself smack in front of me.

"If you paid more attention to where you're going," she said, "you might get a lot further in life."

"And where would I want to go?" I asked cheerfully. "I'm pretty happy right here." I flung out my arms, narrowly missing a light pole.

Denise rolled her eyes. "It was a metaphor."

I wasn't sure it had been, but whatever. I'd learned not to take Denise's comments personally; she was caustic by nature, and there was no reason to think she treated me any differently from anyone else. Denise, if she'd been face-to-face with Bill Gates, would demand to know why Microsoft products locked up so often. If the most famous author in the world moved to Chilson and wanted to volunteer with the Friends, Denise would have asked for qualifications. If the most—

Something jogged in my head and I mentally snapped my fingers.

"Say, Denise. I could do with a favor."

She sniffed. "Maybe. Maybe not. What is it?"

Of all the Friends of the Library presidents in all the world, Denise had to be president of Chilson's. "Do you keep track of who volunteers in the book-sale room?"

Denise tossed her hair. "Of course I do. What kind of operation do you think I run?"

With great restraint, I didn't say what I really thought. "Could you please e-mail me a list of everyone who was working that week the books were thrown off the shelves?"

Denise's eyes came together into narrow slits. "You can't think that one of my volunteers did that. That's just stupid."

"I don't think anything of the sort. But I would like to talk to each of them, ask if they noticed anything different."

"Hmph. It's about time you did something about that." Denise gave me a quick look up and down. "It's because you're getting a new library director, I bet. You're afraid the new guy is going to fire you for letting a murder and two break-ins happen on your watch."

How she'd come to that bizarre conclusion, I had no idea. But since I also didn't care to learn how Denise's thought process worked, I just said, "If you could send me the list, I'd appreciate it."

"Well." Denise sighed. "I suppose. But that stuff is at home, and I'm doing the flowers at church this morning, then I have a volunteer shift at Lake View this afternoon, and tonight my friend Bobbi is hosting a euchre tournament, and she always says she can't play cards without me, so I can't promise when."

"Whenever you have a minute is fine," I said, edging away. "Thanks." And I fled before she could start talking about her Monday schedule. During my hurried walk, I went past Benton's, stopped, turned around, and stepped up to the front door. The store wouldn't be open for almost another hour, but maybe Rianne was in. I knocked loudly and, sure enough, Rianne's head poked out of the back doorway.

She saw my frantic gestures and came forward to unlock the door. "Minnie, what's up?"

"Do you have a few minutes?"

"Sure," she said, glancing outside at the big clock. "Would you like some coffee? I was just going over some inventory numbers. Come on back."

As we settled ourselves in her office, coffee in hand, I trailed my fingers across a few spokes of the ship's wheel. "Do you remember a book about wildflowers at your grandparents' house? It was on the sideboard."

"Flowers?" She blew steam off her coffee. "I guess so, but I was more of a Boxcar Children fan. Why do you ask?"

"Because I think that book is why Andrea was killed."

Rianne stopped midsip. "I don't understand."

"This is going to sound impossible, but the book *Wildflowers*, by Robert Chastain, is potentially worth a lot of money."

"How much is a lot?" Rianne went back to sipping.

"If it's in mint condition, half a million dollars."

Rianne's mouthful of coffee blew out in a spray all over her desk. "Half a *million*? That can't be right. No way did Deke and Granny have anything worth that much. No way."

I told her that Cade himself had seen the book. "Plus, I think that's why Andrea was in the library that night. Somehow she knew the value of the book and was trying to find it. And I think someone is still trying to."

"Why didn't they put it in a safety-deposit box?" She looked around a little wildly. "Get it insured? Something. Anything."

"I'm not sure they believed Cade about its value. To

them it was just a book that had been sitting on the sideboard."

"Now, that I can believe." Rianne pulled a tissue out of a box and dabbed at the coffee-colored spray on her papers. "But why would anyone think the book ended up in the library?"

"Because in her later years, your grandmother gave away a lot of things. Because I'm guessing it isn't on the sideboard anymore."

"Let's find out." Rianne put down her coffee mug and reached for the phone. "Honey? Can you go into the dining room? You know that pile of kids' books on the sideboard? Is there a book about wildflowers in there?"

"*Wildflowers of Northern America*," I said.

She nodded, passed on the title, and, after a few moments, said, "Thanks. I'll tell you about it tonight." She hung up the phone and looked at me. "It's not there. And there's nowhere else in the house it would be. It's gone."

Though that was what I'd expected, it was still a punch in the stomach.

The skin around Rianne's mouth was tight. "Did Granny give it away, or did someone steal it?"

"If someone had stolen it from the house, Andrea wouldn't have been in the library, looking for it." At least that was my assumption. "I think your grandmother gave it away."

Rianne relaxed a fraction, but only a fraction. "So, someone out there is willing to murder for the sake of this book?"

"For half a million dollars," I said.

She blew out a long sigh. "My grandparents had a lot of people in that house over the years. It could be almost anyone. I just . . . I just hope it isn't anyone I know."

For her sake, I hoped so, too.

"Keep your elbows in."

I nodded at Ash's instruction, trying not to think that he sounded like my father had, years back when I was being taught table manners. I still didn't honestly see why it was such a horrible thing to put your elbows on the table when you were eating a hamburger, especially if you were like me and had elbows that ended closer to the tabletop than most people's, but I still couldn't do it without feeling guilty.

Speaking of parents . . . "How did it go at your mom's?" I asked.

Though Ash was about twenty feet away, over the flat water that was between us, there was no need to speak any louder than if he'd been right next to me. We were in kayaks, sitting low, and the world looked different from the way it did from a standing position. Though I'd canoed many times, this was my first-ever kayak outing, and I was already a convert. The only thing I had to unlearn from my earlier canoeing efforts was the elbow thing.

"All set," he said.

He'd gone to his mom's house to help her plant trees that a landscaping company had delivered the day before. Maples, to replace the ash trees that had been killed by the emerald ash borer. Since Ash's name had come from how much his mother had loved those trees, it had only made sense that the human Ash work on the replacements.

"I would have been glad to help." Digging hard into the water with the paddle's blades, I sent the kayak scooting forward fast.

"Hey there, Speedster!" Ash laughed and caught up to me in seconds. "I told Mom you'd be happy to help, but she said she didn't want to bother you."

There was a small kernel of worry tucked away in a corner of my tummy. It was a stone kernel that had the name Lindsey Wolverson etched into its surface, and I had no idea what to do about it. Maybe it was a personality thing and we would never get along. Or maybe it was something I'd done, but I had no idea what. Then again, it was possible that she just didn't like short people.

"What's so funny?" Ash asked.

I glanced over. In the year that I'd known him and the few weeks we'd been dating, the thing I liked most about him was that he kept an open mind. There was no possible way that he had been raised by a mother who was prejudiced.

"Lots of things are funny," I said. "Take the duck-billed platypus, for—"

The low growling sound of a big boat's motor came up fast behind us. "Boat coming up," Ash called. "Turn to face it diagonally, okay?"

Without too much flailing around, I did as he said, and was in proper position to take the boat's wake when it passed underneath us.

The boat itself was a charter fishing boat headed for the channel and the open waters of Lake Michigan. On board were the typical passengers: men in their forties to early fifties, wearing jeans, fleece jackets, and baseball caps with downstate team names. A grizzled man was behind the boat's wheel, his skin crinkled from too many years without enough sunblock. The boat's single crew member was a tall man who was busying himself by stowing coolers and checking fishing gear, joking with the passengers, and constantly adjusting his hat.

Mitchell Koyne.

I watched the boat slide past and stared at Mitchell the entire time. When it had gone by and we'd ridden out the bobbing wake, I turned to Ash. "Did you see that?"

"Yeah," he said, watching the boat's stern grow ever more distant. "A bunch of guys out having a lot of expensive fun."

His tone was a little envious, and I hoped that the next activity he taught me wasn't going to include rods and reels and sharp hooks, because I didn't see the attraction to sitting in a boat for hours on end, hoping you were clever enough to outsmart a fish. "Mitchell Koyne was crewing."

"Heard he was working hard this summer." Ash turned his kayak to run parallel with the lake's shore, and I did the same. "Maybe he's trying to save enough money to buy a house. He's lived with his sister for how long? I bet her husband's ready to see him go."

Though that last part was undoubtedly true, I was fairly sure Mitchell's new work ethic wasn't a product of his brother-in-law's urgings.

"I've been thinking about what you told Hal this morning," Ash said.

For a moment, I had no idea what he was talking about. Hal who? I almost asked, then, at the last second, I remembered that Detective Inwood, unlike Lieutenant Columbo, did indeed have a first name, and that it was Hal.

When Ash had arrived at the marina with two kayaks, I'd given him the same spiel I'd given the detective as we wrestled the boats off the top of his SUV and into the water.

"And?" I asked now. "Please tell me you had a magical leap of insight. A brilliant flash. Any kind of flash."

"Sorry." Ash leaned back and rested his paddle across the kayak's cockpit. "What I was thinking was that almost everybody in town worked for Benton's at one point in their life. I grew up in Petoskey, so I don't know for sure, but from what I heard, the DeKeysers treated all of their staff like family."

"A dysfunctional family?"

Ash laughed. "What other kind is there? No, what I meant was that I've heard people who worked at Benton's say it wasn't unusual for staff to be invited to the DeKeyser's house for lunch or dinner."

Outstanding. "So anyone who ever worked at Benton's could have noticed that copy of *Wildflowers*."

"Yup." Ash glanced over. "Which means the people who might know about the book's value could be anyone from all the DeKeysers to Shane Pratley to Rafe to the mayor."

"Shane worked at Benton's?"

"Well, sure." Ash frowned. "I thought you knew. He was more or less in charge at Benton's when Deke and Talia handed over the management to Rianne. Shane was fine with that until Rianne moved back to run the store hands-on. He quit cold and went to work at the grocery store."

"No," I said. "I didn't know." But suddenly Shane's anger made . . . well, not sense, but at least now I knew there was a reason behind it. But was he angry enough to kill? I looked up at the big blue sky. Though it sent no answers, it was clear that Ash needed to know about Shane's temper. I sighed. "There's something I have to tell you."

When I described the encounter I'd had with Shane

at the grocery store, Ash went still. "And you didn't mention this at the time because?"

I shrugged, because I wasn't sure why. "He was just letting off steam."

"You don't know that."

He was right. "Sorry," I said. "I should have told you."

"Okay." Ash nodded. "I'll tell Hal and see what he wants to do with it." He twirled his paddle in his hands, started to dig the blades into the water, then stopped and looked at me. "Just so you know, we are looking at Steve Guilder."

"Andrea's high school boyfriend?"

"That's the one." Ash nodded. "We're looking, so leave that alone, okay? He moved back to Michigan about a year ago. We're trying to track him down."

"Is he in Chilson?" For some reason I glanced around. "Do you know where he's working?"

"We're trying to track him down," Ash repeated. "We'll find him. Don't worry."

It was a beautiful summer day with hardly a cloud in the sky, and worrying had been the furthest thing from my mind.

Until then.

Chapter 13

The next morning, I woke to the sound of rain pattering on the houseboat's roof. I lay quietly for a moment, trying to decide which was noisier, the rain or Eddie's snores, then reached for my clock to check the time. "It's not even eight," I said, yawning. "What do you think, bud? Option one is get up, get going, and be productive in the four hours before I have to be at the library. Option two is roll over and see what happens."

"Mrr," Eddie said sleepily.

I murmured agreement, rolled over, and went back to sleep.

Two hours later, I blinked and found that I was wide-awake. Eddie tried to convince me to stay in bed, but it wasn't any good. I was awake and going to stay that way.

"You, of course, get to remain in bed if you wish," I told him as I towel-dried my hair, postshower. "That's one of the benefits of being a cat."

Eddie's eyes opened slightly.

"You want me to name all of them?" I pulled on clothes suitable for an afternoon in the library; dress pants, a dressy T-shirt, and a light jacket. "There's no time for the complete list, but I can hit the highlights. A cat's sense of self-confidence, for one. The absolute non-necessity of having to change your clothes. Plus there's the ability you have to purr. What's that all about, anyway? And then there's—"

I stopped, because my audience of one had gone back to sleep. I could tell, because he was snoring again, this time most certainly louder than the rain.

"Have a good day," I whispered. Then I kissed him and headed out to hunt down some food.

The folks at the Round Table were happy enough to stuff me full of cinnamon apple pancakes, link sausage, and some healthy wedges of watermelon. I put up my rain jacket's hood and scooted from restaurant to car, telling myself that driving to the library when I normally walked on nonbookmobile days was okay on a day like this. Far better to use the gas to drive the mile than to walk and end up with wet shoes and socks and pants from which I might never get the mud spatters out.

I arrived at the library long before the noon opening and used the time to catch up on e-mails and to open the snail mail that had been accumulating on my desk. At straight-up twelve, I unlocked the doors and headed across the quiet lobby to the reference desk.

Donna, who was a deacon in her church, wouldn't arrive until half past. She'd worried over me being the only staff member in the entire library, saying that maybe someone else should work on Sunday afternoon. I'd said if I couldn't manage half an hour by myself, that my librarianship should be irrevocably revoked.

And, for the first fifteen minutes, absolutely nothing happened. Not a single soul walked in the door, and I was left free to research a new educational software program for the children's computers. Then, just as I was thinking that I must not have unlocked the doors, I heard one swing open and a troop of children scampered in. A motherly type cast a worried glance in my direction and shushed her charges.

I got up, smiling, and walked toward them. "Hi, I'm Minnie. If you need anything, just let me know."

The woman pushed back her rain-damp hair. "How about something for three siblings and four cousins to do for an hour or two? We're staying with friends and we were all supposed to go out on the boat, but . . ." She sighed.

"I have just the thing," I said with confidence. The brick-and-mortar library might not have a cat, but in addition to books, we had a puppet theater, a tree-shaped resin structure designed to be climbed upon, and jigsaw puzzles galore. I herded the entourage to the children's section, and the kids instantly scattered to various parts of the room.

"Thank you," the woman said. Deep feeling rang in every vowel and consonant. "I promise to remember you in my will."

"No need," I assured her. "All in a day's work for a librarian."

I left them to their devices and headed back to the reference desk, exquisitely satisfied with my profession, glad I hadn't given in to a brief temptation in my sophomore year to switch majors. Though the archaeology class I'd taken had been fascinating, it wouldn't have suited me nearly as much as being a librarian did.

As I neared the desk, I saw that in my absence a man had come in and sat at a computer. "Hi," I said. "If you need any help, my name is—" I blinked. "Oh, hey. I didn't recognize you."

A hatless Mitchell nodded. "Hey, Minnie. What's up?"

"Not much," I said, leaning against the barrier that separated the computer carrels from each other. "But I'm wondering what's up with you?"

"Nothing."

"I don't believe that."

He glanced up sideways at me, then turned his attention to the computer, shrugging.

"You've been working at the toy store," I said quietly. "You're been crewing on a charter boat, and you're working that renovation construction job." From what I'd been told, Mitchell had never held more than one job at time in his life, and often not even that.

"Work isn't so bad," he muttered, whacking at the keyboard.

I thought about what I might say next, trying to choose words that would sound concerned yet lack any hint of condescension. "Mitchell," I said softly, "if your girlfriend truly loves you, she loves you just the way you are."

"Yeah?" He reached up for his baseball hat, but his hand found nothing but air, so he was forced to let his hand flop back down uselessly. "That's what my sister says, but Bianca, she's so great, you know? She deserves someone who works as hard as she does. Someone who's worth something."

"But—"

Mitchell pushed on through my objection. "You told me to stay busy, remember? And I figured working lots of jobs was the best way to do that. And now I see that I can save some money, you know? I need to show Bianca that I'm worth more than just an attic apartment in my sister's house." His voice was full of disgust for himself. "I've wasted so much time hanging around and not doing anything much. I need to change before it's too late."

Negative point to Minnie for not thinking her advice through. I reached out to touch him on the shoulder, but let my hand drop. "Mitchell, I understand that you don't want to lose Bianca."

"She's the one," he said. "I love her."

The stark declaration startled me. I blinked, then said, "It's great that you're making a living. But don't change yourself too much, okay? We like you just the way you are."

Mitchell faced me. "Do you? Do you really? Or are you just saying so because you like to have me around to make fun of?"

His accusation stung. I didn't want to think it was true, but I was the least bit afraid there was some truth in what he said. My mother would have been ashamed of me, and for good reason. I flushed. "Mitchell—"

"And you know what?" he said, interrupting, yet another thing that was very un-Mitchell-like. "It's kind of stupid. All these years people have been telling me to get a real job, and now that I'm working like crazy, people are asking me why I'm working so hard. I can't win for losing."

He had a point. A very good one. And when I told him so, he shrugged again.

"Anyway," he said, "I bet you're working as many hours as I am at your one job than I am at all of mine put together."

"That's different."

"Yeah?" He grinned, and there was the old Mitchell, right there in front of me. "How's that exactly?"

I opened my mouth to respond, couldn't think of anything to say, and closed it again.

Because there was a strong possibility that there was no difference.

"Your splits are getting faster," Ash said.

"My what?" I asked, panting. My body was not made for doing splits. The last time I'd tried had been in third-grade gym class and, if I thought about it, the humiliation still stung, so I'd done my best not to think about it for the past twenty-odd years.

"Splits," he said, not panting at all. "Your mile times on our runs. They're down almost thirty seconds since we started running together."

How nice for me. And as soon as I found the breath enough to say so out loud, I would.

But as soon as I had the uncharitable thought, I tried to unthink it. Most runners wouldn't slow down so much for a friend. This wasn't helping Ash's fitness level at all; he was only doing this for my sake. To spend time with me.

And I did enjoy our morning routine. No matter what I did the rest of the day, I could think back to this run and know I'd done something right.

We were about halfway through our normal route, which started out at the marina and went up the hill, through downtown and its outskirts, toward the high-priced real estate on the point, then back along the edge of Janay Lake along the public walkway.

"How about trying for a fast quarter mile?" Ash asked. "Bet you can do under two minutes."

A few weeks ago, I'd been happy enough to run three miles at all; now I was trying to improve my times. "You think?" I asked, trying not to gasp.

"Sure," he said easily. "Interval training is the way to go."

If I'd had the wind, I'd have asked, "The way to go where?" but I didn't, so I didn't.

"We can start at the next intersection." Ash pointed ahead. "Through the last block of downtown, past the gas station, past the church, and up to the Point Road. That's a quarter mile. I've clocked it."

"Sure," I said. What the heck. I didn't mind pushing myself. I might even learn what an interval was.

His running watch made some beeping noises, and when we reached the upcoming intersection, he said, "Go!" at the same time his watch made another beep.

I put my head down and concentrated on my running. *Don't be a rabbit,* I told myself. *Don't go out too fast. Set a pace you can maintain for a couple of minutes. You can do anything for two minutes.*

So I tried. I really did. But then, in front of the office to the local propane dealer, I saw a man who looked familiar. He must have heard our footsteps, because he turned. "Morning, Minnie," he said.

I slowed to puff out, "Morning!" then worked to return to my former pace, but must have been distracted by trying to remember the guy's name and missed my target time by ten seconds.

It wasn't until I was showered, dressed, breakfasted, and walking to the library that something went *click* in my brain and I remembered why I knew the guy in front of the propane company. Or at least I'd been introduced to him. He was the attorney for Talia DeKeyser's estate, the one I'd met in Rianne's pilot's house of an office. Peter? Paul? Something like that.

For some reason, I was suddenly embarrassed, which made no sense because I had, in fact, said good morning; I just hadn't remembered his name.

And then, since the thing was done and there was nothing I could do about it, I put the incident from my mind.

"Long time no see," Josh commented.

Startled, I jerked the coffeepot and narrowly missed pouring hot coffee all across the counter. "What are you talking about? I was here yesterday afternoon. And all day Friday." I counted back. "And Wednesday and Monday and the—"

"I mean mentally here." He picked up the coffeepot I'd set down and filled his own mug. "The past two weeks you've been walking around like a zombie, hardly paying attention to anything anybody says."

My knee-jerk reaction was to deny all, but I had a sneaking suspicion he was onto something. And it was one of those somethings I would address as soon as I had a spare few minutes. Of course, when that might be, I didn't have a—

"Minnie, I need to talk to you right now." Denise Slade stood in the doorway of the break room, her arms crossed.

"Have fun," Josh murmured. "Hey, Denise," he said in a normal voice. "See you later, okay?"

And he was gone.

"Hello," I said to Denise. "How are you this fine morning?"

"What?" She frowned. "I'm fine. Why wouldn't I be?"

I could have mentioned a number of reasons, starting with the death of her husband less than a year earlier, moving on to the troublesome situation in the Middle East, and ending with the cost of bacon, but I just smiled and asked, "What's up?"

"Here." She uncrossed her arms and brandished a piece of paper. "It's that list of names you wanted, all the Friends who worked in the book-sale room." She flapped the paper up and down, which made a bizarrely loud noise.

I walked around the table and reached out to take the paper from her. "Thanks, Denise. This really—" I stopped. The list, which I'd anticipated to have four or five names, had more like twenty. "All of these people worked in the sale room that week?"

"No idea," Denise said. "Say, can I get a cup of caffeine? I'll even take it if you made it." She laughed.

Silently I took a mug from the cupboard, checked its insides for dust, and poured it full of coffee. When I handed it to Denise, I also pushed over the small tray that held creamer, sugar, and a jar taped with a note that said, *Please donate to our coffee fund*. Ignoring the jar, Denise added two packs of sugar and one pack of creamer to her mug.

Denise stirred the contents of her mug with a spoon and then laid the spoon on the table, where it would leave a small puddle, "That list is all the people who were scheduled to work this month."

Though it was wonderful that the Friends had so many people who volunteered for the good of the library, the task of calling them all would take a while. "I thought you said you'd know who worked that week."

Denise paused in the act of sipping her coffee. "I do. They're on that list."

I almost looked around for the rabbit hole I must have fallen into. "Which ones?"

"Minnie," she said, frowning at my obvious stupidity, "I told you already. They're on that list."

"But you can't tell me which ones?"

"Are you nuts? Of course I can't. Maybe you have time enough on your hands to waste it doing that kind of paperwork, but I have better things to do."

Don't take it personally, I told myself. *She's like this with everyone.*

"Take last week," Denise was saying. "Not only did I have to help my neighbor down the street move around a load of dirt, but I ran into Kim Parmalee downtown, and she was all in a tizzy about a bunch of new furniture. She couldn't decide on fabrics for some upholstery, and if there's one thing I know, it's furniture, so I dropped everything to help her. And if that wasn't enough, my son called and said he was wondering about his dad's power tools." Denise made a *whuff* sort of noise. "So I had to go down to the basement and do an inventory of everything. My son said I didn't need to, that a couple of pictures would been enough, but I know better."

She rolled her eyes and though I was tempted to roll mine, too, I maintained my polite, if stiff, smile.

"I absolutely know better," she said. "First it's pictures, then it's what brand, then what model, then he'll want to know how old everything is. Better off just to do the work now and take care of it at the front end."

Absently, I nodded, which provided her with enough conversational fuel to move to her next topic: the recently appointed city councilman. Denise had nothing good to say about him—surprise!—and wanted to make sure I knew about his vote regarding the purchase of a new snowplow truck.

"Brand new," she said. "Do you know how much those things cost? Why can't they buy a used one? I mean, does that make any sense?"

But I wasn't listening, not really, because I was back at the fabric part of the conversation, when Denise had said that Kim Parmalee, née DeKeyser, a woman who'd been rumored to be close to bankruptcy, was shopping for furniture.

Every time I had a spare moment the rest of the morning, I called someone on Denise's list. I ended up leaving messages at most of the numbers, and every time I did, I wondered if the exercise was a complete waste of my time. The odds of learning something useful felt slim to slimmer.

Still, it was something I could do. I'd considered giving the list to Detective Inwood or to Ash, but they were busy and this wasn't real investigative work; it was just narrowing down the names. I was saving them time and would tell them so if they found out what I was doing and tried giving me The Look, the one that meant I should leave law-enforcement work to the law-enforcement officers. And I would do that, as soon as there was a true law-enforcement task to get done.

All of which meant that I worked through noon and didn't realize until about two in the afternoon that I hadn't had any lunch.

"No wonder I'm hungry," I said out loud. I'd eaten a small breakfast and had no snack, because I still needed to do my grocery shopping. If I didn't get some food into me soon, I was going to be cranky all afternoon.

So I snatched up my backpack—holder of my wallet,

cell phone, and a spare book, among numerous other things—and headed out to the lobby.

"Hey, Holly?"

My friend looked up from the computer and put her index fingers to her forehead in a parody of concentration. "I'm reading your mind," she said. "You've finally realized you haven't had any lunch, and now that your stomach lining is starting to digest itself, you're going to get some food before you keel over from low blood sugar."

"I was more worried about getting irritable."

"As you should be," she said, crossing her arms.

Whenever she did that, she looked like she could be a close blood relative to Denise. But I'd long ago vowed to keep that thought to myself. I smiled and started to walk backward as I said, "I'll be back in half an hour, if not less."

Holly's eyes went wide. "Minnie, you—"

"Twenty minutes, then," I said, still walking backward. "If anybody wants anything from Shomin's, call me on my—"

Bam!

My body thumped into something and my backpack went flying. I staggered, my breath leaving me with an *oof.* My arms wheeled around in circles as I instinctively tried to keep my balance, but it was a lost cause and I dropped to my knees on the tile floor with a wincingly loud *crack!*

"Good afternoon," said a resonant male voice.

I looked up and saw the president of the library board. "Oh. Hi, Otis. Sorry about barging into you. I was just . . . uh. . . ." I glanced around. There were three other people standing there: two library board members and a fortyish man in a jacket and tie.

The contents of my backpack were strewn across the lobby floor; I must not have zipped it closed when I'd grabbed it out of my office. Still on my knees, I scrambled to gather everything without looking like an idiot. It was far too late for that, of course, and I knew it, but since my head boss, my vice-boss, a subsidiary boss, and a possible supervisor were all looming above me, it made sense to make an attempt.

"Here," said a male voice. "Let me help."

I looked, startled, at the guy who might be the new Stephen. He'd crouched down to my level and was gathering up my scattered possessions. "Thanks," I said, accepting a small spiral-bound notebook, a handful of pens, and a set of fingernail clippers and shoved it all into the backpack, along with the things I'd already added.

"Is this yours?" The guy held out a packet of Eddie treats.

"Thanks," I said again, taking the treats. As we stood, me to my five feet of height and him to his not-quite six feet, Otis said, "Graydon, this is Minnie Hamilton, assistant director of the library. Minnie, this is Graydon Cain, one of the candidates we're interviewing for the directorship."

Graydon's face went from politely kind to frozen. He stared down at me. "You're Minnie Hamilton?"

I blinked. Somehow I'd thought he'd known who I was. Somehow I'd figured he'd seen my mishap and understood that these things can happen to competent and intelligent people who sometimes didn't pay quite enough attention to where they were going.

"Yes," I said, lifting my chin. "I'm Minnie."

He nodded but didn't say a word. At least not to me. Instead, he looked at Otis and the other two board members. "Shall we get started? I don't want to take up any more of your time than is necessary."

They walked away without a backward glance.

I watched them go, getting a sick feeling deep in my stomach that my professional future was not as rosy as it had been ten minutes earlier.

Chapter 14

The next day was a bookmobile day. We were in the southeast part of Tonedagana County, and driving the curvy, hilly, narrow roads kept my mind too occupied to tell Julia the tale of the previous afternoon. I'd started to talk about it at the first stop, but we were stampeded by too many children in search of books for me to be able to finish. The moment I started braking for the second stop, however, Julia was pumping me for the rest of the narrative. I obliged, and was to the part where I was walking backward in the lobby, when a carload of white-haired ladies pulled into the parking lot.

"Have to finish this later," I told Julia, nodding at our incoming visitors. "It's the softball team."

Julia's face, which had started to droop, perked up. "All of them?"

I peered out the window. "No, but more than half. Pitcher, catcher, shortstop, left fielder, center fielder."

"Oh, excellent." Julia beamed. "I love these ladies. What shall we give them today?"

A few months earlier, we'd stopped for lunch at a small café in the tiny town of Peebles. The waitress had noticed the mammoth vehicle parked at the curb and asked us about the bookmobile. When I said the phrase "thousands of books," she'd grinned and said, "I have to tell my mother-in-law about this. Do you happen to have a copy of your schedule?"

Since I always carried a few copies, I pulled one out and handed it over.

"Perfect," she said, scanning the list. "I bet you'll see them next week."

"Them?" Julia and I had asked.

The waitress had just laughed and told us that we'd know them when we saw them.

And we did. No question about it.

The waitress's mother-in-law happened to be the pitcher and coach of a local softball team, and the entire team, with the exception of one player, had been playing together since they were in high school. How they'd managed to stay a healthy team was a mystery of immense proportions, but their fifty years of experience—each, not total—pushed them to the top of their league every year. Only the catcher was a newcomer, and that was because the original catcher and her husband had retired to Arizona.

"Still playing ball, though," Corky Grigsby had said that first day, nodding. "What about you ladies?" She flicked an experienced glance over Julia and me. "No time like the present to join a team. Do you play?"

I'd smiled and said I was more the swimming/hiking/bicycling type, but Julia had looked interested.

Now I looked at her as she unlocked the door and pushed it open. "You know Corky's going to ask if you've joined a softball team."

"And I have," she said. "You are looking at the new right fielder for the Chilson Swingers."

"Really? Did you have to try out or anything?"

"They asked how much I'd played, and I told them." Julia pulled down an imaginary baseball cap and pounded her fist into an imaginary glove.

"Which was how much?" I asked.

"Gym class, back in high school." She looked at me and grinned. "I'm going to be horrible, but I'm going to have fun."

Of that, I was sure. If I hadn't known that Julia was a world-class actor famous in theatrical circles around the world, I would have thought she was a fun-loving party girl who'd never grown up. Of course, it seemed as if there was a lot of overlap between those two things.

Corky and her crew came up the steps into the bookmobile. In a line, they went straight to the front to give Eddie his morning greeting, then came back and stood around Julia and me in a semicircle.

"What do you have for us today?" Corky asked. "And, for crying out loud, don't give us anything that'll make us think. It's summer, you know."

"Horror," I said promptly.

The first time the softball team had visited the bookmobile—all nine of them, and I was glad they hadn't brought any of the backup players, because I wasn't sure the vehicle could take it—they'd requested that we give them books they'd never read, or books their mothers would have warned them about, or books that would shock their children. All three, if possible. They'd read *Fifty Shades of Grey* a few weeks ago, and the left fielder said she'd learned only two things, which she thought was pretty good for an old lady.

"Horror? Excellent!" the shortstop said, rubbing her hands together. "This is going to be fun. Give me something that will keep me awake all night. I don't sleep for beans these days. At least this way I'll have a good reason." She elbowed the center fielder in the ribs. "And maybe I'll wake up Joe and tell him I need comforting. What do you think?"

The ladies laughed, and I told Julia to get the bag of books I'd stashed behind the back desk. She opened the bag, peered in, and looked puzzled. "*Lord of the Flies*?"

"Wait a minute," Corky said, frowning. "My kids read this book in school. You're not trying to educate us, are you?"

"My kids read this, too," the catcher said. "It can't be that scary."

I smiled. "Read the first few chapters late at night when no one else is awake. Then come back and tell me how you felt."

Squinting with doubt, they took the books as I reassured them they wouldn't be learning a thing. And they probably wouldn't; they'd all lived long enough to know what people could do to each other.

I pushed away the chill of remembered fear that I'd felt upon first reading the book and turned to greet the person who'd arrived while Julia and I had been busy with the team. He was browsing the natural-history books, and was thirtyish, with long hair pulled back into a tidy ponytail. Though I'd never seen him on the bookmobile before, he looked familiar.

"Hi," I said, stepping forward. "I'm Minnie Hamilton. Is this your first visit to the bookmobile?" Odds were high that it was, but it was also possible that I'd forgotten one face among the hundreds.

"What's that?" The guy looked across the top of my head, then looked down. "Oh. Hi. Yeah. It is. Nice bus you got here."

He smiled, and I got the itchy feeling that he was trying to flirt with me.

"Thank you," I said politely. "Is there anything in which you're interested?" Nothing like perfect grammar to turn off a prospective suitor.

His smile went wider. "My name is Jared Moyle," he said.

The name meant nothing to me, but I nodded. "Nice to meet you, Jared. If you need a library card, either Julia or I can help you with the paperwork. Let me know if you need any help finding a book," I said, stressing the "book" part ever so slightly.

"Mrr." Eddie waltzed past me and thumped Jared on the back of the knees.

In the dog stories I'd read, the narrators often gave their canine friends credit for knowing, at a single doggy sniff, whether or not a newcomer was trustworthy. I did not attribute that power of discernment to Eddie. He was mostly likely after one of two things: either Jared smelled like a cat treat or Jared was wearing pants that looked like something Eddie wanted to shed upon.

"Hey, you guys have a cat." Jared dropped into a crouch and held out his knuckles for sniffing purposes.

"His name is Eddie," I said.

"We could use a cat at the store." Jared scratched Eddie on the side of his neck, eliciting a low but steady purr.

"What store is that?"

"I co-own the used-book store in Chilson." He glanced up. "You been in?"

So that was why the guy looked familiar. "Nice thriller section," I said. "How are things going?"

"Oh, you know." He shrugged. "Not great; not horrible. I'm not going to get rich, but it's a way for me to read a lot without spending a ton of money. Plus, I do caretaking for a bunch of summer people. I get by." He gave Eddie a last pat, stood, and smiled at me.

"My boyfriend does some of that." This was loosely true, since his neighbors were seasonal. Ash gave them a neighborly hand with their cottage-opening and cottage-closing chores, and kept an eye on the place through the winter.

Jared nodded. "Lots of that work around these days. Even high school kids are getting into it." He grinned. "Probably pays a lot better than working at Benton's did. After a couple of summers of that, you'd think I'd stay away from retail, but here I am with my own store."

I'd been starting to slide away, but stopped. "Jared, I have a strange question for you. Have you had anyone in looking for old books on flowers?"

His forehead crinkled a little. "Not that I can think of. Of course, I'm not there all the time."

I was about to warn him about the book-related break-ins—after all, if I'd warned Rianne, I was obligated to warn him, and probably should already have done so, if Ash or Detective Inwood hadn't—but I noticed that he wasn't really paying attention to me. No, he was surreptitiously eyeing the bookmobile's natural-history selection. The part that included wildflowers.

Stooping to pick up Eddie, I said, "We've had some recent interest in books about flowers. I just wondered if you were getting the same thing."

Jared said they hadn't, at least as far as he knew. He kept talking, and I tried to listen, but what I kept thinking, as I inched farther and farther away, was that I'd just added one more person to the suspect list, because who better than a used-book store owner would know the value of *Wildflowers*?

A few hours later, a different man was smiling at me, and the grin on his face was decades younger than the eighty-five I knew him to be. "Now, aren't you a sight for sore eyes?" he asked.

I smiled back. Age and wheelchair notwithstanding, Max Compton was ten times the flirt Jared Moyle had tried to be, and was more than ten times as appealing. "Hey there, Mr. Compton. If I'm looking that good, you need to get out more." It had been a long day, and I knew I was looking like something Eddie had dragged in.

He gave me a look of mock horror. "Mr. Compton? That's my dad—God rest his soul. You call me Max, or I'll start calling you Missy."

"You have a deal." I held out my hand and we shook on it, me being careful not to grip too tightly around the elderly man's arthritis. "Ready for the next couple of chapters?"

Last summer, Cade had spent some time at Lake View Medical Care Facility while recovering from a stroke, and I'd visited often enough that the staff learned what I did for a living. One thing led to another, and in addition to dropping off a rotating selection of large-print books, I'd also ended up promising to stop by Lake View once a month to read aloud to a group of residents. Other volunteers did the same thing, and between us we could read through a book in three weeks. The residents chose the book, and I was curious to see the current selection.

Max pulled a volume from underneath the crocheted blanket that lay across his rickety legs. "Looking forward to hearing you do the voices."

There was a smirk in his own voice, and when I saw the title, I knew why. "*Animal Farm*? Are you serious?"

"No, he's not."

I turned. Heather, a nurse's aide, walked into the sunroom and handed me a copy of Jan Karon's *These High, Green Hills*. "They finished the fifth chapter yesterday—don't let him tell you any different."

Max fell against the back of his wheelchair, clutching at his shirt. "I'm having a heart attack!" he croaked. "I can only be saved by hearing a John Sandford book read to me."

"That's your stomach," Heather said, winking at me, "not your heart. And you know darn well that you got outvoted for John Sandford. Better luck next time."

"Oooh," Max groaned in fake agony. "My heart . . ."

"Is everything all right?" someone asked from the doorway.

"We're fine," Heather said, taking the George Orwell novel from me. "Just a little discussion of book selection, that's all."

I glanced over and saw the lawyer I'd met in Rianne's office, and the guy I'd seen while out running the other morning. "Hi," I said. "Nice to see you again." And then, because he wasn't leaving and I didn't know what else to say, I asked, "Are you here visiting relatives?"

Heather made a very soft but very rude noise in the back of her throat. He smiled and said, "No, not yet. My parents are hale and hearty. But I have a number of clients here, and I like to check on them every week or two."

"Well, it was nice seeing you again," I said.

"Likewise. Say, you still have my card?" He didn't wait for my reply, but fished one from his pocket and handed it over. "You never know when you might need an attorney." Laughing, he turned his hand into a pistol and fired off a quick shot at me. "Catch you later."

As soon as he was gone, Max said, "Now, Heather, you be nice."

"Is it being mean to state an opinion?" she asked. "Because I can't stand that guy. He trolls the halls, looking to sign up clients, but when I ask management to toss him out, they say he's here visiting clients and there's nothing we can do."

I looked at the card. Paul Utley. "Why would anyone here need an attorney?"

"Wouldn't," Max said succinctly. "Not ninety-nine-point-nine percent of them, anyway. Legal affairs are pretty much wrapped up before you check in."

"So . . . ?" I gestured after Paul.

"He's chasing after clients," Heather said savagely. "Convincing them to sign up for services they don't need and pay a retainer they can't afford."

Max smiled. "Tell us what you really think, Heather."

"I think he's the kind of lawyer who gives ambulance chasers a bad name," she snapped.

"If you weren't already married," Max said, "I'd propose to you here and now."

"And if you did it on one knee, I'd agree, husband or no." She grinned at the two of us, her lawyer-inspired anger gone as fast as it had come. "Minnie, I'll go round up the rest of the readers group. Be back in a flash."

Max and I watched her go. "Is Paul really that awful?" I asked.

"He's not what I'd call a force for good," Max said,

"but I wouldn't say he was evil personified, either. In spite of what Heather says, he does help some of the folks here. And not always with legal issues." He rubbed his chin thoughtfully, his two-day whiskers making a scratchy noise against his hand.

This happened to be a noise that, to me, was the equivalent of fingernails on a chalkboard, so I quickly said, "What kind of help would he be giving if it wasn't legal? Do you have a 'for instance'?"

Max took his hand off his face and pointed down the hall. "Paul's the one who noticed that Mary what's-her-name in that room over there can't breathe right if the closet door isn't shut tight. He's the one who realized that Talia DeKeyser was giving away everything she owned to kids she didn't even know. And without Paul, I'm not sure anyone would ever have known that the reason old Robert Smith was so upset—the poor man hasn't had his wits about him in years—was because the picture on his wall was hanging crooked."

Heather bustled in, pushing a woman in a wheel-chair, and half a dozen other folks trailed in after her, and I settled down to read about the doings of the day in Mitford.

But even as I read, my mind kept circling around what I'd learned.

So Paul noticed things.

Interesting.

After I finished reading, leaving the group—and myself—a little on edge on how Father Tim was going to fix things in Mitford, I got back onto my bicycle and headed over to see what Aunt Frances was doing. The traffic was heavy, which, outside of downtown, meant I had to wait for cars at stop signs and had cars passing me on a regular basis. It seemed that one particular sedan passed me more than once, but since I hadn't been paying that much attention, I couldn't have sworn to it. But the third time it passed me, I was sure it was the same one. Unfortunately, the windows were tinted and the license plate was covered with mud.

Though there was undoubtedly a reasonable explanation for that, I cut down a side street, then went through an alley and rolled up to my aunt's place a little out of breath. I leaned my bike up against a handy tree. "Hey, there. Do you want some help?"

My aunt was half buried in the boardinghouse's foundation shrubs, her front end working hard at pulling out leaves and sticks and who knew what else. I called again, and again she didn't hear me, so I walked up next to her and tapped the small of her back.

"Yahh!"

She erupted from the bush, eyes wild and arms flailing. It was then that I noticed the earbuds inserted into her ears and the iPod tucked into the pocket of her oversized gardening shirt.

"Minnie!" She pulled the buds from her ears. "You scared me!"

"Sorry," I said. And I was. It was also a little funny, but I knew how it felt to be startled like that and it wasn't much fun. "I didn't realize you were wired up." I touched my ears.

"Oh. Yes." Aunt Frances poked at the iPod, turning it off. "It's Otto's. Did you know you can download audio books from the library on these things? It's wonderful! Like having someone read you a story. I don't know that I'll ever wash windows again without this little gadget. Talk about taking away the tedium."

I laughed. "Audio books as an aid to housework. I'll have to spread the word."

My aunt smiled. "Of course you know about borrowing audio books. What was I thinking? You have a silly old woman for an aunt."

"Don't you talk that way about her," I said, giving her a quick hug. "She's the best."

"And you're a silly girl." She returned my hug briefly, then eased away. "Getting this close to someone who's been doing yard work all afternoon isn't the best way to keep your clothes clean."

I looked down at myself. Small clods of dirt and specks of leaves covered my front. "Not only is my aunt the best aunt in the world, but she might also be the dirtiest aunt ever."

"Not anymore." She grinned. "I transferred half of it. Now you can't say I never gave you anything."

As I did my best to brush off my clothes, I gave Aunt Frances a thorough but secret visual examination. Fatigue was making her shoulders sag and adding some vertical lines around her mouth.

"Say, what do you think about hiring some help?" I asked. "I bet you could get a high school kid. I could ask Thessie to recommend someone." Thessie, just graduated from high school, had volunteered on the bookmobile last summer. "You don't need to work so hard."

"Minerva Joy Hamilton, you are the best niece in the world, but please do not presume to tell me what to do. I am almost double your age, and I know what's best for me."

Knocking off the last of the dirt from my shirt, I said, "I was just trying to help." It came out sounding sulky, so I added, "And you're not double my age. Just almost."

"I rounded up."

For some reason, I found her firm statement funny enough that, despite my best efforts to stay serious, laughter burbled up and out of me. "You're horrible. Does Otto know what he's getting into?"

"Probably not." The expression on my aunt's face, which had been a smile, faded into a wistful glance across the street. "I just wish . . ."

"What do you wish?" I asked, oh, so gently.

She shook her head. "Nothing. You know what they say about wishes."

"Beggars and horses?"

"Bingo. And if everyone had a horse, how would all the manure ever get cleaned up?"

I thought about Mackinac Island, where, outside of winter, the only motorized vehicles allowed were emergency types. There were lots of horses and the island cleanup crews took their jobs very seriously, but even still, pedestrians spent a fair amount of time watching where their feet went.

Then again, if everyone had a horse, would there even be pedestrians?

I started to puzzle out the problem to my aunt, but she was headed back into the shrubbery. "You sure I can't help?" I asked.

"Go play," she said. "Have fun. Ride your bike along a road you haven't been down all summer."

That sounded like an excellent idea, but still I hesitated. "I can stay."

"Go!"

And so, grinning, I went.

It was a beautiful evening, and if I went home I would feel compelled to clean the bathroom, so I decided to take my aunt's advice and ride aimlessly around town. Off in the distance, I heard the tower clock of the Catholic church chime once. Eight thirty, then. At this time of year there was another hour of daylight left, if not an hour and a half, so I had plenty of time to both bike and clean, if I wanted.

Which I didn't, but if the bathroom went uncleaned for much longer, the ghost of my maternal grandmother would haunt my dreams until I took care of what needed to be done.

But it was hard to care about the cleanliness of bathrooms when the evening sun was golden, when backyards were full of children shrieking with laughter as they played the games children had always played, and when the warmth of summer felt as if it would last forever.

A deep sense of contentment filled me as I cruised the streets of my adopted town. Life was good, would continue to be good, would always be—

"Watch out!"

I braked hard, skidding sideways with a shuddering screech of my tires, trying to avoid hitting the soccer ball that had rolled in front of me.

"Sorry!" A young boy scurried out, snatched up the ball, and ran back to his house. "That wouldn't have happened," he called, "if you'd been paying attention!"

Though this was undoubtedly true, his ire seemed a little harsh. After all, I'd never met him.

"I told you I didn't want to play."

Ah. The kid was yelling at a girl, who looked about seven years old. I hadn't noticed her until now because she was standing in the middle of a lovely country flower garden. The garden almost filled the space between two Victorian-era homes and was bursting with blooms, none of which I could identify except for the daisies the girl was clutching in her hand.

"Better not let Mom catch you picking stuff from there," her brother said.

The girl ignored him and plucked off another white-petaled flower. "It's Mrs. Talia's garden, and she told me I could pick any flower I wanted any time I wanted."

I blinked. Blinked again as I looked at the house next door. Yes, there was the L-shaped front porch. There were the ornamental cornices, fish-scale gable siding, stained-glass windows, and complicated brick-work foundation that Barb and Cade had mentioned. And, if I remembered correctly, Rianne and her family lived in the house now, keeping it in the family for at least another generation.

It was a nice concept and one with a satisfying continuity, but I was glad my family didn't own a house like that. After all, it was hard enough for me to find the time to clean a single bathroom; how on earth would I have managed a house that, when it had been built, had undoubtedly been maintained with the assistance of daily help?

As I stood there, musing about the social changes in the past hundred years, a rattling pickup truck pulled into Rianne's narrow driveway. A man with graying hair got out and gave me a hard look. "You got a problem?" he asked sharply.

"What? No, I was just—"

"Yo, Steve!" The front door opened and another man, one I assumed to be Rianne's husband, came out. "It's about time you showed up, Guilder. The beer's going to get warm if you don't get a move on." He was carrying a cooler and tossed it into the back of the pickup. "There's a bunch of guys who said they're playing tonight. Hope you're up for seven-card stud."

So. Not only was Steve Guilder back in Chilson, but he was a friend of Rianne's husband. Did that mean . . .

No. The police were taking care of this end of things. There was no need for me to get involved. None whatsoever.

I hopped on my bike and pedaled away from the DeKeysers and back toward the marina, where my houseboat and my cat waited for me.

"Mrr!" my cat said.

I looked at him. "You know, when I was riding back through town just now, I was thinking how nice it was going to be to walk in and be greeted by my loving, furry friend, who was longing to be snuggled and petted and perhaps even kissed by his favorite human. Instead, I walk in and find you there."

Eddie, who was sitting on the kitchen counter, sat up even straighter as I finished walking through the door.

"Get down," I said firmly. "There aren't many rules in this house, but No Cats on the Kitchen Counter is one of them and it's at the top of the list."

"Mrr."

"Down," I said, raising my voice.

Eddie blinked at me.

"Down!" I dropped my backpack and clapped my hands. It was a noise Eddie hated. He glared at me and jumped down with a loud *thump!*

"How do you do that?" I asked. "That was a louder noise than I would have made and I weigh . . ." I tried to do some quick math in my head, failed, felt a little embarrassed about the failure, then remembered that I was a librarian and mental math wasn't a required duty. "And I weigh a lot more than you do."

"Mrr."

"Talkative tonight, are you?"

Eddie, who had been walking toward me in a straight line, suddenly swerved and went around my feet in a wide arc, and returned to his straight path, the end of which was to jump on the pilot's seat and sit on top of my backpack. "Mrr," he said, settling in.

"Thanks. A little more Eddie hair on my stuff is exactly what I needed. Because, really, can you ever have enough of—"

From deep inside the backpack, my cell phone rang.

Eddie jumped and scrambled onto the dashboard. When he arrived safely, he turned and gave my pack the evil eye. If the world had been a just place, the backpack would have spontaneously combusted. But since the world was unfair, even for Eddies, I patted him on the head and reached for the phone.

The number wasn't one I recognized, but it was local, so I thumbed it on, "Hello?"

"Is this Minnie Hamilton?"

"Yes," I said. The voice was female and elderly, but it wasn't one I recognized. "This is. How are you this evening?"

"Well, isn't it nice of you to ask," she said, and I could hear the smile in her words. "I'm so glad I decided to call. I knew it was a cellular phone, and in general I don't like to talk to the things—that time lag is wretched if you want to have a meaningful talk."

"I know what you mean." I'd made a strategic error in starting a conversation before I knew who was on the other end of the phone, and it was too late to ask her name. *Nicely done, Minnie. Very nicely done.*

"Anyway," she said. "My Thomas said you'd rung the other day when I was downstate visiting our daughter. He said it sounded important and that I should call you as soon as I got home."

And then I knew who was on the other end of the phone. I stood by the dashboard and gave Eddie a few absent pets, watching stray hairs fly up into the air. "Thank you for calling, Mrs. Panik. It is important."

"Well, then. What can I do for you?"

Lillian Panik was the longest-serving Friend of the Library. She'd volunteered under more presidents than . . . well, not more presidents than Eddie had hairs, but probably more than he had whiskers. I made a mental note to count them later and said, "It's about the break-in in the book-sale room."

Mrs. Panik sighed. "That was so sad. I've never seen anything like it. Such a mess, and for what?"

I had a pretty good idea for what, but said, "I was just wondering if you'd noticed anything unusual in the days just before it happened. Odd phone calls, strange questions, someone in there you'd never noticed before— anything, really, that was different."

"You're sleuthing!" Mrs. Panik exclaimed. "How wonderful! You young girls nowadays will turn your hand to anything."

I didn't think I had a thing on Dr. Elizabeth Blackwell. "Can you think of anything?"

"Well, now." She hummed a tune that sounded a lot, but not quite, like the theme song to Dragnet. "I don't see how this could have anything to do with it, but I know that Monica had someone substitute for her."

Monica? Who was Monica? Denise kept recruiting new volunteers, which was fantastic, but she didn't always bring them around to meet the library staff. I asked for Monica's last name, but Mrs. Panik didn't know it.

"Tell you what," she said, lowering her voice. "I'll make a few inquiries. If I discover anything, I'll call you right back."

I stood straight. "Mrs. Panik, please don't—"

"No trouble at all," she said. "Good-bye, Minnie." And she was gone.

For no good reason, I was uneasy at the thought of the petite, white-haired, and very proper Mrs. Panik playing Bess Marvin to my Nancy Drew. All those stories turned out okay in the end, but there was a time or two in every installment where you weren't sure.

"Well, rats," I muttered. There was no help for it. I'd have to go clean the bathroom.

The shower was almost clean when the phone I'd shoved into my pocket rang. I dropped my sponge and pulled it out. It was Mrs. Panik. I thumbed it on fast. "How are you?" I asked.

"Just fine, Minnie. But how are you? You sound a touch breathless." She paused. "And a little hollow."

I stepped out of the tiny shower stall. "Is this better?"

"Much. Now, I have something to tell you, and it's a little disturbing. I hope you're sitting."

Anyone who'd reached the age she had undoubtedly knew the best way to deliver bad news. I walked the few steps to my bed and slowly sat down. "What's the matter?"

"It's Monica Utley," Mrs. Panik said. "I don't know if this is against the rules or not, but she asked someone to substitute for her the Saturday before the disturbance at the sale room. Someone who wasn't a Friend of the Library."

"Denise would know," I said. "About the rules, I mean." Not that I was going to ask her. "Do you know who Monica asked to substitute?"

"Yes, I do. Now, mind you, I didn't talk to Monica about this. I learned it from Stella, who heard it from Peggy, who talked to Edith about it."

I'd had high hopes at first, but with each degree of separation, my hopes went lower. "I see."

She took in a deep breath. "From what I hear, you have a nice relationship with that fine young Ash Wolverson, so I will assume that you'll take any pertinent information straight to him."

"Yes," I said cautiously. "Of course I will."

"Then that's all right. Now, here's the difficult part." Her words, which had been measured, began to run into each other. "The person who substituted for Monica was Andrea Vennard, that poor woman who was killed in the library, and I know you know all about that, you poor thing, and I'm sorry to have to tell you this, but it's best that you know. You have a good night, and now that I've passed on this information, I'll be able to sleep easier."

I held the phone to my ear long after Mrs. Panik had hung up, thinking about what she'd said. Then I pulled out my laptop and did something a thinking person would have done days ago: used a search engine to look up Andrea Vennard's obituary. It didn't take long, and a paragraph in, I found the name of the business Andrea had owned downstate: VM and Associates. Which didn't tell me much, so I looked that up, too.

"No kidding," I murmured, reading the screen. Andrea

and her business partner, Jayna Molina, owned a company that provided personal assistants and housekeeping staff. E-mail addresses were provided for the partners and key personnel, so I sent a short one to Jayna, telling her I was sorry about her partner's death, that I had been the one to find her, and that if there was anything I could do, to just call.

When the phone rang an hour later, Eddie and I had been about to turn in for the night. "Is this Minnie Hamilton?" a woman asked. "This is Jayna Molina. I wanted to thank you for your kind e-mail. It meant a lot to me."

"Oh. Sure." What, exactly, would Emily Post have recommended in a situation like this? Since I had no idea, I forged ahead on my own. "I'm sure Andrea's death was a shock."

"To all of us." Her voice was a little shaky. "The police told me they're doing everything they can to find her killer, but I thought I'd ask if you knew how that was going."

"They're working on it," I said, which was weak, but it was all I had. "They told me they were looking into her business. Was there anything you could tell them?"

"Nothing useful." She sighed. "Our clients are wealthy and they value their privacy. Everything we do for them is confidential. If we breached confidentiality, we wouldn't have their business any longer. Andrea knew that better than anyone."

"I'm sure she did." I thought a moment, then asked, "Did you have any new clients? Someone who might have wound up with the wrong idea about Andrea?"

"That's funny," Jayna said. "Your nice detective asked that, too."

Nice? Detective Inwood? That wasn't a descriptor I would have used.

"I can't divulge our client list," she was saying, "but I can say we had two new clients last month. One is a very nice lady who spends a lot of time in Europe, and I'm not sure Andrea ever talked to her outside of the time she called to hire us. The other is an elderly man who was an executive at one of the car companies. Andrea went out to meet him because he's not very mobile. She said he was very interesting."

"Oh?" I asked. "Did she say why?"

"Well, he collected books," she said. "Old and rare ones. She said his house was more library than house. But it was his cars that interested Andrea." Jayna had a smile in her voice as she talked about the Duesenbergs the man owned.

I listened and made the right noises in the right places, but I was quietly working the keyboard. A few links later, I was reading about the retired Ford Motor Company executive who had turned from collecting old cars to collecting books, and who had been the last person to purchase a copy of Chastain's *Wildflowers*.

I sat back. Finally, I'd established how Andrea could have learned about the value of her great-aunt's book.

But what was I going to do about it?

Chapter 15

The next morning, after kissing Eddie on the head and getting a sleepy "Mrr" in return, I stopped by the sheriff's office before heading to the library.

"Let me guess," the deputy in the front office said. "You're here to see Inwood or Wolverson."

I eyed him, not sure if he was trying to be funny, if he was trying to be a smart alec, or if he was merely being factual. "That's right," I said. "Is either one of them here?"

"You're that librarian, right? The one going out with Wolverson?"

It was only natural that Ash's coworkers knew whom he was dating. A little creepy, but natural in a small town. "Correct."

The guy's grim visage lightened, changing him from an intimidating uniformed officer you knew was carrying a handgun to a friendly neighborhood cop. "Okay, yeah. He's talked about you."

Even creepier. Sure, I talked about Ash to my coworkers, but that was different. They were library people. "He has?"

"Sure." The guy leaned forward, putting his elbows on the high counter. "He says he thinks you'll be doing buoys by August."

"I will?"

"Not with a short rope of course. That'll take a while. But as soon as you're up to speed, he'll take you through the course. Wolverson figures you'll take to it easy." He grinned.

Ah. Water-skiing. That's what he was talking about.

"Got a competitive streak in you, Wolfie said. Comes from being so short, I bet."

I smiled politely. "Sorry, but I have to get to work. Is either one of them here?"

"Nope." He shook his head. "Both out on calls. You want to leave a message or anything? I can get you into their voice mails."

"Even though I'm not very tall," I said, "I don't think I'll fit. But thank you." I told him to have a nice day and had my hand on the door handle when he started laughing.

"You won't fit," he said, chuckling. "That's a good one. No wonder Ash likes hanging around you."

Once I was out on the sidewalk and moving along, I pulled out my cell phone and scrolled through the phone list until I found Detective Hal Inwood. As the phone rang, I wondered if he was a Henry kind of a Hal, or if his given name was Hal. Of course, I'd never figured out how Hal had become a diminutive of Henry in the first place, same as Bill from William, or—

"This is Detective Inwood," said the recording.

I made a face and left a message, which, according to what I'd just heard, would be answered promptly, then called Ash. The same thing happened there.

I'd done what I could, so I went to work.

*   *   *

Late in the day, my cell, which I'd set in a prominent position on the corner of my desk, started vibrating.

I knew this because the papers that had accumulated on top of the phone started rustling and sliding and were in danger of descending to the floor.

Holding the papers with one hand, I pulled out the phone with the other and looked at the screen. Not Ash and not Detective Inwood. I thumbed it on. "Hey. What's up?"

"I need you."

"Of course you do," I told Kristen. "Why this time? No, wait. Let me guess. It's my soufflé expertise."

"Right. That's about as likely as you needing me to . . . to . . ."

"To come up with an appropriate analogy?"

She laughed. "What are you doing for dinner tonight? If you stop here after seven, I'll feed you."

"How about seven-oh-one?"

"Done deal."

We hung up, I put the cell phone on top of the papers this time, and went back to what I'd been doing.

After work, I walked home, changed into shorts and a T-shirt, and took Eddie out to the front deck for some fun in the sun. He enjoyed a game of Attack Minnie's Shoelaces When She Moves, but the wind came up— which, according to Eddie's glare, was my fault—and he wanted back inside.

"Sorry about that, pal," I told him, but he wasn't mollified until I gave him some treats. I watched him scarf down the tender morsels, and wondered if I'd accidentally created a very bad habit that I would never be able to erase.

As I let myself out, I tried not to think about a future that included a constant stream of "Mrr. Mrr. Mrr. Mrr," whenever Eddie wanted something, and instead tried to think about what I'd learned from Mrs. Panik. I still hadn't heard back from Ash or the detective, so I hadn't had the opportunity to hear them pooh-pooh my new theories.

"Hey, Minnie. You in there?"

I jumped and looked around. Rafe was on the steps of his front porch, along with Skeeter and a medium-sized cooler. Skeeter was a marina rat and couldn't have been much older than I was. Where his name had come from and what he did for a living that enabled him to spend every summer on a boat in Chilson, I had no idea. I'd always meant to ask, but somehow direct conversations with Skeeter were difficult. This made him an ideal companion for Rafe.

"What's up with you two?" I asked.

"Guess what's in here." Rafe slapped the top of the cooler. "Want to bet on it?"

"You've spent the day picking strawberries, and now you're about to start making jam."

The two men looked at each other. "How did she know?" Skeeter asked, his voice full of artificial wonder.

I rolled my eyes. "It's either beer or fresh fish."

"Nope." Rafe flipped back the cover and reached in with both hands. "It's both." He brandished a Miller Lite and what was probably a trout. "Want some?"

While it was tempting to say yes, just to see the look on his face, I shook my head. "Kristen asked me over for dinner. I'll see you guys later."

They called out dinner suggestions to my back until I couldn't hear them any longer. "Morons," I said to myself, but I was smiling.

And I was also early. I'd tried to time my walking pace to arrive at exactly one minute past seven, but something had gone wrong and I was a few minutes early. I didn't want to barge in on the end of the dinner rush, so I decided to extend my walk.

The homes in this area weren't large, but they were old and many had been in the same family for decades, DeKeyser style. I went back to thinking about the implications of Andrea Vennard being in the Friends' book-sale room the Saturday before her murder. Had she intentionally done so to look for the book? While in the sale room, had she discovered something that led her to—

"Hey, Minnie."

For the second time that night, I jumped and looked around. Over to my right, I saw Mitchell Koyne standing behind a running lawn mower. "Hey, yourself. Don't tell me you're working yet another job."

Mitchell turned off the mower and wiped his forehead with a handkerchief. "Nah. I'm just helping out." He shoved the damp cloth into his back pocket and put his baseball hat back on his head. "Mr. Wahlstrom doesn't get around as good as he used to, and I figured I could mow his lawn, at least."

"That's nice of you. Have you known Mr. Wahlstrom for a long time?"

"He was my third-grade teacher." Mitchell glanced at the house. "He gave me a prize at the end of the year. I never got a prize before, you know?"

Part of me wanted to ask the reason for the prize, but the rest of me didn't want to hear that it had been for good grammar. "He sounds like a good teacher."

Mitchell nodded. "Well, I'd better get back at it. See ya." He pulled the cord on the mower and it roared to life.

I slid out my cell phone, checked the time, and hopped up into a fast walk. When I walked in the back door of the Three Seasons, Kristen was standing there, arms crossed, and looking pointedly at the clock on the wall, which indicated clearly that it was three minutes past seven.

"Sorry," I said. "I got talking to Mitchell."

Kristen's blond eyebrows went up. "Mitchell Koyne's conversation is more interesting than my food?"

"I didn't know it was a competition."

"Everything's a competition. I thought you knew." She turned and studied her busy kitchen staff. "Okay, guys. If there are any problems, let me know before they happen, yes?" Half a dozen heads bobbed up and down. "Harve, you'll bring us a couple of specials when things slow down?"

"You bet, Kristen," he said, nodding.

We went down the hallway that led to her office. She plopped herself into the chair behind her desk, and I settled into the much nicer guest chair. "So, what's the problem?" I asked. "You said you need me?"

"Oh, yeah." She pulled out a drawer, pushed back, and put her feet up. "It's more that I have something to tell you."

My ears perked. "Scruffy proposed again, and this time you accepted." For the past three months, on a biweekly basis, he'd been asking her to marry him.

"As if." Kristen slid down in her chair and put her arms behind her head. "The first time he might actually be serious, I might consider it. But he's not, so I haven't, and won't until something changes."

"And what might that something be?" This was where things were going to get a little tricky. Scruffy had started texting me, asking what he could do to get

Kristen to take his proposals of marriage as a serious offer because he was, in fact, serious about marrying her. "It'll take some figuring," he'd said when I'd called him. "She has that restaurant, I have this job in New York, but we could make it happen. I know we could."

"You love her very much, don't you?" I'd asked.

"More than the morning sun," he'd said quietly, and I'd vowed then and there to help him in any way I could, because I knew how much Kristen loved him.

Now she shrugged. "How will I know when he's serious? I'll know it when it happens." She nodded at her computer. "What I needed you for was this. Take a look."

I squinted at the monitor. "Looks the same as always."

"No, you idiot. There's a video clip I want to show you. Here." She swung her feet to the floor, made some mouse clicks, and turned the monitor so I could see it. "Watch it and weep with me."

Curious, I hitched my chair forward. The blank screen dissolved into a moving image of sparkling lake waters. The camera was close in, then pulled back, and pulled back more to show the far side of a lake. I blinked. "Hey! That's—"

"Just wait," Kristen said morosely.

The camera panned Chilson's shoreline, then magically shifted off the water and onto the street, moving along at a pace slow enough to see everything, but not fast enough that it made me queasy.

Soon we were in front of the Three Seasons. Kristen and her staff were smiling and waving in a friendly manner. They stepped aside for the camera, and it came in through the front door and into the restaurant, where a smiling hostess stood with menus in hand.

The screen dissolved to black and I looked at Kristen. "And?"

"It's awful," she muttered, slumping down. "They'll add the sound later, but I don't see how it's going to help."

"Um . . ."

"Didn't you see?" she demanded. "There was gunk in the water next to the boat launch. There was dirt in the street gutters; I asked the city to sweep the streets before the filming, but did they? Oh no, we can't change the schedule for the sake of some little thing like a national cooking show. And I can't believe you didn't notice the dirt on that window of the restaurant, the little one above the stairway. This whole thing was a horrible idea, and I'm sorry I ever agreed to it."

Kristen had been right. She did need me.

"Play it again," I said, and watched it a second time. At the end, when I still hadn't seen any of the things she was obsessing about, I told her to play it a third time. And a fourth.

Finally, I sat back.

"You're absolutely right," I said. "There was one piece of debris in the water. A leaf, I'd say. There was a little bit of sand on the streets closest to the beach, and that window did indeed have a speck of dust in one corner."

"Told you."

I ignored her. "It also took me four times through to see that stuff, and that was when I was looking for it. Your average viewer isn't going to watch it more than once, and even then they won't be assuming that they're going to see the fantasy version of Chilson. The average person recognizes that lake water contains the occasional leaf, you know."

Kristen looked at me, a grin starting to quirk up one side of her mouth. "And that streets near beaches might have sand on them?"

"And that windows might have a speck of dust."

My friend's grin went wide. "See? This is why I needed you. You're the absolute best at making fun of me to my face without me knowing I'm being made fun of until it's too late."

In a convoluted way, I followed her sentence structure. "When will the show be ready?"

She shrugged. "I've decided not to ask for updates. It'll make me nuts."

"How self-aware of you."

"Yes, isn't it?" She twisted the monitor back. "But it's summer. I'm getting too busy to obsess about anything except running this place." She pointed to the kitchen. "Now that you've taken care of me, what can I do for you? I know you don't want any cooking pointers, but how about career advice? Romantic tips?" She waggled her eyebrows.

I thought a moment. Gossip was an unreliable source of information, but it often held a kernel of truth. "Have you heard anything about Kim and Bob Parmalee?"

"Why?"

"Her name came up, that's all."

"Right," Kristen said. "That sounds about as likely as me not obsessing about that video." She turned her hands palm up and made fluttery "talk to me" gestures with her fingers. "Talk, or I'll tell Harvey to wait on dinner until you do."

That was a cruel thing to threaten, but I knew she'd carry it out if pressed. And it wasn't like I wasn't going to tell her everything, anyway. "It had to do with Andrea Vennard's murder . . ."

We were done with the salad and halfway through the main course of seasoned pork tenderloin with mashed sweet potatoes and the last of the season's asparagus by the time I finished talking.

"So." Kristen, who had scooted her chair around to the small table Harvey had brought in with our food, pointed at me with her fork. "At this point, you have four suspects. Kim Parmalee. Jared, the used-book store guy. Paul Utley, the attorney. Shane Pratley, the angry guy. Anyone else?"

"Steve Guilder, the old boyfriend."

"And have you told Ash or your detective friend about this?"

I shook my head, first because it sounded just wrong to hear Detective Inwood spoken of as a friend, and second, because neither the detective nor Ash had returned my calls.

When I said as much to Kristen, she sighed and speared another piece of asparagus onto her fork. "The only thing I know about Kim and Bob Parmalee is that they haven't been in here since I opened for the summer and they used to be regulars."

I nodded thoughtfully. Eating out, especially eating out in a fancy restaurant, was the first thing to go when people had money troubles.

After a moment, our talk turned to other topics, but I couldn't shake the feeling that if I didn't find out something soon, Chastain's book—and the killer— were going to disappear forever.

* * *

The sun had dropped below the horizon by the time I left the restaurant, my tummy full of fine food and my face hurting from laughing so hard at Kristen's stories. How much was pure truth and how much was embellishment, I didn't know and wasn't sure I cared. Kristen wasn't one to let the truth get in the way of a good story, and her winter in Key West had given her a healthy supply.

In the gloaming, I walked along the waterfront, nodding to the occasional passerby, usually a hand-in-hand couple, and thought about what I'd told Kristen.

I'd tried to tell her everything I'd learned in the past couple of weeks, but there was bound to be something I'd forgotten. Kristen had a knack for distilling vast amounts of information down into a single sentence, and she'd done it again tonight, just as I was heading out the door.

"It's not about the book, you know," she'd said.

I'd squinted at her. We'd been talking about her dad, which was the reason we'd had to skip last week's written-in-stone Sunday-evening dessert. Her father was coming along nicely from a recent bypass surgery, but he was getting bored, and I'd been telling her about the books I'd drop off for him to read when she'd interrupted me.

"It's not?" I'd asked, cocking my head. She was wrong, of course. Books were the only thing that mattered.

"No," she said. "It's the value of the book. That wild-flower book."

"Well, sure." As in, "duh."

"What I'm saying," she said, a little exasperated, "is that not everyone puts the same value on things. That book, for instance. It had sentimental value to the DeKeysers and monetary value to whoever is trying to find it. But maybe somebody is attaching another kind of value to it, a kind that we're not thinking about yet."

Although I was sure the monetary value was the only thing that counted—because who couldn't use more money?—it was an interesting idea, and I said so.

"Yeah," Kristen said, already turning back to her kitchen. "That and two bucks will get me half a coffee at Starbucks. Harvey! Have you started the stock for tomorrow?"

But it was interesting, and it sent my thoughts back to the era when Robert Chastain had given away copy of his not-yet-famous book. In those days, the streets would have been dirt. There were no cars. No electric lights. No refrigeration.

And so it was, when the voice came out of the darkness, that my mind was both miles and years away.

"Hey, Minnie."

I jumped, gasping out a silent shriek. After my feet came back to the ground and my breaths returned to normal speed, Rafe said, "You know, if you started paying more attention to where you are and what you're doing, people saying hello won't scare the snot out of you."

Throughout my youth, my mother had told me much the same thing. Not that Rafe needed to know.

"Bet your mom used to tell you that," he said.

"She told me a lot of things," I replied. "Have you been sitting on your porch all night?"

"Far as you know, sure. What's up with Kristen?"

"She's nervous about being on Trock's TV show."

"Figures. She has about the least reason to be nervous as anyone in the history of that show."

True, but I wasn't going to discuss my best friend with Rafe, no matter that he'd known her longer than

I had. "I saw Mitchell Koyne tonight," I said. "He was mowing the lawn of his third-grade teacher."

"Yeah? Who was it?" Rafe opened the cooler that was still sitting on the same spot on the porch and peered in. "Want one?"

"Beer or fish?"

He flashed me a grin, his white smile brightening the darkness, Cheshire Cat–like. "Which one would you prefer?"

"Neither, but I wouldn't mind a water." I sat down next to him.

"There should be one in here somewhere," he said, rummaging around in the cooler. "Hah!" He held it out to me triumphantly. When I reached out, our hands touched and an odd shiver went over me. I put it down to the cold of the water bottle, but when I looked at Rafe's face I saw an expression I couldn't interpret. He'd felt the same chill, probably, and was getting ready to make a rude comment about my chilly personality.

"Mr. Wahlstrom," I said quickly. "That was Mitchell's teacher."

"Wally Wahlstrom," Rafe said, sipping at his beer. "Sure, I remember him. He looked about a hundred years old when we were in grade school, but he didn't retire until after I started teaching at the middle school."

"Mitchell said Mr. Wahlstrom had given him an award at the end of the year." I squinched my nose at the beery smell wafting down the steps. "He seems to have left a big impression on Mitchell. Whatever the award was, I bet Mitchell kept it for years."

I half closed my eyes and saw Mitchell's award. A certificate of some sort, framed by Mitchell's proud mother, for best speller. Or the fastest times-table reciter. His mom would have hung it on the wall in the living room, in a place of honor for everyone to see. What a nice thing for a kid. He would have been bursting with pride.

"Have to tell Wally next time I see him." Rafe laughed. "Bet he never thought his prizes were that memorable."

The young Mitchell of my imagination paused and looked back at me, his lower lip trembling. "What do you mean?"

"Wally gave every kid in his class a prize," Rafe said. "It was a ceremony, sort of, on the last day of school. Wally would call up the kids by name and hand out whatever it was he'd picked out. The kids loved it, but it's not like Wally spent a lot of money. He bought stuff at garage sales and thrift stores, everything from T-shirts to superhero juice cups to comic books."

My dream bubble popped so loudly I almost flinched. "So Mitchell's wasn't anything special."

"Special to him, maybe." Rafe drained the last of his beer and tossed it over his shoulder onto the porch, where it rolled around and hit a number of other empties. "With Mitchell, who knows?"

Who knew, indeed?

Speaking of things I didn't know, I remembered that I'd meant to ask Rafe about Cal DeKeyser's nickname. "Is there some guy named Deke that's famous in hockey?"

Rafe, who was in the act of opening the cooler, paused to look back at me. "What are you talking about?"

"Cal DeKeyser. I heard that people called him Deke, because of his last name and because he played a lot of hockey. Who's Deke?"

"So much learning," Rafe said, sighing and shaking

his head, "but so little knowledge where it really counts. Deke isn't a person, it's a technique. When you fake out a guy and skate around him, that's a deke."

"Weird word."

He shrugged. "They say it's short for decoy, but who knows? Most of us who worked at Benton's were calling Cal by his nickname within a couple of weeks."

"Did Steve Guilder ever work at Benton's?" I asked.

"Don't know for sure, but it's a good bet. That's where he and Andrea first hit it off, right after she and what's-his-name broke up."

"Which what's-his-name is that?" I asked idly, not really caring, though I was yet again astounded at the depth and breadth of Rafe's knowledge of Chilson gossip.

"That Paul what's-his-name. Attorney."

I sat up straight. "Paul Utley?"

"Yeah, that's the guy. Do you know him?"

"We've met," I said, my mind whirling in tiny circles. Andrea had probably known about the value of *Wildflowers* through a client. She had probably known about its existence because she was related to the family and been in and out of the house a hundred times as a kid. Paul, as the DeKeysers' attorney, might have known of the book's existence while making that inventory of the house he'd mentioned in Rianne's office.

So the question was, had Paul and Andrea still been in contact? Could she have told him about the book? Could they have been in cahoots to steal it and he had, instead, killed her?

Rafe leaned over and tapped my head. "What's going on in that curly-haired brain of yours?"

His hand lingered on my hair for a moment, and I felt that odd shiver again.

"You're always thinking," he said quietly. "That's one of the things I like best about you."

This time the shiver went deep into my bones.

Rafe cleared his throat and pulled away. "Of course, there are things I don't like about you, too."

The shiver vanished and was replaced by an uncomfortable feeling in my middle. Was it possible that I cared what Rafe thought about me? "Like what?" My question came out a little squeaky.

"Your taste in cars, for one," he said.

"I don't care about cars."

"Like I said."

I smiled into the dark.

"So, you going to tell me what you were thinking about?" he asked.

Too much, actually. Books and theft and murder, and now I was wondering if Andrea and Paul had been having an affair. Sighing, I got up and dusted off my behind. "Nothing much. I should get back and make sure Eddie hasn't figured out how to get into the microwave." The microwave was one of the few places truly safe from Eddie's reach, and was where I stored the bread.

"Want me to walk you home?" Rafe asked.

I squinted at him. "What would you do if I said yes?"

"Die of shock, probably." He grinned. "How about if I sit here and watch you walk over. If I see a suspicious character, I'll heave this at him." He held up his beer can.

"Sounds like a plan," I said. A stupid plan, but a plan nonetheless. "See you later."

When I reached the dock, I could see Eric standing on the end of his boat, casting a fishing line into the water.

"Catch anything?" I asked.

"Nah." He reeled his line in slowly. "Niswander over there was making so much noise that I swear he scared all the fish."

Either that or the lake bed in a marina wasn't the best fish habitat. "When I left for dinner, he and Skeeter were sitting on his front porch, looking like they were stuck there for the night."

"That would have been nice." Eric whipped his fishing rod back and cast out again with a long, slow ratcheting noise. "They spent the past two hours on their hands and knees, sanding that porch with hand sanders. Horribly whiny things. Sound like dentist drills."

I laughed. "Well, they're probably done now."

"Oh, it'll be something else tomorrow." He watched his bobber for a moment, then started reeling in again. "Is Niswander ever going to finish that place? Chris Ballou said he's been working on it for three years."

"Whatever you do," I said, "don't ask him. Do that and next thing you know, he'll dragoon you into helping. If he's sanding the porch now, painting will be next."

"Painting? Now, that's a job for a surgeon. With hands as steady as mine, you don't need any of that so-called painter's tape." He reeled in fast and clipped the hook to his fishing rod. He plopped his rod across the arms of a chair and stepped off the boat and onto the dock. "See you later, Minnie."

And he was off, headed in Rafe's direction. Thirty seconds later, I heard two male voices, and the *pop* of another beer can.

I shook my head and opened the houseboat's front door. "If you had thumbs," I asked my cat, "would you spend all evening on Rafe's porch, hanging out with the guys?" Not that Rafe had done that, technically, but he'd certainly given a fine imitation of a man who would eschew things that needed to be done for the sake of beer.

"Mrr," Eddie said, simultaneously yawning and stretching.

He was on the dashboard again, and I suspected he'd fallen asleep while watching the seagulls swoop around the marina.

"So, I was a little disappointed," I told Eddie, "learning the truth behind the story of Mitchell's award from his Mr. Wahlstrom. And I was also disappointed that Kristen didn't have any insight into who killed Andrea. I mean, the why is pretty clear—well, to me, anyway—but the who of it isn't coming."

I flopped myself onto the dining bench. "If someone killed Andrea to keep her away from Chastain's *Wildflowers*, hurt Pam while rifling through her store"—the thought made me jump off the bench and walk around the kitchen, fists clenched and jaw tight—"and is willing to set a library on fire and risk the entire building and everything in it, what else is that someone willing to do to get that book?"

Eddie looked straight at me and yawned again.

"Yes, I know I'm boring you." I stopped my pacing about and patted him between the ears. "But do you really have to make it so obvious that I'm not nearly as interesting as I think I am?"

"Mrr."

"Gotcha." What he'd said, I had no idea, but agreeing

with Eddie was usually the best course of action for both of us.

At that point, my furry friend thumped off the dashboard, pawed at the front door, and let himself out.

"Hey! Don't you dare—"

But he was already gone, out into the night.

"Rotten cat," I muttered, although it was my own fault for not making sure I'd shut the door tight behind me. I opened a kitchen drawer, snatched out a small flashlight, and headed after my furloughing feline. "Where are you, Eddie? Here, kitty, kitty!"

"Mrr."

He hadn't sounded far away, but sounds carried across water like nothing else. It wasn't unusual for us to hear a dog barking from the other side of Janay Lake, a mile and a half off. "Eddie?" I shone the flashlight over the front deck, picking out all his usual haunts. Not on the chair, not on the table, not behind the flower pot, not—

"Mrr."

I whipped around and spotlighted my cat. "Eddie! You get off Eric's boat this minute!"

Since he was a cat, he didn't pay attention to a word I said, but instead sat down on the boat's edge, a little sideways, and started licking his back paw. "Nice," I said, stepping onto the dock. "They say cats are elegant creatures. What happened to you? Oh, that's right. You're not exactly a cat, are you? You're a different species entirely. I'm almost sorry I had you fixed. I could have made all sorts of money putting you out for stud. Tens of dollars, I'm sure. Not all at once, but as a total, I can definitely see it."

My babble covered the noise of my soft footsteps, and as soon as I got close enough, I reached out and pulled Eddie into my arms.

"You are a horrible cat," I told the annoying animal, who was already purring. "Jumping over to the neighbor's, acting as if you belonged. You probably hoped Eric would be there, ready to hand out treats and—"

I stopped in the middle of the dock, my words forever lost.

Because I suddenly knew, flat-out knew, what had happened to the DeKeysers' copy of *Wildflowers*.

Chapter 16

The next morning, I wasn't so sure.

Yes, maybe Talia DeKeyser, in her last months of living in the family home, had given away a book about flowers to the little girl next door who had a penchant for picking the things, but what proof did I have?

None whatsoever.

And how seriously would Detective Inwood take this if I toddled down to the sheriff's office and insisted on talking to him face-to-face since he hadn't yet bothered to return my phone call?

Not at all.

Which meant that instead of turning my suspicions over to Inwood or Ash, who also hadn't called back, I flexed my research muscles—I am librarian, hear me type into a search engine!—and thanks to the parcel-search function on the county's Web site, within minutes, I'd tracked down the name and mailing address of the people who owned the property next to the DeKeysers.

"Nathan and Chandra Wunsch," I said out loud. The last name wasn't familiar and it was too early to call my local sources. It wasn't even eight o'clock; Kristen would be sleeping for another hour, as would Rafe, who slept deep and late the couple of weeks after school was done for the summer. It was tempting to call Rafe anyway, just to annoy him, but he'd be groggy and uncooperative, and any information he gave me would be suspect.

So I pulled the phone book out of the back of my bottom drawer and flipped through the flimsy pages. The names went from Wunderlich to Wyant, no Wunsch in sight. No landline, then.

I looked up and down the column of small print, hoping that maybe the phone book people had made an alphabetizing mistake, but saw nothing helpful.

After uttering a short curse, I tossed the book into the spot from whence it came. Lunch. I'd walk over to the Wunsches' house during lunch.

It didn't happen, of course. By the time I caught up on e-mails, the phone calls started, and by the time I finished with those, there were more e-mails to answer. Lunch came, and only the fact that Donna called back to ask if I wanted an order from the Round Table kept me from going hungry.

It was midafternoon by the time I'd taken care of the library's immediate needs. I got up, stretched, and, since it was in the neighborhood of the traditional three-o'clock break time, I grabbed my coffee mug and headed for the break room. Huddled together at the table were Holly, Josh, and Kelsey.

I was about to make a comment about an unholy triumvirate when Holly whirled around. "Oh, it's you," she said.

This was a little deflating, and I was about to say so, but Josh spoke first.

"If they hire a jerk, it'll be your fault."

I blinked at the fierceness of his tone. "'They' being who, exactly?"

Holly blew out an exasperated sigh. "The library board, doofus. If we end up with that Jennifer Walker as our boss, I'm dead meat. She hated me on sight—I could see it."

I frowned, not remembering if Jennifer had been the one Eddie had deposited his stomach contents onto, or if she'd been the one I hadn't met due to being out on the bookmobile. "What was Jennifer like?"

"She was wearing city clothes," Kelsey said. "All sleek and shiny."

The one who'd been Eddified.

Josh got up and started making a pot of decaf. "And if they hire Theodore, I'm giving my two weeks' notice. No way am I going to work for some guy who thinks he knows everything about IT. He was giving me pointers on how to store data on the cloud. Did I ask for advice? No. But he wanted to give it, so I had to listen."

My coworkers continued to vent their anxieties, ranging from Josh's concern that a new director wouldn't want to fund his full-time IT position, to Holly's fear that a new boss would move everybody to part-time, to Kelsey's worry that the most recent hires would be considered unnecessary.

As they talked, I recognized a common theme: all three were afraid of change. It was natural and to be expected, and it was why they'd wanted me to apply for the position. But change was inevitable, and they had to be prepared.

When I told them as much, I received a universally sour expression.

"Don't want to," Josh said.

"We wouldn't have to change if you'd applied," Holly added.

"Just think," Kelsey said morosely. "The next director might be worse than Stephen."

And with that encouraging sentiment ringing in my ears, I headed back to my office.

Hours later, I walked up the steps to the front porch of the house owned by Nathan and Chandra Wunsch. The porch floor's wooden boards had been replaced by composite, one of those materials that didn't have to be painted and wouldn't need to be replaced for a thousand years.

Rafe railed against the stuff being installed on period homes, saying it was nothing but plastic, that if you didn't have time to take care of real wood then you shouldn't buy a period house in the first place. He had a point, but he was so emphatic about it that I'd been compelled to poke at him with a sharp-ended conversational stick. "Okay, but don't people have the right to do what they want with their own house?"

"Not if what they want to do is stupid," he'd said.

This had sent us into a long debate about who got to decide what was stupid—Rafe saying that he should be the ultimate arbiter of any stupidity issue, me saying that no man who ever climbed an extension ladder carrying a sixteen-inch chainsaw should be able to judge someone's stupidity level—and we'd ended up playing rock, paper, scissors for the final decision. He'd tried to cheat, of course, by using the world-destroying-meteor option to win, something I'd banned from the game the year before, so we'd called it a draw.

Remembering all that, I was smiling when I used the lion's-head knocker to rap on the front door.

It opened immediately, and the little girl I'd seen playing in the garden a few nights before looked up at me. She pushed her long sandy blond hair back behind her ears and said, "I saw someone on the porch and my mommy told me to answer the door. She's in the kitchen stirring something."

"Macey?" her mother called. "Who is it?"

The girl squinted at me, then over her shoulder, yelled, "I'm not sure!"

It was so like what I would have done at her age that I almost laughed out loud. "Here," I said, digging into my backpack for a business card. "Take this to your mommy."

"Okay." Macey left me standing in the doorway and scampered back to the kitchen.

There was a murmur of voices, the rattle of pots and pans, and a woman a few years older than me, with hair even curlier than mine, came out of the kitchen and through the living room, drying her hands on a small towel as she walked. "Hi," she said. "I'm Chandra Wunsch. Sorry, but we don't get to the library much."

"Hi," I said. "And I'm sorry to barge in like this, but I have a quick nonlibrary question for you."

Macey appeared and tugged at her mother's elbow. "Mommy," she whispered. "I think this is Miss Minnie. She drives the bookmobile."

Chandra looked down at her daughter. "She does?" She looked back at me. "You do?"

I nodded. "Two or three times a week."

Macey tugged again. "She has a cat."

Her mother put an arm around her daughter's shoulders. "How nice. But the cat isn't on the bookmobile."

"Yes, it is," Macey said. "His name is Eddie and he makes a noise like this: mrr!"

The kid had it down. She must have been in the second-grade class that had toured the bookmobile a couple of months ago. It had been a fun afternoon, and I'd already decided to do it again in the fall with other elementary schools.

"The bookmobile has a cat?" Chandra looked at me questioningly, and I sketched out the story of Eddie and the bookmobile. "How fun," she said, laughing. "Almost makes me wish we lived outside of town so we could visit the bookmobile."

I told her the bookmobile's schedule was on the library's Web site and that we'd be happy to see them at any stop. "But I didn't stop by this evening on account of the library," I said. "This has to do with the DeKeysers."

Chandra glanced toward the DeKeyser's house. "Macey, honey," she said, "I need you to set the table."

"But, Mommy—"

"Now, please," Chandra said firmly. She bent to kiss the top of her daughter's head. "And I'll be checking to make sure you got it right."

"How long do I have?" Macey started walking backward.

Chandra looked at her watch. "Six and a half minutes."

Macey whirled and ran to the kitchen. "Ticktock, ticktock," she sang to herself. "Ticktock."

Her mother smiled after her, then faced me. "So. You're here about Deke and Talia? I was sorry to hear about Talia's passing, but . . ." She sighed.

I nodded, understanding exactly what she meant.

Death was always a loss, but when tied with a person whose memories had long since gone, the loss wasn't quite so bitter. "It's Talia I'm wondering about," I said. "In her last years, she'd given away many of her possessions, and I wondered if she'd happened to give anything to your family."

Chandra frowned. "The daughters put her in Lake View because of that, but if you ask me, Talia had every right to give her things away."

"Even if they were family heirlooms?" I asked. "Things that had been in the family for decades, handed down across the generations?"

"Well . . ." Chandra glanced around her, seeing an antique clock, a framed embroidery sampler, a brass umbrella stand, clearly remembering where they'd come from, who they'd come from, and who she was already intending to give them to when the time came.

"Specifically," I said, "what I'm wondering about is a book. I've been told there was a stack of children's books on the sideboard in their dining room. There was a book on wildflowers in there, too."

Chandra's frown cleared. "Oh, those!" She laughed. "Talia came over last fall and gave them to Macey. They sat on that table over there, but no one ever looked at them."

I glanced at the table, but it was bare of books. "Do you still have them?" I asked. The question came out as a creaky squeak.

"Gave them away," Chandra said, casually. "No point in keeping things around that you don't use, right?"

"Where did you take them?" My words came out so fast they almost ran into each other.

She shrugged. "I could see that some of them were old, so a few weeks ago I dropped them off at the museum."

* * *

I walked downtown, barely knowing where I was, and certainly not thinking about where I was going, because how could I think about that when I'd just been handed a wonderful answer?

The museum. Chastain's *Wildflowers* was in the museum. What a perfect place for it to be. How appropriate! Only, what was the best thing to do with the information? Should I tell the police? Tell the family?

Thinking, I paused in front of Pam Fazio's store. It was past closing time, but she was in the front window doing something creatively cool to the display. I knocked on the glass, and she pointed to the front door. "It's unlocked," she mouthed.

I poked my head inside. "Don't want to interrupt. I just wondered how you're doing."

"As good as can be expected." She adjusted the propeller of a large wooden model airplane and grimaced. "If I used my broken arm less, I'd be better off, but who has time?"

I nodded at the plane. "That's really cool. Where did it come from?"

"Walked in the door just last week," she said. "Closed on a deal for a bunch of fun stuff from . . . Oh, I think you saw me with Kim a while back at Cookie Tom's, standing in line like the rest of the unwashed masses while you sailed to the front."

I ignored the good-natured gibe. "Kim?" I asked.

"Kim Parmalee. She and Bob are selling off a slew of things," Pam said, studying the arrangement.

Yet more evidence that Kim not-a-DeKeyser-anymore Parmalee and her husband were in financial trouble. I murmured good-bye and was out on the sidewalk when things finally went *click* in my head. The woman I'd seen with Pam was the same woman I'd seen at the bookstore, which was the same woman I'd seen at City Park Grill, arguing with her husband, Bob, about a six-figure sum. The sale price of their house? The size of their debt?

I scuffed along the sidewalk, deep in thought. . . . And suddenly there was Ash's mother, Lindsey, closing the front door of a wine shop and turning my way. Tonight she wore a simple midnight blue sheath dress, low heels, and a golden necklace hammered thin and wide.

She looked stupendous.

For a short second, I was tempted to dash into whatever store was closest and hide until she passed by, but I shoved away the temptation and said, "Hi, Lindsey. How are you this evening?"

"Ah. Hello, Minnie." She gave me a quick up-and-down glance, taking in my plain pants, my sensible shoes, my uninteresting shirt, and equally uninteresting jacket. I saw, suddenly and clearly, that though my clothes were eminently suitable for life in the library, they were dead boring.

And, just like that, I went from being the intelligent, competent professional that I was ninety-nine percent of the time to a mumbling preadolescent who knew she would stay an ugly duckling the rest of her life and never come close to being as self-assured as the woman in front of me. "You . . . I–I mean . . . it's j-just . . ." I sighed and gave up.

Lindsey looked at me. Like I was a germ under a microscope. Or a specimen in a bottle of that stinky formaldehyde. I started to shrink, shoulders sagging, head bowing, but something in me reared up. Yes, Ash's mom was beautiful and capable and successful and tall, and I was just a short librarian, but that was no reason for her to look down on me.

I lifted my chin and met her gaze straight on. And, after a moment, she smiled.

"It's time for me to apologize," she said. "I should have realized what had happened and I am truly sorry I let this go on for so long."

At some point this conversation would start making sense. "Let what go on?"

"When Ash introduced us at the Round Table, I could tell you were nervous about meeting me. I should have been more understanding. Instead, I went all proper and uptight and made you even more anxious."

"Well," I said, "I have to confess that I didn't expect Ash's mom to look like she stepped out of a Nordstrom catalog."

Lindsey laughed. "It's a hard thing, being a woman, isn't it? We want to look good, but when we succeed, we can end up intimidating more than impressing."

"You were trying to impress me?" My eyes went wide.

"Good heavens, of course I was. Ash has talked about you for weeks. I couldn't possibly meet you wearing old jeans and a T-shirt."

"Wow. I had no idea."

"How could you? And then Ash was called away and we were left with each other, and I still felt the need to make a good impression. Which was when you started tripping over your words."

I thought back. "I did, didn't I? It's something I do when I'm . . ." I grinned. "When I'm nervous."

She nodded. "You weren't making fun of Ash; you were simply nervous."

"Making fun?" I stared at her, aghast. "No! Of course not!" No wonder she'd frozen me out—she'd thought I was mocking her son, who had had a severe stutter as a kid. "I'd never do a thing like that."

"I know that now," she said. "And that's why I'm apologizing." She stuck out her hand. "Friends?"

Smiling, I shook. "Friends." After the ritual was complete, I asked, "What are you doing in Chilson this fine evening?"

"Working." She made a face. "You'd have thought financial consultants wouldn't need to make house calls."

"Someone win the lottery?"

Lindsey started to say something, then changed it to, "Everyone's financial situation is different."

Which was a lot like what Tolstoy had written in *Anna Karenina*. "'All happy families are alike,'" I quoted. "'Each unhappy family is unhappy in its own way.'"

Lindsey's eyebrows went up. "That's what Monica said, not ten minutes ago."

"Monica?" My brain twitched. It was a Monica Utley who'd switched her stint in the book-sale room with Andrea right before she'd been killed. "Is this the same Monica who volunteers at the library?"

"I couldn't say." Lindsey looked at her watch. "And I'm sorry to interrupt our chat, but there's a roast in the slow cooker at home that's going to be overdone if I don't get there soon. Have a good night, Minnie."

She turned away and I reached into my backpack for my phone. "Aunt Frances? Quick question: Do you know Monica Utley?"

"Not very well," my aunt said. "She grew up downstate. Met her husband in college—he's from Chilson—and they moved up here after they got married."

"What's her husband's name?" I was gripping the phone so tight that my hand hurt. "Do you know?"

"Paul. He's a lawyer."

"Do you happen to know where they live?"

"In that big pale yellow house a block or so from downtown. At least they do for now," she said wryly. "I hear they're having troubles of some sort. Why?"

"Thanks," I said, and thumbed off the phone as a car with tinted windows drove past.

Slowly.

The skin at the back of my neck prickled unpleasantly. Was someone following me?

"Don't be stupid," I told myself, but all the way home, I kept looking over my shoulder to make sure I was alone.

Chapter 17

As far as I was concerned, the answer to the why of Andrea Vennard's death had been answered days ago; she and someone else had been looking for *Wildflowers*, only that someone else had been willing to kill for the sake of an expensive book.

Now I knew who that someone was.

Well, maybe.

Angry Guy Shane Pratley was still a possibility, as was Jared Moyle, the guy who owned the used-book store, and Kim and Bob Parmalee, but things were lining up that Paul Utley was the guy. Or Monica Utley. Or both of them. Because if they were in financial trouble, wouldn't they both be scrambling to find an answer to their problem? And why else would someone be talking to a financial consultant on a Friday night?

I waited until I got back to the dubious privacy of the houseboat to call Ash. No sense in people on the street overhearing what I suspected. Because all I had were suspicions. I had no real evidence and no real proof. Ash and Detective Inwood would have to come up with those. Unfortunately, I'd recently received a text from Ash that they'd both just left for a long weekend of law-enforcement training. But, hey, what were cell phones for if not to interrupt people?

"Hi, this is Ash."

"Hey," I said, "I know you're at that training—"

"I can't talk right now," his recorded voice said, "but I'll call you back when I can. Thanks."

I growled into the phone. When the beep came, I gave him my information about Paul and Monica Utley, that Paul had learned about *Wildflowers* through his role as attorney for the DeKeysers' estate, that Paul and Andrea had known each other from high school, and that Paul could have learned about the value of the book through Andrea, so it might be a good idea to check to see if any of her phone calls had been to him. Or if they'd had any other contact. Or something.

When I was done rambling, I said, "Okay, um, that's about it. Give me a call when you have a minute, okay?"

"Mrr."

I looked down at Eddie. "What do you think? Should I call the sheriff, too?"

My cat put his head down and whacked my shin. It didn't help my decision-making process, but it did encourage me pick him up for a snuggle. "How about if I e-mail the sheriff?" I asked. "She might not check her e-mail until Monday, but this can wait that long." Eddie didn't disagree with me, so I set him onto the dining bench while I did some tapping on my phone.

It didn't take long to find Sheriff Richardson's e-mail address—it was on the county's Web site—and I sent her a note that replicated the voice mail I'd left for Ash. "There," I told Eddie as I hit the Send button. "I've done what I can, and the rest will be up to the law-enforcement professionals. Want to go to the Friday marina party with me?"

"Mrr?" He jumped on my backpack and scratched at the opening until he'd managed to get himself inside.

"A backpack is not a cat toy," I said, pulling him away. This was a little mean of me, because I'd watched him strain with the effort to get in and not done a thing to either help or hinder him, but I tamped down my guilt with the knowledge that he'd be sleeping on my head later that night.

"Mrrrr."

I could hear Eddie latching on to something inside the backpack. I reached out and detached his front claws from whatever it was that he was sinking them into. "Don't ruin my stuff, okay? Some of those things aren't even mine, you know, and it wouldn't look good for me to return books to the library with cat-claw marks in them."

Eddie wriggled out of my grasp, gave me a dirty look, and jumped down. He stalked across the kitchen floor, thumped down the steps, stamped across the bedroom, and launched himself up onto the bed.

"Whatever," I muttered. There were, in fact, two library books inside the pack, and I pulled them out. One looked intact and, after wiping off what might have been a small amount of Eddie spit, I started to slide the other book back inside. This one was nonfiction, with the cover a painting of a single pink rose. Though I'd never admit it to anyone, I'd checked out the book solely for the beauty of its cover art. You should never judge a book by its cover, of course, but it sure could give a hint about—

"Oh," I said out loud. "I am so stupid. I forgot all about calling Amelia."

"Mrr," Eddie called from the bedroom.

I dug out my phone and scrolled down toward the end of the alphabet. "Ha," I said. "Thought she was in there." I stabbed at the button and waited for the phone to ring on the other end.

Amelia Singer had grown up in Chilson, moved downstate to attend college, worked as a teacher, married, had two children, worked as a school principal, divorced, worked as a school superintendent, and had recently retired and moved back to the town of her youth. She'd cast around for something to do and, when the museum director said he'd had enough after eleven years, which was one year too many by most accounts, she'd stepped in with both feet.

"Hi," I said, when she answered. "Minnie Hamilton. How are you?"

"Minnie!" Amelia boomed. She did a lot of that, and I had yet to figure out if she'd always talked that way or if it was a natural result of her career choices. "Couldn't be better if I were twins," she said. "How are you?"

One of the first things Amelia had committed to doing was a faster processing of the multitude of donations that poured in. Not once had she said she'd bitten off more than she could chew, but I'd caught her looking at the vast pile of boxes with more than a small amount of loathing. Still, if anyone could turn the Chilson Historical Museum from a dusty, slightly musty, and ill-lit warehouse of castoffs from the town's attics into a showpiece, it was Amelia.

I pictured her, my height but about twice my weight, her long reddish brown hair rolled up into a bun, her active mind whirring along at a hundred miles an hour. "Got a question," I said. "How caught up are you with the donations?"

"Humor is the last refuge of the scoundrel," she misquoted darkly. "And if you ever remind me that I'd vowed to organize this place by the end of my first year as director, I will never speak to you again."

Laughing, I said, "I would never do that. I value your advice too much."

"Advice?" She sighed audibly. "If I'd listened to my friends, I would never have become director of the museum. Why is it that we refuse to accept the experience of others?"

"Because we think we're going to be different."

"Why are we so often so wrong?"

"It's a survival mechanism. If we were completely honest about our chances at completing any given task, we'd never get out of bed in the morning."

Her laugh was deep and contagious. "How did you get to be so smart at such a young age?"

"It's not me. It's Alexandre Dumas, Elizabeth Goudge, and Charles Dickens."

"Elizabeth Goudge," Amelia mused. "Sad that so few people have heard of her these days."

I was doing my best to take care of that, but I didn't want to get too far off topic. Amelia and I could talk books for hours—we'd met at the library when she'd come in to get a library card—but I had a question for her. "Have you had many books donated lately?"

"You are a cruel, cruel woman," Amelia said.

I smiled. "Not intentionally, honest. I take it you've had a few?"

"Tens of boxes. Hundreds of boxes. Thousands of boxes. Millions of boxes. And none of them are going to St. Ives or anywhere, because they're all in the museum basement." She sighed again. "I would love to look through them. I crave to look through them, but all I have time right now to do is open the flaps every so often and gaze at the contents longingly."

The decision about what to do with my knowledge of the likely whereabouts of *Wildflowers* gelled into action. If anyone from the sheriff's office called back soon, I'd pass the information on to them, but I couldn't tell the family, not when parts of the family were suspects. Which left me, a librarian to the core, with only one possible course of action.

"Amelia," I said, "I have a favor to ask . . ."

The next day dawned hot and humid. I debated leaving Eddie at home to nap the day away in the comfort of the cooler lakeside air, but he parked himself on the top of cat carrier and stared at me, unblinking, and it was easier to bring him along than to argue with him.

"Good thing I don't have children," I said, lugging the Eddie-filled carrier out to my car. "I'm a pushover. They'd be spoiled rotten kids with no manners and a huge sense of entitlement."

"Mrr."

"You're right." I opened the car door, set the carrier inside, and buckled it in. "Cats are different from kids. There'd be no teaching you table manners."

Eddie opened his mouth to object, but I shut the door, for once getting in the last word.

Julia and Eddie and I spent the day trying to find the deepest shade in every parking lot where we were scheduled to stop. Worst was the asphalt lot of a newly constructed township hall whose only shade came from a spindly sapling that looked as if it could use a good watering. Best was the gravel lot of a rural church whose maple trees cast enough shade to cover the entire bookmobile.

Even still, it was a long, hot, sweaty day, and the three of us were glad to return to Chilson, where the ice-cream cones we'd been talking about all afternoon awaited.

I started my car and cranked the air-conditioning while Julia and I lugged crates of books into the library. By the time we were done, my car was cool enough to move Eddie from the bookmobile.

"See you on Tuesday," Julia said, and, for the first time since I'd met her, she looked limp and exhausted and every one of her sixty-some years.

"Double scoop," I recommended. "Mint chip."

She shook her head. "Waffle cone of Mackinac Island fudge." Then she grinned. "With a vodka martini chaser."

The thought of drinking a martini made the inside of my throat go dry as overcooked toast. "I'd rather—" But before I could note my preference for a glass of chilled white wine, my cell phone rang. I pulled it out of my pocket. Amelia Singer, the museum director.

"See you Tuesday," Julia said, waving, and off she went.

I thumbed on the phone. "Hey, Amelia."

"Minnie, I'm so glad you answered."

Amelia's usually expansive voice was tight.

"What's the matter?" I asked. "Are you okay?"

"Me?" She forced a chuckle. "Fine as cotton candy. It's my granddaughter that's the trouble. The thirteen-year-old. She was out skateboarding with friends, tried a fancy somersault, and didn't quite make it all the way around."

My breath caught as I imagined the scene. "How badly was she hurt? Is she okay?"

"No, no she's not." The words were spoken through

sniffles. "Long-term she should be fine—her mother won't let her go to the skate park unless she wears protective equipment—but she broke her femur."

"Oh no." I touched my thigh. "Does she need surgery?"

Amelia sniffed again. "They're waiting for some fancy-pants orthopedic surgeon to get off the golf course and into the hospital."

"Are you on your way downstate?" I asked.

"No, my daughter just called." *Sniff.* "I had to talk to you first. We'd set up tonight for you to stop by the museum to look for your books."

She was worried about me? "Amelia," I said, "go home and pack. This can wait."

"But you said—"

I'd told her the book that might have been donated to the museum might be related to the murder of Andrea Vennard, but none of that mattered when a granddaughter was in the hospital. "It can wait," I repeated.

"Can you come down right now?" Amelia asked. "I'm still at the museum. I'm locking up, but I can wait until you get here."

I glanced at my car. "We'll be there in two minutes."

Five minutes later, I was walking down the creaky stairs to the museum's basement. Amelia had asked if I was familiar with the museum's layout—I was, thanks to time spent volunteering the summer after my high school graduation—and she'd asked me to cross my heart and hope to die if I didn't make sure everything was locked up tight when I left.

When I'd done the crossing and the hoping, she'd given me a long look, full of fear and anxiety. I'd set the cat carrier on the floor and given her a hug. "It'll be okay," I'd said. "They'll take great care of her, and she'll be up and around in no time."

Amelia had returned the hug, muttering, "That's what I'm afraid of."

I couldn't help it; I'd laughed, and, after a moment, Amelia had actually smiled.

Now it was just me and Eddie in the museum, a building that had originally housed a dry goods store. When the owner had moved to Traverse City, about seventy years ago, a hardware store had taken its place. That had gone out of business when the owner had passed away, and a pharmacy had come in next. The pharmacy had lasted until its history-buff owner had retired, and he'd sold it to the museum for far less than it could have brought on the open market.

It was a lovely building. Upstairs were wooden floorboards, hand-plastered walls, and oak trim, but downstairs was a cavernous basement that, for reasons now lost in the mists of time, had a nine-foot ceiling.

"There could be lots of reasons," I told Eddie, hefting the carrier onto a handy chair. "Some people say this building is where the first-ever city council meetings were held. And while that might be true, that doesn't explain why the basement was built so big in the first place."

"Mrr."

"Well, sure, it's possible that the first owner wanted a massive basement for his cats to play around in, but how likely is that, really?"

"Mrr!"

I considered the current Eddie situation. If Chastain's book happened to be in the first box I opened, we'd be out of here in a flash. If it was in the last box I opened, we'd be here for days. The most probable reality was that we'd be here somewhere between those two possibilities. Hours, anyway.

"Promise to come when you're called?" I peered into the carrier through the wire door. Not that he ever had in the past, but maybe today would be different.

"Mrr," he said quietly.

"Okay, then." I unlatched the door and let Eddie roam free. "The door to upstairs is closed," I told him, "so all you can do is wander around down here. And don't even think of asking if you can go up, because you can't. There are too many exhibits that aren't cat toys." A bear rug for one, a native American headdress for another. And then there were the lace dresses, the carved pew from Chilson's first church, and the dugout canoe. "Claw marks in any of that stuff wouldn't be good."

"Mrr." Eddie leaped out of the carrier and onto the concrete floor.

"I agree with you, pal," I said, blatantly lying. "Claw marks make everything look better. It's just some of that stuff hasn't had any claw marks in it for a hundred years or more, and Amelia prefers it that way."

As I talked, I studied the boxes that were strewn about. Some were labeled; some were not. Some were taped shut; some were not. There were boxes on chairs, boxes on tables, boxes on shelves, boxes in the maze of storerooms that some said had once housed alcohol during the Prohibition years.

I turned around in a small circle, trying to make sense of the arrangement. Amelia had started to explain the sorting system, but I'd shooed her out the door, telling her that I'd figure it out. And I would.

Eventually.

"How about this one?" I asked, but Eddie was nowhere to be seen. When he wanted to, he could make himself smaller than a cat hair–covered washcloth. So, without Eddie's assistance, I flapped open the first box and peered in.

I hadn't honestly expected to find *Wildflowers* in the first box, but when I saw a collection of linens, I was still disappointed. "Rats," I said, after reaching inside and making sure there were no books tucked into the folds of aprons and tea towels. "So much for serendipity."

I put my hands on my hips and looked around. "It would have been helpful," I told my invisible cat, "if the date of the donation had been written on the box." Amelia had said they kept a log of the donations, who they were from, general contents, dates, and so on, but they hadn't written any of that nice data on the boxes, since the moment the donations were taken out of the box, it didn't matter.

This made sense, but it wasn't very helpful for someone like me, who was looking for something larger than a needle in something that was bigger than a haystack. Then again . . .

"How big is a haystack, exactly?" I asked.

Eddie didn't answer, of course. I was tempted to whip out my phone and ask my favorite search engine the question, but no. I was here to find a book. A very valuable book. A book that someone had been killed over.

I rubbed my arms, trying to smooth down the goose pimples. "It's chilly down here. Good thing you have a fur coat, Eddie."

"Mrr," came the muffled noise.

And I started opening boxes.

A while later, I was tired of opening boxes. The day had been long and hot, and I was tired and hungry and in need of a shower. "Can we go home now?"

Eddie had climbed onto a set of shelving in a back room and fit himself between the top box and the ceiling. "Mrr."

I sighed. "You're right. This is important, and I shouldn't give up so easily."

"Mrr," he said, and started purring.

"Easy for you to say," I said, but I went back to the boxes and, as I should have expected, I grew fascinated with things I was finding. It didn't take long, and I soon lost track of time, forgetting about food and water and sleep and even ice cream.

"Look at this!" I held out a framed photo so Eddie could see. "It's Abraham Lincoln—I'm sure of it!" The image was a crowd scene, but President Lincoln was front and center, stovepipe hat and all. "I wonder where it was taken?" I looked closely but couldn't see any identifiers in the photo. "But that guy sitting next to him looks familiar, doesn't he? If I could figure out who he is, I might be able to figure out when and where this was taken and—"

"Mrr!"

I sighed. He was right. We were here to look for *Wildflowers*. President Lincoln had waited this long; he could wait a little longer.

"Don't you get tired of being right all the time?" I asked, reaching for the 1974 newspaper in which the photo had been wrapped. "I mean, being perfect must be exhausting. No wonder you sleep so much."

I cocked my head, waiting for his response.

Thud.

I frowned in the direction of the noise I'd just heard, which had sounded a lot like someone stepping onto the bottom creaky step. Amelia had said she'd lock the doors, that I just had to let myself out the side door, which would lock behind me. I hadn't bothered to make sure she'd locked up, and given her state of anxiety, I now realized I should have.

"Hello?" I called out. "The museum is closed." I carefully set Lincoln back into his box and headed for the storeroom's narrow door. "Sorry, but the door must have—"

There was a small *click*.

The basement went black.

I stopped. If given a few minutes, I might be able to think of a dozen reasons why all the lights had suddenly gone out. A power outage, for one.

But combined with that footstep, there was only one reason; whoever was after *Wildflowers* had figured out what I was doing and had followed me.

"This is so not good," I whispered to myself.

Because I was now alone with Andrea's killer.

In the basement of an empty building.

Chapter 18

I edged backward, deeper into the dark, trying to get as far away from the killer as possible, but stopped almost immediately, because the stupidity of that particular action was apparent even to me.

Retreat to a smaller space? One that had a single door and zero windows? Only the dumbest potential victim in the lowest-budget movie would do something like that, and, since I liked to think of myself as smart and resourceful, now would be a good time for that to actually be true.

"You can come out now, Minnie," said a male voice. "I know you're in there."

My last hope, that I'd been mistaken about the killer being in here with me and that the museum's electricity had been shut off because someone had neglected to pay the electric bill, fizzled away into nothing.

"Who else is down here?" he asked. "I know you're not alone; I heard you talking to someone."

Eddie, in a bizarre act of appropriate behavior, remained quiet.

So did I.

"There's no point in hiding." A flashlight beam started dancing around the room. I moved quickly and quietly, and crouched behind a stack of boxes.

What I needed was a plan, and I needed it fast. Ten minutes ago would have been best, so that Eddie and I could have left the basement before the killer even arrived, the killer being . . . who? Shane, aka Angry Guy? Paul Utley? Jared, the used-book store guy? Steve Guilder? Bob Parmalee? Of the five, I hadn't even met Bob, and I didn't know the other four well enough to recognize their voices.

"Come on, Minnie, there's no need to be scared."

If I hadn't been so scared, I would have snorted derisively. No one who barges into a closed museum, tiptoes down to the basement, and turns the lights off on the unsuspecting occupants of said basement had good intentions.

"All I want to do is talk."

And all I wanted was to get out of that basement, cat in hand, but I didn't say so out loud.

The flashlight's beam played over the stacks of boxes, sending long, complicated shadows around the room as it went. "I hear," he said, "that you've figured out that Chastain's *Wildflowers* is down here somewhere." He sighed. "All these boxes! I hope I gave you enough time to find the book. The last thing I want to do is spend my Saturday night digging through a bunch of old dusty crap that should have been thrown away generations ago."

The cone of light came to an abrupt halt. "For crying out loud. Would you look at that? It's one of those hair wreaths. What did some woman do, cut off all her hair to make this thing? Must have taken weeks to make something this complicated, but at the end of the day, it's just creepy to have some dead chick's hair hanging on your wall, don't you think?"

I wanted to ask him if he thought the DeKeysers should have thrown away *Wildflowers* a generation or two back, but managed to keep my mouth shut. He was trying to get me to talk, and I wasn't going to play his game.

Think, I told myself. *Figure this out. Come up with a plan A, have a plan B for backup, then start working on implementation. Shouldn't be that hard.*

In theory.

"Why on earth do people hang on to old crap like this?" The flashlight played over a box I'd opened early on. I saw a hand reach down to flip through the contents. "And then donate it to a museum?" He made a rude noise. "You must have some kind of ego if you think strangers would be interested in your old family photos."

Clearly, the man had no sense of history. I continued to keep my mouth shut and silently vowed one more time to keep *Wildflowers* from this guy. Not that I'd found the book yet, but that wasn't the point.

"So, where is it?" he asked. "You've been down here for hours—you must have found it by now. And I must say, I'm pleased you never noticed me following you the past week. I kept hearing you were asking all sorts of questions. I didn't worry too much about that, but once I found out you're dating Ash Wolverson, I had to make sure you didn't cause me any trouble." He laughed. "On the contrary, I'd say you led me straight to the book."

He moved around the room, but slow enough that I was able to back away, undetected, by hiding behind boxes, old countertops from the pharmacy, and old shelving units from the hardware store. Once again, being under-tall was working to my advantage, since it didn't take much to hide me. Hooray for getting the short end of the genetic stick!

Short end?

My inane thought was suddenly so funny I almost laughed out loud. I slapped my hand over my mouth to keep my nervous laughter inside, and the small noise must have alerted him.

"Heard that," he said casually. His flashlight speared the darkness, and I tried to make myself smaller than I'd been since I was twelve years old. "Look," he said. "We both know you're down here, so why are you bothering to hide?"

I figured the answer to that was obvious, so this time it was easy to keep my mouth shut.

"Come on, Minnie," he said. "All I want is that book. Sure, it was donated to the museum, but they don't even know what they have, so clearly they don't deserve it. We're the only ones who know the value of Chastain's book, so let's talk about this."

I watched the flashlight shift away from me. If I ran now, he wouldn't see the movement. The open stairway was about fifteen feet to my left and it was . . . too far. He was bigger, faster, and stronger than I was, and he'd be on me before I got three steps up the stairs. I had to get closer before I ran.

A lot closer.

Slowly, so very slowly, I stood and wedged myself behind a set of freestanding shelves; old wooden ones with a solid back. If I could inch behind it all the way to the other end, I'd be close enough to the stairs to make a run for it.

"So, here's the deal," my enemy said. "Let's work on

two assumptions. One, that the book is here. Two, that we both want the money it will bring if we sell it to the right person."

I almost yelled at him then and there. Any money the book might bring didn't belong to him and it didn't belong to me. It belonged to . . . well, I wasn't sure who it belonged to, considering that Talia DeKeyser had given it away while in the grips of Alzheimer's, that Chandra Wunsch had given it away without knowing what she had, and that the museum hadn't a clue about its value, but that was for the attorneys to figure out.

And speaking of attorneys, the more this guy talked, the more I was sure it was Paul Utley. Angry Guy Shane didn't have this guy's vocabulary, and, if my first impressions of Jared were anywhere close to being accurate, he didn't have this kind of intensity. Then again, I didn't know anything about Bob Parmalee and hardly anything about Steve Guilder.

"Let's talk about a sixty-forty split," he said. "Sixty percent for me, forty for you. Now, you might think a fifty-fifty split would be fair, or even sixty-forty to your benefit, but let's look at the facts."

This guy was definitely an attorney. It wasn't possible that any other variety of human would talk that way.

"Yes," Paul said, "you've found the book, or at least its approximate location, but would you have even known it existed without the inciting incidents that came before? Incidents that were the result of my knowledge? And Andrea's?"

He had a point, but it didn't matter. "Moron," I whispered. If he thought a true librarian could possibly steal a valuable book, he could think anything.

Paul sighed audibly. "This is getting old."

I edged farther along the back of the wooden shelves,

stabbing myself with tiny bits of raw wood in the process, hoping that none of them were big enough to catch me tight. I had to get to the other end. There was no other choice.

"I'm stronger than you," he said, "faster than you, and I'm certainly a lot bigger than you. There's no way this will be a fair fight, which is the way we lawyers prefer things." He laughed. "So, I ask you: Why are you making this so difficult? I asked Andrea the same the same thing, and look what I had to do to her." He laughed again. "I even had to pretend to love her all over again, for crying out loud."

His words sent my blood pressure soaring. If there was one thing I hated more than people turning down the corners of pages in library books, it was condescension, and this guy reeked of it.

"Come out, Minnie," Paul said, "and let's discuss this like reasonable adults. After all, nothing has happened yet, correct? I haven't done a thing except frighten you, and that was pure accident."

It was?

I sidled sideways a little bit more. The end of the shelves were close now. If I leaned to the left, maybe I could see where Paul was and what he was doing. After all, maybe he did just want to talk. Maybe I'd jumped to a conclusion that I'd laugh about later. Maybe my instincts had been wrong.

Moving slowly, carefully, and quietly, and always, always watching the path of the flashlight's beam, I eased left.

"An accident." Paul was crouching low, sending the cone of light around the room, looking for . . . what? My feet? "You understand that, right? Why would I want to scare you? Come on out, and we'll talk about how to deal with the book."

His lawyer's voice was soothing and monotonous and almost sirenlike. Happily, a short stint as a tele-marketer when I was desperate for cash in college had endowed me with a permanent immunity to sales pitches, and there was no doubt Paul was trying to sell me something.

Groaning, he put his hands on his knees to help push himself upright. As he did, the flashlight dropped out of his hand and clattered to the floor. He cursed and leaned down to pick it up.

But it was too late. When the flashlight had fallen and hit the floor, it had spun around and illuminated what he held in his other hand.

Illuminated the long, shiny, and very sharp-looking knife he was holding with a strong grip.

If there was ever a time to launch Plan A, it was now.

I braced my back against the wall, wedged my knees tight, placed my hands flat against the shelving. And pushed.

Creak!

Paul Utley whirled around, but since I was behind the shelving, there was nothing for him to see.

Though I was pushing for all I was worth, the freak-ishly heavy thing didn't tip over. It swayed a little, though, and I moved instantly into Plan A-1, because I hadn't spent the last four winters in northwest lower Michigan without learning something about how to get my car out of a ditch. The key was to rock it.

Push, release. Push, release. Push . . .

With each cycle, the arc of movement grew wider and faster.

Utley's flashlight danced around the room, but too fast to catch the slow action of the shelves.

C'mon, I urged it. *Tip!*

Push, release. Push, release. Push . . .

Paul's flashlight finally touched on the movement. "What the—"

It toppled over in superslow motion. I heard the boxes on the crowded shelves start to slide forward, heard one thud to the floor, heard Utley shout, and then finally, at long last . . .

Crash!

I didn't wait to hear any more. I was scrambling for the stairs, tripping over boxes, hurling myself forward, trying to get away from that long, shiny, deadly knife. My cell phone was in the back room, but it was only a couple of blocks to city police station. If I ran fast, I could have someone back here in less than—

"It's a freaking cat!" Paul Utley said.

I stopped dead.

"Hey," he said, loudly, "I bet this is that bookmobile cat everyone talks about. What's your name, kitty?"

"Mrr."

"Here, kitty, kitty, kitty."

Now Eddie decided to be Mr. Friendly? *Now?*

But maybe he'd see through Utley's fake friendliness. Maybe cats really did have some of the traits ascribed to dogs. Maybe Eddie would sense Utley's underlying intentions, claw the back of his hand, make him drop the knife, pick up the knife in his teeth, and scamper away with it, and I'd take it in my handkerchief to preserve the fingerprints and—

And that's where my fast-forwarding fantasy came to a screeching halt. I'd never carried a handkerchief in my life.

My hand was on the front doorknob. Outside it was full dark; more time had passed than I realized. The sidewalks were empty of life, and the only car in sight was parked at the far end of the street. I pushed open the door and squinted, trying to see the time on the freestanding clock at the corner.

"That's a good kitty," Utley said.

My cat's purrs were loud enough so that I could hear them from the top of the stairs.

"Just a little closer . . . No, come on now, just a few feet more . . ."

A few feet more and Utley would grab Eddie, my fuzzy friend, my pal, my napping buddy. He'd put that long knife to my cat's white throat and use him as a hostage. Eddie would hiss and howl and claw and scratch, but Utley wouldn't care, because he needed that book and he needed me to keep quiet about it and about him.

Time for Plan B.

Which was unfortunate, because I hadn't had time to formulate more than a rough draft.

I scanned the sidewalk one more time, hoping against hope that I'd see someone coming, someone who could help us, someone who would instantly respond to a shriek for help.

But there was no one.

"Come here, you stupid cat!"

"Mrrrr-RRR!!" Eddie growled and hissed and spat.

I turned and ran pell-mell back down the stairs.

Chapter 19

I screwed my eyes shut and slapped at the light switch. "Leave him alone!" I shouted, then opened my eyes slowly.

I'd turned on the lights in the hopes that the abrupt glare might give me a slight advantage over Utley, but now that I'd followed through on the idea, I wasn't sure what I'd really hoped to accomplish, other than showing him how small and unthreatening I really was.

Because much as I wanted to smash into Utley, head down and racing fast in my best imitation of a football player trying to make the tackle of his life, toppling him to the ground and smashing his head on the concrete floor to give him a stunning blow that would render him unconscious long enough for me to grab my cat and run us to safety, I couldn't risk it, not with that knife being so close to Eddie's . . . to Eddie . . .

I stood like a lumpy rock on the bottom step, swallowing convulsively, so scared for my cat that I could hardly breathe, trying to come up with more ideas that would get Eddie and me out of this alive and unharmed.

"So, here we are," Paul Utley said, smiling.

It wasn't a very nice smile—so wide it somehow reminded me of a snake.

I didn't care for snakes.

"Yes," I said. "Here we are."

"Sorry about your cat." His smile went a little wider, and my heart clutched until a muffled "Mrr" came from under Utley's arm, where Eddie was being held in place by a firm elbow. The knife must have been in Utley's other hand, which was hanging low and slightly behind his back.

By this, I assumed Utley didn't realize that I knew he was armed. I devoutly hoped this gave me some sort of advantage. Too bad I didn't know what kind of advantage that might be. But I'd play along, see if I could get him talking, see if I could make this spin out long enough for us to get away.

"You scared me," I told Utley, "turning off the light. If all you want is that book, why didn't you just ask?"

Utley studied me. "Are you telling me that you're willing to sell *Wildflowers?*"

It wasn't mine to sell, I wanted to shout. The owner, whomever that might be, was the only one who had the right to make decisions about the book. I'd weep myself to sleep if what the owner wanted to do was slice out pages and sell them piecemeal, but it wasn't my choice to make.

But instead of saying all that, I smiled. "It's worth a lot of money."

Utley continued to study me.

"I've checked, you know," I said. "The last time a copy of Chastain's book sold publicly, it went for almost half a million dollars. There wasn't much information about its condition, so we'll have to assume it was pristine. Now, this one was sitting on a sideboard for a hundred years. Not in direct sunlight, which helped keep it from aging, but it wasn't in a controlled environment, either."

"There were undoubtedly private sales of the book," Utley said, still watching me carefully.

"Oh, sure." I nodded, then did one of the hardest things I've ever done in my life: started walking straight toward him. "But I don't know enough about private sales to know if the prices would be higher or lower than a public sale." I raise my eyebrows. "Do you happen to know?"

"No," he said, moving his knife hand further behind him.

"That's too bad." I kept inching slowly forward. "See, what I've been trying to figure out is if it makes more sense to sell the pages individually, or if the whole book should be sold at once. Maximizing its value is key."

"It appears that you've spent a lot of time thinking about this," Utley said, sounding amused.

You have no idea, I thought grimly. "Well," I said, "working in a library pays the bills, but it's no way to really get ahead, if you know what I mean."

Utley grunted. "A lot like being a small-town lawyer, then. Unfortunately, my wife doesn't understand there aren't many multimillion-dollar class-action suits running around Tonedagana County. The money this book could bring would solve all my problems."

It burned me that he was blaming his wife for his own greed, but I pushed that away and stepped even closer. "Say, do you mind letting my cat go?"

"Oh, I don't think so." Utley's smile made my insides clench. "I need some insurance, right, kitty?" He jostled

Eddie, and grinned at the low growl. "Kitty needs a lit-tle work on her manners."

I willed Eddie to stay quiet and still. "She's a he," I said. "And he still has his claws, so be careful."

Utley chuckled. Clearly, he didn't have cats. "Kitty and I are just fine. Aren't we, kitty?" He jostled Eddie again, who gave a drawn-out hiss. "Now, Minnie, you and I need to get down to business. First off, I have to see the book."

"Great idea. It's back there." I gestured at the back room.

"Excellent." Utley smiled, and I really wished he hadn't. "Why don't you go and get it?"

How stupid did he think I was? If I went first, as soon as I laid hands on *Wildflowers*, he'd stab me in the back with that scary knife, I'd fall to the floor dead, he'd grab the book, and he'd hightail it out of the museum.

"Sure," I said, starting to edge past him. "It's right on top, and—"

"What's the matter?"

"Look out!" I shouted, pointing behind him.

When Utley instinctively turned his head to see what I was shouting about, his attention was off me, and that was all I needed.

I gave him a stiff two-armed push with all my weight and all my might, and hooked my foot around his ankles, just like I'd been taught in the self-defense class I'd taken last summer.

"Hey!" He flailed his arms, dropping Eddie to the ground.

"Mrr!"

Eddie bolted away.

The knife flashed bright.

I kicked at Utley, aiming for his soft private parts, and he went down hard.

The sharp blade spun away across the floor, and I scrambled over the top of the fallen man, trying to get to the knife, sorry that Plan A hadn't come together, hoping I'd know what to do with the knife if I got hold of it, knowing that Utley could ruin Plan B by getting to it first. Reaching, clawing, grabbing, praying . . .

"Police!" thundered a large voice. "Get your hands away from that weapon!"

A uniformed city police officer, Joel Stowkowski, the wonderful man who'd told me that no one was going to "get away with breaking into our library," came down the steps two at a time.

Utley, who was lying flat on his stomach, arm stretching out long for the knife, turned his head. "Officer," he said, putting on an awkward smile, "this is all a big mistake. I can explain everything."

"Don't move," Joel ordered. As he pulled his handcuffs off his utility belt he glanced over at me. "You all right?"

I nodded a little tentatively, then, when that didn't seem to set off any fireworks, nodded again with more certainty and slowly got to my feet.

"Need an ambulance?"

I shook my head. "I'm fine." Which wasn't the literal truth, since I felt banged-up and grimy, but I would feel much better after a long, hot shower.

Joel ratcheted the handcuffs into place, read Utley his rights, and spoke into his shoulder microphone.

"What took you so long, anyway?" I asked.

"You were doing such a fine job," Joel said, ignoring the quaver in my voice and hauling a protesting Paul Utley to his feet, "that I didn't want to interrupt. I saw and heard more than enough to put this guy away. You barely needed my help at all, seems like."

In the distance, I heard police sirens approaching, and even though Utley was already incapacitated and unlikely to cause anyone any physical harm ever again, the sweet sound let me breathe easier.

The tips of two cat ears popped up from behind a box. "Mrr?"

"Of course, I see you had some help." Joel pushed Utley toward the stairs. "Well done, Eddie."

I reached out to pull my cat close and covered his ears. "Don't let him hear that—it'll swell up his head even bigger."

"Mrr," Eddie said. He put up a token struggle, but then let me hug him tight and kiss the top of his head.

"Mrr to you, too, pal," I whispered. "Over and over and over again."

"You did what?" Kristen asked loudly.

It was the next day. It was still hot, and we were sitting on Rafe's shaded front porch, catching the breeze off Janay Lake. We'd started out on the marina's concrete patio, but Rafe had called us over, served us cans of soda, and then took off to play golf with some college buddies.

Chilson, on a hot Sunday afternoon in early July, was drowsy with sleep. The weekend tourists had already left, and everyone else was doing their best to avoid getting hot and sweaty. Well, except Rafe and his friends. I leaned back in his chair and propped my feet up on his porch rail, wondering what it was about men that made them do such things.

"You really ran straight toward a guy holding a knife?" Kristen glared at me. "And don't use that self-defense-class excuse. How could you do such a stupid thing?"

"It wasn't as dumb as it sounds," I said, trying not to sound defensive.

"Yeah? How?"

"Lots of reasons." I could see her mouth start to open, so I jumped in before she could get going. "When I'd gone upstairs to the front door, I'd propped it wide open. In summer, a Chilson police officer makes a walking round of downtown every hour on the hour. With the door open and the light on in the basement, I knew someone would be coming soon." To forestall Kristen's next objection, I added, "And I knew it would be less than an hour, because I could see the time on that downtown clock."

"That's one," Kristen growled.

"Another reason rushing Utley wasn't as stupid as it sounds is that I'd been watching him closely. His grip on the knife was loose, and I was sure I could knock it out of his hand without too much trouble." Pretty sure, anyway.

"That's not lots." Kristen held up her index finger and her middle finger in what I had a feeling wasn't the *V*-for-victory salute. "That's two, and the second one was marginal at best. To reach the 'lots' quantity, you need at least four reasons. Give me two more."

"Okay, how about this: I'm so short it would have taken so long for the knife's blade to reach me that I could have grabbed Eddie, found the book, and ran to the police station before the downward stroke even started."

Kristen frowned at me fiercely. "One more answer like that, and I'll call your mother and tell her what you did last night."

And she would, too. "How about this? I was so angry that I'd become invulnerable. Nothing short of kryptonite would have hurt a hair on my head."

"Three." Kristen snapped up another finger. "And that reason wasn't much better. The last one better be bulletproof."

I looked through the leaves of the big maple tree that stood outside Rafe's house and over at the marina, where I could just see the back end of my houseboat. "Maybe this won't fight the stupidity allegation," I said quietly, "but I had to get Eddie away from Paul Utley. At least, I had to try."

Kristen studied me for an eternal moment, then sighed and got to her feet. "Okay. You got me on that one. Be right back."

She went inside, and, closing my eyes, I slouched down in the chair.

It had, after all, been a long night. After Paul Utley had been hauled away in the back of a police cruiser, the city police chief had shown up. He'd taken one look at me and at the mess in the museum's basement, and after I'd made it partway through my explanation of the evening's events, he'd held up his hand and called the sheriff's office.

Since I'd known Detective Inwood and Ash were out of town, I wasn't surprised when the sheriff herself walked in. Sheriff Richardson gave the room and its contents—human, feline, and inanimate—one sweeping glance and said, "Go home and get some sleep. Inwood and Wolverson will be back tomorrow morning. Stop by at ten and we'll take your statement."

She'd crouched in front of the occupied cat carrier, reached through the wires to give Eddie a chin scratch, stood, given us a collective nod, and left.

I'd woken Sunday morning to a cat wrapped around the top of my head and a ringing cell phone. Ash, on his way back north, was calling to make sure I was all right. Groggily, I'd said I was fine, and we'd met at the Round Table in time for a quick breakfast before the ten-o'clock meeting at the sheriff's office.

He'd apologized for not calling me back. "It was part of the training," he'd said. "I didn't know until we got there, and I'm sorry about that, but it was what they call an immersion training session. We had to hand over our cell phones when we checked in."

My mouth was full of French toast, so I couldn't say anything, but he nodded. "Yeah, I know. I should have called right then and said I'd be out of touch. I really am sorry."

And, since it was obvious that he was indeed sorry, I'd smiled and forgiven him.

Now I yawned comfortably. My feet were in the sunshine, staying nice and warm, the rest of me was in the shade, staying cool, and Andrea's killer was in jail. And while waiting for the sheriff the night before, I'd opened one last box and, lo and behold, there was the DeKeysers' copy of Chastain's *Wildflowers*, right on top.

The book was currently in the sheriff's evidence lockup, where it would stay until the ownership question was solved. Sheriff Richardson had contacted Paul Utley's partner, who would now be handling Talia DeKeyser's estate. After recovering from the shock of discovering that his partner had been arrested for murder, he had been, according to the sheriff, flabbergasted to hear that the DeKeysers had owned such a valuable book. The attorney would be contacting the estate's heirs and it would be interesting to hear who would wind up as the book's official owner.

Considering the book's value, there would inevitably be a legal wrangle, but since that didn't have anything to do with me, I didn't have to think about it at all.

What Sheriff Richardson had told me was that the local DeKeysers she'd spoken with had gone very quiet when Andrea's attempted theft was described. "I think Leslie, the oldest daughter, was crying when she got off the phone," the sheriff had said. "That family sticks together. At least they used to."

The other thing the sheriff and Detective Inwood had said was that Monica Utley claimed to have absolutely no knowledge of her husband's activities. Inwood thought Monica was in it up to her teeth; the sheriff disagreed, and it would be interesting to see which one of them was right.

I was glad, however, to have the question of the X-Acto knife answered. Paul Utley, who, as an attorney, should have known better than to talk without representation present, had told Detective Inwood that he'd met Andrea at the library to look for the book together. They'd gotten into a heated argument about when he'd divorce Monica, during which he'd strangled Andrea and then stabbed her with her own X-Acto knife in a fit of rage.

I sank deeper into the chair and sighed. All this, for the sake of money? A life ended, other lives ruined, for what? A new boat? A new car every couple of years? I didn't understand and didn't want to. Even thinking about it was making me tired and sick at heart.

My eyes fluttered open at the sound of Rafe's front

door shutting. That noise was accompanied by the tinkle of glassware and I sat up. "What's that?" I asked.

Kristen set down a pitcher filled with a heavily ice-cubed pink concoction and handed me a glass. "It's medicinal. Drink up."

"Alcoholic?"

"Just the right amount. Cheers."

We *tink*ed the rims of our glasses and drank. At first sip, the sweetness made me shudder, but the second sip went down easier. "This isn't half bad," I said.

"You don't tend bar in Key West and learn nothing. So, what else had happened since I saw you last? Have you saved any small children from drowning? Fended off a nuclear holocaust?"

"I met Bianca Sims."

Kristen's eyebrows went sky-high. "Mitchell's girlfriend? How did that go?"

It had been at the Round Table that morning. Bianca, in real-estate agent mode, had been meeting with clients. I'd waited until they'd left, then slid into her booth and introduced myself.

"It's weird," I told Kristen, "but I think it's going to work out."

"Hang on. You mean . . . ?" She couldn't say the word.

"Marriage?" I smiled. "Probably too soon to say, but she really seems to love him. Loves him just the way he is, and wishes he'd stop trying to impress her with all his hard work. She figures it's just a phase and hopes he'll go back to being the normal Mitchell soon, because that's the man she fell in love with."

"'Weird' is right," Kristen said.

I nodded. "Speaking of love interests, what's the news from Scruffy? Has he asked you to marry him lately?"

"Actually, no, and it's a big relief." But she glanced

at the empty ring finger of her left hand as she spoke. I started drafting a mental note to text Scruffy that progress was being made, when Kristen asked, "What about you and Ash?"

I blinked. "What about us?"

"Any chance of wedding bells? You've been seeing him for a while now. You must have a good idea of what's possible."

"We've only been going out for a few weeks." I shifted my feet, realizing that if I didn't move them out of the sun soon, I'd end up with a very strange-looking case of sunburn. "It's too early to say."

"Sure," Kristen said.

I checked her expression for sarcasm, but couldn't detect anything overt. "It's too early," I repeated. "But at breakfast, we were talking about skiing this winter."

"A week out West?" Kristen rotated her glass, making the ice cubes clink.

"What? Oh. No, we were talking about our favorite places to ski up here." I watched her ice cubes go round and round. "Speaking of ski places, when I was talking to Bianca, I found out how the rumor about Kim and Bob Parmalee going bankrupt got started."

"Yeah? How's that?"

"They have a condo in Colorado. Breckenridge. When their kids were young, they used to spend a lot of family time out there, skiing. Now that the kids are grown and gone, they're selling it and buying a couple weeks in a time-share instead."

"Gossip," Kristen said, rolling her eyes. "The whole bowl contains one grain of truth, but which grain is it?"

"Speaking of gossip, I have a question."

"And I might possibly have an answer. What's up?"

"Dana Coburn. Why haven't I met her before now?

I would have thought a kid like that would practically live at the library."

Kristen looked out at the sparkling waters of Janay Lake, then back at me. "You liked her?"

"I'm annoyed it's taken me this long to meet her. She's obviously smart to the genius level, she's personable, she's . . ." I stopped, frowning. "What's so funny?"

"Peas in a pod," she said, still laughing. "I should have known you two would get along."

"I'm no genius."

"No, but I'll lay down money that you and Dana have more in common than you have differences."

"Not if she's not visiting the library."

Kristen gave me a speculative look. "I kind of don't want to tell you why."

"Then don't." I slid my toes back into the sunshine. "Especially if it's gossip, because we know how true that's likely to be."

"Not gossip," Kristen said vaguely. "It's just, well, Dana has this bizarre condition. She can't stand being touched. She freaks out if anyone other than her mom or dad touches her, and even that she doesn't like much."

"Oh. That's . . ." I searched for a word, but couldn't find the right one.

"Horrible," Kristen supplied.

It wasn't quite right, but it would have to do.

"Anyway," she went on, "that's why she's being home-schooled, and that's why she doesn't go out in public much. Even accidental touches can . . . well, let's just say it's not good. If she's willing to talk to you, that's great. I'm sure her mom was all over it."

"She was," I said, remembering Jenny's grateful tone and eagerness to have me stop back at the house. Any time, she'd said. An exaggeration, of course, but still. "I like her," I said. "Dana, I mean."

Kristen sent me a lazy thumbs-up. "Excellent. You can't have too many friends."

We sat for a while, chatting about this and that, me suffering the occasional pointed comment about running headlong into danger every time it came near, her taking my abuse that her perfectionist ways were going to shorten her life by decades, both of us guessing Rafe's golf score for the day, both of us guessing in the hundreds and laughing ourselves silly.

It was a fine way to spend a hot Sunday afternoon, but eventually, when the pink pitcher was nearly empty and the sun was starting its slide down the far side of the sky, Kristen looked at me. "Is it tomorrow you'll hear about your new boss?"

"Yup."

"Do you know what's going to happen?" she asked.

"Nope."

"Are you going to guess?"

I made a face. "There's enough of that going around without me joining in."

She sighed and poured the last of the pink concoction into my glass. "I hope you know what you're doing."

I grinned. "Have I ever not?"

"Well," Kristen said, flopping back in her chair, "there was that once. The summer when we were fourteen, remember? When you thought Robby Teller was going to be the love of your life forever and you wrote letters telling him so."

I did, and the memory still made me squirm, which was why she'd brought it up. "I'm really, really glad he moved to Hawaii."

"Didn't you hear?" Kristen peered at me through half-closed eyes. "He's in town for a family reunion."

My eyes went wide with horror and my mouth dropped open.

"Gotcha," my best friend said. "You are so gullible."

I took a long drink of pink as I tried to plan an appropriate method of revenge.

"You know what?" she asked.

"What?"

"I'm glad you didn't get sliced up with a big, long, scary knife," Kristen said softly.

"Yeah," I said just as softly. "I know."

Chapter 20

The next morning, I got to the library early and dove deep into the pile of work on my desk. I kept my head down, ignored the footsteps passing my open doorway, and, in general, did all that I could to keep busy and not think about what was happening upstairs in the boardroom.

It didn't work, of course, but I made a valiant effort.

Finally I couldn't stand it any longer. I needed to hear a human voice and, almost as much, I needed caffeine. I grabbed my coffee mug and headed for the break room, which seemed to be packed full of noisy library employees.

I looked around, counting heads and trying to remember how many people I'd scheduled to work that morning. I'd been preoccupied lately, but surely I hadn't put this many people on the calendar. Had I? "Please tell me that someone is at the front desk."

Holly gave me a stern glance. "How can you think about things like that when the Big Decision is about to come down?"

"Kelsey's out there," Donna said, coming by with a full pot of coffee.

"Did you switch with someone?" I asked. "I'm sure I didn't put you on the schedule today."

Donna grinned. "What makes you think I'm on the clock?"

"I'm not working, either," said another part-time clerk a little tentatively. "Um, that's okay, isn't it? To come in if I'm not scheduled to work."

Josh held up his mug for a refill. "Like Minnie would be one to talk about that. She's here seventy hours a week, and she's salaried."

"She's dedicated," Gareth said as he winked at me.

"Or she's stupid," Josh muttered.

"Or both," Donna said, laughing. "Anyone want more coffee?"

"How long do you think they're going to be?" Holly said, pointing at the ceiling.

Trying to guess the length of a board meeting was a pointless exercise. "No idea." A large number of speculative glances were being sent in my direction, so I said, "Anyone want to hear about Saturday night?"

On a normal Monday morning, the first thing we would have done was exchange any significant weekend stories, but this Monday was far from normal.

"That's right," Gareth said. "I heard you were in the hospital with a gunshot wound to the gut." He studied me. "You must be a fast healer."

"What!" Donna turned around so fast I was afraid the coffee in the pot she was holding would swirl out. "Minnie, are you okay? What happened?"

So I explained everything, starting with the passing of Talia DeKeyser, the murder of Andrea Vennard, the break-ins, and Pam Fazio's injury. When I told them that a copy of Chastain's *Wildflowers* had been sitting on the DeKeysers' sideboard for decades, a collective gasp went through the room, and I finished up with the arrest of Paul Utley and the uncovering of the near-pristine *Wildflowers*.

"What about the gun?" Josh demanded. He looked angry and, oddly, protective. "Did that Utley hurt you? That's got to put him in jail even longer."

"No gun," I said mildly, and decided not to talk about the weapon that had been involved. The sharp blade of that knife would haunt my dreams for many nights, and I didn't want to talk about it any more than I had to.

"How's Eddie?" Donna asked. Back in the pre-Julia days, Donna had gone out on the bookmobile a few times and had taken a liking to the fuzzy little guy. "Is he okay?"

"He was fine when I left him this morning," I said. "That is, if being curled up on the middle of my pillow and purring at sixty decibels is an indication of being fine."

The rest of them started pelting me with more questions about the events of Saturday night, some that I could answer (Where's *Wildflowers* now?) and some that I couldn't (How long will Utley be in prison?), and it was when the questions were dwindling to speculation about the ownership of Chastain's book that a polite voice asked, "Minnie, do you have a minute?"

All other sounds in the room stilled. I turned to the library board's vice-president. "Of course," I said, and followed him upstairs to hear who the board had selected as the new director for the Chilson District Library.

*   *   *

My aunt Frances handed me a plate of chocolate-chip cookies.

We were sitting on the creaky metal glider that had been on the screened porch of the boardinghouse for longer than I'd been alive. Birds sang in the trees, leaves rustled in spite of there being no detectible breeze, and the evening sun lit everything with an almost magical golden glow.

I sighed, not feeling any magic inside of me, and took a cookie, which probably wouldn't help, but why risk it?

"What do you think the new director is going to be like?" my aunt asked.

"Jennifer Walker?" I studied the cookie, formulating my approach. The last bite had to have more than one chocolate chip, but so did the first bite. "Remember when Eddie threw up on a candidate's Italian shoes?"

"Oh, dear."

I glanced at Aunt Frances. "You're laughing. How could you? My new boss already hates me, and she most certainly hates Eddie. She's going to ban him from the bookmobile, she's going to get rid of the bookmobile, and then she's going to fire me." Savagely, I bit into the cookie.

"I'm laughing because it's funny," my loving aunt said, now laughing out loud. "The only time Eddie is in the library and what does he do? Urp all over the shoes of your next boss."

"Well," I said, half smiling. "Maybe it's a little funny."

"See?" My aunt bumped me with her elbow. "It'll all work out—you know it will."

Once again, she was right, and I pushed away my concerns. Because things would work out, one way or another, and worrying about it wouldn't help. So I decided to stop thinking about it. Jennifer would start at the library the second week of August, and that's when we'd find out what she'd be like. Why ruin the next few weeks worrying?

I told this to Aunt Frances, who smiled. "Just so you know," she said, "I think you made the right decision about not applying for the director's spot. You're young and you're enjoying what you're doing. When it's time to make a move, you'll know."

"Really?"

Her smile deepened. "Absolutely. It may be difficult in many ways, especially if the decision will create ripple effects for others, but, in the end, you have to think about what's best for yourself. It's no good making life choices based on what other people think."

I looked at her carefully. "We're talking about something else now, aren't we?"

"Minnie," she said, laughing, "you are not the most observant of nieces today." She held up her left hand, and only then did I notice that it was glittering with the light of a thousand suns.

I gaped at the gorgeous ring, which was encrusted with light blue jewels that matched the color of her eyes. "Otto asked you to marry him?"

"He asked me over a month ago," she said. "It took me this long to decide."

Which explained her odd behavior the past few weeks. Hah!

"Well, it's about time," I said, grinning hugely, and reached over to give her a hug. Halfway through, a thought bolted into my brain and I pulled back. "Aunt Frances, what about the boardinghouse? Is Otto going to move here? Or . . ."

"Things will work out," my aunt said, patting my arm. "Don't worry. Everything will be fine."

And, since Aunt Frances was the best aunt in the whole wide world and was one of the wisest people I'd ever met, I believed her.

"What do you think?" I asked.

Eddie, whom I'd just told about the engagement, picked up his head and blinked at me.

"Never mind," I said, giving him a long pet. "You had a long night two days ago and must be way behind on your rest. Go back to sleep."

He sighed and settled in deeper on my legs.

We were sitting on the front deck of the houseboat, watching the sun slip down behind the horizon. Or at least I was, since Eddie's eyes were closed. There wasn't a single cloud in the sky, and the clarity of the air and water was so beautiful it almost hurt.

I watched the colors above me ease from medium blue to dark blue to indigo. As I watched the slow changes, I thought about all that had happened in the past weeks, and came to the conclusion that if people only spent more time watching the sun go down and the stars come out, that there would be less suffering in the world.

The marina lights were just bright enough for me to see the black-and-white tabby cat on my lap. "What do you think?" I asked, my hand on his warm back. "Am I being profound tonight, or what?"

He opened and shut his mouth in a silent "Mrr" just as my cell phone trilled.

To answer or not to answer? That was the question. An even better question, though, would have been why had I brought the cell out here in the first place? I turned it over. *Detective Inwood?* Why was he calling so late?

I snatched up the phone, suddenly worried about Ash. "Detective. What's the matter?"

There was a pause. "Why would you think anything is wrong?"

Which could only mean that Ash was safe and sound. "Because it's ten thirty at night."

"It is?" He sounded surprised. "I apologize. I was working late, catching up on things, and didn't realize what time it was. I'll call you back tomorrow."

I had a sudden sympathy for the man. He'd been gone for a couple of days and his desk must have been piled high with work. "Or you could just tell me now. Then you can cross something off your list."

"Thank you," he said. "I appreciate that. What I wanted to tell you is that all parties involved in the ownership of Chastain's book have agreed on a temporary holding location."

"Oh? That's good." Although why Inwood needed to tell me about it, I wasn't sure.

"Yes," he said. "The location is the rare-books collection of the Chilson District Library."

"It . . . What?"

"You do have a rare-books collection, yes?"

"Well, sure, but . . ."

"And you have proper security for that collection?" When I didn't answer straightaway, he prompted, "Or you can get some in a reasonable time frame?"

"Yes," I said, visualizing various budgets. When I mentally located a line item for contingency expenses that had a four-figure balance, I said, "Yes," again, this time more firmly. "Absolutely yes."

"Excellent," Inwood said, and I was pretty sure I

heard the stroke of a pencil crossing out an item on a list. "Let me know when you have things in place, and I'll have the book delivered."

A copy of *Wildflowers*? In my library? There couldn't possibly be anything I could do that would impress the new director more. Aunt Frances was right: Everything was going to work out. My heart began to sing.

"Nicely done, by the way, Ms. Hamilton," the detective said.

The song came to an abrupt halt. Had he really said what I thought he'd said? "Sorry?"

"Saturday night. You found yourself in a difficult and dangerous situation and were alert enough to do what needed to be done."

"Oh. Um, thanks." He didn't hang up, so I said, "Most people think I was nuts for rushing a guy with a knife."

"Most people." He chuckled. "You are not most people, Ms. Hamilton." His chuckle turned into an outright laugh, and he ended the call, still laughing.

"'Nuts' wasn't the first term that came to my mind," came a voice out of the dark. "'Brave' was the first. Then 'stupid.' Then came 'nuts.'"

I turned off the phone. "Hey, Eric." Over our Sunday-morning newspapers, I'd told my neighbor about the events of the night before. "How long have you been sitting out there?"

"Long enough to hear you ask your cat about being profound. Were you?"

"Doubt it."

"Tell me anyway."

So I shrugged and did, telling him how sunsets and stars might lead us to a better world.

After a long moment, he said into the evening's darkness, "You know what, Minnie? You're probably right. I can't believe your cat didn't say so."

Smiling, I gathered Eddie up into my arms. "See you tomorrow, Eric."

"Night, Minnie."

I carried Eddie inside and set him gently on the bed. I brushed my teeth and changed into jammies, and, finally, slid between the sheets, trying to disturb my sleeping cat as little as possible. "Night, pal," I whispered, and kissed him on the top of his head. "Sleep tight. Tomorrow's a bookmobile day."

"Mrr."

And I would have sworn that he was smiling.

Keep reading for an excerpt of
Minnie and Eddie's next adventure . . .

WRONG SIDE OF THE PAW

Available in paperback from
Berkley Prime Crime!

There are many tasks that I find difficult. Braiding my annoyingly curly hair, for starters. Differentiating equations and putting down a good book before one in the morning are also beyond my capabilities. Another thing I've found hard for all of my thirty-four years? Choosing a favorite season.

Though summer is easy to enjoy with its warm freedoms, winter offers skiing and ice-skating and the sheer beauty of a world transformed by a fleecy blanket of white. Spring is exciting with its daily growth spurts, but right in front of me was a glorious hillside in its early-autumn colors of green with sprinklings of red and orange and yellow, a scene so stunningly beautiful it was hard to look away.

"Fall, it is," I murmured to myself.

I was standing at the bookmobile's back door, the door wide-open to let the unseasonably warm air of late September waft around the thousands of books, the hundreds of CDs and DVDs, the jigsaw puzzles, my part-time clerk, me, and Eddie, the bookmobile cat.

"Mrr," Eddie said. On his current favorite perch, the

driver's-seat headrest, he stretched and yawned, showing us the roof of his mouth, which was the second-least attractive part of him, then settled down again, rearranging himself into what looked like the exact same position.

Julia, who was sitting on the carpeted step under the bookshelves, which served as both seating and as a step to reach the top shelves, looked up from the book she was reading. "What does he want now?"

One of the many reasons I'd hired the sixtyish Julia Beaton a few months ago was her tacit agreement to always pretend that Eddie was actually trying to communicate with us. Julia had many other wonderful qualities, among them the gift of empathy, which was a huge plus for a bookmobile clerk, and an uncanny ability to understand people's motivations.

Those two traits had undoubtedly contributed to her success as a Tony Award–winning actress, but when the leading roles had started to dry up, she'd retired from the stage, and she and her husband had moved back to her hometown of Chilson, a small tourist town in northwest lower Michigan, which was the town where I now lived and worked, and there wasn't anywhere on earth I'd rather be.

Though I hadn't grown up in Chilson, I'd had the good fortune to spend many youthful summers with my long-widowed aunt Frances, who ran a boardinghouse in the summer and taught woodworking during the school year. It hadn't taken me long to fall in love with the region, a land of forested hills and lakes of all sizes, and I soon loved the town, too, with its eccentric restaurants, retail stores, and residents.

Soon after I'd earned a master's degree in library and information sciences, I'd heard about a posting for the assistant director position at the Chilson District

Library, and spent half the night and all the next day working on a résumé and cover letter.

I'd sent the packet off, crossing my fingers as I imagined it being read by the library board, and, after a grueling interview and a couple of nail-biting weeks, I'd been ecstatic to be hired as the library's assistant director.

Since then, not all had been exactly rosy, but the bookmobile program I'd proposed had become a reality a little over a year ago, and in spite of sporadic funding problems, library director issues, and the occasional library board confrontation, I was a very happy camper.

Eddie, on the other hand, did not look like a contented cat. Instead of the relaxed body language he'd been exhibiting moments earlier, he was now sitting up, twitching his tail, and staring at me with a look with which I was intimately familiar.

"What he wants," I said, "is a treat."

"He had treats at the last stop," Julia pointed out.

"Which is why he thinks he deserves a treat at this one, too."

"If he has treats at every stop," she said, "he's going to get as big as a house."

I'd first met Eddie a year and a half earlier. In a cemetery. Which sounds weird, and probably is, but Chilson's cemetery had an amazing view of Janay Lake to the south and, to the west, the long blue line that was massive Lake Michigan.

The day I'd met Eddie had been another unseasonably warm day, and I'd skipped out on the cleaning chores I should have been doing and gone for a long walk up to the cemetery. I'd taken advantage of a bench placed next to the gravestone of an Alonzo Tillotson (born 1847, died 1926) and been startled by the appearance of an insistent black-and-gray tabby cat.

In spite of my commands for him to go home, he'd followed me back to my place. By the time I'd cleaned him up, making him a black-and-white cat, I'd fallen in love. Even still, I'd dutifully run a notice in the local newspaper's lost and found and had been relieved when no one answered the ad. Eddie was my first-ever pet; my father had suffered horrible allergies, and until last year I'd never felt the connection a human and a pet could have. I'd also never realized how opinionated and stubborn a cat could be.

"He's already pretty big," I said, "but the vet says he's a healthy weight."

"Mrr," said the cat in question, starting to ooze off the headrest and toward the driver's seat.

"Thanks so much," I muttered. "I love it when you sleep there and shed all over the upholstery so I get your hair on the seat of my pants."

Eddie thumped himself onto the seat. "Mrr!"

"I think," Julia said, laughing, "that he took offense to that 'big' comment."

"Who you calling big?"

Julia and I turned. Up until that point, the bookmobile's stop had been empty of patrons. I smiled, pleased that we weren't going to turn up completely dry. Of all the facts and figures that my library board scrutinized, the numbers from the bookmobile got the most attention. So far, the trends were upward ones, but I didn't for a moment assume that all would be well forever.

"Hey, Leese," I said to the woman, who was almost a foot taller than my efficient five feet. Her height was the same as my best friend's, who owned a restaurant in Chilson, but instead of Kristen's slender blond Scandinavian inheritance, Leese Lacombe's ancestors had endowed her with a broad build, olive skin tone, and brown hair almost as curly as my unruly black mop.

Leese, a few years older than me, possessed a razor-sharp brain, a quick wit, and a prestigious law degree. She'd spent her time in the corporate trenches in a big downstate firm, and had moved back north a few months ago to start up her own law office, one that specialized in elder law. To keep costs down, she was using her home as an office, and had taken to borrowing books from the bookmobile instead of making the half-hour drive into Chilson.

"What's new with you?" Julia stood and went to get the stack of books Leese had requested online. I was still tweaking the bookmobile schedule, but at that point we were visiting each stop every three weeks. Though that wasn't a very long time to most people, it was an eternity for bibliophiles, and we were getting used to bringing along huge piles of requested books and lugging back the corresponding huge piles of returns. I doubted that any bookmobile librarian had ever needed to buy a gym membership to get an upper-body workout.

"New?" Leese perched the books on the corner of the rear checkout desk. "I'm glad it's almost October, for one thing. My summer neighbors have slammed their trunks for the last time."

Julia and I nodded, understanding the feeling. We lived in a part of Michigan that was the summer playground for a large number of folks from the Detroit, Grand Rapids, and Chicagoland areas. Some people visited for a weekend or a week, while others had seasonal residences they occupied from May through September.

The population of Chilson and the entire Tonedagana County more than tripled in the warmer months, and summer came with a complicated set of issues. Most of us were glad to renew the friendships that had been put on hold the previous fall—not to mention the fact that many businesses depended on the summer dollars—but October was undeniably a sigh of relief. No more parking problems, no more waiting in line for a restaurant table, and no more waiting anywhere, really.

"It is nice to have our town back," Julia said. "We'll be tired of looking at one another by April, though."

Leese laughed, and it was a surprisingly gentle sound from such a large person. "Undoubtedly. But without this quiet time, would we appreciate the busy time?"

The question was an interesting one. I gave up trying to shift Eddie from the driver's seat and walked down the aisle to join the conversation. "So it's part of that old question: How can we value the highs of life if we don't know what the lows are like?"

"Exactly!" Leese beamed at me with a high-wattage smile, and I knew exactly what was going to happen next. She would sit on the carpeted step, Julia would pull around the desk chair, I would perch myself on the edge of the desk, and the three of us would dive into a long, leisurely discussion when we all had better things to do. But it was nearly October, the summer folks were mostly gone, and it was warm enough to prop the door open. What could it hurt to let the bookmobile chores wait a few minutes longer?

Julia pulled the chair around, and Leese dropped onto the step. "It's the swings in life that make things interesting," she said.

"Oh, I don't know," I said, hitching myself up to sit on the edge of the desk. "Isn't that some Chinese curse? 'May you live in interesting times'?"

"Would you rather live in a boring era?" Leese challenged.

Julia laughed. "Minnie Hamilton couldn't live a boring life if she wanted to. She's just attracted to trouble."

"Am not," I said automatically. "I'm just—"

"Do you know what this tiny woman did earlier this spring?" Julia demanded of Leese. "In the middle of a massive power outage, she managed to hold a very successful book fair."

Leese looked at me with interest. "You did that? Wasn't Trock Farrand the headliner?"

"Minnie's show, from top to bottom," Julia said. "When the original big-name author pulled out, Trock heard about it and flew out from New York."

"He's a friend. That's all," I said, knocking my shoes together. "He wanted to plug his new cookbook." Trock, host of a nationally televised cooking show, owned a summer place just outside of Chilson and in spite of the differences in our ages, backgrounds, and interests, we'd struck up a solid friendship.

Another solid thing was the relationship between Trock's son, Scruffy, and my friend Kristen. I had the inside scoop that a proposal was in the near future, and I was having a hard time keeping quiet.

"Whatever." Julia waved off my comment. "And just a couple of months ago, Minnie figured out that—"

"Hey!"

Julia frowned. "I'm on a rant, Minnie. Please don't interrupt me when I'm in full flow."

But it wasn't Julia who I was scolding. I shifted on the desk and called to my cat, "Where are you going?"

We'd felt free to open the bookmobile door because for the last year, Eddie had completely ignored it. When we were en route, my furry friend traveled in a cat carrier strapped to the floor on the passenger's side, but once I set the parking brake, Julia unlatched the wire door, allowing him to roam free about the interior. Though he'd run outside a couple of times the first year of the bookmobile's service, since then he'd shown little interest in leaving the bus before we did.

Eddie, being a cat, paid no attention to my question, but continued to sniff at the open doorway.

"Is he going to make a run for it?" Leese asked, amused.

"Not a chance," I said. "He wouldn't want to get too far from his cat treats."

Eddie's ears flattened and Julia laughed. "I think you hurt his feelings. You should apologize before he does something drastic."

"I shouldn't have to apologize for telling the truth."

But she did have a point. A miffed Eddie was not a good situation. He had claws and knew how to use them, especially on paper products. Paper towels, toilet paper, facial tissues, newspapers, and even books weren't necessarily safe when Eddie was in the mood for destruction.

"I am sorry," I told my cat, "that you take offense to a fact-based statement."

"Huh," said Leese. "Not much of an apology, if you ask me. And from the looks of him, he doesn't think much of it either."

Eddie was standing at the top of the stairs, intent on ignoring everything in the bookmobile, twitching his ears and nose.

"Hey, pal," I said, sliding off the desk. "Inside only. You promised, remember?"

"That was before you insulted him," Julia said. "All previous deals have now been canceled."

"Come here, Eddie." But just as I leaned down to grab my fuzzy friend, he hopped out of my reach, jumping down to the bottom step.

"That'll teach you to make fun of a cat," Leese said, laughing.

"Especially an Eddie cat," Julia added.

We were parked in a large church parking lot, at least a hundred feet from the closest road, which hadn't had a car pass in the last ten minutes, so I wasn't overly worried about Eddie getting dangerously close to traffic, but there was a long line of shrubs at the far side of the lot and I could just see Eddie crawling into that prickly mess and not wanting to come out until long after we should have been at the next stop.

"How about a treat?" I crouched at the top of the stairs. "Come back right now and I'll give you a whole pile of treats." Not a big pile, but still. "Here, kitty, kitty, kitty."

Eddie, catlike, was bent on his new mission, whatever that might be, and launched himself off the bottom step and into the bright late-September sunshine.

I groaned and went after him. Over my shoulder, I called, "Can someone bring me the treats? He might come if I shake the can."

Once outside, however, I realized that Eddie wasn't headed for the shrubbery. Or the roadway. Instead he was trotting straight for the only vehicle in the parking lot, a battered pickup truck. Dents and scrapes of all shapes and sizes were scattered all along the doors and sides, some serious enough to have scoured the paint down to the metal.

I leapt to the stunningly obvious conclusion that the vehicle was Leese's and wondered what a former corporate attorney was doing with an open-bed truck, since at previous bookmobile visits, I was pretty sure she'd been driving a midsized SUV.

Mentally shrugging—I paid about as much attention to cars as I did to the daily temperatures in Hawaii—I trotted across the parking lot, ten yards behind my cat in a very short parade of two. "Eddie, come back here, will you? I thought I only had to run on workout mornings with Ash. I'm not sure I'm ready for more. Think of me, will you? I'm sure you've done that once or twice."

Most days, my inane conversation caught Eddie's attention, slowing him enough for me to catch up to him. This time, if anything, he sped up. Then he sniffed the air and trotted ever closer to the truck.

"Here kitty, kitty, kitty," Leese called as she climbed down the bookmobile's steps. "Come get a kitty treat." She rattled the cardboard can of annoyingly expensive moist morsels, but Eddie trotted onward.

"Is that your truck?" I asked, pointing.

"For now," she said, still rattling the can. "It's a long story."

Eddie, still ignoring the siren call of cat treats, jumped onto the truck's rear bumper, then up onto the edge of the tailgate. I slowed from my half-run and started planning how best to snatch him up into my arms. Cornering Eddie was a lot easier than capturing him. "I think he wants to go for a ride."

"Ha." Leese, with her long-legged strides, reached my side. "I'll give it to him with my blessing as soon as my SUV is fixed."

Eddie's ears swiveled. Laughing, I edged a few feet closer to the truck. "I think he's rejecting your generous offer."

"He's a cat of good taste." Leese gave the treat can an extra-hard shake. "That thing's a piece of junk."

"Mrrr," Eddie said, then slid off the tailgate and into the truck's bed.

Reaching the side of the truck, I stood on my tiptoes and peered in. All there was to see was a large tarp and a black-and-white cat walking over the top of it in an ungainly fashion.

"Fred Astaire, you are not," I told him. "And please don't make me come in there after you."

"Mrrr," he said, but his tone was different from the usual communicative chirp he gave. It was low and long and almost a growl. He started pawing at the edge of the heavy canvas and trying to poke his little kitty nose under the edge. Of course, he was standing on the edge, which made things difficult, but Eddie didn't always like to do things the easy way.

I turned to look at Leese, who was now standing next to me. "What's under your tarp?"

"No idea," she said shortly. "It's not mine. Tarp or truck."

Two minutes earlier, she'd been ready to give away a truck she didn't own? "I don't—"

"Mrrroooo!"

I winced as Eddie's howls penetrated my skull and sank deep into my brain.

Enough was enough. I walked around to the back end of the truck, put one foot on the trailer hitch and pushed myself high enough to grab the tailgate's edge with both hands.

I swung one foot over into the pickup's bed, then the other. Eddie was now howling for all he was worth and had managed to burrow his top half under the tarp. I crouched down and took a gentle hold of his back half. "Come on, pal. Let go of whatever it is you're after, okay?"

But when I stood, cat in hand, his claws were still

extended, and they snagged the tarp's edge, yanking the canvas to one side and revealing what Eddie had been after.

"Oh . . . !" I stumbled backward. "Oh . . ."

Because Eddie had uncovered a body. A dead body. Of a man. A man about sixty years old. With staring eyes of blue.

I scrambled over the tailgate, holding a squirming Eddie close to my chest, and dropped to the ground, panting, and not wanting to see any more.

Leese was standing quiet and tall, her hands gripping the edge of the truck, her mouth working as if she was trying to say something. For a long moment, nothing came out, but when it did, her voice was a raw whisper.

"It's my dad."